W9-CAA-417

Slowly, wanting to savor every moment of this, he lowered his mouth to hers. He heard her sharp intake of breath as his lips brushed hers and felt something jam in his chest. His lungs? His heart? He didn't know, but everything seemed to start aching.

She tasted so damned sweet, he wanted more. Nay, he *ached* for more.

He brushed his mouth over her velvety lips again. So soft. So incredibly soft. He had to let his mouth linger, press a little harder, but that was it, he assured himself. He held his mouth there, giving her the kiss, but not giving in to the urge pounding through his body. The urge to pull her up against him, open her lips under his, and taste every inch of that silky, sweet mouth with his tongue.

Pull back. You have to pull back.

But God, it felt so good, and he'd been wanting to do this for so damned long. Just a moment longer and he swore—

She moaned, and whatever promise he'd been about to make to himself was lost in the surge of lust that shot through him as her mouth opened under his.

He dropped his hand from the gentle hold on her chin and plunged it into the knot at the back of her head, to bring her mouth more firmly against him, while his other hand slid around her waist to bring her body against his.

Oh God, yes. He groaned as sensation crashed down over him in a hot wave and dragged him under. There was no holding back.

One kiss? He was a damned fool.

By Monica McCarty

The Arrow
The Raider
The Hunter
The Recruit
The Saint
The Viper
The Ranger
The Hawk
The Chief

Highland Warrior
Highland Outlaw
Highland Scoundrel

Highlander Untamed
Highlander Unmasked
Highlander Unchained

Books published by Random House are available at quantity discounts on bulk purchases for premium, educational, fund-raising, and special sales use. For details, please call 1-800-733-3000.

THE
Arrow

A HIGHLAND GUARD NOVEL

MONICA
McCARTY

Northfield Public Library
210 Washington Street
Northfield, MN 55057

BALLANTINE BOOKS • NEW YORK

Sale of this book without a front cover may be unauthorized. If this book is coverless, it may have been reported to the publisher as "unsold or destroyed" and neither the author nor the publisher may have received payment for it.

The Arrow is a work of fiction. Names, characters, places, and incidents are the products of the author's imagination or are used fictitiously. Any resemblance to actual events, locales, or persons, living or dead, is entirely coincidental.

A Ballantine Books Mass Market Original

Copyright © 2014 by Monica McCarty

All rights reserved.

Published in the United States by Ballantine Books, an imprint of Random House, a division of Random House LLC, a Penguin Random House Company, New York.

BALLANTINE and the HOUSE colophon are registered trademarks of Random House LLC.

ISBN 978-0-345-54395-0
eBook ISBN 978-0-345-54396-7

Cover design: Lynn Andreozzi

Cover illustration: Franco Accornero

Printed in the United States of America

www.ballantinebooks.com

9 8 7 6 5 4 3

Ballantine mass market edition: September 2014

To all the readers who have been asking
for this book from day one,
and who obviously know how to appreciate
a little eye candy. This one's for you!
And to "tomboys" everywhere
(the OED has the first use in 1592!)
who discovered that it was okay to prefer sports
to Barbies, and still wear the occasional skirt :)

ACKNOWLEDGMENTS

It's hard to believe this is my fifteenth book with Ballantine. Since December of 2005, when I signed my first contract, I've been extremely fortunate to work with some incredible people. After so many books I've named them all many times, but a huge thanks again to everyone in editorial, production, art, and sales and marketing who have worked on my books and turned a raw manuscript into a published book on a shelf at your favorite retailer.

I do need to give one more shout-out and thanks, however, to Scott Shannon, who took that initial "water cooler" pitch for the MacLeod trilogy from my agent Andrea Cirillo (it might not have been an actual water cooler, but you get the idea), Gina Wachtel, who has been a source of such incredible support for my books over the years, Lynn Andreozzi and the art department for an unbroken record of fifteen(!) exceptional covers (and for beating down the door of every muscular model in the business), and my fabulous former editors Charlotte Herscher and Kate Collins, as well as my current one Junessa Viloria. Junessa, I don't think editorial letters are supposed to be fun to receive, but somehow you've made it that way!

From day one, I've had the ladies at Jane Rotrosen taking care of the business side of things so I can concentrate on the important thing: writing. Thanks to Andrea Cirillo and Annelise Robey for always having my back, for the long talks about "the business," and for bringing out the pompoms when needed. One of these days, I'm going to buy you guys cheerleader costumes for Halloween!

And finally, a huge thanks to Jami Alden who has been my "alpha" (not beta, of course!) reader for every book I've ever written, and who helps me talk through story or character issues when they arise, you are the best. I'd insert the "you can never quit me" line from *Brokeback,* but our husbands might have some questions.

THE HIGHLAND GUARD

Tor "Chief" MacLeod: Team Leader and
  Expert Swordsman
Erik "Hawk" MacSorley: Seafarer and Swimmer
Lachlan "Viper" MacRuairi: Stealth, Infiltration,
  and Extraction
Arthur "Ranger" Campbell: Scouting and
  Reconnaissance
Gregor "Arrow" MacGregor: Marksman and Archer
Magnus "Saint" MacKay: Survivalist and
  Weapon Forging
Kenneth "Ice" Sutherland: Explosives and Versatility
Eoin "Striker" MacLean: Strategist in "Pirate" Warfare
Ewen "Hunter" Lamont: Tracker and Hunter of Men
Robert "Raider" Boyd: Physical Strength and
  Hand-to-Hand Combat

Also:
Helen "Angel" MacKay (née Sutherland): Healer

FOREWORD

The year of Our Lord thirteen hundred and twelve . . . For six years Robert the Bruce and his secret band of elite warriors known as the Highland Guard have been waging a new kind of war against the English, who have sought to wrest the crown from King Robert's head and make Scotland a fiefdom with England's king as its overlord.

To defeat the most powerful army in Christendom, superior in number, weaponry, and training, the Bruce has forsaken the fighting style of the knight and adopted the "pirate" warfare of the fierce warriors from the Highlands and the Western Isles. Like the Norsemen who had descended on Britain's seashores hundreds of years before, the Bruce has struck terror in the heart of the enemy with his surprise attacks, ambuscade, and scorching of the earth to leave nothing behind, winning the battle for Scotland's countryside.

But with English garrisons still occupying Scotland's important castles, and little in the way of siege weaponry at his disposal, the Bruce will have to become even more inventive, using cunning, trickery, and the special skills of the men in his Highland Guard to take them back.

Prologue

Moss Wood, Lochmaben, Scotland, March 1307

Cate thought nothing could be worse than the hideous wails and screams of the dying, but she was wrong. The silence of the dead was infinitely worse.

Huddled in the damp blackness of the old well, she rocked back and forth in icy, shivery terror, trying not to think about where she was or what might be crawling around her.

Her eyes burned with tears that had run out hours ago. She'd screamed and cried for help until her voice was a thin rasp. She was so thirsty, but she dared not pray for water. She was only too conscious of what would happen if it rained. How much water would it take for the old well to fill, inch by horrible inch, as she waited for someone to find her?

But the English hadn't meant for anyone to find her. After the soldiers' murderous rampage, they'd left her here to die. To slowly starve to death or drown—they cared not which. It was her punishment for trying to save her . . .

A sob choked in her throat. Heat swelled her eyes. Her mother. *Oh God, Mother!*

She closed her eyes, trying to shut out the memories. But alone in the darkness there was nowhere to hide. They came, barreling through her mind in an avalanche of fresh horror.

Cate had been at the river fishing when she'd heard the sound of horses. It was the number that made the hair at the back of her neck stand up. In their small, isolated village tucked into the forested hills on the outskirts of Lochmaben, they had few visitors. In these dangerous times, with the outlaw Earl of Carrick (King Robert, as he'd crowned himself) recently returned to Scotland after being forced to flee the year before, so many riders could be only one thing: bad. It was either more of Bruce's men seeking refuge in the outlaw king's ancestral lands—putting the small village of mostly women and children in more danger—or worse, the English soldiers who'd garrisoned the nearby Bruce stronghold of Lochmaben and were turning over every stone and village looking for the outlaws or the "rebels" who gave them aid.

She didn't bother with her net or fishing line (or her shoes, which she'd removed and left on the bank); she just ran. Fear had taken over, with the stories of the fresh wave of English terror racing through her mind. Men drawn apart by horses, women raped, children beaten, cottages ransacked and burned, all in the effort to make neighbor turn on neighbor. To find the rebels and punish them. Cate had no love for "King" Robert, but even he was preferable to their English "overlords."

God help them, if the English ever learned her village had given shelter to the handful of Bruce's men who'd survived a massacre a few weeks ago at Loch Ryan. Cate had warned her mother—to whom the other women deferred—not to do it, but Helen of Lochmaben would not be dissuaded. It was their duty, she'd said; even dispossessed, the outlaw king was their lord.

Cate was halfway back to the village when she heard the first scream. Her heart leapt in panic, and she shot forward through the trees and brush, heedless of the branches scratching her cheeks or the stones digging into her bare feet. While fishing she'd tied the skirts of her kirtle around her waist, revealing the more comfortable breeches she sometimes hid underneath so as to not upset her mother.

The first cottage on the edge of the village came into view; it belonged to her friend Jean. She opened her mouth to shout for her, but the scream died in her throat. Cate stopped dead in her tracks and felt her stomach turn, and then heave. Jean's mother lay on the ground with blood still flowing from the bright red gash across her neck. Jean lay across her, pinned to her mother where she'd fallen with a pike through her back.

It was as she'd feared. A dozen English soldiers were swarming over the small cottage like mail-clad locusts, a black plague leaving only death in its wake.

"If there is nothing worth saving, burn it," one of the soldiers said. "The next village will think twice about offering shelter to rebels."

Cate's heart jolted in horror, his words leaving no doubt of what they intended. It was more than punishment; it was a lesson in what came to those who helped the outlaw king.

Fear unlike any she'd ever known gripped her. Her mother. She had to find her mother. Had to reach her before the soldiers did. Although the sounds coming toward her told her it might already be too late. The English were everywhere.

Careful to avoid being seen, she crept through the trees, each step, and each cottage she passed, confirming her worst fears. It was a vicious, bloody massacre. The soldiers were sparing no one. Old men, women, children, even babes were cut down before her stricken gaze. Twenty-seven. That's how many people remained in the once thriving village. People she had known and cared for her whole life.

Don't think of that now. Her stomach turned again, her body wanting to rid itself of the horror, but she knew she didn't have time. She had to reach . . .

There! Finally, she spotted the small cottage that she had shared with her mother and her stepfather—her second— until he'd been killed last summer. If any breath had been left in Cate's lungs, she would have heaved a sigh of relief.

Unlike the other wattle-and-daub cottages, there were no soldiers swarming around it. It was eerily quiet. Thank God, she'd reached her mother in time.

A scream pierced the illusion of peace like a dagger. Her heart froze in sheer terror. Though she'd never heard her mother make a sound like that, instinctively she knew it was her.

Cate might be only fifteen, but she had seen enough of war and English atrocities to have her mind immediately fill with ghastly images. But she pushed them forcefully away. *Don't think about it. The scream means she is still alive. That is all that matters.*

It was all Cate focused on as she crept toward the cottage, at any moment expecting men to burst forth and capture her. Her heart had stopped beating, and she seemed to barely be breathing, as she circled around back.

"No, please!" The terrified, pleading voice of her mother stopped Cate cold. "Please don't hurt my baby."

Cate bit her lip to prevent the sob that gurgled up the back of her throat from escaping. Her mother was more than eight months pregnant with her dead stepfather's child. Her second child, which she'd had to wait over fifteen years to conceive. Between Cate and her mother, it was hard to tell who was more excited about the new baby. A brother or a sister, Cate didn't care. She would finally have a sibling.

Please don't hurt them.

Crawling over the fence that penned in the few animals they had left—a pig, an old goat, a few hens, and one mean cockerel—she looked around for a better weapon than the small knife she carried in the belt at her waist to gut the fish. From the few farm instruments stacked near the back door, she grabbed the most threatening looking: a long-handled hoe. A sharp sickle for reaping the grain would be better, but here in the woods they didn't have any crops other than the few hardy vegetables they could get to grow in their small garden.

She heard a loud grunting sound and her imagination could no longer be contained. She knew what it meant, but it still didn't prepare her for the sight that met her eyes when she moved from the back room where the animals were kept in the winter into the living area.

Her mother was lying on the table where they'd broken their fast a mere hour ago, a soldier in mail and a blue-and-white surcoat leaning over her. He had his back to Cate, but from the thrusting movement of his hips between her mother's spread legs it was obvious what he was doing. He had his forearm pressed across her mother's throat to prevent her from talking—and breathing.

Her mother's already wide eyes bulged wider in fresh panic when she saw Cate over his shoulder. Cate heard the wordless plea to leave, to run and not look back, to stay safe, but she could not heed it. Her mother was the only person in the world she loved. She couldn't let her die.

Cate's fingers squeezed around the wooden handle, her muscles tensing with readiness. Not for the first time, she wished she were bigger. She'd always been small for her age, and the famine of war and English occupation had made her slender frame scrawny. But she worked hard, and what flesh she had on her bones was muscle.

Calling on every bit of strength she possessed, Cate lifted the hoe high and swung as hard as she could across the soldier's head. But he must have sensed her approach and turned his head just enough to avoid the strike to the temple she'd intended. Instead, the iron of the hoe connected with the steel of his helm. The force was enough to make him stagger, knocking him off her mother, but unfortunately not off his feet.

He cursed and turned on her with a look of such rage and menace that she could live a thousand lifetimes and never forget it. His features—twisted though they were— fixed in her memory. Dark, flat eyes, a sharp aquiline nose, a thin mustache and neatly trimmed beard. He had the finely wrought face of a nobleman, not the thick, heavyset features of a brute she'd expected. Norman, she would wager. If not by birth then by heritage. But his refined looks could not hide the evil emanating from him.

He was cursing at her and shouting.

Her mother was crying, "No, Caty, no!"

Not hesitating, Cate lifted the hoe again. She was so focused on her task, she didn't hear the two men approaching from the other side of the room—men she hadn't even noticed—as she brought it down hard again on his shoulder.

He let out a grunt of pain. "Get the little bitch off me!"

One of the soldiers grabbed her arm. The other wrenched the hoe from her hand. The brute who'd been raping her mother lifted his steel-gauntleted hand and brought it down hard across Cate's face before she could turn away. But she noticed with satisfaction the blood streaming down his arm. At least she'd done some damage.

Her mother screamed and lunged for Cate, trying to protect her with her body.

That was when the true nightmare began. The handful of seconds that would play over and over in Cate's mind. It happened so fast, and yet each second ticked by in haunting precision.

Out of the corner of her eye Cate saw the flash of silver as the brute pulled his sword from the scabbard at his waist. She opened her mouth to scream a warning, but it was too late. The blade came down in one vicious stroke across her mother's body, splitting her side to the waist in an instant. Her mother's expression went from stunned to horror to pain, where it stayed for what seemed an agonizing length of time. "Love you . . . father . . . *sorry* . . ." Her voice faded; she staggered and slid to the ground.

Cate wrenched free from her captor with a primal scream and tried to catch her. But the second soldier stopped her before she could reach her mother. Cate fought like a wildcat, but he was simply too strong.

"What should I do with her, Captain?" he said to the monster who'd just cut down the only person in the world she had left.

The brute bent down to wipe his sword on her mother's sark, leaving a sickly streak of red on the creamy linen. "Kill the mongrel's bitch. I'd use her to finish, but I need a woman, not a pathetic chit in breeches. Find me one," he ordered the first man.

The man who was holding her reached for his blade. He had his arm wrapped around her like a vise. Though she knew it was hopeless, she kicked and screamed, trying to free herself.

The captain watched her with a predatory smile on his face, clearly enjoying her terror. "Wait," he said. "I want the rebel brat to pay for what she dared. Toss her in that old well outside." His smile deepened, his white teeth flashing across his face like a wolf's. "Let her suffer before she dies."

That was hours ago. How many, she didn't know. It had been morning when Cate had gone fishing, and the skies had been dark for some time. The last embers of the fires the soldiers set had burned themselves out some time ago.

Everything was gone. Her mother. The babe. Her friends. Her home. All that was left was ash and this hideous pit of death.

She'd given up trying to climb out. Though freedom was only a precious six feet away when she stood, what handholds and toeholds there were in the stone walls crumbled with her weight. She'd tried to wedge her back against the wall, but her legs weren't long enough to exert enough pressure to inch her way up.

Tired, cold, and wet, she knew she had to conserve her strength. Someone would come for her. Someone would find her.

But how long would it take?

Every minute in this pit felt like torture. Her heart raced in her chest. She hated the dark, and icy fear had become a companion to her grief.

"There's nothing to be scared of, Caty Cat. The darkness won't hurt you."

The laughing voice—familiar even all these years gone past—came out of the darkness like a ghost, haunting her with cruel memories.

What made her think of *him* now? she wondered. The father—the *natural* father—who'd soothed her nightmares when she was a child, but who'd left her and never looked back when she was just five? He certainly wouldn't come for her.

A tear slipped from the corner of her eye and she angrily brushed it away. He didn't deserve her tears.

Her eyes burned fiercely. For a while her anger kept her fear at bay. But by the next night it had returned. By the following it had turned to panic. By the next it had turned to desperation. And by the fifth it had turned to the most horrible feeling of all: hopelessness.

Gregor MacGregor gazed around the charred shell of the village, a grim set to his celebrated features. The past year of war had shown him some of the very worst of mankind, but this . . .

Bile rose to the back of his throat. He had to fight to keep the contents of his stomach down. His companions—especially Eoin MacLean and Ewen Lamont, who'd been here not a month ago—seemed to be having the same struggle. When MacLean disappeared behind one of the burned-out buildings, Gregor figured he'd lost the battle.

"It's true," Lamont said. "Bloody hell, it's true. Who the hell could do something like this?" The gruff tracker's eyes were stark with disbelief as they met his. "All those women and children." His voice cut off and then dropped to a ragged whisper. "They killed them all."

Lamont turned away. He didn't seem to expect a response and Gregor didn't have one to give him. What could he say? It was true. The blackened bodies they found at each holding left no doubt.

Rage replaced some of his horror. *No more,* he vowed. Once Bruce was on the throne, nothing like this would ever happen again.

The importance of this mission to Bruce was evident by the man who spoke next. Tor "Chief" MacLeod, the leader of the king's secret band of elite soldiers known as the Highland Guard, hadn't left the king's side for more than a few hours in recent weeks. Personal bodyguard, enforcer, protector, advisor, MacLeod was everything for Robert the Bruce. Yet the king had sent his most trusted man to check on the loyal villagers who had given a handful of his men shelter after the worst disaster of a short reign that had been filled with disasters.

The fearsome West Highland chief cursed, his stony expression revealing a rare glimpse of emotion. "For once I wish our informants had been wrong."

Gregor nodded. "As do I."

They'd come as soon as they heard the first whisper of rumor that the English had retaliated against the village that had given the "rebels" aid. Leaving their temporary base in the hills and forest of Galloway, they'd raced the forty miles or so east through Dumfries to Lochmaben. But they'd never had a chance to prevent the slaughter that had taken place here.

As soon as MacLean rejoined them, MacLeod turned to

him and his partner, Lamont. The two Guardsmen were among the handful of men who'd escaped the disaster at Loch Ryan and taken refuge here. "No one could have foreseen this. This is not on you—either of you. Do you understand?"

His voice was hard and commanding, without a hint of compassion or reassurance. Lamont and MacLean were warriors; they understood orders, not coddling.

Neither man responded for a moment. They exchanged a glance, and then Lamont gave a short nod, one that was mirrored a moment later by his partner.

"Good," MacLeod said. "Then let us give the villagers a proper burial and return to the king to tell him what we have found. But do not doubt that what has been done here will be avenged." He turned to Gregor. "Gather the bodies and bring them here." They were standing in what had been the village kirk—identifiable by the scraps of the robe left on the body of the priest. "The three of us will dig."

Gregor nodded and began the grim work of gathering the charred remains of the dead.

Someone will come for me . . .

Cate dreamed of knights from troubadour's tales. Of strong, handsome warriors on white chargers with shimmering mail, colorful tabards, and banners streaming in the wind as they rode in to the rescue. Noble knights. Valiant knights. The knights of her childhood. The knights she'd once believed in. A knight like her father.

"My father is the greatest knight in Christendom!" The boast she'd made when the other children teased her about being a bastard had only provided more fodder for them after he'd left.

"Where's the greatest knight in Christendom now, Caty?" they'd taunted.

Not here.

She woke with a start. Delirious with hunger and thirst, barely strong enough to unfurl from the ball that she'd been rolled in for God knew how long, at first the sound of voices confused her. She'd prayed so hard and for so long without response that when it finally came, just when she'd resigned herself to her fate, it seemed a cruel taunt of her imagination.

But then the voices grew stronger. *Men's* voices. Was it the English soldiers? Had they come back to torment her? To finish what they'd started?

A fist of irrational fear gripped her, and her raw lips—which had parted to cry for help—clamped shut. But then she realized she had to take a chance. If the men were friends, it might be her only chance of rescue. And if they were English . . .

Perhaps they would put her out of her misery.

She opened her mouth to cry for help, but in some kind of cruel, twisted irony, her voice strangled in her throat. Tears of desperation and frustration sprang to her eyes. She willed her voice to work with everything she had left, but it wasn't enough for more than a faint whisper. "Help! Please, help me." She started to cry at the futility, precious fluid rolling down her cheeks. "Help me."

God, this couldn't be happening! She was strong. She wouldn't give up. She didn't want to die.

She thought of her mother, of the brother or sister she would never have a chance to know, of her friends and neighbors she'd known her whole life. Someone had to remember them. Someone had to see that the men who did this paid.

She tried again. "Help!" It was louder this time. Not much, but enough to give her encouragement. She sat up a little straighter, looked up through the tunnel of light, and tried again. And again.

Her efforts were rewarded by a shout, a voice that

seemed to be coming closer to her. "I think someone is down there."

It wasn't her imagination. She cried out again, sobbing with both hope and fear. *Don't go . . . Please don't go! I'm here.*

With a burst of energy, she wobbled to a stand, using the mossy stones of the wall to help keep her upright. She looked up as a shadow crossed over her head. A man's face appeared above her, peering down.

She gasped. Blinked. Felt her knees grow wobbly—and not from exhaustion or starvation.

From his face. The most perfect she'd ever seen.

Sunlight blazed behind him like a halo, bathing his tawny hair in golden light. His nose was straight and strong; his jaw firm, lightly clefted, and not too square; his cheeks high and sculpted; and his mouth . . . his mouth was wide and full of sin. His eyes were light in color—blue or green, she could not tell—set below brows arched like the wings of a raven. There wasn't one part of him, not one bone or one inch of golden skin, that had not been put in exactly the right position.

Dear Lord, he wasn't a man, he was an angel.

And that meant . . .

I'm in heaven.

It was her last thought as the ground rose under her feet.

"Is she alive?"

A deep voice pulled her from unconsciousness. She had the sensation of floating. Nay, of being carried. A man's arms were around her. Arms that were strong and safe.

He put her down on the ground. The gentle warmth of his breath as he leaned over her caused her eyes to flutter open.

Their eyes met: hers and her angel's.

"Aye," he said softly, brushing a clump of matted hair from her forehead. "She's alive."

The gentleness in his voice made her chest swell with emotion. She opened her mouth to speak, but all she could do was lick her dry lips. The next moment a skin was brought to her mouth and the first precious drops of water slid down her parched throat. She drank hungrily—greedily—until he murmured for her to slow; she would make herself ill.

When he pulled it away a moment later, she would have tried to snatch it back had she not been distracted. He was cradling her against his chest, and his heavenly face was so close, all she had to do was reach up and touch it. Green. His eyes were green and framed by the thickest, most glorious lashes she'd ever seen. Unfair—even for an angel.

Alive? She frowned as his words penetrated. "But you're an angel."

She heard what sounded like a sharp laugh coming from behind her. "Hawk is going to have fun with that one."

Her angel shot an angry glare in the direction of the man who'd spoken, but his words and gentle voice were for her. "You are alive, child. And safe."

The reminder of what had happened made her clutch at him in renewed terror. With her head pressed against his leather-clad chest—a very hard and broad chest—she glanced behind her, for the first time seeing the three men standing there.

She gasped, shirking in fear. They were massive. Clad in black leather *cotuns* studded with bits of steel and darkened nasal helms (her rescuer's was on the ground next to her, she realized), the tall, muscular warriors made her shiver. Good thing she hadn't seen them first or she might have thought she'd died and gone rather south of heaven.

Who were they? Not English, she knew by the soft burr in her rescuer's voice. She looked again, seeing the dark plaids they wore around their shoulders. *Highlanders.* But which side were they on? The clans from the Highlands fought on both sides of the war: some with Bruce and some, like the MacDougalls, against him, making them reluctant allies of Edward of England, the self-proclaimed "Hammer of the Scots."

Were these men with the English?

Her rescuer seemed to sense her fear. "It's all right, lass—we are not your enemy. We were sent by King Robert to help when he heard the English had retaliated for the shelter your village gave to his men."

Help? Her mouth drew tight. Bruce was the one who had put them in this position. He was the one who'd done this.

But these men were proof that Scotland's would-be king hadn't completely forsaken them. Not that it gave her much comfort; Bruce's men had come too late.

And there were only four of them! Her heart started to race again, pounding against her chest like a drum. "What if they come back?"

"Who?" he asked. "Who did this, child?"

Tears streamed down her cheeks and a fierce sob tore from her lungs. "English soldiers from the castle. The Earl of Hereford's men. They . . ."

She started to cry harder when she remembered what they'd done. He drew her closer to his chest, soothing her with soft words, telling her it would be all right.

But it wouldn't be all right. It would never be right again. Her mother was gone, and Cate had no one. Unconsciously, her fingers gripped the steely muscles of his arms harder. Except him. This man who looked like an angel sent from God to save her from certain death. As long as he was holding her, she had him. And Cate didn't want to ever let him go.

Gregor thought he might need Robbie Boyd (or at least his fellow Guardsman's inhuman strength) to pry the lass's bloody fingers from his arms, but eventually the mite grew so exhausted from weeping, she dozed off, enabling him to help the others finish their grim task.

But he kept a close eye on her where he'd left her, wrapped in his plaid by the horses. The wee lass was traumatized, and as he was the one who'd found her, he felt strangely responsible for her. Strangely, because it was an entirely new experience feeling any sort of responsibility toward a woman—even one who was still a child.

But when he thought of what she'd been through, it roused every protective bone in his body. Bones he hadn't even known existed.

God's blood, how long has she been in that hellhole? Four days? Five? She'd been close to death—was *still* close to death. Without food and water for so long . . .

He grimaced. It would be bad enough for a grown man, let alone a young girl with little meat on her bones to spare. Her shredded fingers from trying to climb out of the well were evidence of the torture she'd endured and how desperate she'd been to escape.

He'd thought he'd seen just about every injustice and barbarous cruelty the English could mete out. But who could do something like this to a child? It seemed calculated and almost personal.

Gregor didn't have much experience with young lasses, but he did have two younger brothers, and she couldn't be more than eleven or twelve. Still more young girl than young woman. One side of his mouth curved up, recalling the breeches he'd been surprised to discover under her skirts when he'd carried her over his shoulder to climb out of the well.

She weighed next to nothing. Practically skin and bone. Fragile, but with a surprising strength to her skinny limbs. Aye, the lass was a fighter. With what she'd survived, she had to be.

It was MacLean who finally asked the question they all

were thinking. "What are we going to do with her? We can't take her back to camp. It's too dangerous."

That was an understatement. They'd been back in Scotland for less than a month after being on the run in the Western Isles for the past six. Bruce's army had won one minor victory against the English at Turnberry, but they were one lost battle away from being forced to flee again. After the disaster at Loch Ryan, where over two-thirds of Bruce's force had been killed, they'd been left with fewer than four hundred men in the entire army.

A lost cause it might seem to some, but they didn't know Robert the Bruce. Gregor would fight by his side for as long as it took, even if they were the last two men standing.

"Was she able to tell you anything that might help?" MacLeod asked.

Gregor shook his head. "Nothing more than what we'd already guessed. It was Hereford's men." Though Lochmaben was part of the Bruce ancestral lands of the Lordship of Annandale, its castle was again in English hands after being retaken by Bruce last year. King Edward had given it to Sir Humphrey de Bohun, Earl of Hereford, and the earl and countess (one of King Edward's daughters) had arrived not long ago to occupy it. "She is still in shock. She couldn't even tell me her name. She just kept crying over and over that he killed her mother, and now she was alone."

Lamont winced. "She witnessed her mother's death."

Gregor turned to him grimly. "Aye, it sounds like it."

"Poor lass," MacLean said. "She's too young to have seen something like that."

An odd look crossed MacLeod's face. It took Gregor a moment to realize it was compassion. "I was ten, probably only a couple of years younger than her, when I witnessed my mother raped and murdered. I still remember every damned moment of it."

The men were silent. Apparently Gregor wasn't the only one to be strangely affected by the lass's suffering; it had penetrated the stony shell of one of the most feared swordsmen in Scotland—hell, probably in Christendom. Until MacLeod's marriage last year to Christina Fraser, Gregor didn't think the Chief of the Highland Guard was capable of smiling.

"Perhaps she has relatives nearby?" Lamont asked.

"No!" The lass's voice rang out, and the next moment she'd launched herself into Gregor's arms. Her raw and bloodied fingers were digging into his arms again, clutching tighter if it were possible. "Please, you can't leave me here. They'll find me and kill me."

"Shhh," he soothed, stroking her head. "No one is going to leave you here. But isn't there someplace we can take you? An aunt? An uncle?"

She shook her head furiously. "There is no one. My mother is my only family."

He didn't correct her tense. "What about your father?"

A hard look crossed her face. "Dead." From her tone, he gathered her memories were not fond ones. "At Methven."

One of the many disasters that had felled Bruce's and his men last year. "What's your name, lass?"

She hesitated. "Caitrina."

"And your father's name?"

Another pause. "Kirkpatrick."

A common enough clan name around these parts. "You have no brothers or sisters, Caitrina?" Gregor realized it was the wrong question to ask when her face collapsed in grief.

"My mother was eight months pregnant. He was hurting her. I had to try to make him stop."

Gregor felt rage flare inside him, suspecting the kind of "hurting." Sick bastards! He squeezed her tighter, though he knew there was no comfort he could give her that would take the pain away.

"I hit him with the hoe, but I missed, and then he . . ." Tears glimmered in the big brown eyes that dominated her small face. She was a cute little thing (even beneath the dirt) with a wide mouth, slightly upturned nose, softly pointed chin, and dark hair and brows to match her eyes. "He killed her. It was my fault. He killed her because of me."

Gregor's voice turned hard as he shook her by the shoulders and forced her to heed him. "It was not your fault," he said in a voice that brooked no argument—much like MacLeod had spoken to MacLean and Lamont earlier. "You fought back and gave her a chance no one else in this village had."

"But I wasn't strong enough."

"You were strong enough to try, and that's what counts. Fighting isn't just about physical strength. Quickness and knowing where to strike can compensate for size."

She eyed him skeptically. "But I'm a girl."

He mocked disbelief. "I must have been confused by the breeches."

A fiery blush stole up her cheeks. "I just wear those sometimes to make it easier to move around." She paused and looked at him. "Do you really think I could learn to defend myself?"

He nodded, guessing the direction of her thoughts—to prevent a man from doing what had been done to her mother. "I'm certain of it."

Her dark brows gathered across her nose, and her mouth screwed down tightly in an expression that was oddly fierce. "Then I'll do it. Will you teach me?"

Ah hell. He looked to his companions for help, but they gave him a look that told him he'd gotten himself into this.

"Please," she begged. "Can't you take me with you? I've nowhere else to go."

She looked up at him with such hope in her eyes, he instinctively wanted to turn away. No one should pin their hopes on him.

There had to be someplace he could take her. A church? Perhaps a home for foundlings in Dumfries?

But something inside him rebelled at the idea. What would become of her? Who would protect a young girl? And what would happen to her when she wasn't so young?

Not your concern. Not your responsibility.

He grimaced. She wasn't, but he couldn't force himself to turn away. No matter what MacLeod said, they all bore some guilt for what had happened to this lass and the other villagers.

Perhaps there was somewhere he could take her. Someplace where she would be welcomed—loved, even. His mother had always yearned for a daughter. Since the death of his father and two older brothers, she'd been so lost. He knew his softhearted mother would take one look at the lass, hear what had happened to her, and melt.

"Please," the lass said with just enough desperation to make his chest pinch.

Though every instinct told him he was making a mistake, Gregor didn't heed the warning. "My home is in Roro—near Loch Tay in the Highlands. You can stay there with my mother, if you wish. You will be safe there."

The look on her face was one he'd seen many times before—a cross between adulation and love—and he instantly regretted whatever impulse it had been that compelled him to make the offer.

But it was too late.

"Do you mean it? You will really take me with you?" She launched herself against his chest and wrapped her arms around him. "Oh thank you, thank you, thank you!"

Bloody hell, what had he done?

He looked over the dark head that barely reached midpoint in his chest to see his friends watching them and trying not to laugh—even MacLeod.

"Breaking hearts wherever he goes," MacLean said to Lamont with a laugh. "Looks like you've made yourself another conquest, MacGregor. Though this one's a little young even for you. The curse of a pretty face, I suppose."

"Bugg—" Conscious of the lass, Gregor bit back the rest of his normal response.

Instead he gave MacLean a deadly look. It wasn't funny. Especially as Gregor suspected it might be true.

What had he gotten himself into?

One

❧

Berwick Castle, English Marches, 6 December 1312

There is nothing wrong with me.

Gregor drew his arrow back and let it loose. One shot. One kill. He wouldn't miss.

He didn't. The soldier froze in paralyzed shock as Gregor's arrow found the narrow patch of skin between his eyes—one of the few places unprotected by mail and the steel kettle-cap the soldiers favored. The old Norse nasal-style helm that the Highland Guard wore would have served them better. But even at this close range— Gregor was no more than thirty yards away—such a small target required skill to hit. Skill like that possessed by the greatest archer in Scotland.

A moment later, the Englishman's mail-clad body toppled to the ground like a felled tree. Before he'd even hit the ground, the next target already had appeared on the rampart. Gregor took quick aim and fired. He didn't appear to think; his movements were as smooth and precise as a finely tuned engine of war. But the cool, effortless facade masked the intense focus and concentration underneath. Everyone was counting on him, but under pressure was when Gregor MacGregor was at his best.

Usually.

The second soldier fell as the arrow found its mark.

After nearly seven years fighting in the Bruce's elite

Highland Guard, no one was better at eliminating key targets in advance of an attack than Gregor. Targets. That's how he had to think of them. An obstacle in between him and his objective that needed to be eliminated to achieve victory. And there had been plenty of obstacles over the past seven years.

But they were making progress—*real* progress—and the victory over the English that most had thought impossible was inching closer to reality. Since returning to Scotland from the Western Isles, where Bruce and those loyal to him had been forced to flee six years ago, the king had made steady gains in wresting his kingdom from English occupation. He'd defeated his own countrymen to take control of the North; Robbie Boyd, along with James Douglas and Thomas Randolph, had a firm grip on the lawless Borders; and the isolated former Celtic kingdom of Galloway was about to fall to the king's only remaining brother, Edward Bruce.

All that were left were the English garrisons entrenched in Scotland's castles, and one by one those were falling to Bruce as well. But none would be more important than Berwick Castle. The impenetrable stronghold in the Scottish or English Marches (depending on who currently had control) had seen more than its share of this war and had served as the English king's headquarters on his previous campaigns. Taking it would bring them one step—one *big* step—closer to victory. But without siege engines, Bruce and his men had to rely on more inventive methods. Like the grappling-hook-and-rope ladders two of Gregor's fellow members of the Highland Guard were waiting to toss over the wall, as soon as he cleared the battlements of the enemy.

Gregor peered into the darkness, scanning the wall patiently, his pulse slow and steady. There had been three soldiers patrolling this section of the wall. Where was the third?

There! His reaction instantaneous, Gregor let loose the arrow at the first glimpse of steel as the soldier emerged from the shadows of the guardhouse. The man fell to the ground before he even knew what hit him.

Pop, pop, pop, and it was done. The targets had been cleared.

Gregor never missed. Which was why he was so valuable. When stealth was key, the Highland Guard could not risk an errant arrow or one landing in a part of the body that might give the enemy a chance to raise the alarm. Bruce's success depended on subterfuge. And Gregor would do whatever he had to do to see Bruce permanently entrenched on Scotland's throne.

Except that he had missed. Gregor bit back a curse of frustration. The third arrow had landed in one of the soldier's eyes, not between them. To anyone else it might be on the mark—dead was dead—but not for him. For him, it was a miss.

And it wasn't the first. The past few weeks—months— he'd been off by a few inches more than once.

It's nothing, he told himself. *A temporary rut. Everyone has them.*

Everyone but him. He couldn't afford to be anything but perfect. Too much was riding on this. The king was counting on him. And the small misses bothered him more than he wanted to admit.

Gregor took one more look before using hand gestures to let the others know that it was all clear. Leaving their position hidden in the shadows of the riverbank, the five men crept toward the White Wall. They were the advance guard. The men handpicked by Bruce to go over the wall first and open the gate from within to let in the rest of them. In addition to Gregor and his fellow Guardsmen Arthur "Ranger" Campbell, Lachlan "Viper" MacRuairi, and Erik "Hawk" MacSorley, Bruce had chosen James "the Black" Douglas for the honor of taking Berwick.

This was the most ambitious—and dangerous—attempt they'd made to take a castle by subterfuge yet. Two stone guard towers along the riverbank of the Tweed were linked to the main fortifications atop the motte by the steep winding wall with the apt name of "breakneck stairs." So scaling the wall and taking the lower towers was only the first challenge; they would then have to climb the breakneck stairs and take the upper guard tower before the English became aware of what was happening.

Their task would be aided significantly by the ingenious ladder. Sir James Douglas or, depending on whom you talked to, Sir Thomas Randolph (the good-natured rivalry between the two men for the position of the king's most trusted knight was becoming legend, and they often vied for credit for the latest escapade) had come up with the idea of attaching iron grappling hooks to a rope ladder fitted with wooden footboards. It was light enough to be carried by two men and far easier to hide than the fixed wooden ladders used to scale walls. This would be their first attempt at using one.

Gregor scanned the area of the rampart above for additional soldiers, as Campbell and MacSorley—who as a seafarer had plenty of experience with grappling hooks—went to work tossing the hooks over the wall and securing the ladder into position. With the fierce Island chieftain's uncanny ability to slip in and out of shadows, MacRuairi would go up first, and Gregor would follow, setting up in position along the wall to observe and, if necessary, get rid of any unexpected problems while the rest of the men made their way up the ladder.

Observation was Gregor's secondary role. It was his job to make sure they weren't the ones surprised.

The first part of their mission went smoothly—too smoothly, which always made him twitchy. He'd been on enough missions to know that the only thing you could count on was that something *always* went wrong.

But the ladders worked better than they could have hoped. Within five minutes, Gregor was in position along the wall where he could see both guard towers, and the other men had cleared the wall and dropped down beside him.

With the dark leather light armor, the blackened nasal helms, and skin darkened with ash, they blended into the moonless night. Only the whites of their eyes stood out as they looked to him, waiting for his signal. Scanning the area one more time, he gave it.

The men spread out. MacRuairi and MacSorley went toward the guardhouse leading up to the breakneck stairs, while Douglas and Campbell headed down the stairs of the lower tower to open the sally port to the sea, where the rest of their men—a force of fifty, given the size of the garrison at Berwick—would be waiting.

Gregor kept his eyes on the wall, ready to loose the next arrow if necessary, knowing the next few minutes would be the most dangerous. Discovery now would leave the five warriors at their most vulnerable: inside the castle with nowhere to go, surrounded by two towers of sleeping soldiers. Silence was imperative until the towers could be taken, and the gate opened.

Gregor's ears pricked at a faint sound. His gaze shot to the second guard tower, where MacRuairi and MacSorley were a few feet from entering. His brethren heard the light clicking sound, too, and froze.

Gregor had his arrow nocked and ready. He drew it back, poised to let it sail as soon as the first glimpse of the white of a man's eyes emerged from the shadows.

Tick, tick, tick.

Damn it, that didn't sound like footsteps. It sounded like a . . .

Dog.

A moment later, a mangy-looking terrier—its head no more than a foot off the ground—trotted out of the shadows toward the two warriors. It had probably been scavenging the castle for rats when it heard something and decided to come investigate.

With Gregor's gaze fixed at the height of an average man, it took him a moment to make the adjustment down. *Bloody hell.* The thing was so ugly it was almost cute.

The dog scampered to a sudden stop. It was about a dozen feet from MacSorley and MacRuairi, giving Gregor such an easy mark he could shoot it with his eyes closed. But he didn't. He looked at the pathetic excuse for a dog and hesitated.

The dog seemed to be having second thoughts about approaching the two imposing-looking warriors, proving that it was smarter than its half-starved, unfortunate appearance suggested. Appearing to lose interest, it started to turn away, when something flashed in the moonlight.

The blade from MacRuairi's drawn dagger.

The dog darted into the shadows of the guardhouse like it had just seen a ghost, letting out a torrent of terrified yapping behind it.

God's bones! The dog might be small, but in the quiet night air the shrill, high-pitched bark might as well have been a thunderclap. It had the same effect: disaster.

Gregor unfurled the arrow, but it was too late. The dog was lost in the shadows and the damage had been done. They might as well have rung a bell inside the towers, as soldiers poured out to investigate.

The quiet, sleeping castle had become a hornet's nest.

With them caught in the middle.

He swore, knowing that not only had the dog cost them their chance at surprise—and the chance of taking the castle—but they were also going to have a hell of a time getting out of here without being caught.

But he'd be damned if he let his friends die because of his mistake. Drawing his sword, Gregor turned to face the onslaught of soldiers who were almost on him and shouted the words that had become feared across Christendom. The battle cry of the Highland Guard: *"Airson an Leòmhann!"*

For the Lion!

King Robert the Bruce sat behind the large table that dominated the small solar off the Great Hall of Dunstaffnage Castle and stared blankly at the three warriors.

Why the hell did Gregor feel like squirming? Bruce wasn't his father—the king was only seven years his elder—but Gregor hated to fail at anything, and having to explain it to the man who was the last person he ever wanted to let down made it that much worse. There was no one he believed in more than Robert the Bruce, and Gregor would fight to his dying breath to see him claim his throne.

A claim that could have been much closer if Gregor hadn't buggered up.

A damned dog. They'd lost the chance to take one of the most important castles in the Marches because the best archer in the Highlands had hesitated to shoot a little flea-bitten ratter.

Elite warriors didn't miss and they sure as hell didn't hesitate. Gregor was still furious with himself even a week later. Furious, aye, but that wasn't the worst of it. The worst was how *after* he, MacSorley, and MacRuairi had narrowly—very narrowly—managed to escape the hornet's nest stirred up by the damned dog at Berwick, Gregor had nearly gotten them captured a few days later in the village. Or rather, his damned face had nearly gotten them captured.

The king finally spoke. "We lost our best chance to take back one of the most important castles in the Marches from the English because of a dog?"

MacSorley winced. "Aye, well, it wasn't much of a dog

to speak of, but it could have raised the dead with that bark."

"It was a bit of bad luck, that's all," MacRuairi interjected.

If Gregor needed any more proof of how badly he'd erred, the fact that a mean bastard like Lachlan MacRuairi was trying to cover for him said it all.

"I didn't think any of you fell prey to something so human as bad luck?" the king said with a wry turn of his mouth.

"It wasn't bad luck," Gregor corrected. "It was my fault. I hesitated."

Bruce lifted a brow. "To shoot a dog?"

Gregor gritted his teeth, humiliation burning inside him. He was an elite warrior, the best of the best—he wasn't supposed to make mistakes like this. He *didn't* make mistakes like this. Bruce was counting on him. But he had, damn it, and it had cost them. He met the king's gaze unflinchingly. "Aye."

"In his defense, sire, it was kind of a cute little blighter," MacSorley added with a grin. "And we did find out one thing that is important."

"What's that?" the king asked suspiciously, expecting the jest.

"The rumors are wrong: he doesn't just break hearts, he actually has one."

"Sod off, Hawk," Gregor bit out under his breath. But the blasted seafarer just grinned.

The king appeared to be fighting doing the same. Gregor's reputation was well known. But that wasn't the way of it. If women wanted to throw themselves at him for something as silly as how he looked, he sure as hell wasn't going to stop them. What was he supposed to do, fall in love with all of them?

"And there were no other problems? Campbell and Douglas reported how they managed to hold off the English long enough to open the sally port gate and escape. But they feared you might have been trapped trying to go after them."

That was exactly what had happened, but with the Highland gift for understatement, MacRuairi just said, "It was nothing we couldn't handle, sire."

Robert Bruce hadn't won his crown by being a fool. He narrowed his gaze on the man who'd been one of the most feared pirates in the Western Isles before he'd agreed to join the Highland Guard and fight for Bruce. "Yet it took the three of you a week to return, my best seafarer is hobbling, my best marksman can't lift his arm, and you are wrapped up around your ribs as tight as a mummy?"

"I didn't say there weren't any problems," MacRuairi clarified. "I said it wasn't anything we couldn't handle."

"I think you've been around my little sister-by-marriage for too long, Viper; you're beginning to sound like a damned lawman!"

Janet of Mar, the sister of Bruce's first wife, was married to their fellow Guardsman Ewen Lamont, and the lass could talk her way out of a shite-storm.

Gregor had had enough. The embarrassment of telling the king what had happened couldn't be more painful than listening to these two try to cover it up.

He stepped forward and gave a brief summary of how they'd gone in to rescue Campbell and Douglas, fearing they'd been trapped, and instead become surrounded themselves. They'd managed to fight their way out through about thirty soldiers, but he had taken a blow to the arm with a sword, MacRuairi had broken a few ribs when a war hammer connected with his side, and an arrow had landed in the back of MacSorley's leg while they were running from the castle. As the other men had been forced to flee, leaving them without a quick means of getting away, with the English swarming and MacSorley's leg gushing blood, they'd thought it best to lay low at a safe house in the village until the English gave up their search.

"A sound plan," the king said with a nod.

Gregor held back a grimace. "It should have been."

"But?"

Christ, this was like pulling his own teeth. "But our presence became known and the English surrounded the cottage where we were hiding. Fortunately, the previous occupants had dug a hole under the floor to preserve their winter stores, and we hid in there while the soldiers searched."

"That couldn't have been too comfortable."

That was putting it mildly. Three well over six-foot-tall, broad-shouldered warriors jammed in a space no more than five feet by five feet for nearly an hour had been hell.

"Good thing my cousin smells so sweet from all that bathing," MacSorley said, referring to MacRuairi's well-known penchant for cleanliness. "The whole place smelled like roses."

MacRuairi gave his cousin the cold, I'm-going-to-stick-a-knife-in-your-back-when-you-least-expect-it look that had earned him the war name "Viper."

"You were damned lucky not to be taken," Bruce said.

No one argued with him.

The king sat back in his chair, crossing his arms contemplatively. "So is anyone going to tell me how your presence in the village became known?"

Gregor didn't need to look to know that MacSorley was fighting laughter and dying to make some kind of jest—especially as it was one of his favorite topics to jest about. You'd think that after seven years he'd grow tired of it.

Gregor should be so damned lucky.

Usually, it didn't bother him, but this time it could have gotten them all killed. His mouth fell in a hard line. "It seems the farmer's young daughter couldn't keep a secret and decided to tell a few of her friends we were there."

"A few?" MacSorley said. "The enterprising lass sold nearly a dozen tickets to see the 'most handsome man she'd ever seen in her life.'" He added the last in the dreamy, singsongy voice of a sixteen-year-old lass that made Gregor itch to put his fist through that gleaming grin.

"Tickets?" Bruce asked incredulously. "You can't be serious."

MacRuairi nodded, smirking. "Aye, at a half-penny apiece. And all these years, we've been getting to look at him for free."

Gregor shot him a glare. Now MacRuairi was making jests? Christ, hell had truly frozen over.

"I told you not to remove your helm," MacSorley said, still smirking.

"For three days?" Gregor replied exasperatedly, raking his hair back with his fingers. It was so bloody ridiculous. It wasn't the fact that he was an elite warrior in the Highland Guard taking on the most dangerous missions that was going to get him killed, it was his cursed face.

Although he had to admit there were times when it wasn't a curse—in the alehouse last night, for example, with that pretty, buxom serving lass who'd crept into his bed—but it sure as hell didn't have a place in war.

Just once he'd like to meet a woman who didn't take one look at his face and pledge her undying love. Or at least one who wasn't married to one of his brethren.

Gregor stood silently as MacSorley and MacRuairi exchanged a few more barbs pointed in his direction. By the time they were done, even the king was chuckling.

Aye, it was bloody hilarious. He supposed there were a lot worse things than having women throw themselves at him, but sometimes it began to wear.

After a minute Bruce sobered. "So how long do you think it's going to be before someone connects 'the most handsome man she's ever seen' who was part of the failed attack on Berwick with Gregor MacGregor, the famed archer and 'most handsome man in Scotland'?"

Gregor cringed again. Christ, he hated that moniker. "I don't know, sire."

That his anonymity in the Highland Guard had possibly been jeopardized was one of the worst parts of the whole fiasco in the village. They were all still reeling from the traitor Alex Seton's defection to the enemy. He'd betrayed them all. God help their former brother-in-arms if they ever came face to face with him in battle. Although Seton's former partner Robbie Boyd had been certain Seton would inform the English of their identities, thus far he hadn't. But with what had happened in the village, Gregor knew it was only a matter of time before he was unmasked.

Having his identity hidden was one of the reasons he'd been so eager to join the Highland Guard. The anonymity— the mask—gave him freedom. He would earn a name for himself by his sword—or rather, his bow—and nothing else. There were no distractions like there were at the Highland Games. No well-meaning relatives like his uncle Malcolm, chief of the MacGregor clan, telling him how to help his clan by marrying one of the women who were only too eager to take him for a husband. Gregor would defeat the English, help see the man who had been more a father to him than his own secured on the throne, and do his duty to his clan on his own merit. By deed and skill alone.

"Aye, well, neither do I," the king said, "but I think it's best if you stay out of sight for a while." Gregor started to protest, but Bruce cut him off. "Only a few weeks. It will be Christmas soon anyway. I will send for you when we are ready to take Perth." The king intended to begin laying siege to Perth Castle in early January. He smiled appeasingly. "God knows we can all use a little break. A few weeks to relax and clear our heads. I need you all at one hundred percent."

The words were directed at all of them, but Gregor wasn't fooled. The king knew Gregor had been struggling of late. That was the real reason for this "break." Gregor had let him down. Shame twisted in his gut, but all he could do was nod.

"Besides," Bruce said, handing him a folded piece of parchment, "this arrived from your brother a few days ago."

Gregor let out a groan of deep dread, eyeing the note as if it carried the plague. Bloody hell, what had she done this time?

He took the note with reluctance, not wanting to know. Gregor hadn't had much schooling, but his younger brother John had been meant for the church before their two older brothers had died, and he could write as well as read. Gregor had only a bit of the latter skill, but it was enough to make out the short missive. "Come as soon as you can. Emergency."

Rather than raise alarm, the note only made him curse.

"Problems?" Bruce asked innocently.

He might be king, but that didn't mean Gregor couldn't glare at him from time to time. "It seems I'm needed at home."

"Something wrong, Arrow? Don't tell me those golden wings of yours have finally tarnished in your adoring wee ward's eyes?" MacSorley said, guessing, as the king had, what had provoked the curse.

"She's not my ward, you arse!" He ignored the reference to the lass's mistaking him for an angel. Thank God for Helen MacKay. Until she'd arrived and assumed the nickname, MacSorley had called him Angel.

"Then what is she?" MacRuairi asked.

Hell if he knew. A termagant? A penance? God's test of his sanity? The lass was always landing in some kind of trouble. From the moment he brought her home, she'd been causing "emergencies" of one sort or another.

Like the time she'd entered a local archery contest dressed as a boy in a hooded cloak and bested every one of the local lads, nearly causing a riot. Damn it, that was probably his fault. But he'd never imagined when he told her that she could learn to protect herself that the lass would take to warfare quite so enthusiastically. John, who'd been teaching her, said she was better than some men he knew. His brother was exaggerating, of course; she was only a lass—and not a very big one at that.

But his first impression of her all those years ago had been right. The lass was a fierce little thing. A real fighter. She was also stubborn, proud, opinionated, bossy, and overconfident. All fine characteristics in a man, but not in a young girl.

It was hard to stay angry with her, though. She wasn't a beauty by any means, but she was cute in an unassuming fashion. Until she smiled. When she smiled, she was as cute as the devil.

She also adored him. Which made him bloody uncomfortable. Especially lately, as she grew older. She'd become a . . . distraction. Which was exactly what he needed to be rid of.

"So when are we going to meet this wee lass?" Bruce said. Not such a wee lass anymore, Gregor recalled uneasily. The last time he'd been home—a year ago, when his mother had died—that fact had been brought home to him in an embarrassing fashion, when Cate had broken down crying and somehow ended up in his arms. And on his lap. "What was her name? Caitrina?"

Gregor nodded, surprised that the king remembered. Six years ago, when they'd returned to camp after leaving the lass with his mother, Bruce had been horrorstruck by what had happened to the villagers. He, like the rest of them, had been deeply moved by the lass's tragedy and had taken a personal interest in her.

"Aye, Caitrina Kirkpatrick." Though his mother had called her Cate.

"How old is she now?" Bruce asked.

Gregor shrugged. "Seventeen or eighteen."

"Hell, Arrow," MacRuairi said. "If you want to be rid of the chit so badly, why don't you just find her a husband?"

If he weren't such a mean bastard, Gregor would have hugged him. Of course! Marriage! Why hadn't he thought of it earlier?

There was only one problem. He had to find someone fool enough to take her on.

Two

🌿

Dunlyon, Roro, Perthshire, Scottish Highlands

This time when Gregor came home, Cate was going to be ready. She could no longer be patient.

As she'd done every day for the past week since John had sent the letter, she dressed with particular care. As she normally didn't take *any* care, this was quite an extraordinary undertaking. The "boyishly" short, just-past-her-shoulder, dark hair that she usually kept tied back with string, a piece of leather, or whatever else she happened to have on hand had been brushed and brushed until it was as glossy and shiny as polished mahogany to hang loose around her shoulders.

A simple circlet of gold, given to her by Lady Marion before she'd succumbed to the fever, rested upon her head, securing the gossamer-thin pink veil that covered—but did not hide—the dark tresses. Her hair was one of her best features, and she had to take advantage of whatever she could.

Cate didn't need to pinch her cheeks as some girls did; hers were rosy enough from all the time she spent outdoors. Her lips, too, didn't need any color, as they were naturally a dark, vibrant red.

She wrinkled her nose. Unfortunately, the freckles she couldn't do anything about. Cate told herself they added character, but she'd never convinced her mother or Lady Marion to agree.

She stepped back from the looking glass procured from the bottom of one of Lady Marion's trunks, held out the deep rose velvet skirts of her *cotehardie,* and chewed anxiously on her lip, not knowing quite what to make of her attempts.

She hadn't been sure about the color—she'd never liked pink—but Lady Marion had insisted it would be "beautiful" on her. That was an exaggeration, but it did seem to flatter her coloring. The gown was one of three that Lady Marion had insisted on buying her two years ago on Cate's eighteenth saint's day. *"You are a lady now, sweeting,"* the older woman had said with a fond smile. *"You need at least a few fine gowns."*

It had been so important to her, Cate hadn't had the heart to argue, but she'd never seemed to find the occasion to wear them. Frankly, dressing in such fine things made her feel a little silly. Like she was pretending to be someone she was not.

Her father had given her a beautiful dress once. It had made her feel like a princess. When he left, she'd shoved it under the bed and never looked at it again.

Her chest squeezed with a longing she refused to acknowledge. She wasn't a lady, no matter who her father happened to be.

Her attention returned to the strange woman in the looking glass.

"Men want a woman to act like a woman, my love." Her mother's voice mingled with Lady Marion's in her memory—in so many ways they'd been one in the same. Both gentle, sweet ladies. Nothing like Cate.

Her chin set with determination. She would be soft and feminine if it killed her. But goodness gracious, did being a lady have to be so blasted uncomfortable?

She tugged at the fabric around her bodice, trying to pull

it up. Two years had added a certain dimension to parts of her body that she was not quite used to, making the gown a bit tight in the bodice. But as that was the fashion, she supposed no one would notice.

Cate had given up the breeches under the skirts when Lady Marion nearly fainted the first time she'd seen them, but she'd made few other concessions. She would wear shoes in the winter but not in the summer. And no matter how plain, the simple "peasant lad's" clothes were what she felt comfortable in while training.

She'd just finished her critical appraisal when the door burst open behind her. Assuming it was Ete, who was supposed to have helped her with her hair and veil but was called away when Maddy started crying (screeching, actually), Cate didn't turn right away. It was only when the silence became noticeable that she looked and realized that it wasn't the maidservant but John.

He was staring at her slack-jawed, with a slightly dazed look on his face.

Cate wrinkled her nose. Whatever was the matter with him?

Suddenly, the blood slid from her face, and her heart started to pound—gallop, more accurately. "Is he here?"

John didn't seem to hear her. "You look . . . you look beautiful."

Despite the rather unflattering level of surprise in his voice, a warm blush spread up her cheeks, and she grinned with unabashed delight. Cate didn't have any real pretensions toward beauty, but she could not doubt the admiration in John's eyes. And it gave her the confidence that until that moment she hadn't realized how much she'd needed.

She had never doubted her appeal to men—they liked her. Indeed, she had more male friends than she did female. But they treated her like a little sister they were fond of, which was *not* the way she wanted Gregor to think of her.

She was determined that this time he would notice her as a desirable woman. Of course, she'd told herself the same thing last year, but she was confident that it would be different this time. This time she had more than herself to consider. This time she was going to act—and look—like a lady.

From the first moment he'd looked down at her in that well, Gregor MacGregor had stolen a piece of her heart. When he'd taken her to his home, he'd stolen a little more. As the years passed, each time he came home—of which there had been precious few—he claimed more and more, until eventually he held it all. Her love had matured from that of a young girl's to a woman's, but it was the one constant in her life since that horrible day, and she held to it like a lifeline. (That and the resolve to discover the identity of the man who killed her mother. But after five years, Gregor had been unable to find out anything about the English captain.)

A less determined person might have given up in the face of Gregor's obvious disinterest. Well, not disinterest really, more a lack of awareness. He still thought of her as the "child" he'd rescued, or the young girl he was forced to acknowledge when some kind of trouble arose (which, to be clear, wasn't always her fault), and not the strong woman she'd become.

The woman who was perfect for him.

It was that certainty that kept Cate going when she became discouraged. And with Gregor MacGregor it was very easy to get discouraged. She knew he wasn't perfect, but sometimes he certainly seemed that way. Not for the first time, she wished he weren't so handsome. Or so charming. Or so good at everything he did. It made him feel out of reach. Elusive. Like trying to catch quicksilver.

It wasn't arrogance, exactly. Or superiority. More a separation. He would laugh, flirt, and jest with everyone (except for her), but there was always an arm's length between him and the world. An air of caution.

To the uninformed, hers might seem an impossible quest—the most handsome man in Scotland and a cute-ish twenty-year-old bastard who was better with a sword than with a needle?—but Cate knew there was a connection between them that defied logic or explanation. A connection that went beyond skin-deep.

She might not be a raving beauty, but she did have many other good qualities. She was loyal and trustworthy and would fight to the death for the people she loved. People *liked* her—except for Seonaid and her friends, but they weren't nice to anyone.

If only Cate could curb her temper. And her passionate nature. And behave more like a lady. But she was working on those things.

That she and Gregor were meant to be together might seem a rather bold claim for someone who'd seen him no more than a handful of times in five years, but she had faith. She understood him like no one else. Not even his mother—perhaps *especially* his mother. God knew Lady Marion had loved him, but she hadn't understood his drive. "*He's so handsome,*" she would say. "*He can have whatever he wants. Why must he put himself in danger for a man who might never be king when he could marry a king's ransom?*"

But Gregor was a man of deeds and accomplishments. He wanted to earn his way. That was why he fought so hard. Indeed, his dedication, loyalty, and integrity were the things she most admired about him. There was no man she believed in more.

She'd learned so much about him from his family, including John, who was still staring at her.

Cate laughed and, in what must be some primitive feminine instinct that had previously never been seen in her, she twirled. Twirled! "Do you think so?"

A broad smile spread across his familiar features. John was so much a brother to her, sometimes she forgot how handsome he was. Not outrageously so like Gregor—who could be?—but his strong, masculine features were warm and pleasing. Especially now when he was laughing (rather than scowling) at her.

"Aye, I've never seen you look so fine." Suddenly, his eyes narrowed. "What's this about, lass?"

Cate looked away, pretending to adjust her gown, so he wouldn't see her embarrassment. "Nothing. Has Gregor arrived? Is that why you came to fetch me?"

He paused for too long before responding, as if he'd guessed exactly what this was about. She plastered an innocent look on her face and turned back expectantly. She didn't think he was fooled, but then he swore, remembering his purpose. "Ah hell, it's the lad. Have you seen him? I sent him into the village three hours ago with some coin to purchase some spice for the wine. If he's gambled it away again . . ."

Cate stiffened. "Pip didn't gamble away anything. It was stolen from him by that horrible Dougal MacNab."

"So he says. But Iain saw the lad playing raffle at the alehouse that day."

"I gave Pip that money from his share of the fish we caught; it was his own to do with as he liked. And Iain shouldn't be tale-telling. Perhaps I should mention to Iain's wife that he was at the alehouse the day the rents were paid?" Their old retainer had a fondness for Annie and her ale. His wife had barred him from both. Cate gave John a knowing look. "Besides, you shouldn't be so quick to jump to conclusions. For example, I might think that you had sent Pip for some spices because you were drinking Gregor's good wine again and trying to cover it up."

John's eyes narrowed. "Cate . . ."

The warning fell on deaf ears. He couldn't intimidate her even if he tried. "It won't work, you know. He will know the difference."

Gregor had a taste for the fine things in life—from food, to drink, to horses, to women. The last would change when he found the right woman. In other words, her.

Was she being a fool? Was it ludicrous to think he could ever love her back?

John muttered a curse and dragged his fingers back through his dark-blond hair. "Damn it, I know. But he shouldn't leave it here for so long if he doesn't want someone to drink it."

Cate tried not to laugh. "Let me know how that excuse works."

John shook his head. "You'll know." He grimaced, unconsciously rubbing his shoulder as if already feeling the thrashing he would take on the practice yard. "I hope he hasn't learned any more new wrestling moves. The last time I had bruises for a week."

Cate laughed, walked over to him, stood up on her toes, and placed a fond peck on his cheek. "Poor John." When she drew back, his eyes looked a little odd. She hoped he wasn't coming down with the ague. Maddy had been sick for a week.

"Don't worry about the money," she told him. "I'll see where Pip has gone. He's probably on his way back with your spices right now."

Despite what she'd told John, Cate wasn't so certain about Pip's location. After searching the tower house and the handful of wooden buildings inside the peel, she hurried along the path in the woods the short distance to the village. If she happened to be heading toward the alehouse, she told herself it didn't mean she didn't trust him. Pip— Phillip—was a troubled, confused fifteen-year-old lad who'd been abandoned by his mother. He needed someone to believe in him. And Cate did. Really. She was just being diligent in her covering of all possible locations.

As it turned out, Cate's faith in him was warranted, although she would have rather found him at the alehouse.

Barely had the old wooden motte-and-bailey tower house of Dunlyon, built by Gregor's grandfather on the site of an ancient hill fort, faded into the distance when she heard a burst of laughter followed by the excited shouts and cries of children playing, coming from the River Lyon on her right.

She smiled and continued on her way. But a small prickle at the back of her neck made her stop and listen again. In the cacophony of noise she tried to sort out the different sounds. A chill spread over her skin, and she started to run. It wasn't laughing, but jeers. And it wasn't the excited shouts of children playing, but the inciting chants of a mob.

Her heart pounded as she ran through the canopy of trees and burst out into the bright sunshine of the boggy riverbank. Her stomach dropped seeing the circle of boys— although two or three of them were already the size of full-grown men—gathered around watching something.

Please don't let it be . . .

"Get him, Dougal!"

The hard thump of a fist in the gut, followed by a sharp "umph" and moan, were enough to confirm her suspicions, even before she caught a glimpse of the black hair caked with mud and the bloody too-big nose.

Rage stormed through her. "Get away from him!" she shouted, running toward the not-so-little brutes.

The sound of her voice parted the circle of spectators like Moses at the Red Sea. The thugs-in-the-making gaped at her as if she were a madwoman. Which, as furious as she was, wasn't far off.

Be smart. John's admonitions came back to her. *Lead with your head, not with your heart.*

She scanned the faces. She knew most of them and wasn't surprised by any, except for one. Willy MacNee met her gaze and quickly turned away, his face as red as a ripe tomato. Willy was the younger brother of one of her friends, and a sweet boy. She'd expected better of him, and he knew it.

But her attention was soon focused on the two boys at the center of the spectacle. One was big, thick, and mean; the other was small and thin, and didn't know when to back down. After assuring herself Pip was all right beyond the obvious broken nose (the last thing the already over-large feature on his small face needed), she turned to Dougal. "What is the meaning of this, Dougal? How dare you hit him!"

The boy obviously wasn't used to being taken to task by a woman. Recalling the bruises she'd seen on his mother's face, she wasn't surprised. The father was just as brutish as the son.

But when he looked her up and down, she realized it wasn't just her sudden appearance that had startled him; it was also her clothing. She'd forgotten about the fine gown and realized he'd never seen her dressed like a lady before—like the daughter of a chieftain. Except she wasn't the daughter of a chieftain, and everyone knew it.

They thought her an orphan rescued by the absent MacGregor laird. Not a peasant, but not a lady either. Somewhere in between. By not telling Gregor the truth about her father, the stain of her bastardy had not followed her to Roro.

Seeming to remember her status, Dougal puffed up and thrust out his chest like a preening peacock. " 'Tis none of your affair, mistress. This is between us men."

She lifted a brow at that, making the seventeen-year-old boy flush.

She took a step toward him. Though she was about half

his weight and a full head shorter, the fierceness of her expression must have startled him. Instinctively he moved back. "Pip *is* my business," she said firmly. "He is my family."

"He's a worthless, thieving no-name bastard!"

Rage expanded every vein in her body. Pip, too, let out a roar that belied his size and launched himself at the other boy, fists pummeling. "I'm not a thief. It was you who took my money. I was only trying to get it back!"

Pip's advantage of surprise didn't last long. He landed only a few blows before Dougal retaliated with an upper-cross to his jaw. Blood sprayed out of his mouth as Pip's body went flying back through the air like a sack of bones.

Cate didn't think; she reacted. Dougal's fist had barely returned from his side when she took hold of his arm and twisted it around his back.

Leverage, position, and hitting the right spot, she reminded herself, *not physical strength.* Still, her pulse was racing. This wasn't the training yard.

But it was working. She couldn't believe it was actually working! She was really doing it.

Dougal let out a yelp of pain and stared at her as if she'd suddenly sprouted a second head. Levering her foot around his body, she pulled his arm until his eyes started to water and sweat poured off his reddened face. His knees were buckling to absorb the pain, so when she leaned toward him their noses were only inches apart. "You are nothing more than a big bully, Dougal MacNab. A weak boy who preys on those physically smaller than you. But size doesn't equal strength." She tugged his arm a little harder until he cried out. "I hope you've learned your lesson because if you touch one hair on his head again, I will find you and ensure you do."

Suddenly, she was conscious of the other boys. Coming out of their shock, they'd started to murmur and shift back and forth a little uneasily, as if they knew they should do something. She'd been so carried away by her success that she'd forgotten about the others. But Cate was painfully aware that using what she'd learned on one man was vastly different than on a half-dozen.

"Please," he said, the crack in his voice reminding her of his age. "You're going to break my arm."

"You'll remember?"

He nodded vehemently.

"Good." She released him and took a few steps back. He was rubbing his shoulder, staring at her with a mixture of disbelief, embarrassment, outrage, and hatred. "Being mean doesn't make you a man, Dougal. And fear is not respect. I hope you will remember that as well."

Deciding it might be prudent to get out of there as quickly as possible, she turned to help Pip up. The next thing she knew, she was facedown in the mud. It wasn't the first time she'd been knocked down from behind, but it was the only time she'd ever wanted to cry. The sodden, muddy edge of her pink veil reminded her of what she was wearing. Her gown was ruined.

The gown Lady Marion had bought for her.

The gown she'd wanted to impress Gregor with.

The gown that had made her feel . . . pretty.

She heard Pip shout in outrage, spewing a litany of inventive threats that almost made her smile.

Making a show of slowly dragging herself to her knees, she waited, her pulse racing. *Just like practice . . .*

Dougal's feet appeared by her side. "You stupid bitch. I'll show you who is a real man."

His words unleashed a twisted flurry of anger and pain, his threat a brutal reminder of what had happened to her mother. She wanted to lash out. She wanted to cry. She wanted to punish any man who would ever think to rape a woman.

But John had warned her that her weakness wasn't in

her limbs but in her quick temper. So instead she waited patiently for what she hoped was coming.

He didn't disappoint. Dougal moved his leg to kick her in the ribs, and she caught it, using the momentum to catapult him onto his back with a ground-smacking thud. A moment later she had her knee on his chest and her blade pressed against his thick neck. "You are a bully *and* a coward, Dougal MacNab."

He looked at her wide-eyed. "What kind of lass are you?"

"The kind who has a blade to your throat, so unless you want to continue this, I suggest you take your friends and go on home."

This time when Cate let him up, she made sure to keep an eye on him as he rejoined his friends. They whispered back and forth, and every now and then Dougal would cast a scathing glare in her direction.

She still had her dagger drawn and ready, but when they didn't leave right away, she felt the first prickle of sweat on her brow. It was the worried look Willy sent in her direction, however, that made her pulse flutter. They were planning something, and there were so many of them. Six, not including Willy. If they chose to fight as a group . . .

Cate swallowed, her mouth suddenly dry. Her advantages were surprise and quickness. She'd lost the first, which would seriously impact the second, even with one opponent. With six . . .

Deciding that she'd made her point, and perhaps she should be the one to back off, she motioned for Pip to come to her side.

Before he'd reached her, however, the sound of an approaching horse did what her threat had not, sending Dougal and the other boys scurrying off toward the village.

Cate let out the breath she didn't realize she'd been holding. She turned to face their unwitting rescuer just as the rider drew his horse to a halt on the edge of the riverbank.

She froze, the blood slowly draining from her face in horror.

No . . . Please, no. Not like this. He couldn't see her like this. She'd wanted to impress him.

Her throat tightened, and a misty sheen of hot tears blurred her mud-streaked vision, as she took in the familiar white charger and the muscular, leather-clad warrior who sat atop the magnificent beast, staring down at her like some golden hero in a bard's tale.

She blinked, feeling the urge to put her hand up as if she were staring straight into the sun. He didn't need to wear chain mail to shine; he caught the light in a blinding array all on his own. But for once she did not feel like sighing.

It wasn't fair! Did he always have to look so perfect? So shiny and polished? Always impeccable, as if dirt wouldn't dare stick to him.

While she . . . she was a muddy mess. She wanted nothing more than to sink into the boggy ground and disappear.

He pulled off his helm and shook out his hair. It fell in spectacularly tousled waves around his face. Her heart squeezed at the unfairness. Her hair after being in a helm looked like it was plastered to her head.

"What in Hades have you done this time, Caitrina?" His mouth twitched. "Or do I want to know?"

Caitrina. He was the only one who'd ever called her that, and it wasn't even her real name. *Catherine.* She shouldn't have lied about her identity—or, by omission, her age (she realized he thought her younger)—but she'd been fifteen, traumatized, and desperate for him to take her with him. She'd known that if she'd told him the truth, he would never have done so. By using her dead second stepfather's name of Kirkpatrick, there was no chance *anyone* would connect her to the bastard daughter of Helen of Lochmaben. And that was the way she wanted it. No more pitying looks. No more teasing. No more secret prayers that her father would come for her. She'd been given a chance to put that life behind her, and she'd taken it.

Any twinge of guilt she might have felt, however, was quickly forgotten when she saw that mouth twitch. How could he be so ungallant as to laugh at her? *Because he thinks you are a child.* A child who needed rescuing from a well. Not a woman full grown.

His amusement seemed the final slap of injustice on her mud-strewn indignity. She adored him, but the man could be a thoughtless horse's backside at times. The tears that had threatened were forgotten; instead she fought the urge to put her dirty hands on him and knock him off that pristine white horse into the mud. Usually she admired his cool unflappability, but just once she'd like to see him ruffled.

Pip had obviously taken umbrage at the newcomer's attitude as well. He angled his thin body in front of her. "She saved me, that's what she did. One of those boys took my coin, and when I tried to get it back, he and his friends came after me. But Cate nearly broke his arm. And when he pushed her down, she pulled a knife on him."

"She *what*?" Gregor exploded incredulously.

Cate tried to stop Pip, but apparently mistaking Gregor's anger for admiration, he was eager to continue the story. "Aye, she flipped him on his back like a dead chicken and had her dirk right up to his neck." The boy whose nose had swollen to the size of a turnip looked at her with unabashed adoration, and then back over to Gregor. "You should have seen her."

Gregor looked at her as if he didn't know whether he wanted to take her over his knee or be ill.

She winced; he definitely wasn't impressed with her

skills. She suspected there was going to be hell to pay for this—and not just from Dougal's father.

Gregor gave her a hard look before turning to Pip. "And who perchance are you?"

Pip flushed. Seeing the boy's discomfort, Cate thrust her chin up and met Gregor's gaze. "He's your son."

Three

In retrospect, perhaps it had been a bad idea to laugh, but, damn it, Cate looked so adorable and fierce with the mud streaked all over her face and clothes—an unusually pretty dress for her, actually. Seeing her look so refreshing *girlish* had been something of a relief, after the uncomfortable and far from guardian-like thoughts Gregor had been having about her since his last time home.

But he hadn't meant to hurt her feelings and would have apologized had he not been struck by what could only be described as sickly panic when he heard what she'd done (she could have been hurt, damn it!), and then momentarily struck dumb by her announcement.

"My w-what?" he sputtered.

"Your son," she replied calmly.

The words didn't lose any impact on repeating. If Gregor had been more shocked in his life, he couldn't recall. She might as well have proclaimed herself the Queen of bloody England. She had about as much chance of claiming that position as he had of having sired this whelp.

Aside from the fact that the boy looked nothing— *nothing*—like him, he was at least fifteen or sixteen years old. Gregor was thirty-one, and the only woman he'd had relations with before he was twenty hadn't given birth to this boy. He should know, since she married his older brother a few months after their relationship had served her purpose.

He gritted his teeth, casting a sharp glance at the blood-ied, mud-splattered youth. "I don't know what hard-luck story he's told you, but that boy is most assuredly *not* my son."

The whelp shot him a black scowl, looking as if he'd like nothing more than to stick a blade between Gregor's ribs. Cate, however, acted like the wee blackguard had just been grievously injured and hastened to protect him by wrap-ping her arm around his shoulder.

"Of course he is. Just like Eddie and Maddy."

"Who in the hell are they?" Gregor exploded. He'd given up trying not to swear and blaspheme around her years ago. Not even God would have enough patience and re-straint for Cate.

"Did John not tell you? Congratulations—you have two sons and a daughter!"

This was the "emergency"? The lass wasn't only trouble, she was mad—especially if she thought he'd ever have a son named after the English king.

He told her so, and what skin on her face wasn't covered with mud turned red. She turned to the boy. "Pip, you go on ahead. *Your father* and I have something to discuss."

This Pip could give Viper a contest in venomous glares. The lad looked like he wanted to argue, but when Caitrina added, "Please," he nodded and left—though not without a few more black scowls cast in Gregor's direction.

Christ, did the lad think he would hurt her? Gregor hadn't strangled her in the five years he'd known her; he sure as hell wasn't going to start now. With any luck, in a few weeks she'd be out of his hair for good. Although in light of today's events, his plan to marry her off was going to be even more of a challenge than he'd thought. He shook his head. Brawling in the dirt like a . . . he didn't know what, but it certainly wasn't befitting a marriageable young lass.

She turned on him, hands on her hips, as soon as the boy

moved out of earshot. "How could you say that in front of him? You hurt his feelings!"

Gregor jumped off his horse, preparing to square off for the battle he knew was coming. If he didn't know better, from the way the blood was racing through his veins, he might think he was actually looking forward to it.

"Hurt *his* feelings? My good name is the one being *dragged through the mud*." Her eyes flared at that. "The little charlatan has lied to you and taken advantage of your kindness. How old is he?"

"Fifteen."

Gregor smiled; it was as he suspected. "It's impossible for him to be my son."

"How can you be so sure?"

"I know how to subtract."

Clearly, she didn't understand, and he was in no mind to explain. His age when he'd first been intimate with a woman was not a proper topic for a young lady's ears. But that wasn't the only reason. She'd closed the gap between them to a few feet—which, as it turned out, was too damned close.

He was feeling it again. The heat. That strange tingling of his skin. The blasted awareness. The blasted *inappropriate* awareness.

The top of her head only came to his mid-chest, but he could still remember how it had felt tucked under his chin. How warm and silky her hair had been. How she'd smelled like wildflowers. How firm but undeniably feminine she'd felt in his arms.

What the hell was the matter with him? This was *Caitrina*. The lass he was responsible for, no matter how unwittingly—the lass he was supposed to protect from men like him. Bloody hell, he needed to find a little self-control.

Drawing his hand through his hair, he made a sound of

frustration. Returning to the subject at hand, he said, "How did he come to be here?"

"His mother left him at the gate. She told him he was to find you and inform you that he was your son, and that it was time for you to take care of the lad, as she could no longer do so on her own."

He might have felt a pang of sympathy for the boy at his cruel abandonment by the woman who'd given birth to him had Gregor not been so certain every word of it was a falsehood. The boy and his mother were probably in league together. God knew what they hoped to gain by their trickery. "What was this woman's name?"

She shrugged, as if the question wasn't important to her. "You'll have to ask your son."

He tried to control his temper, he did. But Caitrina—Cate—had a way of bringing out the worst in him. She was so blasted stubborn and too damned free with her opinions. He was her guardian, for Christ's sake! She should defer to his opinions. Respect her elders.

"He is not my son," he reiterated, emphasizing each word.

"So you've said."

His jaw clenched at her smile. "And the other two children? Let me guess—they were abandoned as well, not long after word of Pip's arrival spread, I would wager."

She flushed, tossing her muddy hair as regally as any queen. "There is no cause to be sarcastic."

"No cause? Christ, did you not think the timing just a little suspicious? Suddenly I go from having no progeny to three in the space of a couple of months? You are lucky there haven't been more showing up on my doorstep."

Her eyes widened and blinked. "You mean you have more natural children out there?"

Gregor squeezed his fists, praying for patience. Though she said it innocently enough, sometimes he could swear she was purposefully being obtuse just to get a rise out of him—irritation, not the other kind of rise, although regretfully she had managed to do that as well. Being around Cate was beginning to make him feel like an old lecher.

"I do not have *any* children. Get rid of them, Caitrina."

Her eyes narrowed. "I won't 'get rid' of them; you are responsible—"

He didn't let her finish. "I have no more duty to them than I do to any child off the high street of any village in Scotland."

She gasped, gazing up at him with a vulnerable expression on her face that he hadn't seen in a long time. The look that made his *cotun* feel like it was too tight. "Like me, you mean?"

He cursed with frustration at the inadvertent hurt his words had caused. Of course she would sympathize with these foundlings. She knew what it was like to be left all alone in the world. "Ah, hell, I didn't mean it like that. You were different."

"Why?"

"Because we were responsible for what happened to you."

"*You* weren't responsible. *You* weren't even there when the men sought shelter. If anyone was responsible, it was your king. Robert Bruce was the one who told those men to seek refuge in our village. So why did *you* offer to take me?"

He knew what she was trying to wrest from him, but it wasn't going to work. He wasn't what she thought he was. Cate wanted to see him as some kind of noble knight. A man she could rely on. That sure as hell wasn't him. One of the reasons he'd stayed away so much over the years was because he didn't want to disillusion her—even though he knew without a doubt that one day he would.

"Because it made sense, and it was the easiest solution. I knew my mother would love you, and I hoped you would be happy here."

"I have been, and so will they—"

He stopped her, suspecting where she was heading. "It won't work, Caitrina. They aren't staying here. If you don't find a place for them, I will. God knows there are a lot of mothers struggling to care for their bairns in this war, but that doesn't mean I'm going to let Dunlyon be used as a refuge for foundlings or claim children who aren't mine."

After the unwelcome tenderness he was feeling toward the lass, he was almost glad to see the irritation returning to her dirt-smudged features.

Her eyes narrowed. "How can you be so certain they aren't yours? From what I hear, you are not lacking in bed partners. Is your seed incapable of bearing fruit?"

Gregor could only stand there and gape. How was it that this young girl managed to do what no one else could and so thoroughly, so maddeningly, disconcert him? He didn't know what was worse: that she'd been listening to gossip about the number of women he took to bed (or rather, the number of women who took him to *their* bed) or that she'd just questioned the potency of his "seed." Both were inappropriate topics for any young woman, let alone his . . . his . . . whatever the hell she was!

"I am perfectly capable of siring children, damn it! When I want them."

She wrinkled her nose, causing the dried mud to crack. The thin whisker lines it made on her face made her look like a bedraggled kitten. But any warm, fuzzy feelings were quickly quashed when she spoke. "I don't see how you can know that unless you've tried. And with all those women, one would think—"

He took a step toward her, fighting a losing battle for patience. "Caitrina . . ."

Wisely, she took a step back. "So you are telling me that it's completely out of the realm of possibility that you could have made a mistake?"

"I don't make mistakes."

She gave him a look that was filled with more understanding than he liked. "Everyone makes mistakes."

"Not me. Not that kind." He was always careful. Very careful. Although there was always the smallest, tiniest possibility . . .

Hell, she'd done it again. Turned him inside out. Upside down. Confused him. Rattled him, blast it.

Like any born warrior, she sensed the weakness and went in for the kill. "Just meet them, Gregor. You'll see—"

He put up his hand, trying to tell himself it wasn't like a white banner. So much for *Bàs roimh Gèill*. Death before Surrender, the motto of the Highland Guard—and his before he'd met Cate. "I've already met one of them, and I know for a fact he is not mine. It will be the same for the other two. I will see them, but it will not change my mind."

"Oh Gregor, thank you!"

She'd apparently ignored the "won't change my mind" part, proving she wasn't immune to the skill possessed by so many of her sex to hear only what they wanted to hear.

When it looked as if she might throw herself into his arms, he took a step back.

Mistaking the cause, she made a face. "I suppose I should get cleaned up first."

It wasn't the dirt; he just didn't trust himself to touch her.

"They aren't staying, Caitrina."

The smile quickly slid from her face. He regretted it, but it was necessary. He didn't want any misunderstandings.

She held his gaze, and after a moment, nodded. He wasn't foolish enough to mistake it for acquiescence; it was more temporary acceptance. But in this he would stay firm. No more foundlings. Worrying about her was distracting enough; he sure as hell wasn't going to take on any more. His responsibility toward Cate was always hanging over him; even when fighting he thought of her.

More so of late, the reasons for which he didn't want to examine.

He was supposed to be clearing his head, damn it. Getting rid of all distractions, not adding to them.

Leading his mount, they walked the short distance to Dunlyon in silence.

It was one of the things he liked most about her. Unlike most women, Cate didn't feel the need to fill the silence with chatter.

It was hard not to like the lass. That was part of the problem. When she wasn't irritating him or making his life difficult, she was passionate, loyal, no-nonsense, and refreshingly straightforward. *Too* straightforward sometimes, he thought, recalling her reference to his bed partners.

So she thought him a profligate. Hell, he probably was—more by happenstance than by effort. What was he supposed to do, refuse the women who jumped in his bed? What man in his right mind would do that?

And why did he care what she thought?

He was still frowning when they entered the gate. She started to run off, but after a few steps stopped to turn around. "Have you found him yet?"

Gregor stiffened at the mention of the familiar subject. Damn it, did the lass never give up? He hated having to lie to her, but God only knew what Caitrina would do with the information. Actually, he suspected he knew *exactly* what she would do, which was why he'd never shared it with her. He'd learned the name of the man who'd attacked her village shortly after it happened. Unfortunately by that time, Sir Reginald Fitzwarren had already been recalled to London—where he'd stayed out of Gregor's reach. But one day, he would find him and the lass would have her vengeance.

"Not yet," he said.

She sighed disappointedly, and he felt a sharp stab of guilt in his chest. "Maybe I could—"

"You promised to let me handle it, Caitrina. I want you to trust me."

She smiled. "I do."

Somehow the blind faith only made him feel worse.

"I'd better hurry, if I'm going to have time for a bath before the meal," she said, starting to turn away again.

A surge of unwelcome heat rushed through him. He shouldn't think of her in the bath, those pert breasts that had felt so firm against his chest bare, the taut, shapely buttocks smooth and . . .

Wrong, damn it.

"Caitrina!" he snapped.

She turned with an uneasy smile at his tone.

"There is still the matter of that knife to discuss."

There, that was good and guardian-like.

But his forbidding frown seemed to have no effect. The lass actually looked pleased. Aye, her lips were definitely curved upward. "It was your idea."

Cheeky brat.

"Don't remind me," he muttered, but she was already gone.

For the second time that day, Cate finished making the final adjustments to her gown. This time she chose the moss green. Though she regretted the loss of the rose dress—Ete had taken one look at the ruined gown and nearly burst into tears—Cate thought the green might be even more flattering. The gold ribbon that lined the bodice, hem, and sleeves seemed to pick up the lighter flecks in her eyes.

She didn't bother with a veil. It would only get wet, as her hair was still sopping from her bath. But with only an hour until the midday meal, she didn't have time to sit before the brazier brushing it until it dried.

She replaced the circlet atop her head and gave herself another quick once-over in the looking glass before stepping away. She might not look quite as primped and polished as she had this morning, but she looked a good sight better than she had with mud splattered all over her face. The humiliation of being seen like that by the man she so desperately wanted to impress was painfully fresh. But she would do what she always did: get up, dust herself off, and try again. Bruised and battered perhaps, but ready to fight again. Not just for her, but for the children. They needed him and the stability she'd never had.

She hustled from the room, wanting to make sure the children were looking their best for their "presentation." Her mouth pursed. She tried not to be disappointed by Gregor's cold reaction—no doubt suddenly being told you were the father of three would be a shock to anyone—but she was. For the first time that she could remember, he'd let her down.

His harsh words still rang in her head. *"Get rid of them."*

As if they were rubbish. As if she could just send them away and not care what happened to them. They were children, for heaven's sake, not stray cats!

Once he saw them and came to know them, he would change his mind. She just had to be patient. He'd taken her in, hadn't he?

Cate had enough faith in him for them both. As his mother had told her, ties didn't come easily to Gregor, but once formed they were as unbreakable as steel.

Cate ought to know; she'd put them to the test enough.

She gnawed on her lip guiltily. Had she done so on purpose? Maybe once or twice. But eventually the fear that he would send her away abated. Now, she tested him just because it seemed to be the only way to get him to come home—not to mention it was rather fun. She liked pricking beneath the charming, roguish facade to see those gorgeous green eyes darken, that sinfully delicious wide mouth harden, that tiny muscle beneath the perfectly formed jaw start to flex.

But pricking his temper wasn't good enough anymore. She wanted him to notice her the way a man does a woman. She wanted him to take her in his arms and kiss her the way she'd seen him kiss the previous seneschal's widow the last time he was home. She wanted him to realize that she was the one for him.

When she reached the top floor of the tower, she found that Ete and Lizzie, one of the kitchen maids, had Eddie and Maddy temporarily under control, but Pip was nowhere to be found. He hadn't returned to the tower house or to the garret chamber where he slept with Eddie.

Leaving the younger children to the capable hands of the servants, Cate went in search of Pip. She suspected where she would find him. He'd slept in the barn for nearly three weeks, before she'd been able to convince him that he belonged inside. The barn was still the place he retreated to when the chaos of the house grew too much for him.

It was where he would go to lick his wounds.

Not that she blamed him. Cate had worked so hard to make Pip feel like he belonged, and with a few sharp words, Gregor had undone it all.

Her heart squeezed for the proud boy who was trying so hard to be tough and pretend it didn't matter that his mother had abandoned him on the doorstep of strangers. Trying so hard to believe in a story that even Cate conceded left room for a few questions.

She'd wanted to believe it was true nearly as much as Pip had. But the boy's age had always bothered her. She knew Gregor had just turned one and thirty, and although she wouldn't put it past him, fifteen was awfully young to father a child.

Gregor's certainty—at least about Pip—left little room for error. She only wished Pip hadn't had to hear it.

What had she thought, that Gregor would take one look at the boy and his heart would go out to him as much as hers had? Perhaps. Though she knew it wasn't fair. Gregor hadn't been eager to be saddled with her; she shouldn't have expected that he would welcome three children with open arms.

Even were she to believe him that they weren't his children—and there seemed little room for doubt about Pip—it didn't matter. He couldn't turn them away; they needed him.

He would come around.

Having reached the barn, she drew open the door. The pungent, earthy smells accosted her at once, but she didn't mind. She'd spent a lot of time in the barn when she first arrived, too.

"Pip?"

She heard what sounded like a muffled sniffle, and then a bit of shuffling around. "Back here," he said. "With the pup."

One of the dogs in the village had given birth to pups a few weeks back. The bitch had ignored the sickly runt, and the farmer had been about to drown the poor thing, when Pip had come to its rescue and brought it back to the tower house. Remarkably, not only did the creature seem to be thriving, but their old, stubborn barn cat, who didn't like anyone, seemed to think it was the pup's mother.

Cate moved toward the far end of the barn, finding Pip sitting against the wall of the last stall.

Her heart squeezed, seeing the telltale streaks down his swollen, bloodied face. But she pretended not to notice. His pride was a tender thing right now. He was so full of bluster and bravado. But it had helped him survive, and she would not destroy it with comfort. Not until he was ready.

"How is he?"

Pip shrugged. "I brought him some scraps of meat from the evening meal last night, and he seemed to like them."

"Have you named him yet?"

The boy shook his head. "No." She understood. He wouldn't name him until he was certain the pup would live. His eyes scanned her dress, and then narrowed angrily. "That's for *him,* isn't it? You've dressed like that for him."

Cate hoped she wasn't blushing, but her cheeks felt suspiciously hot. Good gracious, was it that obvious? "No, I—"

"You like him, don't you? Well, I don't. I hate him—and he's not my father!"

Cate pulled over a stool that was used for milking the cows and drew it over to sit by him. "Why do you say that?"

For a moment he looked stricken, but then he looked away and mumbled, "My mother said he was handsome. That we looked just alike. I don't look anything like him. He's cold and arrogant and ugly."

He looked so upset, Cate didn't have the heart to smile. She doubted anyone had ever called Gregor MacGregor ugly before. "He didn't mean what he said, Pip. He was surprised, that's all. Once you get to know him—"

"I don't want to get to know him. I hate him!"

Dear Lord, had she actually thought this would be easy? Her plan to bring them all together had the makings of a disaster. "You both started off on the wrong foot, that's all." Not wanting to leave any more room for discussion, she stood. "It will be time for the midday meal soon—you have just enough time to wash up." He started to protest, but she stopped him in a voice that brooked no argument. "I will fetch some salve for your cuts."

He looked down at the dog and nodded.

Again she wanted to put her arms around him, but she remembered all too well how she'd been at that age. Lady

Marion had been patient with her, and she would do the same for Pip.

She turned to leave, but he stopped her. "How did you do what you did to Dougal today?"

Her mouth twisted. It had been rather amazing. She hadn't really been convinced all of her practice would pay off. But it had, and she was proud of herself. "Practice."

His eyes darkened again. "Did *he* teach you?"

She shook her head. For years she'd pestered Gregor every time he came home to teach her how to defend herself, but he always put her off "until next time." Finally, she grew weary of waiting and asked John. "No, John taught me."

Pip paused for a moment and looked up at her uncertainly. "Do you think that maybe you could teach me?"

She grinned. "You wouldn't mind taking lessons in warfare from a lass?"

He thought for a minute, obviously taking her question seriously. "Not if you can teach me to do that."

She laughed. "Well, why don't we see what you can do tomorrow?"

He stared at her, a look of cautious excitement on his bruised and battered face. "Really?"

She smiled. It was still so hard for him to believe that anything good would be coming his way, but she was determined to change that. "Really. But you'll have to work hard."

His black head was nodding so enthusiastically, she feared he might start his nose bleeding again. "I will, I promise."

She hid a smile. "Then come to the practice yard after your chores. John and I should be done by then."

A few times a week—more if she begged him hard enough—John found time to squeeze in a few practice sessions with her in between his other duties. With Gregor and their youngest brother, Padraig, off fighting, it had been left to John to keep watch over their holdings for the time being. Although John was anxious to return to the battle, Cate looked forward to their training more than anything—except for Gregor's visits.

Reminded that the very man was likely waiting for her and the children in the Great Hall, Cate hurried to get the salve and see what could be done about Pip's poor face. She had to ensure that Gregor's second impression was better than the first. A wry smile turned her lips. Given the first meeting, that shouldn't be too hard.

Four

With Cate requisitioning the tub, Gregor made use of the river to wash away the two days of grime from the saddle. On a hot summer day, a dip in the River Lyon was invigorating and refreshing, but about a week from mid-winter's day, it was like jumping into ice water. Cold enough to freeze your bollocks off.

He hoped.

The prurient thoughts about his wee "ward" weren't just an annoyance, they were also bloody embarrassing. A man of his experience should have some control over his thoughts and his body, damn it. But apparently, he was reduced to relying on cold water until he could find a husband for her.

To that end, the first thing he'd done after meeting with John was make a list of suitable men in the area—not too old, not too young, not too rich, not too poor, not too noble of blood, but not a peasant either. He was seeking a man who would appreciate the generous tocher that Gregor intended to provide, but who would not require an important family alliance. Although Cate would benefit by her connection with him as her guardian, her father had been only a man-at-arms of one of Bruce's vassals.

It was a delicate balance, but Gregor intended to make the best connection for her that he could. It was what she deserved. He couldn't see her with a simple husbandman or cottar. There was something oddly noble about the lass.

She certainly acted like a queen sometimes—or at least with all the bloody authority of one. Perhaps one of his retainers? A member of a local chieftain's *meinie*? The second or third son of a local chief?

In the end, he'd come up with a half-dozen names. He would have the clerk start writing to them immediately. As Gregor was home for the holidays for the first time in years, he would be expected to hold a feast for the Hogmanay celebration, which would be as good a reason as any to bring them here. With any luck, the betrothal would be all wrapped up by the time he was called back in early January.

But he feared it was going to be a long few weeks until then.

Returning to the tower house, Gregor started to climb the third set of stairs before catching himself and going back down to the second. Christ, he'd been chieftain for six years, and he still had to remind himself that he was "the laird."

It was a position that had never been meant for him as the third son. God knew, he wasn't cut out for the responsibility. His father would have hated to see the clan under Gregor's leadership. After Alasdair's death, his father had put all his faith in Gregor's second-oldest brother, Gille. It probably would have killed him to know that Gille had fallen not long after he had on the same battlefield, leaving his "useless" third son as his heir.

There were two chambers on the second floor, the laird's—now his—being the larger. John slept in the other. Cate slept on the third floor (with his mother before she'd died), in the chamber Gregor had shared with his brothers as a boy.

He'd never paid much mind to the size of the tower house before, but now he regretted that his father hadn't had time to begin the plans he'd made to build a new, modern keep of stone. The old wooden walls had seen better days, and the building—although serviceable—was simple and rustic, not fitting for the laird of the most important chieftain of the MacGregors. Isolated in the Highlands as they were, the wooden palisade fortifications had been adequate until recently.

But it was the other defenses that Gregor was thinking about. Distance and separation were what he needed, but the small tower house—the small, *intimate* tower house—provided little of that. He was far too conscious of that single flight of stairs.

After exchanging his war clothes for a fresh tunic, surcoat, and leather breeches, Gregor knew he'd delayed long enough. But he relished the first precious few hours of peace before the throng descended. It was always that way when he returned after so many months away. He knew it was expected—and partially his fault for staying away for so long—but sometimes he felt like a carcass in the sun with the buzzards pecking away at him. The men wanted a decision about some dispute, requests for delays in the payment of rents, or to put off their service, and the women . . .

He groaned. They wanted a piece of him, too. Some a bigger piece than others. He sometimes thought it would be worth getting married just to avoid having to evade all the "offers" that came his way. But then he would remember that getting married meant he would have a wife.

MacSorley, who was the king of the nicknames (it was how many of the Guardsmen had ended up with their *noms de guerre*), had taken to calling him "Slick" or the "Sorcerer," referring to Gregor's propensity to "magically" evade the traps of the more marriage-minded lasses who threw themselves in his path. According to MacSorley, Gregor had slipped out of even more bonds than MacRuairi, who was an expert at getting in and out of anywhere. It wasn't too far from the truth. Eventually, Gregor knew he would have to get married—he might not like responsibility, but he recognized when he had it—but right now his only focus was on the war.

As he was leaving his room, he caught a glimpse of the bed and was tempted—damned tempted—to collapse on it, draw the fur-lined blanket over his head, and forget about everything for a while. Maybe Bruce was right. Maybe he needed this break more than he'd realized.

How long did he have before it started? If the noise coming from below in the not-so-Great Hall was any indication, not long. Damn, it sounded like a feast in there.

A moment later, standing inside the entry and scanning the crowded room, he groaned. There were already at least forty of his clansmen in the room. By tomorrow morning, there likely would be twice that many.

He picked John out in the crowd, standing next to the dais with some members of Gregor's *meinie,* talking with an attractive woman. A *very* attractive woman, he noticed on second glance, taking in the slender but shapely curves in the snug green gown, the silky cascade of wavy, dark hair that edged just past her shoulders, and the pretty profile.

Gregor brightened, suddenly feeling a little lighter, and started toward them. A little distraction. That's what he needed. He hoped his brother didn't have a prior claim. He'd learned the hard way what could happen if two brothers desired the same woman—that was a mistake he would never make again.

No matter how shapely a set of breasts or sweet a bottom—

He stopped mid-step, feeling as if he'd just slammed into a stone wall.

It couldn't be.

John caught sight of him, waved, and said something to the woman at his side. She turned, and Gregor felt something in his chest drop to the floor. His blood followed hard after it. He felt as if Raider had taken one of those giant cabers he liked to throw and slammed it across his chest.

No, damn it, no!

But it was Cate. Looking . . .

Lovely. And not like a young girl at all. His jaw clenched. Nay, she looked very much like a woman full grown. She smiled, and the sense of dread that had begun to crawl over him grew crushing. Suffocating. A woman full grown *and* far too attractive for his peace of mind. Who would have guessed that the mud-soaked urchin could look so damned pretty?

Mud he knew how to handle. But this—*this*—what the hell was he supposed to do with glossy, dark hair, eyes so bright and lively they seemed to sparkle across the room, wide crimson lips that suddenly looked naughty in an entirely different way, and breasts? *Breasts*, damn it! Breasts that weren't just in his imagination anymore, but were now being displayed to perfection in a snug, figure-molding gown. Sized to fit perfectly in a man's hand, they were firm, round, and mouthwateringly sweet. Every bit as sweet as he'd imagined after they'd been pressed against his chest. But now they weren't in his imagination; they were right there, perched under his nose where he couldn't deny them.

His "wee ward" had grown up, and Gregor couldn't do a damned thing about it.

The inconvenient attraction he felt for her, however, he could do something about. Ignore, distract, and be rid of her as soon as possible—that was his plan.

But securing a quick betrothal had taken on a new urgency.

Cate's heart caught when she saw him across the room. This was it. This was the moment for which she'd been dreaming. She waited for lightning to strike. For him to see her for the first time as a woman—a *desirable* woman.

She waited. And waited. But his gaze skimmed over her without the barest flicker before returning to his brother.

And just like that, the moment passed.

She blinked, stunned. She'd been so certain that this time he would notice her, it seemed impossible that he hadn't.

She tried not to be disappointed, but Gregor's lack of reaction to her appearance crushed her newfound confidence in her femininity like the bud of a flower under a boot.

Maybe there was something wrong with her? Maybe she didn't have what other women had that made them attractive to men—sensually attracted, not "you're a great friend" attracted.

Wait. Perhaps he hadn't recognized her or couldn't see her from the distance across the Hall?

Sadly not. He crossed the Hall, greeted them both, and didn't make one comment about her dress or hair. She might as well have been wearing a sackcloth, for all that he noticed. Indeed, his notice seemed to have been diverted elsewhere. Namely to the bodice of the gown of the prior seneschal's widow, Màiri, whom Cate knew had shared his bed on more than one occasion in the past.

Cate's mouth tightened. Perhaps the change in her appearance had not been as dramatic as John's reaction had led her to believe, and Gregor needed a little help to see it?

The moment the widow walked away, Cate diverted Gregor's attention from the other woman's sashaying hips back to her by stepping slightly in front of him to block his view. "I'm wearing a new dress," she pointed out.

His jaw appeared to tighten before he turned his gaze to meet hers. The quick once-over he did of the gown was hardly longer than the passing glance he'd given her earlier. "It's nice."

It's nice? Not even a *"you* look nice"? Good gracious, the man handed out compliments to every other woman like they were sweets to bairns, and all he could manage for her was *nice*?

She glared at him. "Do you think the color flattering? Your mother thought so when she bought it for me, but I wasn't sure."

She saw the telltale tic of annoyance appear on his jaw, but as she was rather annoyed herself, she paid it no mind.

"It's certainly an improvement over the brown you were wearing earlier."

Cate gasped in outrage. The beast! He meant the mud!

Her eyes narrowed, anger replacing her earlier disappointment. Was he purposefully being dense? Didn't he realize that she was practically banging him over the head to get him to notice her?

Apparently, her banging was too subtle. She straightened, sticking her chest out the way Seonaid did whenever she came within fifty yards of him. "You do not think it's too tight? I've grown quite a bit in the past two years."

For one long heartbeat his eyes dropped. She sucked in her breath, feeling singed, as if a slow-moving wildfire were sweeping across her chest. Yet, oddly, her nipples hardened the way they did in a cold bath. The heat and hardness were a heady sensation, making her skin flush with a heavy tingle. It was as if her body were the string of a *clàrsach* that had just been strummed.

She felt her knees grow weak. Something hot and powerful fired between them. Something that made the air feel thick with tension. She knew she would see heat reflected in his gaze—the desire that she'd longed for.

But his eyes when they returned to hers weren't hot at all—they were cool and distant.

"If the gown is uncomfortable, you can go change," he said indifferently. "We will wait to start the meal. But don't take too long—I'm hungry."

He turned back to John, who'd been listening to the conversation with an odd expression on his face, and Cate didn't know whether to cry or kick the handsome clod in his leather-clad backside.

She was saved from making the decision by the appearance of Ete, who stepped out from the wooden partition behind the dais that separated the Hall from the corridor leading to the kitchens and the small room that served as the laird's solar. Cate gave her a questioning look and the other woman nodded. The children were ready.

Anticipating that Gregor would not want this meeting to take place in public, Cate had asked Ete to bring the children to the laird's solar.

She put her hand on Gregor's arm, startling him from his conversation with his brother. He stiffened, the muscles in his arm turned as rigid as steel. Moss-green eyes fixed on hers with an intensity that made her shiver.

She dropped her hand, the tension emanating from him startling her. Good gracious, what was the matter with him? He acted like she had the plague.

"They are waiting for us," she said hastily.

"Who?"

She tried not to lose her patience, reminding herself how important it was that this went well, but it wasn't easy. How could he have forgotten about them already? "Your children."

Gregor shot a look to John, who just shrugged and gave him a "don't look at me" look. "I told her you wouldn't like it," John said.

"And I told him," Cate said with a tight smile to John (the traitor), "that you wouldn't deny your own flesh and blood."

Gregor's mouth tightened, and she knew he wanted to argue with her premise but was holding his tongue—presumably because he knew his shouting would enable others to overhear their conversation.

"Where are they?" he asked impatiently, clearly eager for the meeting to be done with.

"In the solar."

He gestured with his hand for her to lead the way.

"Watch your feet," John said with a snicker.

Cate shot him a chastising glare, and pulled Gregor along when he would have turned to ask his brother what he meant.

"Perhaps you can pour Gregor some wine for when we get back, John," she said over her shoulder with a sugary smile.

The solar was small and without a window to let in natural light. Even with the circular iron candelabrum lit, the room was fairly dark. It wasn't until she closed the door behind them, however, that Cate realized her mistake. The two younger children took one look at the big warrior, and their eyes went wide with fright. Only Pip didn't look like he was about to burst out in tears. Nay, Pip was too intent on scowling and projecting an air of surly indifference to notice how the room seemed to suddenly fill with the big, strapping warrior.

Having become accustomed to his size, Cate forgot how physically intimidating Gregor could be. At three or four inches over six feet, he was a head taller than most men. Five years ago he'd still possessed some of the lean muscle of youth, but not any longer. Nay, now his build was all hard, solid man. His muscular chest and arms didn't need to be clad in armor to look intimidating; they were steely and forbidding all on their own. As her eyes skimmed over the broad shoulders and bulging arms, taking him in as if for the first time, an odd little flutter of awareness tingled low in her belly. She felt . . . *funny.*

Maddy's whimper, however, knocked her from her stupor with a frown.

"You're scaring them," she said under her breath.

One very finely arched brow lifted. "I'm just standing here."

"Aye, well try not to look so big." He stared at her as if

he couldn't figure out whether she was serious or not. Not knowing herself, but realizing how nervous she was, she began the introductions. "You've already met Phillip," she said. "And this young man is Edward—Eddie." She knelt down and held out her hand to the little boy. He eyed Gregor uncertainly, looking as if he wanted to bury his head in Ete's skirts. But after Cate's encouraging nod, he released the nursemaid's hand, slid the fingers into his mouth, and slipped his other hand into Cate's.

"He has red hair," Gregor said incredulously. "And freckles!"

Cate stood, meeting his accusing stare. "How very observant of you," she said, with a sharp look of warning not to say anything more in front of the children.

She'd known the bright red hair and freckles would be a problem. The coloring, although common enough in the Highlands, did not run in Gregor's immediate family. It was the first thing John had pointed out.

But surely with the plethora of women Gregor had been with, there had been at least a handful of redheads?

If the darkening look on his face was any indication, it seemed perhaps not.

She knew she was searching for a straw to clutch, but even if she'd harbored more than a big twinge of doubt about Pip, she'd held out *some* hope for the little ones. It would be so much easier to convince him to let them stay if there was a possibility they were his.

Proving that he wasn't a completely unfeeling brute, however, Gregor bent down on a knee to address the little boy. "How old are you, Edward?"

Cate winced at the same time that Eddie jumped. Even lowered, Gregor's voice was deep and authoritative. Scary to someone not used to being on the other side of his questions. Cate, of course, had plenty of experience with that.

Eddie, however, did not. When the little boy decided to use her skirts as a curtain to hide behind, Cate gave him an encouraging nudge forward. "It's okay, Eddie. This is your new laird. Remember I told you about him? He's been off fighting the nasty old English in the war. He won't hurt you. He just wants to ask you some questions."

The little boy looked up at her with his big blue eyes and nodded. Peeking out from behind her skirt, he held up three fingers.

"Come here, lad," Gregor said in a gentler voice.

Cate put her hand on the boy's head. "I'm not sure that's a good—"

Gregor shot her a glare. "I'm not going to hurt him. I just want to ask him a few questions."

That wasn't why she'd tried to stop him.

"It's okay, Eddie," Pip said with a devilish grin.

Cate shot him a look and started to explain to Gregor, but it was too late. Gregor had taken the boy's hand from hers and drawn him forward.

Cate said a silent prayer the little boy didn't get too scared or upset.

"When is your saint's day, lad?" Gregor asked.

Eddie gave him a big gap-toothed grin and Cate heaved a sigh of relief. Maybe it would be all right after all. "All Saint's Day. Pip gave me a new ball 'cause I was sad."

"Why were you sad?"

The smile fell as quickly as it had appeared. "I missed my mummy."

Gregor's voice was even softer yet, and Cate felt her heart tumble from her chest. "What's your mummy's name, Eddie?"

"Mummy." His little jaw started to tremble. "I want my mummy."

Cate would have moved toward him, but Gregor put a firm hand on his back. "I know you do, lad. And I would like to find her for you, but I need to know her name. What did other people call her? Janet? Mary? Elizabeth? Christina . . . ?"

Eddie brightened with understanding. "Ellen! That's what my Gram called her."

"And did your mum have nice red hair like you, lad?"

Eddie nodded furiously.

Gregor smiled, gave the boy a pat on the head, and stood. The smug look on his face did not bode well. The boy's answer seemed to have convinced Gregor that he was not his father.

The matter decided in his mind at least, Gregor turned to the little girl, who was wiggling in Ete's arms. "And who is this?"

"Mathilda, my laird," Ete said. "A right heavy handful this one is."

Gregor frowned. "Doesn't she walk?"

Cate and Ete exchange a look. "Not really, my laird," the older woman answered dryly. "It's more of a run."

As if on cue, a determined "Down!" was added to Maddy's wiggling.

Gregor looked at Cate. "She talks?"

Cate shrugged. "A few words here and there. We think she's about sixteen months—give or take a few." Cate held out her arms to a struggling Ete. "Here, I'll take her."

But for once, Maddy didn't seem to want Cate to hold her. She'd apparently overcome her temporary fear of Gregor and was eyeing him intently, while squirming and saying "no" over and over to Cate. Her face was growing redder and redder, and Cate feared those "no's" were about to turn to a screech. That had to be avoided at all costs.

"Here, you take her," Cate said, thrusting the child into his arms and not giving him a chance to refuse. "I think she wants you."

The stunned look on his face would have been comical if Maddy hadn't immediately quieted and started making a sound Cate had never heard from her before. In between sniffles from the cold she was still getting over, the cranky toddler—the *very* cranky toddler who hadn't done much but scream for the past week—started to coo and goo, making eyes at him like . . .

Good lord, did he have the same effect on females of all ages? It appeared so. The little girl was flirting!

"I think you've made another conquest," Cate said dryly.

Some of Gregor's shock had worn off, but he was still holding the little girl out like she had the plague. He did, however, grin. A devastating grin that made Cate suck in her breath. It was a grin that had made countless women fall at his feet, her included.

"Apparently the lass has good taste. I guess that is something." He examined her like a piglet at market. "She's a cute little thing, if you like white-blond hair and big blue eyes."

She would have wagered he did, but something about the way he said it made her wonder.

Gregor asked Cate what she knew of the child, and Cate started to tell him, but apparently Maddy had other ideas. She started kicking and bouncing up and down, reaching for Gregor to pull her closer. "My!" she said, then louder, "My!"

"I think she wants your brooch, my laird," Ete said. "She likes shiny things."

But it wasn't the large gold broach set around an onyx stone securing the plaid he wore around his shoulders that Maddy wanted. It was the *other* shiny thing.

As soon as Gregor pulled the little girl in closer, she reached for his face, putting her no-doubt drooly hand on his cheek. "*My!* Pretty!"

There was a moment of stunned silence at the child's proclamation.

But then Cate and Ete took one look at Gregor's horrified face, exchanged glances, and burst into laughter. Seeing Gregor's horror at being called "pretty," even Pip joined in.

Perhaps it wouldn't have been so bad if Eddie hadn't started laughing, too. Thus they found out the hard way that the little boy didn't release his bladder *only* when he was scared or upset.

"Oh, no," Eddie whispered, tugging her skirts. "I have to go."

Cate looked down and tried not to groan. "I think you already went, sweeting."

"What the hell?" Gregor yelled, jumping back and nearly dropping Maddy as the stream of liquid headed for his feet.

Cate took one look at his face and knew the chance for a good impression was long gone. With nothing to lose, she gave in to the laughter and grinned. "John warned you to watch your feet."

After nearly having had his foot pissed on, the midday meal was blissfully anticlimactic. But Gregor was painfully aware of the woman at his side.

As if it weren't bad enough that his body was humming with attraction, she was aggravating his edginess with laughter. Hers, at his expense.

"This is quite a pretty bowl, isn't it, Gregor?" and "What a pretty dress that is, Màiri, don't you agree, Gregor?" followed by "The heather was so pretty a couple of months ago, Gregor—too bad you could not have returned then."

Each time she said "pretty" with such teasing laughter dancing in her eyes, he itched to throw her back against the "pretty" tablecloth and kiss that impudent grin right from her mouth. Kiss her until those golden flecks in her dark eyes were soft and hazy with passion. Kiss her until the laughter in her throat turned to soft moans and whimpers. Kiss her until she knew just how far from pretty he could be.

Wrong, he reminded himself. But the voice was weaker

this time. Or rather the desire hammering through his body for her was getting louder.

Normally, he wouldn't mind the prodding—God knew he'd heard far worse from MacSorley—but he was wound so damned tight, he felt ready to explode.

To avoid that, he distracted himself with Màiri. The seneschal's widow had slid into John's seat after his brother had disappeared when Gregor called for the wine. At his first taste of the spiced swill, Gregor knew why. He would deal with his wine-poaching brother later, but for the moment all his attention was on the pret—damn it, *lovely* widow. He found himself relaxing. Enjoying the food— which was exceptional—and the easy, flirtatious banter.

Cate he largely ignored. Or tried to ignore, which was easier said than done, since she seemed to poke or nudge him for something every other minute. It was the oddest thing, though. Rather than getting all prickly or annoyed by his curt-bordering-on-rude responses, she was unusually calm and solicitous. "Is the lamb to your liking?" (It was exactly how he liked it, actually—roasted with lots of mint.) "Can I get you more wine?" (No. God knew he needed all his senses sharp to deal with her.) "What do you think of the new piper?" (He was the best Gregor had ever heard.) "Can I get you another trencher?" (No, he and Màiri didn't mind sharing this one.)

Once or twice he thought she was about to lose her temper, but then she would mumble something under her breath and smile at him instead. A very demure, maidenly smile that he couldn't recall ever seeing on her face before. That made him uneasy. The lass was up to something, and he suspected he knew what.

Cate's adoration for him had always made him uneasy, but now that she was older it was worse. The last thing he wanted was to be the object of a young girl's first love. She would only get hurt, and he didn't want that. He cared about her. As any man put in his position would, of course.

By the end of the meal, he and his bruised ribs were looking forward to the evening, when he intended to rid himself of the edginess for good. He thought Màiri was looking forward to it as well, which was why he was surprised when he found himself walking back from the stables alone after she didn't appear for their assignation.

He passed through the Hall, where the trestle tables had been replaced by bedrolls for the sleeping clansmen, on the way to his room.

"Did you have a nice walk?"

Recognizing the voice, he stiffened. Cate was seated on a wooden bench before the fire with John, a chessboard set out between them. They looked . . . *cozy*. He frowned.

"It's rather cold for a nighttime jaunt, isn't it?" she added.

Though it was an innocuous question, something about the way her eyes sparkled in the firelight made that frown deepen. Had she been aware of his foiled plans? And why the hell did her knowing about his liaisons bother him?

"I like the cold." Especially when he felt so damned *hot*.

He strode toward them and glanced down at the chess pieces that had been carved by his father. His father and his eldest brother, Alasdair, had loved to play. Gregor, on the other hand, had never had the patience for the game— another mark of many against him to his father's mind.

Striker, Raider, and Chief played, as did Bruce. Indeed, some of their matches had been more fierce and contested than the battles with the English of late.

He frowned at the board. From the looks of it, Cate appeared to be winning. His gaze met hers. "You play chess?"

She smiled. "A little."

John snorted. "Don't let her fool you, brother. She'll take the shirt off your back if you aren't careful. The lass is ruthless, with no mercy for a man's pride. She's been crushing mine for years. Padraig won't play with her anymore. Last time he was home, she had him helping Ete with hanging the laundry after he lost."

Their youngest brother, who fought for Bruce under their uncle Malcolm, the Chief of the MacGregors, was nearly as good a chess player as their father had been.

Cate grinned. "John exaggerates."

His brother grunted. "The hell I do."

Gregor shook his head. "You shouldn't have taught her if you weren't willing to lose."

There was an awkward pause. John shot Cate an uncomfortable glance. For some reason, the intimacy of that silent communication bothered him.

Cate seemed to stiffen slightly, but when she responded her voice was light and breezy. Perhaps too breezy. "John has taught me many things"—Gregor didn't like the sound of that—"but not this. I learned chess from my father."

Chess was a nobleman's game. Though it wouldn't be unheard of for a man of Kirkpatrick's birth to learn the game, it wasn't usual. Something about it pricked. But the subject of her father wasn't one she wished to discuss. Ever. Gregor had broached the subject a few times over the years, but Cate shut down so completely, he'd stopped. He hated seeing her upset.

She stood. "I think I shall retire." She looked at John. "We can finish the game tomorrow."

"It shouldn't take long," John said wryly.

Both men watched her cross the Hall and slip into the darkness beyond the partition. The Hall seemed suddenly . . . less.

John was watching him. "The lass has grown up."

Sensing there was more to the statement than there appeared, Gregor gave an inconsequential, "Aye."

"I didn't think you noticed."

He shot his brother a withering glare. "I noticed." When she'd stuck out her chest earlier, he'd nearly swallowed his tongue.

"Then why didn't you say anything about the gown? It isn't like you to be so ungallant around a lady."

"What gown?"

John's face darkened. "Don't be an arse, Gregor. I saw your reaction, even if she didn't. You noticed. The question is, what the hell are you going to do about it?"

"Find her a husband."

The blunt response took his brother aback. John thought for a moment, and then shook his head. "She'll never agree. She loves it here and belongs here, maybe even more than you or I. This is her home. You can't send her away."

Gregor steeled himself against the guilt, but it came anyway. "What would you have me do? With Mother gone, she can't stay here. She's not our sister."

"No," John said evenly. "No, she's not."

There was something in John's voice that set Gregor's already frayed nerve endings on edge. "What the hell is that supposed to mean?"

John returned the hard stare. "I don't know. Maybe I should ask you?"

The two brothers gazed at one another in the firelight in some kind of challenge neither one of them wanted to acknowledge. But feeling as if he were wading damned close to something he didn't want to step in—a mess he'd been in before—Gregor was the one to look away.

"What about the children?" John asked.

"They aren't mine."

"You are certain?"

"Aye." Their ages had left no doubt.

John nodded. "I suspected as much."

"Then why the hell did you let her take them in?"

"I wasn't sure, and . . ." John looked up at him, and then gave a helpless shrug. "She wanted them."

Gregor understood more than he wanted to. Cate was making the foundlings her family—*their* family. But he couldn't let her do that.

God, he hated this. Hated feeling responsible for someone else's happiness. He assuaged his guilt with the knowledge that she would likely have her own family soon
enough. And he would get back to doing what he did best:
fighting. Without anything—or anyone—else to weigh on
him. John could handle the clan and act as chieftain. The
position should never have been Gregor's anyway.

"I'll see you in the morning. Right now all I want to do
is sleep."

John's mouth curved on one side. "Then you might want
to find another bed."

"What?"

John shook his head and smirked. "You'll see."

Five

❧

Gregor was too tired to pay his brother's vague comments any mind. He fell asleep as soon as his head landed on the pillow.

But instead of relaxed and sated (as he surely would have been had Màiri shown up in the barn), his sleep was restless and definitely *un*-sated. He dreamed of dancing golden-brown eyes, delicate dark brows, a turned-up nose, and a naughty mouth. A naughty mouth with soft, dark red lips that were wrapped around him, sucking—

A scream tore through the night, piercing like icy nails driven through his ears. He shot awake, the lustful dreams that had gripped his body instantly cooled by shock.

His first thought was that Cate was having another nightmare. The first couple of years at Dunlyon she'd been plagued by them, but they'd grown less frequent as the years went on. But Cate's screams were of terror—they weren't the shrill, high-pitched wail of the banshee that went on and on until his skull felt like it was going to explode.

Not Cate, he realized. Then what the hell was it?

By the time the second scream came hard on the heels of the first, this one longer and—if possible—shriller, he was already out of bed, pulling on his breeches. He threw open the door and was about to bang on his brother's door, when it suddenly opened. A ghostly figure in white came flying out of the darkness toward him.

Instinctively—so as not to be barreled over—he caught
the apparition to him. His body shocked at the contact.
A rush of awareness poured through him like molten
lava, hot and heavy through his veins. His nerve endings
flared, his senses sharpened, and the heat . . . the heat engulfed him.

It wasn't a ghost. The very real body pressed against
his—nay, molded into his—was achingly female. Unusually
firm and surprisingly solid for a lass, perhaps, but still un-
mistakingly soft and sweet.

Cate.

Her gasp of surprise tangled with his groan of something far more primal. Lust. Raw, physical, primitive lust
that took hold of him and wouldn't let go.

She looked up, and their eyes met in the semi-darkness.
He saw her confusion, her innocence, and her desire. Her
very *womanly* desire.

For a moment that was all he saw. The connection was
so strong, so visceral, it seemed everything else faded away.
The horrible screeching. The time. The place. The voice of
reason. His thoughts became a dark tunnel of need that
led only to the woman in his arms.

He wanted to drown in her. To push her up against the
wall, cover her mouth with his, and give in to the desire
roaring through his body. He didn't know what the hell
was happening to him. The control he always felt had deserted him. He was wild.

The arm wrapped around her waist instinctively tightened, drawing her even closer. Her eyes widened, as she
no doubt felt what he did. Bodies plastered together, her
breasts crushed against his chest, her stomach nestled
against the substantial bulge of his manhood, their legs
entwined. Like a lock that had slipped into place, each
part had been fitted together precisely.

Perfectly.

Christ, it felt incredible. *She* felt incredible. The heat

started move to lower, to swell in his groin, to fill his cock and tighten his bollocks.

Every muscle in his body went rigid to battle the urges racing through him. The lust came on him so quickly and powerfully, it seemed impossible to hold back—especially for a man who'd never had to hold it back before. It had always been so easy for him—maybe too easy. When he wanted a woman, he never had to ask.

But this was different. He couldn't recall the last time he'd ever wanted a woman this intensely. It must be some damned perverse bone in his body making him want her precisely because he couldn't have her.

You can't have her. The voice penetrated the haze that had engulfed him.

But he didn't want to let her go. How could something that felt so damned right be so damned wrong?

Cate had wanted *him* to be struck by the lightning bolt, but instead she was the one who felt as if her entire world had shifted.

Her knowledge of love and romance was the bards' tales of a young girl. Sweet and tender, the gentle flutter of heartstrings at the thought of his lips touching hers for the first time in a chaste, reverent kiss. The kind of kiss a knight might give his lady after championing her on the tournament lists. That was what she'd pictured it would be like between them. That was all she knew.

But when Gregor caught her in his arms and held her against him, the picture changed forever. What she felt wasn't sweet or romantic or chaste at all. The cravings of her body weren't gentle flutters but a torrential thunderstorm of need, hot and powerful and a little—maybe a lot—wicked.

The images flashing through her head weren't of gallant knights bowing over their fair maidens' hands proclaiming their undying love, but of dark, sultry chambers and naked limbs entwined in bedsheets.

Sweet heaven, he was naked! Or rather, half of him was naked. And with her wearing only a thin linen shift, the feel of his powerful chest against hers was unlike anything she'd ever imagined. It made her hot and flushed and weak all over.

Instinctively her hands had slid around his shoulders when he caught her to him, and that was where they stayed, molded to the smooth, bare skin and hard, bulging muscle. He was so warm. She wanted to sink into him and never let go.

She'd known he was strong and powerfully built, but seeing him in the flesh was an entirely different kind of knowledge. The kind of knowledge that once awakened would never be put to rest again.

He'd been forged like a weapon of war, all lean, rigid muscle and tight sinew, without an ounce of spare flesh of which to speak. His shoulders were square and broad, his arms thick with rounded slabs of muscle, his waist narrow, and his stomach lined with layer after layer of tight rope-like bands. He was as hard as granite, yet impossibly warm—almost hot—to the touch. Especially where their bodies met.

She was hot, too, her skin flushed and strangely sensitive. She'd never felt like this before. The sensations—her thoughts and desires—shocked her. Confused her. Making her feel like she was seeing him for the first time.

She'd never imagined what the sight and feel of a man's naked chest could do to her. She'd never imagined the hot flush that would claim her body. The heaviness in her breasts and loins. The unmistakable flicker of awareness between her legs, and then the strange dampness. She'd never imagined wanting to run her hands all over some-one's body, wanting to feel the hard ridges and muscular bulges tightening under her fingertips.

But his naked chest did all of that.

It was just as perfect as the rest of him, glowing warm and golden in the light from the single torch that lit the hall. How was it possible for one man to be so blessed? It was as if God had set out to create a man who would make women fall to their knees.

She'd wanted Gregor MacGregor from the moment she'd seen him staring down at her in that well. But this was a different kind of want. It was much more powerful. It was the want of a woman for a man that came not just from the heart but from somewhere bone-deep and elemental. It was the want that could make a woman lose her virtue.

Until this moment, Cate had never really understood what could have made her mother—such a perfect lady in every other respect—do what she did. Now she had an inkling of just how easy it would be to lose herself in a man's arms.

Did Gregor feel it, too?

When their eyes met, Cate saw a myriad of emotions crossing his face, none of which she could decipher.

The screaming stopped as abruptly as it had started. Yet for a long heartbeat, neither of them moved. "Gregor, I . . ."

She didn't know what to say. Her emotions were too big to put into words.

He dropped her so suddenly, her legs almost didn't have enough time to find their bones.

"What was that noise?"

Cate blinked. The question was so matter-of-fact, his expression so neutral, had she not been there, she would have never guessed that a moment ago he had been holding her as if he would never let her go.

She felt like she'd been knocked over by a battering ram. Her body was still flushed with arousal—her skin prickling, her nipples throbbing, her belly fluttering—and he was as cool and unruffled as always. Even without clothes on to ruffle!

Had he felt nothing? Was the fierce attraction not between them at all, but one-sided? *Her* sided? Did nothing touch him?

She stared at him, peering closer in the darkness. This time she detected the faint tightness around his mouth, the clenching of his fists, and the stiff set of his shoulders. His muscles, too, every God-blessed one of them, seemed to be slightly flexed and rigid. Like those of a man fighting for control. Holding himself back.

Her eyes narrowed. Perhaps he wasn't quite as unaffected as he wanted her to think.

As if he could read her mind, his expression hardened. "Go back to your room, Caitrina. I will track down the source of the screaming."

She bit her lip and gave an apologetic smile. "There is no need. It was Maddy. She has an earache and wakes up sometimes."

He cocked a brow. "Sometimes?"

Her apologetic smile turning wincing. "Sometimes every night."

He groaned, raking his fingers back through his hair. There was some kind of marking on the top of his arm, but that wasn't what made her suck in every gasp of air in her lungs. Good God in heaven! The flex of muscle in his arm . . .

Her stomach did a little flip and dove straight for her toes.

"Can nothing be done?" he asked.

She forced her eyes from the ripped ball of arm muscle, trying to grasp a thread of coherent thought in her head. "Uh, the healer gave us a poultice, and warm blankets seem to help. But from the sound of it, Lizzie has it under control now. She sleeps in the room with her."

His gaze pinned hers. Obviously, he didn't like something she'd said. "And who do *you* sleep with, Caitrina? Why do I find you coming out of John's room?"

It took Cate a moment to realize what he meant. When she did, all she could do was stare at him with her mouth open. He thought she and John . . . ?

She straightened. How dare he! Unlike certain people in this corridor, she did not share her bed with whoever happened to be conveniently around. She had not been the one spoon-feeding Màiri bites of food all night. Food that Cate had gone to all that trouble to have prepared, including the special sugar-and-cinnamon biscuits she'd made herself. All his favorites. Everything perfect. Not that he'd noticed, blast it. How could he, when his face had been in Màiri's bosom all night?

He wasn't usually so obvious with his liaisons, but this time was different. It was almost as if he wanted her to notice.

Now Cate was the one clenching her fists. She wanted nothing more than to tell him exactly what she thought of his accusation, but her mother's (and Lady Marion's) words came back to her as they had all night long. "Ladies don't have tempers, Caty. Men don't want a shrew for a wife."

Apparently men wanted a giggling ninny with big breasts! But Cate kept her unkind thoughts about the widow to herself.

Cate's smile was so forced and brittle she thought her face might crack. "I moved down here to make room for the children. John slept in your chamber until Maddy became sick, when he decided he preferred the barracks."

"So you are sleeping in the . . ."

"In the room next to yours, yes," she finished. Why did he look so gray? "Is there something wrong with that?"

The muscle below his jaw started to tic from being squeezed so tightly, but he shook his head. "Nay."

She frowned. "Are you all right? It sounds like you have something in your throat. Oh goodness, I hope you are not coming down with a—"

"I'm fine," he growled, grabbing the wrist of the hand that was reaching for his forehead.

He shoved her hand back to her side and let go, but she could still feel the imprint of his hand around her wrist like a manacle.

"You don't sound fine, you sound angry. If it's about the sleeping arrangements or you holding me in your arms earlier—"

"I wasn't holding you in my arms, damn it!"

Cate tried not to smile, but his reaction made her so happy, she couldn't help it. If he hadn't felt anything, he wouldn't be so angry.

He *had* noticed her. He might not like it, but he had.

"You weren't?" she said innocently. "I could have sworn your arm was around my waist and my chest was against yours for a good three minutes—"

His face darkened. "Cate . . ."

Heeding the warning, she grinned and slipped back into her room. She'd made her point. "Good night, Gregor. Sweet dreams," she couldn't resist adding, closing the door in his face.

It was a thick, solid door, but she could still hear him curse as he moved away.

Cate flopped back on her bed and gazed up at the wooden beams and trestles of the ceiling in the moonlit darkness with a huge smile on her face.

She wasn't going to wait for lightning to strike after all. Nay, she was going to make a little storm of her own. She could afford to be patient, but the children could not. They needed him. He would see it . . . soon.

Six

Thanks to the short days of winter, it was still dark when Gregor woke to the sound of movement in the hall below. Although "woke" suggested sleep, which he'd had precious little of the past few days.

If it wasn't Maddy's crying (which had improved since he arranged to have a healer stay with her), it was his own dreams disturbing him. Sinful dreams. Wicked dreams. Dreams from which he'd wake hot and hard, poised on the edge of release. Hell, he'd taken himself in his hand so many nights this week, he felt like a sixteen-year-old lad again.

Since the night she'd ended up in his arms, his inconvenient lust for Cate had only gotten worse. *Much* worse. The lass seemed to be going out of the way to drive him half-mad. Nay, completely mad. Teasing him. Tempting him. Tormenting him with the desire for him that she didn't bother to hide. Coming home was supposed to clear his head, giving him his edge back, not putting him on it.

He'd done his best to avoid her, but within the small confines of Dunlyon, it was virtually impossible. She tracked him down with some excuse whether he was locked away in his solar, in the stables, or training in the yard with the men. The only time he had a moment of peace was when he rode out with his men to scout or to see to some of his more distant clansmen.

It certainly wasn't the first time he'd been the target of a less-than-subtle invitation by a young lass who was pandering to his every need, entrancing him with her smiles, accidentally brushing her body against his, or using any excuse to touch him. He'd been subject to such games and machinations since he was a lad. He saw through them and knew how to deal with them.

Usually. But with Cate it was different. With Cate he might see through it, but it didn't stop him from wanting her. She was the only one he'd ever had to resist, and doing so was proving more difficult than he ever could have imagined.

Twice he'd arranged other distractions, but twice his plans had been foiled. Once when a few of the men returned to the barracks unexpectedly, and another time when the servants decided to clean the storage room (at night, which seemed an odd time for housework).

Dunlyon was too damned small and the places for privacy few. There was his solar, of course, but with Cate right next door . . .

It made him uncomfortable. Cognizant of her tender feelings for him, he'd always tried to be somewhat circumspect in his dealings with other women while he was home. But he wondered how much longer he could keep that up in his present state. Exhausted and on edge were putting it mildly.

If it weren't Sunday, he would have pulled the pillow over his head and rolled back over.

Sunday. Damn it, he had to get ready for mass in the village. With a groan of resignation, he fished around groggily for his braies. He could wash and dress practically in his sleep. The last seven years of war had taught him to be ready at a moment's notice, and his movements were so engrained as to be rote. Cold water from the urn splashed on his face, a quick wash of his body, a paste of mint and salt and a rinse of white wine for his teeth, a comb through his hair (when he had a comb), tunic, hose, breeches, surcoat, plaid all nicely folded (which he couldn't remember doing), and boots. Boots . . .

He squinted again at the foot of the bed. Damn it, where the hell were his boots?

Jerking open the door, he was about to call for one of the servants, when Seamus, the son of a local chieftain who John had agreed to foster and who served as something of his squire, came hurrying up the stairs, the missing boots in his hands.

"Sorry, my laird. You were probably looking for these. I was supposed to have them back before you woke."

Gregor took the boots from the lad, noticing that they were no longer thick with mud. "You cleaned them?"

"Aye, Cate thought you would like them freshened up for mass this morning."

"She did, did she?" How bloody thoughtful of her! How she managed to anticipate his every need before he did was damned disconcerting.

The boy took a step back. "Did I do something wrong? Should I check with your brother next time first?"

Gregor gritted his teeth. "They aren't John's boots, damn it, they're mine."

He was the laird.

The boy's eyes widened, and Gregor swore, realizing what an arse he sounded like. This was what she'd reduced him to. Churlishness. He'd never been churlish in his life—until now. But it seemed that every time he turned around he was hearing "Cate sees to that," or "John already did that," or worse, "John and Cate took care of it." *Together.*

Clearly, John was proving a capable laird in Gregor's absence and Cate had taken over his mother's household duties with nary a misstep. Actually, if anything, the lass was doing an even better job. The place was spotless, the food was improved, and efficiencies had reduced the monies spent in the household accounts. According to the seneschal, Cate could barter a deal from the most tightfisted of merchants and suppliers. She probably bullied them until they gave up—something he was intimately familiar with. She was like a one-woman siege engine when she wanted something.

Gregor should be pleased that things were running so smoothly. Being laird was a job he'd never wanted or been destined for. He was glad he could focus on the war with the knowledge that his clan would be well looked after. He was. But being superfluous in his own tower took some getting used to.

"I'm sorry," Seamus repeated anxiously.

Gregor swore. He shouldn't take his irritation with Cate out on the lad. "Nay, 'tis I who am sorry, lad. I am ill-tempered this morning. You did a fine job—thank you."

The boy beamed and was about to run off when the door next to his opened and out walked the source of Gregor's ill-temper, looking fresh and sweet and too damned lovely for his not-so-peaceful state of mind in yet another snug-fitting gown—this one dusky blue.

She turned her bright-eyed gaze to his. Did she have to look so damned *cheery*? "Is something wrong? I thought I heard raised voices."

"It's nothing," Gregor said at the same time the lad offered, "I was just returning the laird's boots."

She dimpled. Since when did she have dimples, damn it? "We'd hoped to surprise you."

"You did," Gregor said. Turning to Seamus, he added, "You can return to your other duties, lad. Tell my brother we'll be leaving soon."

Cate was studying his face with concern. "Are you sure you are all right? You were tossing and turning rather restlessly when I came in to bring your clothes—"

"When you *what*?" Gregor exploded furiously, taking a step toward her before he remembered how foolish that was. Christ, she smelled good. Plenty of women used heather to scent their soap, but none had ever smelled like this. None had ever made him want to bury his nose in her neck and inhale.

Rather than be intimidated by his anger, however, she looked up at him and smiled. "Freshly washed, brushed, and folded." She shook her head. "You still leave them on the floor, I see."

Whether it was the intimacy of how much she knew about his personal habits or the intimacy of knowing she had been in his room when he was sleeping, Gregor didn't know, but he felt the walls closing in on him. Nay, *she* was closing in on him, and he didn't like it. It made him want to lash out as he always did when a woman set her sights on him and tried to corner him. "Stay out of my room, Cate—especially when I'm sleeping."

How she'd managed to sneak up on him was alarming on many different levels.

Her brows furrowed. "Why?"

"Because it isn't right, damn it!"

She lifted a brow. "Isn't right? I'm like a daughter to you—or a sister. Aren't I?"

The hell she was! She was . . .

Clever. He stopped, realizing what she was doing: forcing him to acknowledge something he didn't want to acknowledge.

He couldn't let her keep doing this to him. It was time to untwist the knots the lass had him all tied up in. She'd grown too bold after what he'd inadvertently revealed the other night. But he'd been playing this game a hell of a lot longer than she had. He smiled slowly. "Aye, you're right."

She blinked. "I am?"

"Perhaps not a daughter—I'm not quite that old—but definitely a younger sister." She looked properly horrified. He shrugged as if it no longer mattered to him. "I was only trying to protect you."

She swallowed uncertainly. If her closeness weren't firing every nerve ending in his body, he would surely have enjoyed it.

"Protect me from what?"

He gave her his best roguish grin. "Seeing something that might shock your maidenly sensibilities in the event I have company."

She sucked in her breath, stricken, the thought obviously never having occurred to her. But if he thought she would so easily be discouraged, he'd underestimated her. The lass was far too stubborn and proud. Nor, as her little brawl at the river had proved, would she back down from a fight, even when the odds were not in her favor. And betting on him was bad odds indeed.

The stricken look slipped away, and the gaze that held his was far more knowing and determined than he would have liked. "There is very little privacy in a castle, Gregor. I'm sure you've nothing that I haven't seen before." The eyes scanning his chest and reminding him of exactly how much she'd seen were narrowed—and didn't seem impressed. Though why the hell that grated, he didn't know. He didn't want her admiring him or his body. But who the hell was she comparing him to? Admittedly he'd bulked up in the past few years, but it was all muscle—

He stopped. Good God, what was she doing to him?

"Although for the children's sake," she added, "I hope you will keep your 'company' to a minimum."

She'd done it again. Put him on the defensive. Making him feel like an arse. A *profligate* arse.

Whom he shared his bed with was his business. He didn't owe her any explanations. He would bring a woman to his chamber if he wanted to.

But damn it, it would hurt her, and something inside him rebelled at the idea.

Her words, however, reminded him of another problem. Every time he tried to talk to her about "the children," she kept putting him off. It seemed the only way to be rid of her was to mention that he'd been on his death-bed with an arrow through his neck when Eddie was conceived and patrolling the Western Isles hunting down John of Lorn in the months during Maddie's conception. "Speaking of the children, have you made arrangements yet for their removal—"

"There they are now," she said, cutting him off. He could hear her relief at once again being saved from discussing the matter by the arrival of Ete, Lizzie, the scowling black-haired charlatan, the child who had a propensity to release his bladder every time Gregor was near, and the banshee in the guise of a blond-haired poppet. "We had best go, if we do not want Father Roland angry at us for being late."

She tried to flounce off, but he caught her arm. "We aren't done with this, Cate."

She looked up at him, and something about her expression—hell, everything about her expression—made him want to cover her mouth with his. "No." Her eyes searched his, probing. "No, we're not."

He might have been pleased by her agreement, except he knew she wasn't talking about the children.

He didn't know what Cate thought she knew about him, but she was wrong. And it was becoming very clear that one way or another, he was going to have to prove it.

Company. The one word had shaken Cate's confidence to the core. He wouldn't bring a woman to his room . . . would he?

With the way Gregor had been fighting acknowledging his attraction to her since the night in the corridor, she suspected he just well might.

Cate was going to have to up her vigilance and her efforts, it seemed, until he was ready to accept that there was something between them.

It was thoughts of how to save him from himself that kept her occupied during Father Roland's long "popular" sermon given in Gaelic rather than Latin. Perhaps ironically, the subject was chastity, and the priest, after giving an example of the nun who'd gouged out her own eyes and had them sent to a king rather than be the object of his lust (Cate thought his point would have been stronger had the king gouged his own eyes out), was going on *ad nauseam* with long passages from the Gospel (these in Latin), which she didn't understand.

Not surprisingly, Gregor had decided to sit a few benches away from her and the children. He was proving intractable on the subject of being "rid" of them, and she was finding it harder and harder to convince herself that he would change his mind. But as she had no intention of changing her mind either, they were at an impasse.

Patience, she reminded herself. But it was difficult. On all accounts. Not just the children, but waiting for him to acknowledge what was between them—especially with all the other women with whom she had to contend.

Feeling as if a rock were sitting on her chest, she watched as the instant the mass was over, the women descended on him like locusts. It had been the same for the past three mornings at Dunlyon, since news of his arrival had spread throughout the small village and surrounding countryside. His arrival *always* caused a sensation, with women arriving at Dunlyon to see the laird under all kinds of ridiculous pretenses.

He took all the attention in stride, smiling, flirting, and charming every one of them. Every one of them but her, and for the first time it bothered her. Cate was jealous. And no matter how many times she told herself the women were nothing to him, she couldn't stop the little voice from saying that neither was she.

Yet. Lady Marion's words came back to her. *"Be patient, sweeting. Those women don't mean anything to him. When he gives his heart to the right woman it will be forever."* It was giving it to the wrong woman that had been the problem. Gregor's mother had guessed Cate's feelings, and trying to give her hope—nothing would have pleased her more than to see them together—told her what had happened with his brother's wife. How the woman had used Gregor to make his older brother jealous and elicit a proposal from him.

Cate followed John outside, where the villagers were taking advantage of the sunny winter morning to gather in the churchyard. One of the reeve's sons—Farquhar, she recalled his name—stopped to talk to John, and Cate took the opportunity to look back at Gregor, who was still in the church trying to make his way outside.

Seeing whom he was talking to, she wished she hadn't. Cate stiffened, her teeth grinding. Seonaid MacIan, the favored daughter of the wealthiest chieftain in the area, had befriended Cate when she'd first arrived but had turned on her once it became clear their friendship wouldn't get her any closer to Gregor.

Blond, blue-eyed, and curved in all the places men seemed to like curves, Seonaid was the most beautiful woman in the area. Just ask her. As such, she thought that made her destined for Gregor. That he didn't seem to agree, Seonaid blamed on Cate—though Cate had never said a word against her (and she would have had plenty of words to choose from).

Turning her gaze from the girl who'd done her best to make her life miserable for years, Cate was pleased to see Pip talking with some of the village lads, including Willy. Ete had Eddie in hand, but Lizzie looked exhausted from holding a squirming Maddy for so long, so Cate offered to spell her for a while. Finding a little space in the back of the churchyard, she let the little girl run for a bit, and then scooped her up in her arms and spun her around until they both were flushed and laughing.

"How sweet."

Cate stiffened at the sound of the mocking voice.

Holding Maddy close to her chest as if to protect her from the venom, she turned to see Seonaid. As always, a couple of her followers were at her side. Alys and Deidre never said much, their purpose simply to echo Seonaid.

"What have you done to yourself, Caitrina?" Seonaid's big blue eyes scanned her gown. "You actually found a pretty dress to wear? After what you did to Dougal MacNab, I thought to find you in armor with a sword." She laughed, though there was no humor intended in the scornful tones. On cue, Alys and Deidre's snickering followed.

Seonaid always had a way of making Cate feel awkward and unfeminine, and she knew it. Seonaid's rich gowns were always trimmed with rows and rows of ribbon and embroidery, her hair always curled and artfully arranged, her skin looked like she bathed in milk, and there was never a speck of dirt under her nails. She was soft and lush as a pillowy confection, while Cate was hard and strong as a stick of dried beef.

When Cate looked at Seonaid she saw everything she wasn't and could never be—on the outside. But underneath the pretty picture, Seonaid was selfish, spoiled, and spiteful, and any man who didn't see that was a fool. Beef might not be flashy, but it had substance.

Cate was done letting the other woman make her feel bad about herself. "What do you want, Seonaid? As you can see, I'm busy."

Seonaid's lip curled with distaste as she looked at Maddy. "With one of the bastards? Why you would let them under the roof, I can't imagine. If I were lady of the keep, I would have sent them away."

Cate's temper notched up at the word "bastard" and the familiar disdain. Disdain she'd heard far too many times as a child. "But *you* aren't lady of the keep and certainly aren't likely to be in the future, so it really is none of your concern."

Seonaid's cheeks flushed with anger, and her expression lost any pretense of equanimity. "Are you so sure of that? That's not the impression I had a few minutes ago. I'd say the laird seemed very interested in a closer relationship."

The way she emphasized "closer" made Cate's chest twist. *He wouldn't.* "I sincerely doubt that."

"Why? You can't think he'd prefer a boyish lass who plays at warfare to a woman like me—no matter what gown you are wearing."

Cate clenched her fists. Knowing how to use a sword or defend herself didn't make her "boyish." But Seonaid's barb had pricked what little there was of her feminine vanity. "It isn't the dress but the character underneath. No matter how fine the linen you bundle it in, rotten fish still stinks."

Alys and Deidre gasped. Seonaid turned florid, her eyes blazing with hatred. "Character? What a naive fool you are, Caitrina. Beauty and a bosom are what men want."

Cate pursed her mouth stubbornly. "Not Gregor."

She knew him. He wasn't like that. She knew how little importance he put on his own looks, and how much it bothered him when other people did—though he never showed it. When he married, it would be for substance, not for superficial charms.

Seonaid might be cruel and spiteful, but she was also surprisingly astute, and something in Cate's expression must have given her away. Her gaze pinned on Cate like a predator who'd just picked up the scent of blood. "My God, you are in love with him!" The sharp burst of laughter hurt more than Cate would have thought possible. "You don't actually think the most handsome man in Scotland would ever marry a woman like you? A foundling he felt sorry for with nothing to recommend her but 'character,' a plain face, and a boyish figure?"

She wasn't plain or boyish. She knew Seonaid was just

being cruel, but the words still stung—and made her want to sting back. Gregor did care for her. And one day he would marry her. She knew it deep in her soul.

It shouldn't matter that no one else knew. But like the taunts of "bastard" that had followed her as a child, Seonaid's words had hit a tender spot—a defensive spot. *"My father is the greatest knight in Christendom."* The old boast rang in her ears, and she felt the same compulsion to make them sorry for teasing her rise inside her.

"He will marry me," she said fiercely. "And not because of a pretty face or big bosom, but because he loves me. The most handsomest man in Scotland will be my husband— you'll see."

The unwavering confidence in her voice seemed to take Seonaid momentarily aback, though she recovered quickly enough. "The only way you will ever get Gregor MacGregor to marry you is if you trap him," her gaze swept over Cate's modest bosom, "and you lack the proper enticements for that."

Cate smiled, recalling the attraction simmering between her and Gregor a few nights ago. "Which only proves how little you know of enticing. You don't have any idea what's between us. If you don't think I can do it, you are wrong!"

Seonaid's eyes widened, hearing her confidence.

Suddenly Cate cringed. The conversation was deteriorating, leaving her feeling as if she needed to jump in the loch to wash. She shouldn't stoop to Seonaid's level, no matter how well baited.

Holding Maddy tightly, she swept regally past the three women before Seonaid could muster her verbal weaponry for another attack.

Cate had barely turned the corner into the churchyard where everyone had gathered when she ran into John and Farquhar. "There you are," John said. "We wondered where you had gone to."

Cate's smile was strained; she felt drained from the episode with Seonaid and her friends. "Maddy needed to stretch her legs after the sermon."

"It was rather a long one," Farquhar said with an understanding smile.

The easygoing smile surprised her. The reeve's eldest son was something of a scholar and had recently returned from university study on the continent. From what she remembered of Farquhar before he left, he'd always seemed rather dry and serious.

They exchanged a few more pleasantries, and Cate was surprised when Farquhar offered to escort her back to Dunlyon. John seemed surprised as well, but mentioned that he and Gregor had business elsewhere. Cate was about to refuse when she chanced a glance at Gregor and reconsidered. She froze. He hadn't moved very far from where she'd seen him last, but it was to whom he was talking, and the darkening expression on his face, that made her rather in a hurry to leave.

It was Màiri, which meant Cate was in trouble.

Seven

If Cate thought she could escape from him that easily, she'd better think again. Gregor now knew whom he had to thank for interfering with his assignations the past few days. God's bones, the lass could give Robert the Bruce lessons in sabotage!

It took him a moment to recognize the man with whom she'd made her escape. He didn't recall the reeve's eldest son as being so tall—or so broad of shoulder. For a scholar, he looked like he spent most of his days out in the field or with a smith's hammer in his hand. The observation wasn't a welcome one. That Farquhar was both suitable and seemingly interested should have gladdened him— Farquhar was one of the men on Gregor's list of potential suitors for her—but Gregor didn't like the way the man was looking at her.

A lass could be disarmed by that friendly smile. Who knew what kind of trouble an innocent like Cate— inexperienced with the wicked ways of men—could find herself in? If Farquhar touched her, Gregor would string the pup up.

The vehemence of his reaction took him aback. He was only being protective—as her guardian, he told himself. He should be glad to find a suitor to take her off his hands. Then he could get down to focusing on getting his head back on straight. The next time the king needed him, he'd be ready. He wasn't going to let him down again. But it took a long time for his fists to unclench after she'd made her swift escape.

As tempted as he was to go after her, his tenuous truce with the neighboring MacNabs required his attention.

He and John rode out to Lochay after church, but the meeting did not go well.

Kenneth MacNab of Lochay, a kinsman of the MacNab chief who'd stood with John of Lorn against Bruce at the Battle of Brander, was practically foaming at the mouth with outrage. "The termagant drew a dagger on my son when his back was turned. A dagger! The lass should be put to the stocks for what she did. You are fortunate I do not demand her arrest."

Gregor's jaw hardened, the only indication of how close he was to slamming his fist through the other man's teeth at the idle threat. They both knew that there was no way in hell MacNab would draw more attention to his son's humiliation—the incident had become public enough. And it was one thing for Gregor to call her a termagant; it was quite another for MacNab to do so.

"The lass is my responsibility," Gregor said with surprising evenness. "If anyone is to punish her, it will be me."

"And just how do you intend to do that?"

Gregor's mouth thinned as he eyed the battle-scarred chieftain. Coarse, thickly built, and more wild and rough-shod than most, MacNab was a handful of years older than Gregor and had retired from the battlefield, but was still a warrior with whom to reckon.

"Caitrina recounts the events differently." As he'd been trying to avoid her, he'd actually gotten the story from John, along with confirmation from a surly, defensive Pip. "According to her, it was your son who pushed her down when her back was turned. She defended herself with the knife when he attempted to kick her while she was on the ground."

"And you believe that? My son is twice her size. Not to mention the fact that she is a woman."

If the bruises Gregor had seen on Dougal's face when they arrived were any indication, MacNab believed it as well. But the clan's pride had been damaged enough by a lass getting the better of Dougal in a fight, and MacNab was obviously trying to put his son in the best light by re-arranging the facts.

"The lass is more than capable of defending herself against a lad Dougal's size," John said. "I taught her myself."

MacNab turned on Gregor with fury. "And you permit this aberrant behavior? What kind of unnatural lass practices at warfare?"

Gregor's eyes narrowed in warning. He understood MacNab's anger, and the blow to his pride, but he would not hear Cate maligned. "I not only permit it, it was at my suggestion. I find nothing unnatural about a lass learning to defend herself against cowardly men who think it acceptable to hurt women."

MacNab turned scarlet at the jab, which he knew was aimed at him as well. His wife's bruises were well known.

If it weren't for the meeting being held under truce, Gregor suspected MacNab would have drawn his sword—despite Gregor's superior skill. "So you plan to do nothing?"

Gregor's jaw hardened. As much as he disliked MacNab and would prefer to tell him to go to the devil, he didn't want to leave John to have to contend with a renewed feud. Still, diplomacy didn't come easily to a man who'd done nothing but fight for seven years, and the words tasted sour in his mouth. "I will speak with her."

"You need to put a harness on her. The lass has been running wild for years. She needs a strong hand—"

"The lass is not your concern," Gregor snapped.

MacNab made her sound like a horse that needed to be broken. Caitrina wasn't wild, she was spirited and ... unique. She was unrestrained. Self-confident. *Honest*. She never held back, having that same no-holds-barred approach to life that he and every other great warrior he knew had. She was strong and unpretentious, with an easy grace and natural appeal that was impossible to resist. If she was at times a little too brazen, it was done without artifice. He wouldn't have her any other way, and he sure as hell wasn't going to turn her into something else to please the likes of MacNab.

Attempting to smooth the waters, John added, "She is to be married soon anyway."

"Married?" MacNab scoffed. "I hope you plan to include a scold's bridle with her tocher. Or perhaps her husband will find something else to put in her mouth to prevent her from opening it."

Gregor saw red at the crude remark. Diplomacy and the truce forgotten, he would have broken more than just a few of MacNab's teeth if John hadn't grabbed his arm to hold him back.

Perhaps realizing that he'd gone too far, MacNab let the matter rest. Still, it was with superhuman effort that Gregor managed to get a rein on his temper and not only refrain from killing MacNab, but also continue negotiations to successfully extend the truce.

By the time they returned to Dunlyon, he was tense, foul-tempered, and looking for a fight. In other words, he was more than eager to hunt down his wee "ward" and have a little chat about her interfering in his private life.

He should have guessed she was the one responsible for Màiri missing their assignation and the two other interruptions. Unfortunately, it seemed that for once the lass was avoiding him. She'd retired early for the evening—the coward—and even in his present mood, he wasn't fool enough to knock on her bedchamber door.

Nay, he had a better plan. He would wait for her in the stables early the next morning and intercept her before she went on her morning ride.

He was barely through the open door to the stables the next morning, however, before he was the one intercepted.

"There you are!"

Gregor stifled a groan. The last thing he wanted to deal with right now was another young lass who thought she "loved" him. Seonaid MacIan was undoubtedly a beauty, but she was a perfect example of everything he tried to avoid. She'd left him no doubt of what she wanted from him, and what she would be willing to give up to get it—as if her maidenhead were some kind of prize to be bartered. He wasn't interested. Not on those terms. Hell, not on any terms. But he was never cruel unless he had to be, and she was Cate's friend.

"I thought I'd missed you," Seonaid added. "I went to the Hall, but they said you'd just left."

From her pink cheeks, he guessed she'd come running after him.

The lazy smile slipped onto his face without thought. "I thought I'd go for a ride."

She peered out at him from under her lashes, a coy smile curving her pretty mouth. "I imagine you are a very good rider." The way she emphasized "rider" left no doubt about the kind of riding to which she was referring. "I'm afraid I do not have much experience. But I'd be willing if you'd like to teach me—most willing."

Good God, this had to be one of the most ridiculous conversations he'd ever had. Still, he returned her naughty smile. "I shall remember that. But I'm afraid I shall be riding alone today."

She pouted prettily and moved close enough to him for the tips of her breasts to brush against the leather of his *cotun*. They were very ample breasts and the cut of her gown gave him a nice view of the deep crevice between them, but the display (surprisingly, given his deprived state) failed to stir him.

"Did you need something?" he asked, cognizant of the time and wanting to rid himself of his unexpected "company."

"I brought you some sugared buns. You mentioned you liked them yesterday. I left them with your maidservant."

"Thank you," he said. "That is very thoughtful of you. I'll have one when I return."

He started into the barn, hoping she would take the hint. She didn't. Instead, he felt her hand on his arm.

Her coy, innocent expression had turned hard and impatient. "I thought you might perhaps thank me another way."

He pretended not to understand, quirking a brow. "What did you have in mind?"

"This." She tilted her face to look up at him, offering him her perfectly parted lips.

The lass was unflatteringly brazen, but her not-so-subtle invitation gave him an idea. Cate would be here any minute. Kissing Seonaid would be as good a way as any to put a decisive end to Cate's infatuation with him.

He told himself it had to be done. Cate was like every other young girl who'd taken one look at him and fancied herself in love. She thought she *knew* him. But she didn't know him at all. He wasn't the man for her—hell, he wasn't the man for anyone. The sooner she realized that, the better. It would save her more heartbreak later.

With something burning in his chest that felt surprisingly like regret, he lowered his mouth.

Half-expecting Gregor to be lying in wait, ready to pounce on her the moment she left the safety of her chamber, Cate didn't leave her room until she heard the door open and close across the corridor, and the familiar heavy fall of footsteps down the stairs.

Of course, she'd known there would be hell to pay for her interference; she'd just hoped to have more time before paying it. But her plans to have him realize how perfect they were together hadn't progressed as quickly as she'd hoped, and she could not stand by and do nothing while he took more women to his bed.

God knew, there had been enough of them. Cate could not change the past, but she was no longer willing to make excuses for him: *you aren't old enough,* she would tell herself, *he doesn't see you yet; just be a little more patient, and it will be you.*

She was tired of being patient, and she wouldn't let him do anything to break her heart before she'd had a chance to give it to him.

He would thank her for it.

Eventually.

She hoped.

But his expression yesterday at the kirk definitely hadn't been thankful. It had been more an "I'm going to give you an ear-blistering lecture" kind of look. Until he had a chance to calm down a bit, she thought a little evasion was prudent. There was a difference between cowardly and not stupid.

Perhaps she'd go on an extra-long ride this morning? After checking with Ete that Eddie and Maddy were taken care of, and swiping an apple and a piece of cheese from the kitchens since she'd missed the morning meal, Cate clambered down the wooden stairs of the tower house into the bailey below in search of Pip. Though he'd never sat on a horse before arriving at Dunlyon, the lad had taken to riding like a fish to swimming. As she thought she might ride out to Loch Tay to visit her friend Anna, Willy's older sister, she wanted Pip to accompany her. It would give him a chance to build on their conversation of yesterday.

Assuming she would find him in the barn with the pup, she ducked inside and was about to call out when she came to a hard stop, feeling as if she'd just slammed into a stone wall.

Her breath caught, her heart lurched and hung weightlessly in the air, and the blood racing through her veins drained to the floor. The shock was so profound, it took a few blinks to process what she was seeing. And then she wanted to close her eyes and block out the image forever.

No. He can't be kissing her. Please let it not be Seonaid. Anyone but Seonaid.

But there was no mistaking the perfectly coiled plaits of long blond hair beneath the veil, the fine dark blue velvet gown, and the generously curved backside. Seonaid was standing on her tiptoes, her arms twined around his neck, her body stretched out against his. His head was bent, silky golden-brown hair slumped to the side, as he deftly tipped Seonaid's chin with his fingers to tilt her mouth to his.

The wide, sensuous mouth that Cate had imagined so many times pressed against hers was kissing another's. No, not just another's, *Seonaid's.*

She'd seem him kiss other women before, but this time it was different. This time the hurt was bigger and more powerful. The white-hot knife of pain stabbed through her heart and stayed there burning, twisting, digging deeper as the kiss went on.

Stop. Please, stop.

She swayed, her legs suddenly weak. They want to crumple to the floor like she did.

God, it hurt. How could he do this? This wasn't supposed to happen. This wasn't what she'd planned.

It's supposed to be me.

Seonaid's taunts came back to her. Was this what he wanted, then? Someone like Seonaid?

This is the kind of man he is.

No. It couldn't be. But then why was he doing this?

Cate felt the tears threatening to storm, hot and tight in

her throat. She wanted to turn and run before he saw her, but her feet had turned to lead.

Then it was too late. A fierce barrage of yapping rang out as the pup came tearing across the barn toward the embracing couple. The tiny terrier obviously didn't like what he saw either, because he started to growl ferociously (as ferociously as a five-pound pup could) and nip at Gregor's heels.

Gregor had to push Seonaid back to break the kiss. That he seemed to do so with obvious relief didn't make Cate feel any better.

"What the hell?" He tried to move his feet around to untangle the pup, but the pup had no intention of letting go.

Seonaid, who at first seemed furious to have been disturbed, started to wail as if terrified by the tiny ball of fur who was barely big enough to fill two hands. "What is it?" she cried. "Oh God, kill it!"

Pip appeared out of nowhere to pluck the dog from Gregor's heels to the safety of his arms. "It's only a dog," he said scornfully to the whimpering woman.

Finally, Gregor turned in her direction. Their eyes locked, and the blow landed anew, reverberating through her chest in a heavy drum of hurt, pain, and disappointment.

But now there was also anger. She'd believed in him, defended him to this very woman, and he'd made her look like a naive fool. She'd thought there was more to him than the handsome heartbreaker. More to him than the untouchable rogue. She'd thought she understood him. That they had a special connection, and that one day he would see it.

But maybe one day would be too late. Maybe she didn't understand him at all. Maybe the only connection they had was in her mind. Maybe he was just as untouchable as he seemed. And maybe, just maybe, all he would do if she let him was break her heart.

But she wasn't going to let him. If Seonaid and her big breasts and beautiful face were what he wanted, he could have them.

"Aye," she said, looking straight at him. "It's just a dog."

Gregor knew she meant him, and not the demonic scrap of fur that had done its best to sink its tiny teeth into his boots.

The barb was well aimed. He felt no better than a dog when he saw her face. She'd looked shattered, and he felt like a man who'd just taken a hammer to her fragile dreams.

Christ, this was what he'd been trying to prevent. He'd never wanted to hurt her. But one look at her face, and he knew just how badly he'd done that.

It was the disappointment, however, that cut him to the quick. He hadn't realized how much her belief in him mattered until it was gone. From the first, Cate had looked at him like some kind of hero. God knows, he'd never wanted it, and had always known he would somehow tarnish that shining-armor image she had in her mind, but he hadn't realized how much he'd come to depend on it, how much it would bother him when it was gone, and how much it would remind him of the other person he'd disappointed.

His father had been ashamed of Gregor's "pretty face" from practically the day he'd been born, yet ironically it was all the man ever saw. "Christ, just look at him!" his father would say to Gregor's mother. "The lad will never have to work hard for anything. See how people bend over to make him happy. He'll be a wastrel and a popinjay for the rest of his life."

His father's portent had proved true. In Gregor's youth, it seemed that whatever he tried to do, it always went wrong. By the time he'd turned fourteen or fifteen he'd given up trying and entered a period of full-fledged rebellion, where he took great pains to throw his irresponsibility in his father's face. That had changed when he'd gone off to join the fighting at eighteen, but by then it was too late. No matter how hard Gregor worked to prove himself, his father had never seen him as anything other than weak and unreliable. And now Cate was looking at him the same way, and he hated it.

But it was her own fault, damn it! He'd never asked for her faith. Hell, he'd never wanted it. Why was she so surprised? So what if he kissed another lass? He could kiss whoever the hell he wanted!

Although next time it wouldn't be *this* lass clutching his chest as if a swarm of rats were circling around her feet.

Nay, not rats, *rat*.

His gaze fell on the scraggly-looking pup tucked protectively against the chest of another scraggly-looking creature. Both were black-haired and scrawny, and both were looking at him as if *he* were filth under their feet. The lad was silent; the pup, however, was not, and its frantic, high-pitched yapping was too reminiscent of another terrier he'd rather not remember.

"Shut that thing up," he snapped.

"Which one?" Pip replied, with an eye to Seonaid.

Gregor might have cracked a smile—Seonaid's high-pitched wail was just as annoying as the pup's—if he hadn't heard Cate muffle a sharp laugh.

Shooting them both a quelling stare, while silently agreeing, he attempted to calm the lass whose arms had taken on the distinct feel of tentacles.

He never should have kissed her in the first place. It had felt wrong from the very beginning. If it wouldn't reinforce everything Cate thought about him, he might admit that he didn't even like Seonaid. In fact, he would have pulled back the moment their lips touched if he hadn't heard the footsteps and sharp intake of breath that had identified Cate.

No matter how unpleasant, however, the kiss had served

its purpose. Cate had been disenchanted. She was no longer looking at him with the heart-in-the-clouds adoration of a young girl. No, the way she was looking at him was far too clear-eyed.

It was what he wanted, wasn't it?

"Here," Cate said, reaching for the tiny beast. "Let me take him. He's probably just scared by all that caterwauling."

Seonaid had calmed enough to narrow her eyes on Cate. "That thing, scared? It was the one who attacked us."

The pup had quieted, and was nuzzling its small head into Cate's hand like it couldn't get enough of her touch as she petted it.

What would it feel like to have those hands on him? Gregor's blood surged. *Incredible.* God, he knew without a doubt that it would feel bloody incredible.

Oblivious to Gregor's unwanted and illicit thoughts about where he would like to have those nimble fingers stroking him, Cate looked back and forth between Seonaid and the pup. "You must have been terrified," she deadpanned. "He is quite vicious."

Seonaid's gaze hardened, and there was something cruel in her eyes that made Gregor uneasy. Had he unwittingly struck deeper than he intended?

"Fortunately, I didn't need to act like a man to protect myself." Seonaid latched onto his arm again. "I had a real one by my side to do so." She blushed, casting him a coy glance from under her lashes. "Well, not exactly at my side." She laughed and turned to Cate. "As I'm sure you saw."

The gloating in her voice left Gregor no doubt of just what a big mistake he'd made. If they'd been friends once, they weren't any longer.

"I hope you are not too disappointed, Caitrina," Seonaid added. Cate's face went white. She seemed frozen in place, her fingers stiff in the dog's fur. Seonaid batted her lashes at him, and he wondered how he'd ever thought her pretty. "You know she has a little *tendre* for you. But I told her a man like you would be more . . . *discerning*." She laughed as if him desiring Cate were the most ludicrous thing in the world.

If she only knew.

Gregor's eyes shot to Cate's. He didn't know what he'd expected. To see her embarrassed? Humiliated, as Seonaid had intended?

But he hadn't given her enough credit. Cate didn't look like an immature girl at all when she lifted her chin almost regally and looked down her nose at the other woman. "It wasn't a *tendre*, Seonaid. I said I loved him."

The soft, matter-of-fact declaration shocked the blond viper into silence.

She wasn't alone. Gregor felt as if he'd just been struck in the ribs with a war hammer. The air seemed to have left his lungs. He'd heard countless declarations of the like from many different women, but none had ever affected him like Cate's simply spoken words. Hell, for a moment they almost sounded true.

In contrast to the gloating Seonaid, who'd cornered him in the stable to offer her body up as a ploy to a wedding ring, Cate's straightforward admission was a breath of fresh air and the polar opposite of the coy games and schemings he'd come to expect from women who thought sleeping in his bed would earn them a proposal. How many times had he walked into a room and heard some woman boast about how she would be the one to trap the elusive warrior?

" 'Tis no secret," Cate continued. "I'm sure Gregor knew my sentiments just as well as you." Her gaze flickered to his only for an instant, but it was long enough to make something in his chest tighten.

He pulled his arm away from Seonaid's, reaching for her. "Cate, I—"

"Sorry for the interruption," she said too chirpily, quickly stepping away from him. "Come, Pip, let's take the pup to the kitchens to see if we can find him something to eat."

She was gone before he could stop her. But what could he say? "I'm sorry you think you love me? I didn't want to break your heart? I'm not the man for you?" All were true, but none would ease the sting of what had just happened.

Time was the only thing that would do that. Aye, in time she would see it was all for the best.

Eight

❧

Two days was long enough.

Hearing the clatter of swords on the opposite side of the bailey beyond the barracks, Gregor quickened his step as he descended the tower house stairs. Although he was curious to see all the improvement John kept talking about, it was Cate—and not her swordplay—that he was anxious to see.

He couldn't take the tension any longer.

Cate wasn't ignoring him or avoiding him . . . exactly. But the way her mouth pursed when their gazes happened to meet, or the way the bland smile never seemed to reach her eyes when he tried to make her laugh at the midday meal, or the way her chin came up as if bracing herself whenever he addressed her directly, told him that she was still furious with him. Maybe more than furious. Maybe he'd finally succeeded in wresting every star from her eyes.

It was exactly what he'd wanted. He should be glad she was no longer going out of her way to try to make him notice her. No longer trying to entice him with those little smiles and gentle touches. No longer looking at him as if she wanted him to push her up against the closest wall and ravish her senseless.

He *was* glad of it. Just like he was glad she wasn't trying to interfere in his assignations anymore. Nay, he'd followed one of the maidservants to the storeroom for more wine last night after the evening meal, and no one had come after them. He could have tapped far more than the cask, but it turned out all he'd wanted was the wine.

Guilt, he told himself. That was what was wrong with him. Once he and Cate cleared the air between them, everything would return to normal.

Or would it?

"I said I loved him."

He could still hear her voice, damn it. The feelings he'd never wanted to acknowledge had been spoken and could not be unheard.

Deep down he knew it would never be the same between them, and that was what really bothered him. He *liked* Cate. He looked forward to talking to her because she didn't prattle and pander to him like every other woman. At least not usually. But even the solicitous Cate of the first few days of his return had been amusing rather than annoying. He'd liked prodding her and seeing how far she would go. He'd liked the way she'd tried to mask her rising temper beneath a forced smile.

Aye, he'd liked it a lot. It had made him want to see whether he could make those dark eyes spark with another kind of heat. It had made him wonder whether she would be just as fierce and passionate in bed.

She would. He knew she would, and the knowledge taunted him.

These were the kinds of unwelcome thoughts that had made him so eager to find her a husband. A task that was proving more difficult than he'd anticipated, but not for the reasons he expected. There seemed to be plenty of interest in having Cate for a wife; it was Gregor who was having trouble finding anyone who he thought worthy of her.

Cate was special, and she needed someone who understood that. Who understood the demons that lived in her nightmares and drove her to the practice yard with John. Who wouldn't push her to be something she was not.

With Christmas in a few days, the Hogmanay feast would be here before he knew it. Time was running out.

The din of swords had quieted. As Gregor rounded the corner of the barracks, he expected to see them taking a break or finishing up.

That wasn't what he saw.

What he saw was John and Cate circling each other in the frost-covered dirt like two men might do in the wrestling contest of the Highland Games. Neither wore a helm or armor. Cate's dark hair had been twisted into some kind of knot at the back of her head, and despite the cool winter's day, she wore a simple belted *leine* of brown wool that came just past her knees over her thick hose and boots. John had removed his *cotun* and only wore a linen shirt tucked into his leather breeches.

They were both streaked with dirt, flushed, and a little sweaty, as if they'd been working hard, and something about that set Gregor on edge.

Christ, she looked like she'd been romping in a bed all night!

They were so focused and looking so intently at one another, Gregor didn't think they realized he was there—except that he knew his brother was too good a warrior not to have noticed.

John feigned a move toward her, trying to get her to react, but she didn't bite. He was goading her with words also—words Gregor couldn't hear—but from the look on his brother's face she was giving them right back.

Gregor felt his temper prick. He didn't like not knowing what they were talking about. It felt too damned *intimate,* which was ridiculous given what they were doing.

He never would have believed what happened next if he hadn't seen it for himself. John lunged for her, jabbing his fist toward her face. Taking advantage of his momentum, Cate blocked the strike by bringing her left arm up and grabbing his wrist as she turned, pulling John's arm down to roll him over her hip and flip him to the ground. From there, with control of his wrist and John on his side, she jerked the arm back to brace it against her thigh. If she'd wanted to, she could have snapped it. Instead, she pinned him with her knee and feigned a palm thrust toward his face that would have sent John's nose straight to the back of his skull, possibly killing him, if it had been real.

Gregor was stunned. She'd moved so quickly, and with such certainty. She'd looked . . . strong. She looked like a real warrior.

Cate—little Cate—was doing some of the same defensive maneuvers that Boyd had taught him, and that he'd passed on to John. Except they looked different when she was doing them. His jaw clenched. *Very* different. Bodies-touching-too-closely different.

But he couldn't deny that she'd impressed him.

"Perfect," John said. "No hesitation, with plenty of intent. If you are going to get in the fight, you have to be ready to hurt someone."

She grinned and started to get up. But as soon as she removed her knee, John grabbed her wrist and pulled her down on the ground, rolling on top of her and pinning her hands above her head.

Gregor's heart was in his throat with what could only be called fear. God, was she hurt? He started forward, but his brother's laugh stopped him.

"Now what?" John challenged.

"You cheated!" she said, struggling, her eyes shooting daggers at him. Clearly she wasn't hurt; she was furious.

"I what?" John said, leaning down to pin her harder.

Gregor's hands fisted at his sides, unable to pull his eyes away from the way her body was straining against his brother's . . .

Bloody hell, John looked like he was thinking about kissing her!

Gregor's mouth fell in a hard line. Perhaps his brother

hadn't seen him, after all. It seemed like John was oblivious to anyone else in the world but the lass underneath him.

She mumbled what Gregor suspected were a few decidedly *un*-maidenly words, and then to his surprise, started to laugh. "There is no cheating in warfare," she said, mimicking his brother's deep voice. "I know."

I should have been the one to teach her this. The knowledge landed somewhere in his gut and twisted. She was his responsibility, not John's. But John didn't look as if he knew that. John was looking far too possessive.

"So what are you going to do?" John taunted.

Gregor was going to put a stop to this. John had made his point. Cate was helpless. She would never be able to overcome his strength and weight. John was nearly as big as Gregor. Damn it, he was probably crushing her. If there was one bruise on her body . . .

"This," she answered. With John's legs positioned on either side of her hips she used her right knee against his arse to knock him forward, wrapped her arm under his chest, and then brought her heels under her bottom to lift her hips up and roll him so that she was now mounted on top of him.

Bloody hell. Gregor couldn't believe it. She'd extricated herself with shocking ease.

His brother had taught her well. Gregor had underestimated her and never imagined that a tiny lass could fight a trained warrior—despite what he'd said.

"That's my lass," John said with a smile.

The hell she was. Gregor's reaction was so fierce and instantaneous that had he been thinking rationally, it might have concerned him. But he wasn't rational at all. He was furious. There was something about the way his brother was looking at her that sent warning bells off in Gregor's head and made him want to go over there and rip them apart. Actually, what made him want to rip them apart had been seeing his brother on top of Cate, and now seeing her on top of him.

He didn't like seeing *that* one damned bit. It was too reminiscent of a position that had nothing to do with fighting. And if his brother's expression right now was any indication, he was aware of it as well.

Cate wasn't for him, and Gregor was going to put a stop to this before his brother started to get other ideas. If anyone was going to train her, it would be him. John was about to be relieved of duty.

"I think that's enough," he said, stepping forward.

Both Cate and John startled. That obviously neither had been aware of his arrival only made him angrier.

John must have caught something in Gregor's glare, because he frowned.

Cate was frowning, too, as she stood and reached a hand down to help John to his feet.

"Is something wrong?" she asked.

"No," he snapped.

"Then why are you glowering?"

"I'm not glowering."

She acted as if she hadn't heard him. "Didn't I do it right?"

She sounded so anxious for praise, he felt like an arse. She'd done fantastically.

Of course, his bloody brother came to the rescue first. "You did it perfectly," John said, glaring at him.

Gregor glared back. "My brother has taught you well, but there are some things he doesn't know. If you'd like, I can show you."

John looked like he was about to argue, but then Gregor shot him a look that said he would be happy to prove it.

Cate's eyes sparked, her eagerness to improve her training apparently outweighing her recent aversion to him. "Really? When?"

"Tomorrow. Right now I need to talk to you."

"But I promised Pip . . ." Her gaze slid over to the boy who was sitting quietly on a rock, hidden in the shadow of the barracks, and who until now Gregor hadn't noticed. Christ, dark and sinister, the lad was like MacRuairi slinking in and out of the shadows.

Pip stood. Though he didn't look in Gregor's direction, Gregor could feel the animosity pouring off him. Apparently his "son" didn't harbor any lost love for him either.

"I need to find Eddie anyway. I promised I'd let him kick the pig's bladder around today if he made it to the garderobe every time he had to go yesterday."

"It was a brilliant idea," Cate said. "I never would have thought of it."

The boy shrugged as if the compliment hadn't meant anything to him, but Gregor could see that it had. It had meant a great deal, suggesting that the boy had received very little praise in his life. Gregor almost felt sorry for him, until he reminded himself that the lad was here under false pretenses.

John gave Gregor a look that said they would talk later, and put his hand on the lad's shoulder. "Come, Pip. I'll show you a field just beyond the wall where my brothers and I used to kick the ball around."

"Make sure to stay away from the water," Gregor said sternly, having no idea where the compulsion to say that had come from.

John raised his brow, and Cate glanced up at him as if he'd just slain a dragon.

Perhaps some of the stars were still there after all.

For the past couple of days, Cate had thrown herself into her practice and her duties around the tower house to avoid thinking about what had happened in the barn. Though she would rather not have had an audience the first time she told Gregor her feelings, she knew the words had needed to be said. Besides, as she'd told Seonaid, it was hardly a secret how she felt, and she wasn't ashamed of her feelings.

Nay, it wasn't Seonaid's cruel attempt to humiliate her that made her want to avoid thinking about it; it was her own confused emotions. What she'd witnessed between Gregor and Seonaid had shaken her faith and made her wonder whether she was wrong about him. Was she deluding herself that a man who'd had women throwing themselves at his feet for his whole life would ever be content with one woman, let alone her? Was he just as attracted by superficial charms as the women he discounted for the same thing?

And the question that haunted her more than anything: was he a man she could rely on, or was he like her father?

She saw similarities between the two where she'd never seen them before—or maybe hadn't wanted to see them. Handsome, charming, noble, bigger-than-life, intense and driven—the kind of men who never did things halfmeasure—they changed a room just by entering it. Was Gregor no more than a re-creation of the great noble knight to fill the gaping hole left in her heart by the one who'd abandoned her? Would he love her and then leave her when someone better came along? Or would the "heartbreaker" be able to give her the kind of commitment she needed?

The questions pecked away at her confidence, leaving her feeling vulnerable and unsure of herself. The man who she thought would never disappoint her had done just that. Gregor had been the anchor in her mind for so long that without him, she was foundering.

Although she might feel like she was drowning, Cate wasn't ready to give up. The hard part about faith was believing even when there wasn't a basis for it, and she believed in him—in them—even if he didn't.

And that faith had just been rewarded. Cautioning Pip not to take Eddie too close to the water might seem like nothing, but to Cate it was a sign. She hadn't been wrong about him. He cared even when he didn't want to care. He was a natural protector and nothing at all like her father. Gregor had taken her in and never turned his back on her—even when she'd given him plenty of reason to do so. He would bluster and complain, but he wouldn't turn his back on the children, either.

She had to be patient. Perhaps it had been unrealistic to expect him to change overnight. This wasn't a faerie tale. He wouldn't take one look at her and never look at another woman again—no matter how much she might wish it. But once he realized his feelings for her, it would be different. Good gracious, he hadn't even kissed her yet!

Yet.

As soon as John and Pip had walked away, she turned to face him. Sometimes she forgot how handsome he was and other times—like now—it would strike her somewhere between the ribs like a thunderbolt. Golden-brown hair shimmering in the sunlight, eyes such a deep sparkling green they looked like emeralds, a face so strong and perfectly formed it would make the angels sing—God, was she fooling herself?

She took a deep breath. "What did you want to talk to me about?"

Perhaps "want" was the wrong word. Although the white lines around his mouth and tightness in his jaw had started to dissipate (he'd been angry about something, but whatever it was, it seemed to be directed at his brother and not her), there was a certain resolve and determination to his expression, like that of a man about to perform an unpleasant task that had to be done.

She being the unpleasant task.

Still, the gaze that met hers was not without compassion—not exactly what she wanted from him, however.

"About what happened in the barn the other day. I don't want there to be any . . ." He hesitated. "Awkwardness between us."

She tilted her head to the side and held his gaze. "Then what *would* you like there to be between us?"

For one moment something hot and possessive flared in his eyes. Something fierce and primal that sent a shudder of awareness racing through her. Something that left her a little shaky and wondering if she really had any idea of what she was asking for.

The flare quickly turned to irritation, however. "Nothing, damn it." He dragged his hand through his hair as if were exuding all the patience of Job. "Christ, Cate, I don't want to hurt you."

"Then don't."

He shot her a glare and ignored the comment. "What you want is impossible."

"How do you know what I want?"

One side of his mouth lifted in a wry smile. "What do all young girls who fancy themselves in love want? The faerie tale. Marriage. Children. A husband who loves them back. But that isn't me, Cate. I'm not the settle-down-with-one-woman type. When you are a little older you will understand."

Now it was Cate who was angry. "Do not patronize me, Gregor. I'm twenty, not a fifteen-year-old girl anymore. I'm old enough to know my own feelings. I do not 'fancy' myself in love. I love you, whether you choose to accept that or not. Although the rest sounds nice, and I do think you are the settle-down-with-one-woman type— the right woman—all I want from you right now is to acknowledge that you feel something for me."

"What I feel is lust, but I care too much about you to give in to it. Damn it, I'm trying to protect—" Suddenly, he stopped and looked as if he'd just been shot with one of those arrows he was so good with. "*How* old are you?"

She winced a little sheepishly. "Twenty."

His gaze narrowed. "Why did you let me think you were younger?"

She shrugged. "You never asked. Your mother thought you'd guessed but didn't want to know."

He swore again, dragging his fingers through his hair again but this time more harshly. "Christ, *twenty*?" He dragged out the word accusingly, scanning her up and down as if she were some sort of strange creature from a menagerie that he'd never seen before.

"Is it really that important?"

"Yes," he snapped. "No! I'm still your guardian, and you're still too young."

Cate's nose wrinkled. Was that what this was about? Was that why he was fighting his attraction so hard? Because of some misplaced sense of responsibility toward her? She was no longer a foundling in need of rescue. "As you have just seen, I don't need a protector anymore, Gregor. I can take care of myself."

"Like you did with young MacNab? Do you know his father wanted to arrest you?"

"For what, defending myself?"

"For humiliating his son."

She gaped at him as if he were jesting. "So I should have let him strike me?"

"Of course not. You shouldn't have intervened in the first place."

"He was hurting Pip."

"There were a half-dozen of them, Cate. You should have gone for help. What would have happened if I hadn't shown up when I did?"

She would rather not think about that. "Have you never fought when the odds were against you?"

His mouth fell in a hard line—a hard *defensive* line. "That isn't the point."

"What is the point, then? We are not talking about my fighting, we are talking about why you won't act on this . . . lust." She moved closer, putting her hand on his chest—which he promptly removed. "You don't need to feel responsible for me."

"I *am* responsible for you, and taking advantage of your youth and inexperience would be wrong."

Cate clenched her teeth to keep her temper in check—barely. She wanted to touch him again, but squeezed her fists at her sides in frustration instead. "Yet you had no problem kissing Seonaid, and she is a year younger than I am. What about her youth and inexperience?"

He clenched his teeth right back at her. "That was a mistake."

That he knew it just as well as she made it somehow worse. She stared up at him. "How can you do that, Gregor? How can you share intimacies with women when they don't mean anything to you?"

He barked out a sharp laugh. "Quite easily. The fact that you can ask that question shows just how little you understand of lovemaking. Believe me, caring is not required."

Cate hated the flush that rose to her cheeks—hated that he could make her feel so silly and naive. "It doesn't sound like lovemaking at all if you don't care about the people you are making love to. Does it not bother you to break all those hearts?"

He laughed, actually laughed. "Oh, Lord, you are sweet. Do you think the women I take to my bed care about me? I assure you when a woman is making herself available two minutes after meeting me, it is not me she has fallen in love with but 'the most handsome man in Scotland.'"

"Because that is all you ever let anyone see."

He smiled, that dazzling roguish smile that had probably felled many a heart but to her felt like a slap. "And you think there is something else?"

She held his gaze steady. "I know there is."

Her quiet certainty seemed to bother him. He frowned.

"Don't look for something more, Caty. You will only be disappointed. I am quite happy with my life as it is."

She stiffened at the childish diminutive. "It doesn't bother you to have them use you like that?"

"Use me?" He laughed again, shaking his head, and then in mock seriousness said, "Aye, it's a hardship having women eager to jump in my bed, but somehow I manage to carry on."

But she knew it did matter to him, and that he was making fun of her made her want to lash out and prove it. "And when your sister-in-law used you to make your brother jealous, that didn't matter either, did it?"

His expression went so cold for a moment she felt a whisper of fear. She thought about stepping back, but his fingers latched around her arm like a vise. The change that came over him was blood-chilling. Gone was the handsome heartbreaker and in his place was a deadly warrior. "Who told you about that?"

She bit her lip, not wanting to give away the confidence.

Guessing the source of her conflict, he pushed her away disgustedly. "Mother. She's the only one who could. John and Padraig know nothing about it. What did she tell you?"

"Enough to know that it wasn't your fault. That you cared for Isobel, and she manipulated you."

He laughed harshly. "So being stupid and gullible is an excuse for bedding my brother's future wife?" Cate's eyes widened, and he laughed harshly. "Aye, I'd wager my mother didn't know about that. But that's the risk when two *young* people start playing a game in which they don't know all the rules." That warning was directed at her. "She played me perfectly. I thought she loved me, and she thought flirting and allowing a few liberties to the laird-to-be's 'useless but beautiful to look at'—her words— younger brother would make Alasdair jealous. Imagine her horror when we were both carried away by a few liberties. More than once. But her plan worked. Alasdair heard the rumors—or some of them—and came home."

Cate reached for him, but he shrugged her hand off.

She tried to ignore the stab of hurt provoked by the rejection. "He didn't know that you and she . . . ?"

The gaze he turned on her was full of pain and self-loathing. "Not right away. I left to fulfill my service for my uncle, thinking I would be announcing our engagement when I returned home; instead she was married to my brother. But he must have learned the truth at some point. The brother I'd idolized could barely stand to be in the same room with me." He shrugged as if it didn't mean anything, but she knew it meant everything. "He left not long after I returned and was killed during the siege of Bothwell Castle a few months later. My father blamed me, of course."

"That's ridiculous! You had nothing to do with it!"

His eyes were hot and empty as he glared at her. "Didn't I? The truth destroyed my brother. You see, it turned out he really did love her. She needn't have used me at all—he'd intended to marry her all along. Her betrayal—my betrayal—drove him to the edge, and he volunteered for every dangerous job he could. Eventually one killed him."

"That isn't your fault, Gregor. You cannot be responsible for your brother's actions—or Isobel's."

He held her gaze a long time. Eventually his mouth quirked. "My father didn't agree. After we buried my brother it was as if I ceased to exist. Turns out disdain was better than being invisible. So when Bruce was looking for men to join him, I left."

"What happened to Isobel?"

"She died in childbirth a few months after we buried my brother. In case you were wondering, it wasn't mine. She and Alasdair had been married for over a year before I returned."

"You cared for her, Gregor. What happened wasn't your fault."

He gave her a long, slow, wicked look meant to scare her away. "As I said, caring had little to do with it."

"So because you care about me and don't want me to get hurt, you will not act on your 'lust,' but because you do not care about those other women it's fine to take them to your bed? Do you not think that is a bit backward?" She moved closer. "Why don't you just pretend I'm Seonaid?"

He obviously didn't appreciate her sarcasm. "You are nothing like Seonaid."

That they could both agree upon. But the tension she could feel rolling off him in hot waves egged her on. She wanted him to take her in his arms and show her all the passion her body was clamoring for.

"If caring is not required, what is required?" she challenged, standing so close to him their bodies were almost brushing. "Are my breasts not large enough for you? Is my face not pretty enough?"

He uttered a curse she'd never heard from him before. She could feel the tension reverberating off him like a drum. The tic in his jaw pulsed angrily. "Stop it, Cate. It won't work. I told you I am not the man for you."

She heard the heavy warning in his voice, but she did not heed it. He was close to giving in; she could feel it. She pressed the tips of the breasts he seemed determined not to look at against his chest, forcing him to try to deny the attraction sparking between them. "Why am I so different? Am I not willing enough? Must I throw myself down at your feet like everyone else?"

He grabbed her arm, jerking her against him, his eyes hot with anger—and something else. "Is that not what you've been doing since I returned?"

Cate gasped. Was that what he thought? She'd never meant . . . She hadn't thought he would see it that way. She didn't want to be anything like those women. "I was trying to get you to notice me because I love you."

"As if I haven't heard that before."

He glanced down at the breasts poking into his chest, and the heat of it scorched her. For a moment she thought he was going to kiss her. She thought his body was drumming with a need as powerful as hers. That the pull would be as irresistible for him as it was for her. That she had what it took to attract a man like him.

Instead, his mouth curved in a slow smile. "I'm not so easily trapped, little one. Believe me, if a pretty face and a pert pair of breasts were all it took, I would have found myself standing at the church door years ago."

Cate wrenched away, drawing back in horror. My God, what had she been thinking? She hadn't been trying to trap him into anything except maybe a kiss. But had she actually thought to use her body to do so?

She wasn't sensual or entrancing. She didn't captivate or intrigue. She wasn't the type of woman men couldn't resist kissing (as evidenced by the fact that she was twenty and had never been kissed!). She was "cute," not beautiful. Her body was taut and strong from fighting, not soft and lush for lovemaking.

And his rejection reminded her of that. It crushed her womanly confidence, and worse, made her feel silly for trying.

She hoped the tears choking her throat hadn't reached her eyes. "I wanted you to kiss me because I love you. Because every time I close my eyes and dream of what my first kiss will be like, yours is the only face I ever see. Because I'm twenty years old and I've never wanted any other man but you. And because I thought you wanted to kiss me, too. So if you are going to accuse me of anything, have it be for being a fool to think I had what it takes to tempt you."

Nine

❧

Gregor was fighting on his last gasp of air. He couldn't fucking breathe. Have what it takes to tempt him? Did the lass have any idea how hard it had been for him to pull away? How that feel of her breasts against his chest had set off nerve endings he never even knew he had? How his skin had tightened, his blood had heated, and his cock had thickened until it was hammering against his stomach with need he hadn't felt since he was her age? How much he wanted to push her up against the wall of the barrack and give her exactly what she was asking for—and probably a whole hell of a lot more?

Nay, he realized, looking into her shimmering eyes. She didn't. She had no bloody idea. She was innocent and sweet and despite what he'd said, without any feminine wiles of which to speak.

He would be glad she was so in the dark if it weren't for the tears. Tears she was fighting to hide. Tears that told him he'd hurt her in a way that he hadn't intended, in a place that was vulnerable. The air of womanly confidence was all for show. The dress, the hair, the perfect lady of the castle—Cate was testing her femininity in a way she never had before. All he had to do was look at her now, and see how comfortable she was in her peasant's rags on the practice yard, to know that it couldn't have been easy for her. Just as he knew that if he let her think she wasn't desirable, it would crush her feminine pride to dust.

If he were honest with himself—which he didn't want to be, damn it—he would also admit that, selfishly, he wanted to be the first to kiss her. That he knew how close his brother had been to kissing her, and just picturing it still drove him half-crazed and filled him with a new emotion: jealousy. Not even when he'd returned to Dunlyon and seen the woman he thought he would marry by his brother's side had he felt this way. That had been more shock—and then stung pride and shame when he realized she'd used him. Perhaps he knew better than anyone how fragile a young man's—or woman's—pride could be.

He squared his shoulders as if preparing for battle as he stared at the freckled, dirt-smudged face turned to his. *One kiss,* he told himself. He could manage one kiss for the sake of her fledgling confidence.

"Come here, Cate."

His voice was so gruff, she eyed him warily. "Why?" He didn't answer, but just held her stare. Nervously biting her lip, she edged closer to him. "What do you want?"

He tipped her chin back with the crook of his finger, holding her gaze with his. Christ, she was pretty. Big doe eyes under straight, delicate brows, a slender nose, high cheekbones in the perfect oval of her face, a pointy chin and softly curved lips that were almost too red to believe they hadn't been stained with crushed berries. Even mussed, with her hair pinned back and dressed in some of the most hideous garments he'd ever seen on a woman, she took his breath away.

"You have more than enough to tempt me, Cate, and I'm going to prove it."

The delicate line of her brows drew together. "How?"

She looked so befuddled he had to smile. "By giving you your first kiss."

Her eyes widened. "You are?"

He nodded.

"What do I do?" Her voice wobbled a little.

Christ, *now* she was uncertain? He laughed and shook his head, thinking if he didn't shut her up this could go on all day. "Close your eyes."

She did as he bid, but then immediately peeked one eye open at him. "Are you sure? Since this is my first time, I don't want to miss anything."

He chuckled huskily; just the anticipation of kissing her was making him throb. "Do you want me to kiss you or not, Cate?"

The eye immediately snapped shut.

He stilled, arrested by just looking at her. *Breathe,* he thought to himself, but his lungs couldn't seem to take in air at the sight of her face turned to his with such trust and innocent surrender.

His heart pounded and his *cotun* suddenly felt like it had been made for Pip. Just a kiss. Something he'd done hundreds of times. But he wanted to make this good—really good. She deserved something special, and he would muster every bit of his skill to give it to her.

Slowly, wanting to savor every moment of this, he lowered his mouth to hers. He heard her sharp intake of breath as his lips brushed hers and felt something jam in his chest. His lungs? His heart? He didn't know, but everything seemed to start aching.

She tasted so damned sweet, he wanted more. Nay, he *ached* for more.

He brushed his mouth over her velvety lips again. So soft. So incredibly soft. He had to let his mouth linger, press a little harder, but that was it, he assured himself. He held his mouth there, giving her the kiss, but not giving in to the urge pounding through his body. The urge to pull her up against him, open her lips under his, and taste every inch of that silky, sweet mouth with his tongue.

Pull back. You have to pull back.

But God, it felt so good, and he'd been wanting to do

this for so damned long. Just a moment longer and he swore—

She moaned, and whatever promise he'd been about to make to himself was lost in the surge of lust that shot through him as her mouth opened under his.

He dropped the hand from the gentle hold on her chin and plunged it into the knot at the back of her head, to bring her mouth more firmly against him, while his other hand slid around her waist to bring her body against his.

Oh God, yes. He groaned as sensation crashed down over him in a hot wave and dragged him under. There was no holding back.

One kiss? He was a damned fool.

Cate's breath stilled as she waited for his lips to finally touch hers. The first brush was so light and feathery soft, she actually wondered whether she'd imagined it. But then he brushed against her again and the heat of the contact singed her all the way down to her toes.

She felt her heart try to jump out of her chest, but she caught it and dragged it back down. Yet she could not control the fluttering. The budding excitement. The overwhelming euphoria of knowing that she was being kissed by the man she loved.

Finally.

Cate had dreamed of this moment so many times, she thought she knew what to expect. But the feel of his mouth on hers was unlike anything she'd ever imagined. It was warm and possessive, tender and sweet, and so exquisitely perfect a thousand dreams could not have captured it.

She'd never dreamed how good it would feel. How soft his lips would be. How she would be able to taste the faint tinge of mint from the paste that he'd used to clean his teeth. How the heat of his body would envelop her. How her skin would tingle. And most of all, how the gentle brush of his lips could stir such a powerful craving inside her for more.

A craving that only grew more intense when his lips pressed against hers and held. Softly at first, and then with increasing pressure that made her heart start to thud against her ribs with instinctive anticipation.

The sensations intensified and stirred faster. Hotter. Wonder and euphoria turned to burning desire and scorching need. She didn't know what she wanted but sensed it hovering just beyond her reach.

She moaned in silent entreaty, and that was all it took to find out. It was as if a dam broke, and all the passion he'd been holding back came crashing out in a tidal wave.

She was suddenly in his arms, her body pressed against his. His fingers were digging through her hair to grip the back of her head and bring her mouth more fully—more possessively—against his.

Her gasp of surprise was followed by an even bigger one, when he took advantage of her open mouth to fill it with his tongue. Long, slow, incredible pulls of his tongue that demanded a response.

Tentatively she gave it to him, and the low groan that emanated from somewhere low inside him was all the answer she needed to know that it was the right one.

He kissed with the skill of a master craftsman, the experience of a rogue, and the expertise of a scholar. He knew *exactly* how to elicit every ounce of pleasure with each deft stroke. He showed her how to circle her tongue against his, how to stroke, how to thrust, how to tease, how to slant her mouth and take him deeper and deeper.

She became bolder, returning the kiss with a growing fervor that matched his own. But it wasn't enough. Even when he bent her back and took her even deeper into the crook of his body, the hunger and craving only seemed to grow worse. The fervor became a frenzy—a violent storm of heavy breaths, pounding hearts, clashing mouths, and tangled tongues.

It was nothing like the controlled kisses she'd seen him give before. It was raw and intense and fiercely passionate. Ravenous. He kissed her like he was starving and would die if he didn't have her. Like she was the only woman in the world for him, and he would never get enough of her.

And she knew she would never—ever—get enough of him. Gregor MacGregor would be the first man she ever kissed and the last. If she'd ever needed proof that they were meant to be, she had it. She belonged to him, and he could not longer deny it. The hot possessiveness of his embrace did not lie. He branded her with his mouth, his tongue, his hands, claiming every part of her.

The sensations were coming harder now, barreling through her in a fast-moving panoply of feeling and perception. The scratch of his jaw against her sensitive skin. The wet heat of his mouth as it devoured her neck and throat. The crush of her breasts against his chest. The tender throb of her nipples as his thumb brushed over them. The imprint of his hand on her hip. Her bottom. Cupping her and lifting her against his . . .

God have mercy.

Her stomach dropped at the size. She could feel him between her legs, thick and hard. A long column of steel riding up against her that sent a hot rush of dampness between her legs. Knowing what happened between a man and a woman, she would have thought the fit impossible.

But once he started to move, she reconsidered. The heat flooded. Her breasts grew heavy, and her body turned soft and melty. Pliant. Supple. *Ready.*

She caught her hands around his neck before her legs gave out. She was tingling—throbbing with something. She could barely stand and yet she needed to . . .

Move. Cate nearly cried out in relief, it felt so good. *He* felt so good. The gentle circling of hips became a hard grind as her body sought more pressure, more friction, more pleasure.

And God, how he gave it to her! His mouth, his tongue, his steely thickness.

Yet still her greedy body wasn't satisfied. The ache intensified. Grew more insistent. Her soft moans quickened into gasps, pleading—begging—for relief from the frantic restlessness building inside her. She could feel his muscles straining under her fingertips, as he, too, fought the demands of his own desire.

Something wonderful was about to happen, and Cate couldn't wait—she *really* couldn't wait—to discover what it was.

Gregor had descended into madness. That was the only explanation for what was happening. What else but madness could explain the dark frenzy of need that had overtaken his mind, stripping him of rationality and turning the vaunted steel of his control to dust?

He knew he should stop, but he couldn't force his limbs to pull back. She tasted too good. Her lips were too soft. Her skin was too sweet. Her mouth too warm. Her body too tight and firm.

Responsive? What a damned understatement. She was like a keg of Sutherland's black powder, her passion ready to explode at the first spark. *His* spark. And the power of it—the danger—sent a thrill racing through him, even as he knew the threat.

Just one more taste—one more touch. But it wasn't enough. It wouldn't be enough until he was inside her and she was screaming his name as her body shattered around his.

And even then it might not be enough.

He pushed the errant thought away. That was ridiculous. It was lust—that was all.

But he'd never felt lust like this before. Lust that was raw and primitive and filled him with a blind need to make her his. Lust that knew no bounds of honor. Lust that rose inside him and wouldn't let go. It took hold and gripped—hard.

Aye, he was hard. So damned hard. And the feeling of her sliding against him, riding up on him as she made those breathy little gasps of pleasure, knowing how close she was to shattering just from the sensation of his cock between her legs, almost took him over the edge.

Right there in the practice yard, in the shadow of the barracks, in the middle of the afternoon where anyone could come upon them, he nearly made her come and lost himself like a squire with his first maid. The realization—the small intrusion of reality in his lust-crazed brain—gave him just enough strength to pull away. Harshly. With a few choice curses.

She stumbled, but managed to steady herself before she fell—which was a good thing, as he was in no condition to react.

His body was on fire. Every muscle was flexed and taut, as he fought to control the desire still coursing through his blood like wildfire. He felt as tight as one of his bowstrings, primed, drawn, and ready to unfurl. One touch, one push, and she'd be back in his arms again.

He couldn't do that. He could never do that again. But he wanted to do that again right now. Especially when she looked up at him with her flushed cheeks, kiss-bruised lips, and dazed-from-passion-filled eyes. God, she was sweet. Responsive. Eager. Passionate. As passionate as he'd known she would be. Nay, more.

"What happened?"

I almost made you shatter. I lost my mind and almost went too far.

But he didn't say that. He found a grip on his sanity and forced his blood to cool. "I gave you your first kiss."

And very nearly a whole hell of a lot more.

"Why did you stop?"

"Because it was over."

Her brows drew together over her nose. "It didn't feel over."

God help him. He nearly groaned. It would be nice, really nice, especially right now when he was trying *not* to think about it again, if she didn't say exactly what was on her mind. "Well, it was. You'll have to take my word for it."

She stared at him, looking as if she were going to argue. But then a slow, maybe even slightly shy, smile turned her mouth. "It was wonderful, but maybe next time you could keep going—"

"Next time?" Something remarkably like fear made his voice come out louder and more forcefully than he intended. "There isn't going to be a next time."

The smile fell. "What do you mean? I thought . . ."

Her voice fell off and she gazed up at him with such confusion in her eyes, he almost reached for her. Almost. But nothing had changed—except now he knew how dangerous it was to touch her. He was not the man for her, and no matter how much he wanted to be the one to show her passion, he would not be the one to do so.

His instincts rebelled, but he pushed them aside. "It was just a kiss, Cate. Don't read anything more into it. Nothing has changed."

Cate stared at him in shock, noting the stubborn set of the jaw that she could still feel scratching against her neck and throat as he ravished her. Just a kiss? Nothing has changed? How could he say that after what happened? She might be innocent and inexperienced, but she was not stupid. That kiss had meant something—and not just to her. He had felt it, too, though he might wish her to think differently.

Aye, that's exactly what he wanted. Her eyes narrowed. "So you felt nothing special, is that what you are saying?"

She was rewarded by a wicked spark of green in those heavenly eyes. "I think you know exactly what I felt."

Her gaze dropped instinctively, and even knowing he was trying to embarrass her didn't stop her cheeks from heating at the memory of how he'd felt between her legs. An ache fluttered low in her belly, but she wouldn't let him distract her. "Ah, yes, only lust, isn't that right? You know it's funny, but I don't recall your kiss with Seonaid or Màiri or any of the other women I've seen you with looking quite the same. But then again, I'm no expert on the subject." She smiled. "Although I hope that will not be the case for long."

His expression changed so quickly, she didn't have time to react. He grabbed her by the arm and pulled her toward him, his gaze penetrating. "What are you talking about? I told you there won't be a next time."

She smiled sweetly, despite the fingers digging into her arm and the furious, gritted-teeth expression of the menacing-looking warrior trying to stare her down. "With you, perhaps."

His eyes turned so dark they almost looked black. "What the hell is that supposed to mean?"

Carefully, she unfurled his fingers from around her arm, and then brushed at the spot as if his touch had been merely an annoyance and was not like a brand upon her skin. "What do you think it means? Now that I've had my first kiss, I wonder what I've been waiting for. It was quite nice."

"Nice?" he blustered, obviously not happy with her choice of adjective.

"Aye, *quite* nice, but then again, unlike you I have nothing to compare it to. Yet." She quirked a brow, eyeing him suspiciously. "I'm also rather curious as to what comes next. I do have the feeling you were forgetting something."

For one moment she thought she'd pushed him too far. He looked like he couldn't decide whether to shove her up against the nearest wall and finish what they'd started or bend her over his knee.

He did neither. But his gaze pinned her like hot green stakes. "I didn't forget a damned thing. And you won't be finding out what comes next until you are married. As long as I am your guardian, you will not be kissing anyone—*anyone*—do you understand me? I'll not have your reputation besmirched—"

She gave a sharp laugh. "That is a bit ironic coming from you, isn't it? It was just a kiss, remember? And as the only man I would consider marrying has made it clear he has no wish to marry me, I will not be marrying anyone. I'm sure my reputation can withstand the potential damage of a few harmless kisses."

Her skin prickled from the heat of his gaze. "Do not press me, Cate. I know what you are trying to do, and it won't work. I will not change my mind."

She met the challenge with one of her own. "Is that so?"

His jaw clamped down so hard, she thought his teeth might crack. "Aye."

She held his gaze. "We shall see." She started to walk away, turning back when she remembered what he'd said. "What time should I be ready?"

Clearly, she'd confused him. For once he looked ruffled, and she decided she liked it—liked it quite a lot. The thought that she could unbalance the untouchable Gregor MacGregor sent a distinctly heady thrill of feminine power shooting through her.

"For what?"

"You were going to teach me some new moves." She paused. "On the practice yard."

"I know what you meant," he snapped, although it was clear he'd been thinking about moves in a different place.

"After the midday meal. I have some business to attend to in the morning."

"I'll be looking forward to it," she said.

By the way he gritted his teeth, she assumed the feeling wasn't mutual. That he was obviously not looking forward to being in close proximity to her put a distinct bounce in her step as she walked away.

Just a kiss, *ha*! She'd never thought she'd see the day, but Gregor MacGregor, the most feared archer in the Highlands, was scared—*of her*. He was fighting the inevitable with everything he had, but it wouldn't be enough. She knew that as well as he did, although he wasn't ready to admit it yet. But he would. It might take a few more of those "just" kisses to prove it to him, but what was between them was special. For the first time, Cate felt as if her dreams were truly within reach.

Ten

Gregor watched her flounce away and wondered what the hell had just happened. He looked around the practice yard, expecting to see trees unearthed, crates turned over, and hay scattered all over the place. All signs of the maelstrom that had just knocked him off his feet. Maelstrom Cate.

What had come over him? This was Caitrina. *Little* Caitrina. The lass he was supposed to be responsible for. The lass he was supposed to protect. From the beginning, he'd felt a strange protectiveness toward her, but that sure as hell didn't include nearly ravishing her in the courtyard.

What could he have been thinking to kiss her like that? He hadn't been thinking. That was the problem. He'd been too busy feeling—bloody incredible, as it turned out. Nothing like that had ever happened to him before. He'd never lost control like that. He didn't lose control. And sure as hell not from a kiss.

The worst part was that she knew it, and thought it meant something.

It meant something, all right. It meant he wanted to take her to his bed and swive her senseless, not marry her. But as he couldn't do the first without the second, he was going to have to pretend that kiss had never happened.

As if that were possible, when every time he looked at her he'd be thinking of how sweet her mouth had tasted, how silky her tongue had been sliding against his, how tight her body had felt under his hands, how firm her breasts had been, and how she'd made all those eager, breathy gasps in his ear as she'd rubbed against him. *Wantonly*.

Don't think about it.

Right. It was all he could think about. Kissing her had been an even bigger mistake than he'd feared. A little damaged womanly pride on her part was nothing compared to the torture he'd be suffering until he could return to Bruce.

Stalking across the yard, he ducked into the armory to retrieve his bow. He stood there looking at it for a moment before picking up a throwing spear instead. He'd been idle from warfare for too long. That was his problem. Once he was back on the battlefield, he would forget all about Cate and her madness-inducing kisses and concentrate on what he did best: eliminating targets and seeing the man whom he'd come to believe in more than any other secure on his throne.

Gregor might have joined the Guard to get away from Isobel and prove himself more than a "pretty" face, but he'd stayed because of Robert Bruce. It was Bruce he believed in, Bruce he fought for, and Bruce whom he never wanted to fail.

There wouldn't be another disappointment like Berwick.

But he wasn't ready for his bow yet. If anything, he was more distracted than when he'd arrived, damn it.

He cursed and was about to step out of the armory when a man blocked the doorway.

"What the hell was that about?" John asked.

For a moment, Gregor thought his brother was referring to the kiss. But realizing that was only his own guilt at work, he forced the instinctive defenses that had risen back down. "Perhaps I should be asking you that question? What did you think you were doing with Cate out there?"

John's eyes narrowed. "What did it look like? I was training her."

"It looked like more than training to me. It looked like you were thinking about kissing her."

John's eyes sparked dangerously. But Gregor didn't heed the warning. His younger brother was a good fighter, but Gregor was one of the best.

"So what if I was? She's a cute girl."

This time it was Gregor who threatened. He stepped closer to his brother, his arms tensing and flexing for a fight. She wasn't a girl, and she wasn't cute. She was more than that. "You aren't going to deny it?"

"Why should I?"

"Because she's our responsibility, damn it. She's under our protection. Taking advantage of her like that is wrong."

"Who are you trying to convince? Me or yourself?"

Gregor threw a fist at his chin, which John deftly blocked. The follow-up blow to his ribs, however, he did not, and it landed with a satisfying thud. Satisfaction wasn't long, though, as John recovered quickly and retaliated with a blow to Gregor's side. After a few more exchanges of fists, an elbow, and a knee, they were both bloody, bruised, and breathing heavily.

Gregor felt better already. This was just what he needed. "Stay away from her, John. I'll be taking over her 'training' for now. She's not for you."

"Then who is she for? One of the men you've been writing to? Have you found her a suitable husband yet?"

Gregor gritted his teeth, not sure whether he wanted to answer or throw another punch. "Nay, not yet."

"You know what I think? I think you're jealous. I think you haven't found her a husband because you can't stand the thought of her with someone else. Even me."

Gregor saw red. "So you do want her?"

"I might, if I weren't convinced she was in love with someone else."

Me. Gregor stepped back, the fight suddenly out of him. *John means me.*

"*Thinks* she's in love with someone else," he amended.

"And you're so sure she's not?"

Hell, he didn't know what to think. "It doesn't matter."

John gave him a long look that reminded him too much of their father. *Weak. Never amount to anything. A disappointment.* But he'd proved him wrong. The king of Scotland trusted him, damn it.

"If that is true, then do everyone a favor and find her a husband before you do something you will regret."

"I don't need a lecture from my little brother. I know how to control myself. I've had a little experience with women, you know."

"Aye, but none of them are Cate."

With words that were far truer than Gregor wanted them to be, John left him standing there. Cate *was* different, damn it. He couldn't deal with her in the same way he did other women, which meant he didn't know how to deal with her at all. He was used to giving women what they wanted—in other words, a night or two of pleasure—but that wasn't an option with Cate. Which left him on the unfamiliar ground of being attracted to a woman and having to deal with it outside the bedchamber.

He never should have brought her here in the first place. He had no business taking responsibility for a young girl. But it was five years too late for recriminations. Now the best thing he could do was get her out of here before he did something they would both regret.

Not even Gregor's noticeable absence from the evening meal could put a damper on Cate's happiness. If anything, perhaps it bolstered it. That he was avoiding her only proved that the kiss had meant something to him. She assumed he'd gone out with his bow—although oddly, she hadn't seen him with it since he arrived.

Gregor always disappeared for hours with his bow when he was upset or needed to think. His mother had been convinced that he'd become such a good archer because of all the arguments Gregor had with his father when he was younger. Cate thought there probably was some truth to that, but natural ability, determination, and drive to be the best factored into it as well.

She wished his father were alive to see it. Though Duncan MacGregor had been dead for a number of years before Cate arrived, she knew how much his opinion—his disregard—had motivated Gregor. But he'd proved his father wrong.

His skill was truly extraordinary. She loved watching him practice and wished she'd seen him compete at the Highland Games before the war. Although from the stories of the female entourage that followed him around, perhaps she wouldn't have enjoyed it so much.

Speaking of female entourages, when she entered the Hall for the morning meal, she wasn't surprised to see it crowded with women hoping for a glimpse of the handsome laird. It would only grow worse in the next few days with the Christmas festivities, and then the Hogmanay feast, which was maybe why she was looking forward to neither. She wanted him to herself. Would they ever leave him alone, or would women flocking around him constantly be something Cate would have to get used to?

The thought was mildly disconcerting. She wished she'd had the foresight to fall in love with someone who didn't make women cast their hearts—and the rest of their bodies—at him wherever he went. It certainly would be much easier on her temper. Cate had a feeling she'd be walking into many Halls over the next few years, wanting to toss more than one pretty maid out on her ear.

It bothered her to think that Gregor could equate her

with the fawning masses. She wasn't like them. She bit her lip, recalling her not-so-subtle ploys of the first few days he was home. She hadn't been trying to trap him; she'd been trying to get him to notice her.

With the handsome laird conspicuously absent from the high table, John appeared to be holding court in his stead, but when he caught sight of her, he waved her over to take a place beside him on the bench.

"Busy morning," she said with a smile. "I hope I am not interrupting anything?" She lowered her voice. "I don't think Lizzie was too happy to make space for me on the bench."

John grinned back at her, glancing at the pretty, blond-haired daughter of the porter who had returned to her place beside her father at one of the other trestle tables. "Aye, well, it wasn't me she wished to see anyway."

Cate quirked her brow. With the way the blonde was eyeing him, Cate wasn't so sure. John didn't need to be in his brother's shadow, and one day soon he would realize that and step out of it. Eventually he would tell Gregor that he wanted to fight—not stay here and take care of his holdings for him.

"Where is Gregor?"

John shrugged, looking as if his *cotun* wasn't sitting on his shoulders comfortably. "He had some business to attend to this morning."

"More missives? I've seen more messengers around here since he arrived than we've had in the past year." Her expression suddenly drew concerned. "You don't think it's about the war, do you? Is the king planning something?"

Bruce had better not call him away again, she thought bitterly. Initially, Cate had assumed Gregor was one of the many Highland warriors who had joined Bruce's army, under their chiefs. But he did not seem to fight often with his uncle Malcolm, Chief of the MacGregors. More often than not, he seemed to be near the king himself. But whenever she questioned him or John about Gregor's role in the king's army, they answered vaguely. As the subject was not one she liked to discuss, she didn't pursue the matter, but sometimes she wondered if he was closer to the king than he let on.

Not wanting to think about that, she turned back to John.

"I'm sure it has more to do with the feast," he said.

Cate relaxed. "Ah, you are probably right. Has he invited many of the neighboring clans?"

"I believe so."

"He's been so secretive about it. Almost as if he's planning a surprise of some kind."

Strangely, John didn't seem to be avoiding her gaze. "I'm sure it will be quite a surprise."

"What?"

He shook her off. "Nothing, just . . ." His voice fell off as if he'd changed his mind about what he was going to say. "There are going to be some changes around here when my brother leaves, and I do not want to see you get hurt."

The blood drained from her cheeks. "Then he *has* been called back?" Gregor had told her he'd be home until the first week of January.

John shook his head. "Nay. Not yet. But it will come in the new year, and I want you to be prepared."

Clearly, he was trying to tell her something. "Prepared for what?" Suddenly, her heart dropped. "Has Gregor said something about the children? Does he mean to send them away?"

John immediately put a hand on her arm to calm her. "Gregor has said nothing to me about the children, although I warned you that I do not think he will allow them to stay."

"You should have more faith in him," Cate admonished. "He is not as uncaring as he wants everyone to believe."

John studied her. "Perhaps not, but that does not mean he will be the man you want him to be, Cate. There is such a thing as blind faith, and I do not wish to see you get hurt."

"I won't," she said, believing it. "You don't need to worry—I know what I am doing."

John didn't look convinced. "Promise me you will be careful, Caty." She stiffened at the endearment, although he didn't notice. "You deserve someone who will make you happy."

It was clear he didn't think Gregor was that man.

She caught the direction of his gaze and frowned. "I wonder what Farquhar is doing here so early this morning? He has been around Dunlyon quite a bit of late."

Indeed, after he'd escorted her from church that day, he seemed to make a point of exchanging a few words with her before seeking out John. This time, however, he appeared distracted and didn't even nod in her direction as he passed through the Hall, apparently on the way to the laird's solar.

"He's a good man," John said.

She frowned at the odd way he was looking at her. "He is. Does he have business with Gregor?"

"Aye, I believe he does."

If his tone was slightly ominous, Cate told herself it had nothing to do with her. It turned out she was wrong.

"I will be able to provide for the lass," Farquhar said, looking Gregor squarely in the eye from his seat opposite the table. Despite his youth and Gregor's black stare, the reeve's son didn't look nervous or show any sign of backing down. Gregor might have admired that if it wasn't annoying him so much. "More than provide," he continued. "I have been offered a position as clerk in the Earl of Lennox's household with the steward, who is a distant kinsman of my mother's. As the steward has no son, he will be training me to take over after him."

Gregor should be ecstatic. The wife of the future steward of the Earl of Lennox was far beyond anything he might have hoped for Cate. That the reeve's son had been able to secure such a position was testament in itself to his ambition, acumen, and promise. Even with the family connection, he must have impressed someone greatly to have so distinguished himself. So why wasn't Gregor impressed? And why did his jaw hurt from being clamped down so hard while the other man presented his offer?

Because the entire time Farquhar was speaking, it was Cate's voice he was hearing. *"I have nothing to compare it to."* Would Farquhar be the next man to kiss her? Gregor's hand closed around the pewter goblet he was holding, until his fingers turned white. *"I'm also rather curious as to what comes next."*

He bit back a curse and slammed back the contents of the cup, barely tasting the fine and expensive claret that he and Hawk had intercepted on its way to Berwick Castle last summer for King Edward. The second English king by that name might not be half the king his "Hammer of the Scots" father was, but he did have outstanding taste in wine.

Realizing that the other man was staring at him, waiting for him to say something, Gregor forced back the instinctive refusal that sprang to his lips. "Why Caitrina?" Gregor said instead. "You can barely know her."

Farquhar must have heard something in Gregor's voice. His brows drew together and his gaze intensified. "Everyone in this village knows Caitrina. I have been away a few years, but she has not changed."

"Some would not consider that a good thing."

Farquhar's mouth hardened. "Then some would be fools. Caitrina is everything I admire in a woman—she's strong, smart, straightforward, loyal, kind, and without an ounce of pretension. Both my parents adore her, and they do not think there is a lass in all of Perthshire who would make me a better wife. There is something real about her. She's confident and at ease with all walks of people—laird, merchant, peasant. She will be at home in a cottage or in a castle."

Gregor's mouth fell in a thin line. It was all true, although why it bothered him that Farquhar so easily identified her finer points, he didn't know. "And what of your temperaments?"

Farquhar frowned. "I don't understand."

"You are serious and scholarly; Cate is . . ."

"Lively of spirit and passionate?" Farquhar finished for him with a wry smile. "That's part of what attracts me to her. I admire in her what I do not have in myself. But I do not think it means we are ill-suited, rather the opposite. It would be a very dull life indeed with a wife who was exactly like me. What man wouldn't want more passion in his life?"

Gregor knew the lad didn't mean it the way it sounded, but it took everything he had not to reach across the table, grab the pup by the collar of his tunic, and put another dent in his nose. Though a scholar, Farquhar looked as if he'd been in more than one brawl.

His fingers were going to bear the relief pattern of the pewter goblet, but otherwise he did not react. "And Cate's unusual pursuits?"

He was rewarded with the first uncertainty on the younger man's face. However, true to his contemplative nature, Farquhar thought a moment before he responded. "I have not been trained as a warrior, but I know how to fight and can protect my wife if the situation arises."

"And what if your wife *has* been trained as a warrior?"

"I would be glad she could defend herself when I was not around."

"So you would not object to her continuing her training?"

Farquhar's jaw hardened. It was clear he didn't like being forced into a corner. "I would hope that she would not feel the need to continue. I would hope to make her feel safe enough to put her training and weapons aside." He held Gregor's stare. "I assume there is a reason she feels compelled to learn to defend herself."

Astute as well as learned. Gregor nodded.

Farquhar returned the nod. "Then I would hope she would confide in me, and together perhaps we could find a solution that will make us both content."

The lad's answers were almost too perfect to believe. Ninety-nine percent of the men Gregor knew would never allow their wife to train at warfare, and the exception had just walked into his solar? How the hell did he get so blasted lucky?

Gregor was running out of excuses. *Bloody hell.* Was that what he was doing, trying to find excuses? "Where would you live?" he asked.

"A cottage near Balloch Castle at first. Later, in the steward's tower." *Not too far away, but far enough.* Farquhar paused, obviously wanting to put an end to the interrogation. "So do I have your permission? I would like to have the matter settled before I leave for Balloch in the new year."

Gregor tapped the stem of his now empty goblet absently. *Think.* But bloody hell, he couldn't think of any reason to refuse the man. It was the perfect solution to his problem. With Cate taken care of, he could leave his clan in John's capable hands and return to the Guard without any unwanted responsibilities to distract him. There would be no more worrying about her at inopportune moments, no more guilt for not being there more often, no more fear of disappointing someone. Not Cate and not the king.

That was what he wanted, wasn't it?

He wasn't cut out for anything else. Not to be the laird, and sure as hell not to be a husband. He liked being on his own, doing what he wanted without having to explain himself to anyone. He wanted the freedom of not having anyone rely on him. He liked not having attachments in his bed partners. Hell, he liked variety.

He would only disappoint her, and probably break her heart. He couldn't do that. Not to Cate. No matter how much the idea of her married to someone else bothered him. No matter how special she was, or how hot she'd made him from a kiss. He would forget all about it when he returned to war.

She didn't *really* love him. The reeve's son would be perfect for her. He was near her age at two and twenty, appealing in countenance, smart, and with a future position that would elevate her standing considerably. Clearly, Farquhar admired her and would do his best to make her happy. What more could Gregor ask for?

He took a deep breath, fighting the sudden tightness in his chest. "Aye, you have my permission. I will inform Cate of your offer, and if she agrees, the betrothal can be announced at the feast."

The lad was watching him carefully—too carefully. "Is there a reason she would not agree? Another suitor, perhaps, whom she favors?"

Aye, definitely astute. Gregor knew what the other man was asking. "There are other men I have considered, but yours is the offer I will bring to her. I am her guardian; she will accede to my judgment and do her duty."

Cate was like him in that regard. She might not like doing her duty, but she recognized when she had one. But Gregor sure as hell wasn't looking forward to telling her of his plans.

Eleven

❧

Cate held the plaid around her neck so it wouldn't slide off her shoulders as she darted through the trees. Though her cheeks were warm from exertion, and the sun was starting to break through the clouds, it was still cold and blustery from the storm that had blanketed the forest and glen with a few inches of snow the night before.

"I hear you, you wee devil. I'm going to get you!"

A startled cry, followed by a fresh peal of excited giggling coming from a tree ahead of her (not to mention the tiny, well-formed, and easily trackable bootprints in the snow), told her that she was closing in on her quarry.

"Where is he?" she said in her best bogeyman voice, creeping closer. "Where is Eddie . . . ?"

Realizing she was closing in, the little boy gave another piglet squeal and shot out from behind the tree in a frantic effort to escape. She lurched forward and wrapped her arms around the nearly three-foot-high wool-covered bundle, lifting him high in the air. "Ha! I've got you now, and you'll never get away!"

She kissed his cold, freckled cheeks, tickled his belly, and spun him around until the bairn was wiggling and screaming with laughter.

She could kiss those soft cheeks forever. The outpouring of affection from her toward the little ones had been unexpected—it awaited Pip, too, when he was ready for it. She'd not spent much time around small children before and had been surprised at how easy they were to hug and kiss. Warm and snuggly, with their soft skin and silky hair, holding them was like holding a puppy or a kitten: irresistible.

She felt a sharp stab between her ribs as the memory of her mother round with child took her. Was this how it would have been to have a brother or sister? Was this what she had missed? Would they have played hide-and-seek? Would they have had stick battles and kicked balls around, and played with the puppy in the barn, like she did with Eddie (and Maddy when she wasn't sick)?

It was rare that Cate allowed herself the pain of remembering, but for one moment she thought of her mother and the sibling that had been taken from her. The sense of loss was not as sharp as it had been, but it was still there. It would always be there, she realized, but Pip, Eddie, and Maddy had made it somehow easier to bear. They had to stay. They belonged here with her—and Gregor, when he came around.

Mindful of Eddie's unpredictable bladder, she decided she'd better stop before she went home with damp clothes. The wee laddie was getting better at making it to the garderobe, though, and she knew it was because he was beginning to feel safe and secure.

Gregor wouldn't send them away. But the odd conversation she'd had with John still bothered her. Clearly he'd been trying to warn her away from Gregor, and she'd gotten the feeling it had been for a reason. Was it the children, or something else?

With one last kiss on Eddie's cheek and a tight hug around his narrow ribs, she set him down. "Should we find a tree?"

He nodded and grabbed the area between his legs so anxiously, she realized she'd probably stopped just in time.

After a minute, the little boy said proudly, "I made the snow lellow!"

For some reason, he thought this was hilarious and proceeded to break out into giggles all over again. "Lellow snow, lellow snow . . . Maddy can't make a line like that. Girls have to squat, did you know that? Standing is much better."

Goodness gracious, the conversation topics of a three-year-old boy! Privately, she agreed with his conclusion—boys definitely had it easier in that regard. "It is quite a talent," she said wryly, glancing over at the artistic accomplishment, which was actually more of a jagged spray than a line. Neatness would have to come later, she supposed. "But perhaps you had best keep it to yourself. We wouldn't want Maddy to feel badly."

He sobered, considering her words with a gravity that made her want to squeeze him all over again. He nodded his gingery head. "Aye, you are probably right. What about my fa—" He stopped, amending, "The laird?"

Her chest pinched at the telling slip. The boy had been told by his mother before she'd abandoned him that Gregor was his father, but even at three he was old enough to understand that Gregor hadn't claimed him. That was one thing she'd never had to face. Her father had never denied his parentage. But like Eddie, even at a young age, she'd understood that she was a bastard. She'd been given a chance to leave the public ridicule behind when she'd left Lochmaben, but the memories were not so easy to erase.

Her heart went out to the boy, wishing she could shelter him from the inevitable hurt that label would bring. It would have been so much easier if he'd been Gregor's. No matter what "the laird" said, she knew he would not deny his own flesh and blood. But what about children who weren't his, yet needed him all the same?

And what about a wife? It was a question she'd never asked herself. Would her bastardy make a difference to him, if he knew? She didn't want to think so, but for the first time, the fact that she'd lied to him didn't sit well. She'd been thinking about herself when she'd given him a different name, not a future marriage. She was still the same person, whether her parents had been married or not. What did it matter if her father was technically alive? He'd been dead to her since she was five.

It might matter.

Pushing aside her uncertainty, she smiled at the laddie. Gregor would do the right thing. "I'm sure the laird would love to hear about it. Should we go find him?" It was getting close to the midday meal anyway.

Eddie nodded, and with his tiny hand in hers, they started winding their way through the trees. While Eddie continued to jabber on about his new talent, Cate's thoughts veered toward the afternoon practice session with Gregor. As much as she was looking forward to the prospect of spending time with him and learning from him, she was also eager to match wits—and skills—with him. She wanted to impress him. She wanted to show him that he'd been right to encourage her. But most of all she wanted him to take her seriously. She knew that he'd always thought her pursuits something of a game, but they weren't to her. She was proud of her accomplishments, and she wanted him to be proud of them, too.

She wanted him to see her as strong. Not as a young girl who needed protection. She didn't want to be the little girl in the well anymore. She wanted him to care for her not because he *had* to, but because he *wanted* to.

She must have chased Eddie deeper into the forest than she'd realized. They were still a good furlong from Dunlyon when she felt a prickle at the back her neck. Instinct made her tense and glance behind her. She had the distinct sensation of being watched.

Not seeing anything, she nonetheless held Eddie's hand a little firmer and quickened her pace.

The feeling grew more pronounced as they went on, and

her heart started to pound faster. Every few steps she shot a furtive glance around, but even in the winter, the trees and snow-covered limbs were dense, preventing her from getting a clear view in any direction. She was being ridiculous.

But the sudden flap of birds, disturbed from their roost in the tree limbs, signaled that it wasn't her imagination. Who would be watching her and trying to scare her? Dougal? She wouldn't put it past the lad to seek vengeance, but he didn't seem to have the patience or cunning to lay in ambuscade or the deviousness to devise a plan of fear.

Could it be brigands? They were so isolated in the glen, it was easy to forget the troubles that faced other parts of Scotland: roaming bands of outlaws in the war-torn lowlands, war parties of English soldiers near the English garrison-held castles, and the clans who still opposed Bruce, like the MacDowells in the southwest.

This part of the Highlands had largely been free from conflict since the MacDougalls had lost the Battle of Brander to Bruce four years earlier. Most of the time the war felt very far away from Roro and Dunlyon. If it weren't for Gregor's part in it, she could almost forget the danger. But she felt it now, lurking out there, hidden in the trees. It reminded her of her childhood. Lochmaben in the south of Scotland had always been right in the heart of the war. Of the many things Gregor had given her, perhaps peace was the most significant.

"Too fast, Cate. My wegs 'urt."

She muttered a curse and tried to mask her rising panic. Slowing, but not stopping, she gave Eddie an encouraging smile. "I'm sorry, sweeting—I just didn't want you to miss it."

"Miss what?"

"I asked cook to make a special fig tart—but you know how Pip likes them, too."

The incentive of losing out on the tart was all he needed

to give him a fresh boost of energy. Eddie's little "wegs" started to move so fast he was practically running.

It was with great relief that the edge of the tree line appeared ahead of them. She could see the tower house now in the distance beyond. Almost there . . .

A sound behind her made her turn. About twenty yards away, a rider broke through the trees. Realizing she'd seen him, he stopped.

Cate stopped, too, paralyzed in horror. Terror spread a sheen of ice over her skin, freezing her limbs. She couldn't move. For one heart-stopping moment, she thought it was the soldier from her nightmares, the man who'd killed her mother. He had the same dark hair, the same finely trimmed beard, the same Norman aquiline features . . .

But no. The haze of raw panic cleared. It wasn't him. This man was younger. His build was not as thick. His face was not as outwardly handsome, his expression not as coldly arrogant. He wasn't dressed in mail and the surcoat of an English soldier; rather he wore the leather *cotun* and plaid of a Highlander. But the resemblance was eerie.

Why was he following her?

A sudden frantic yapping in the opposite direction drew her gaze. She turned back toward the castle to see the pup and Pip rambling over the snow-covered landscape.

Pip laughed when he saw her. "I wondered what he was so excited about. The pup took off like an arrow, and I didn't know where he was going."

She was about to shout a warning to him not to come any farther, when she glanced back to the rider and realized he was gone.

"Did you eat my tart, Pip?" Eddie said angrily.

"What tart?" Pip came to a stop before her, breathing hard. Her expression must have made him forget Eddie's odd question. "What's wrong? Why is Eddie against the tree?" Cate looked down, not realizing she'd pushed Eddie behind her to protect him. "You look as pale as a ghost."

"You didn't see him?"

"Who?"

"The rider."

Pip frowned. "I didn't see anyone. Did he threaten you? We should tell John."

Not Gregor. Pip's instant dislike of Gregor seemed to have settled into permanence.

Cate thought for a minute, recalling the events without the terror. Had the rider threatened her? She'd thought he was following her, but he could have just been passing through the woods. He'd done nothing overt, except stare at her and have the misfortune of bearing a marked resemblance to the man who'd haunted her nights for five years.

She shook her head. "He didn't do anything. He just startled me, that's all." She'd overreacted. Suddenly, feeling silly, she forced a smile on her lips. "It was probably just a messenger. The laird seems to have a new one every day."

Pip gathered the pup, who'd begun to yap when Eddie started to "play" with him, ignoring the reference to Gregor. "Remember, he doesn't like it when you pull his tail, Eddie. You have to be gentle with him if you want him to play with you."

"I was bein' gentle," the little boy whinged.

Listening to Pip explain the finer points of dog care to Eddie as they walked back lightened her spirits considerably. She forgot about the rider and concentrated on the mismatched pair of foundlings who'd begun to sound like brothers.

It didn't take Gregor long to regret his promise to train her. About thirty seconds, to be precise. He'd ordered Cate to attack him with a knife. She was surprisingly quick and moved without hesitation. Still, he'd had years of reacting to threats. He grabbed the hand holding the weapon and twisted her arm around her back, where the dagger clattered harmlessly to the ground.

The problem was that he was now wrapped around her, holding her from behind with his arm around her neck, and their bodies were touching in all the wrong places. As she struggled against the strain of her pinned arm and the chokehold around her neck, her taut backside rubbed against him in a way that his cock—the brainless idiot—mistook for erotic.

Unable to take any more, and not wanting to hurt her, he let her go.

She immediately turned on him, dark eyes shooting like the dagger she'd just dropped. "Why did you do that?"

He frowned, having no bloody idea why she was so furious. "Hell, did I hurt you? I didn't mean to."

"Of course you didn't hurt me! You didn't give me a chance to escape."

She looked so outraged, he had to struggle not to smile. For once he didn't mind seeing her all riled up. She'd been oddly quiet at the midday meal earlier, and he'd wondered if something was wrong. She'd looked . . . upset. Which had distracted him from his conversation with Aonghus, his *Am Marischal-tighe* seneschal, whom he'd put in charge of sending out enquiries about the children, some of which had begun to yield results.

Then, as they walked to the practice yard, she hadn't smiled or joked with him at all. She'd been oddly intense and focused. All business. Which was exactly how he should be acting, not like a lust-crazed lad who stiffened just from the feel of a lass pressed against him.

He cocked a brow. "I had one arm around your neck and the other was twisting your arm behind your back. Exactly how did you intend to escape?"

Her eyes narrowed, hearing his amusement. "I was thinking."

"You didn't have time to think—I could have crushed your throat with my arm."

Her eyes fell on the limb in question, lingering a little too long and appreciatively over the thick spans of muscle. He nearly groaned. Not all business, apparently. She'd been aware of him as well. Why did that only make him hotter?

She lifted her gaze back to his, which didn't do anything to cool his desire. Damn, she was cute. Especially when she was annoyed with him like this. Why he found that cute, he had no bloody idea. Nothing about his feelings for Cate made any sense. There was something about her fierce determination, her stubbornness, her direct, matter-of-fact manner, and her self-assuredness that just appealed to him. She carried herself like a noble lady but lacked all the superficial gloss of pretension and rigid adherence to convention.

Such as those that would have kept her from the practice field.

She was still glaring at him. "I thought it was you who told me physical strength wasn't everything."

"It's not. But there are times when it can be."

"But I wasn't overpowered yet. I had my chin tucked to protect my neck. Here, I'll show you."

Reluctantly, he let himself be put back into the frustratingly intimate position. He was holding her for demonstration now, and she wasn't struggling, but his awareness crackled all the same. She felt good against him. *Really* good. Small and distinctly feminine, even though there was very little that was soft about her. She wasn't lush and curved, but taut and firm. When he'd held her arm, he'd been surprised to find that she actually had muscles—not thick and round like his, but long and sleek like those of a courser bred for speed.

He wondered what those muscles looked like naked.

"I have my chin tucked so you can't . . . Gregor, are you paying attention?"

"Aye," he lied gruffly.

"You're not doing it right. You have to hold me harder."

Christ, not the thing to say right now!

He did as she asked, although it wasn't the way he wanted. If it had been the way he wanted, they both wouldn't have any clothes on, the hand that was around her neck would be dipped between her legs, and the other would be cupping her breasts as he slowly slid into her from behind. It would be "harder," all right. Hard and deep.

He cursed silently, as the image sent a fresh rush of blood to a place that had no need of it. They were pressed together again, her tucked into the shield of his body. He caught a whiff of a soft fragrance from her hair and was trying to figure out the flower in her soap when something—the heel of her boot, he realized later—slammed down hard on his instep.

He groaned in shock and not a small amount of pain, his body naturally buckling forward in surprise.

She was ready and took advantage of the slack in the arm around her neck, twisting just enough to free the arm from its locked position at her back, pivot her foot behind his, and knock him on his arse.

He didn't know whether it was the ground or shock that slammed the air from his lungs—perhaps both.

Jesus! Lustful thoughts about his opponent was definitely a new distraction for him on the battlefield. But he was sure as hell paying attention now.

She stood over him, looking down. Though the sun was behind her head, he didn't need to see her expression to know she was angry. He could hear it in her voice. "That's how I'd do it. Now are you going to start taking this seriously, and stop holding me as if I'm a porcelain poppet?"

He rolled off his back and jumped to his feet. "I'm taking it seriously, Cate. I don't want to hurt you."

She heaved a heavy sigh, releasing some of the anger along with it. "I know, but it will happen. I've had plenty of bruises and scrapes with John."

His face darkened. "If John hasn't been careful—"

The exasperation was back. She looked like she couldn't decide whether to shake him or stomp on his foot again. "Of course, he's careful, but accidents happen in training. You can't tell me you didn't wobble home a few times after practice when you were learning."

Hell, he still did—especially when Boyd was teaching them something new. "That's different."

"Why?"

"Because you're a . . ."

"Lass," she finished for him. "Well, you're going to have to forget that. How else can I learn? I went through all of this with your brother. Isn't it better to suffer a few accidental bruises from you than be defenseless against someone who is intent on doing me harm?"

Hearing the rising agitation in her voice, he said in a gentle voice, "You are safe here, Cate."

"Am I?" Their eyes met and held. "You can't guarantee that. Just today I—"

She stopped, trying to turn away, but he wouldn't let her. He caught her arm and forced her gaze back to his. Had someone tried to hurt her? Was that why she was so upset? God, he'd kill him!

His voice was as hard as the steel that had just filled his veins. "What happened today?"

She lifted her eyes to his. "I was in the forest playing with Eddie, and I saw him—or thought I saw him."

"Saw who?"

"The man who attacked my mother."

He let her go, his expression automatically shuttering.

"You were mistaken," he said flatly. End of subject. End of conversation.

But Cate wasn't finished. "Yes, but he looked so much like him." She shuddered at the memory, and the momentary glimpse of vulnerability made him want to reach for her. But it lasted for only an instant before the fierce expression returned to her face. "I don't want to be scared."

"Did he threaten you?" The menace in his voice only hinted at the fury roaring inside him. Gregor rarely lost control. As an archer—a marksman—he had to be cold and methodical. Precise. Perfect. But just the idea of Cate in danger made him want to lash out wildly around him, striking indiscriminately and uncontrollably at anyone who would harm her.

Where had that rage come from?

She shook her head. "I thought he might be following me, but I must have been mistaken. He did nothing more than stare at me for a moment before continuing on. Did you perchance have a messenger today?"

"Nay. In which direction was he heading?"

"East, I think."

He questioned her a little more until he was satisfied that it was probably nothing. Solitary riders avoiding the road and traveling through the forest were not common, but neither were they that unusual. He would do some checking into it, however, just to be sure, and insist she take an escort if she was going to stray too far from the castle. Guessing how she'd react to that, he kept it to himself.

At least now he had an explanation for her quietness at the midday meal, and perhaps also for her intensity on the practice field.

She bent down to pick up the knife, slipping it in her hand for a moment before handing it to him. "Would you do something for me?"

Anything. But that was not a promise he could make. "If it is in my power."

"I don't want to presume . . ." She caught her lip between her teeth and peered up at him uneasily. "Am I right in thinking that you know the king fairly well?"

He schooled his features to impassivity, the question startling him. She'd never asked him about his role in the king's army, so he'd never had to lie to her. He didn't relish the idea of having to do so now. Bruce and his followers were a topic that she normally avoided. He sensed she still had no love of the king and blamed him for what had befallen her village. "Why?"

"Do you think you might ask him to make some enquiries? I know you've tried to find out his name, but maybe the king would have better contacts . . ."

"I've done everything that can be done."

"I don't understand why the soldier's name should be so hard to discover. Surely there can't have been that many captains with the Earl of Hereford in Scotland at the time?"

He didn't want to talk about this, damn it. "I thought you agreed to let me handle it."

"I did. It's just that it's been so long, and I know you've been busy." She stepped forward, putting the hand that wasn't holding the knife on his arm. "I don't want to keep looking over my shoulder for the rest of my life. He has to pay."

Gregor agreed, but he wouldn't risk her going after him herself. Just the idea of it made his blood run cold. She was too stubborn for her own good. "So what do you plan to do when you find out, Cate, kill him?"

Her eyes narrowed at the hint of scorn in his tone. "Why shouldn't I? He deserves it."

"You think it's just that easy to take a life? You think you can kill him and escape unscathed? You think it won't change you?"

He realized he was shouting only when she released his

arm and stepped back. She was staring at him with far more understanding than he would have liked.

Feeling as if he'd just revealed more than he intended, he forced his temper to cool. Taking the dagger from her, he slipped it into the belt at his waist. "I don't want that for you, Cate."

"But what about you?"

It was too late for him. "It's what I was trained to do."

"To kill?"

He didn't answer. "You have been trained to defend yourself. There is a big difference between the two. You are not trying to win—"

"I am trying to get away, I know." She finished with a roll of her eyes. "You sound just like John."

Relieved at the excuse to end the subject, he smiled. "Good. Let's see what else my brother has taught you. Shall we see how well you do if I am the one wielding the knife?"

She nodded. "But if you are going to go too easy on me, I'm going to go find John."

The hell she would. The lazy smile that curved his mouth revealed nothing of the vehemence of his thoughts. "Careful what you ask for, Caty—you just might get it."

Gregor wasn't his brother. John was good, but Gregor was something else entirely. He seemed to have no weaknesses, his skills as sharp and deadly as the blade he kept getting past her defenses. If this were real, Cate would be dead ten times over by now.

She'd given the outside of his wrist a quick double slap, the way John had taught her, but the dagger didn't come flying out. She'd attempt to block the arm coming toward her and change the direction of the wrist, by putting pressure on it and twisting to release the knife, but she wasn't fast enough to get her hands into position before he stopped her.

He left Cate no openings and seemed to anticipate what she was going to do before she did it.

And then there was his strength. She would have had more luck trying to bend steel than break his hold on her. His arms were . . .

A ripple of awareness shuddered through her. Rock solid, bulging with raw masculine strength, and unbelievably warm. They felt so good wrapped around her, they made her knees weak. Which didn't exactly help her ability to concentrate any.

After another embarrassing failure, which landed her in the dirt on her back, she had to drag herself back to her feet.

He definitely wasn't taking it easy on her, but neither did she sense he was trying very hard. It was infuriating to realize that he was probably using only half—maybe three-quarters—of his strength and skill to defeat her soundly. She felt like a pesky midge being slapped away.

Although Robert the Bruce had waged a whole war on being "pesky," after what happened this morning with the rider, it was humbling. She was supposed to be a warrior, yet all it took was a man who looked like the soldier who'd raped and killed her mother to turn her limbs to ice.

"Again," he said.

She muttered a furious "why bother" under her breath. He would just put her on her backside again, which was bruised and sore already.

Apparently, he didn't just have super strength; he had super hearing as well. "Are you giving up, Caty?"

Cate had never glowered before, but there was a first time for everything. Her mouth pursed tightly, and if she could have killed him with a look, she would have.

The slightly smug smile was the worst. He knew how frustrated she was. God, what she wouldn't do to wipe that smile off his face. "I will never give up."

He chuckled. "I didn't think so." Shaking his head, his

gaze suddenly grew more pensive. "You remind me of someone when you do that, but I can't think who it is."

She was so shocked, her mouth fell open before she recovered. "A jealous husband, perhaps, who'd like to see you gelded?"

He shuddered dramatically. "God's bones, Cate. Let's not use the word 'gelded' when there is a dagger within reach."

"That's assuming I could ever get it out of your hand."

"You don't have to sound so disappointed."

She dropped her gaze to the area in question. She thought she might have heard him swear. When she glanced back up at him, she was smiling. "Oh, I wouldn't geld you."

"Well, that's a relief." There might have been a touch of lingering huskiness in his voice.

She dimpled, her smile turning sugary sweet. "Not without cause, at least."

To her surprise, he laughed, swiping a strand of hair from her lashes. She didn't think he even realized what he'd done. But she did. The unconscious gesture was both tender and intimate, and worth every minute of being tossed on her backside all afternoon.

"You're a fierce little thing, aren't you?"

"Thank you," she said primly. "I think that is the nicest compliment you've ever given me."

He frowned, as if he couldn't quite figure out whether she was serious. Deciding she must be, he shook his head. "You are an unusual woman, Caitrina Kirkpatrick."

Hating the sound of the false name she'd given him, she wanted to correct him. Instead she smiled. "And that was the second nicest. Perhaps we should resume before I'm overcome by too much flattery?"

He gave her bottom a playful slap. "Saucy brat, get over there. This time try not to project your intentions so much. Look at my arms, not at my face." As if that were easy. But he was right. The moment their eyes met, she lost some of her concentration. "You are quick and agile, but you also have to make every movement count—you aren't going to get many of them against a skilled opponent. And with a weapon coming at you there isn't much room for error. You won't beat me skill to skill or strength to strength—no matter how badly you want to." She flushed, realizing that was exactly what she'd been trying to do. She'd wanted to impress him by besting him, and in doing so, she'd forgotten what John had taught her. Her goal wasn't to win; it was to get away. She'd let her pride interfere. "What else can you do?" he challenged her.

She thought about it as they squared off again. She could trick him or distract him somehow. But how? By preying on his weaknesses. Not that she could think of any. Suddenly, she smiled. She had an idea. Maybe he did have a weakness.

The next time he came at her, she kept her eyes low, avoiding his gaze and concentrating on his shoulders. It was a good thing, too, since he decided to switch hands, the blighter—the knife was in his left, not in his right.

But she was ready. When he stabbed with the knife, instead of trying to block, she jumped back out of the way and cried out as if he'd skimmed her.

"Oh God, Cate!" Instantly, forgetting the battle, he lunged toward her.

She locked her hand on the wrist still holding the knife and immediately controlled his hand with her other, twisting it and locking his wrist. He grunted in pain, having no choice but to move toward the ground with the torquing pressure. The knife clattered to the ground. Knowing she wouldn't be able to get him fully on the ground like this, she immediately followed up with a solid kick in the place where John had told her a man was especially vulnerable. As soon as he groaned and collapsed forward, she let his arm go, grabbed the knife, and stood over him.

She'd done it!

He was sure making a lot of noise, though, rolling on the ground and moaning. She took a few tentative steps closer. "Gregor, are you all . . . ?"

Right. She didn't get to finish her question.

As soon as she was in reach, he swung one of his legs around her ankles, taking her legs out from behind. An instant later, she was on the ground with him on top of her, her hands were pinned atop her head, and the knife was lying harmlessly beside them.

"That was a dirty trick, Caty." He smiled. "I like it. But you forgot one thing. Once I'm down, you are supposed to run away."

She glared at him. "I was worried. I thought I'd hurt you."

He lifted a brow. "Is that so? I think I know the feeling." She bit her lip, realizing he'd used her distraction against her. "And if it's any consolation, it hurt like hell. That was the most solid shot someone has landed on me in a long time."

She burst out into a wide smile. "Really?"

"You needn't look so pleased about it."

But she was. She wriggled a little to try to free herself, but it felt like she was pinned down by a ton of rocks.

His eyes darkened. "Now what are you going to do? I'll not be so easily distracted this time."

She struggled against him, using all the tricks that John had taught her. But she couldn't knee him, couldn't use her head to strike his, couldn't lift her hips—she couldn't move her limbs or body enough to do anything.

He was solid and heavy on top of her, crushing. At least he should be crushing her, but he wasn't. Somewhere in the midst of her struggles a different kind of awareness had taken hold.

He must be feeling it, too, because when their eyes met,

the heat in his gaze made her feel as though she'd just stepped too close to an inferno.

Her breath caught.

His eyes dropped to her parted lips. She could feel the tension radiating through him. He wanted to kiss her, but something was holding him back.

Twelve

Gregor had been wrong. She could distract him again—easily. All she had to do was gasp and part those soft, red lips of hers, and all he could think about was kissing her. Of course, there was also the fact that she was under him, and it wasn't very hard to imagine what it would be like to be inside her.

It would be incredible. He didn't need an imagination to know that—he could feel it. Desire swelled hard and heavy inside him, threatening to drag him under. He wanted to kiss her so intensely, he could practically taste her on his lips.

She wanted it, too. He could see it in her eyes. Eyes that held his with anticipation, arousal, too much damned trust, and an emotion that he was beginning to think might actually be real.

Fuck.

He pulled back and rolled off her, not realizing he'd uttered the curse aloud until her eyes widened.

"I can't do this," he said, getting to his feet.

He turned to help her, but she had already done the same. She stood there staring at him, confusion and hurt replacing the anticipation and arousal—though unfortunately the trust and that *other* emotion were still there.

"Why not?"

There was nothing accusatory in her tone, but he felt it

all the same. Or maybe it was his guilt at work. His mouth hardened. "It isn't right."

"Because you still think of yourself as my guardian? I told you, I'm a twenty-year-old woman; I'm capable of making my own decisions. You aren't taking advantage of me."

"That's not it, damn it," he snapped. Or not all of it.

"Then what is it?"

He dreaded telling her and wished it hadn't happened like this, but she needed to know what he planned for her. He couldn't avoid the discussion any longer. He told himself to stop being such a damned coward. As her guardian, or stand-in father, or whatever the hell he was, it was well within his duty to do what he'd done. "I've made arrangements."

She eyed him hesitantly. "What kind of arrangements?"

"For your future." She stiffened, but he continued. "I've been remiss in my duty. Had I been aware of your true age, I would have begun discussions years ago. But perhaps it is better that I waited, as the perfect suitor has come forward."

"The perfect *what*?"

Her shock and outrage were not limited to her tone—nay, they shook from every part of her body, from the combative stance, to the fists tightly balled at her sides, to the dark fury blaring at him from her eyes.

"The reeve's son, Farquhar, has asked for your hand in marriage; I have given him my permission."

She took a step back, her face white. The look of stark betrayal made him wish for a return of the shock and outrage.

She continued to stare at him for a long time. It wasn't easy, but he restrained himself from turning away or shuffling his feet. Why that minor feat felt like a major victory, he didn't know.

"You have it all arranged, then?"

The dull stoniness of her tone turned that urge to shuffle into an urge to squirm. Damn it, he knew she wasn't going to like it. But he hadn't anticipated being made to feel like an ogre—and a traitorous one, to boot.

He raked his hair with his fingers. Christ, this was exactly what he'd hoped to avoid. He was doing this for her own good. She might not see it now, but she would.

"I told Farquhar that if you agreed, he could announce the betrothal after the Hogmanay feast."

He filled her in on the position awaiting Farquhar at Ballock Castle, and his future prospects as steward. She listened expressionlessly, as his enthusiastic presentation of the lad took on the characteristics of a farmer presenting his prized bull at market.

"If I agree?" she repeated. "Do you mean I am to have some say in the matter? How very considerate of you."

She didn't bother to hide her sarcasm; it dripped coldly from her voice like droplets of ice. "Of course, you have a say, damn it. I want you to be happy."

Those big brown eyes turned on him as if he were crazed—which was exactly what she made him. "Yet you arranged all this without letting me know what you intended. I assume that is what all the messengers have been for?"

He acknowledged it with a nod. "There will be other men at the feast. If there is someone else you would rather wed . . . ?"

"There is no one," she said flatly. "As I told you, I have no wish to marry anyone else, but apparently my wishes—my feelings—mean nothing to you. Have you been planning this since you returned?" He must have done a piss-poor job of masking his guilt because she said, "Of course you have. How eager you must have been to finally have the chance to be rid of me."

He muttered a curse. "Damn it, Cate. It isn't like that."

"Isn't it? You took me in, but you never wanted the responsibility. I knew that, but I thought . . . I thought . . ." Her voice caught. "I thought this was my *home,* but you were just waiting for me to be old enough to marry off."

The way she was looking at him made his chest burn, but he couldn't turn away. He almost reached for her. Almost. But he feared what would happen if he touched her again. How easily comfort could lead to something else.

"It is your home," he said gently. He just couldn't give her the family she wanted to replace her lost one. "But now that my mother is gone, with you and John alone . . . it wouldn't be right for you to stay here."

For one moment he thought she might slap him. "How dare you insinuate . . . I told you, John is like a brother to me."

"But he is not your brother, and others will start to realize that as well." Especially if John kept looking at her like he might kiss her all the time. "You had to know that you couldn't stay here forever. Don't you want to marry and have a family?"

"Don't you?"

It was his turn to stiffen. "This isn't about me."

"Why not? I'll marry when you do."

"It doesn't work like that, Cate, and you know it. I have the luxury of waiting; you do not."

"Then you *will* force me?" Her eyes were too bright and shiny. *God, please don't cry.* If she cried, he didn't know what he'd do. "Do you wish to be rid of me so badly? My feelings mean so little to you?"

"Of course not."

"If you planned to marry me off, why did you kiss me?"

Because he was a damned fool. "You looked so upset." He shrugged helplessly, unable to explain himself. "I told you, it didn't mean anything."

*   *   *

He felt sorry for me. That is why he kissed me.

Cate wanted to collapse in a wounded heap and bawl her eyes out like a baby. But her pride wouldn't let her.

She didn't know what was worse: discovering that the man she'd given her heart to had been trying to find a way to be rid of her since he'd arrived, or that he'd kissed her because he felt sorry for her. Both were worse. Both felt like a betrayal.

"It meant something to me," she said softly.

His expression looked truly pained, not that it helped ease hers any. "I'm sorry, Cate. Truly. I never meant to hurt you."

"But you don't love me, have no intention of marrying me, and would see me wed to a man I barely know just so you don't have to worry about me? I understand."

But she didn't. How could he have been planning this and said nothing? John must have known about Gregor's plans for her betrothal—that was what he'd been trying to warn her about. She was such a fool.

Oh God, the children. What about them? They'd needed her, and she'd let them down.

"Cate . . ."

He reached for her, but she stepped away to avoid his grasp. She straightened her spine, hurt turning to anger. "You don't need to explain. It is my fault for falling in love with the wrong man. Of course you've no wish to marry me. You're the most handsome man in Scotland, with your choice of brides. You could have a kingdom. I'm a bastard." Seeing his shock, she added, "Aye, a bastard, some nobleman's by-blow. Kirkpatrick was my stepfather."

He was clearly taken aback. "Why didn't you tell me the truth?"

"Because I was tired of being ashamed of the 'noble' father who deserted me when I was five."

"Who is he?"

"What difference does it make? He's dead to me. *Dead.*

Bastard or orphan, I have little *to* recommend me and much *not* to recommend me. I'm surprised you managed to find someone to marry me at all."

His eyes flashed dangerously. He was angry now. *Good.* If the man known for breaking hearts managed to feel one-tenth of the emotion she felt right now it would be enough.

"If you want to know, there were plenty of men eager to marry you."

He didn't sound happy about it—not that she believed him anyway. "But not the only one who matters. Would it be so horrible to let yourself love me, Gregor?"

He looked pained—uncomfortable—as if he would rather be anywhere than here, having this discussion. "I've no wish to marry anyone right now. But if I did, it sure as hell wouldn't be for a 'kingdom' or to a woman who wanted to marry 'the handsomest man in Scotland.' And if you don't know that, you don't know me at all."

Was he mad? "Know you? I know you like your beef rare, your pork lightly pink, your sauces savory, and your vegetables firm. I know you prefer plums to pears and oranges to apples. I know you like oysters raw and eggs from salmon spread on crusty bread—which is disgusting by the way. I know you can tell where a wine is from from the first sip, and would rather go thirsty than drink the sweet wernage your mother loved. I know you drink more when you are unhappy, which I suspect has been a lot of late."

Taking advantage of his shock, she continued. "I know you hate accepting anything unless you've earned it. I know your father was an arse and made you think you would never amount to anything, but that you've proved him wrong. I know you think you need to be perfect but that you never will be. I know that a man who is the best archer in Scotland, and who has fought loyally beside Robert the Bruce for years—even in the lowest part of his reign—is not irresponsible but a man to count on. I know you don't want to be a protector but you are. I know you let John do your duty as chieftain because you don't think you deserve it. I know that the enemies you kill in battle mean something to you, and that's why the stack of stones on your father's grave and the coin in Father Roland's offertory basket grow higher every time you come home."

She drew a deep breath. "I know you think that you are better off alone and don't want to care about me, but that you do. I know that I'm the only woman you *really* talk to, and that means something. I know that when I sent Lizzie to the wine storage room with you, you didn't touch her, even though you could have. I know you've bedded many women but the only one you really cared about hurt you. I know you think that you will hurt me, but that if you loved me, you'd be loyal and true to me to death—just as I would be to you."

Their eyes met, and she dared him to stop her. "I know that being a notch in a bedpost bothers you more than you let on, but you don't think anyone can see beyond that perfect face of yours to the flawed man underneath. Maybe you're right, but you'll never know because you won't take a chance and trust your feelings. Because I *know* you feel this, too, Gregor. Just as I know that one day you will regret marrying me to another man, but by then it will be too late, and you will have no one to blame but yourself."

He just stared at her. "Jesus, Cate, I . . ."

Didn't know what to say. That was clear. Suddenly, the storm of emotion drained out of her. What was left was a sense of futility and hopelessness—and maybe a need to strike back. "Marry me to whomever you want, Gregor—it doesn't make a difference to me. None of them are you. But when you are lying there in the dark tonight, trying to go to sleep with your body aching for me as mine will for you, think about this: The next man I am lying under might be my husband, and unlike you, he will not pull back."

The pulse below his jaw jumped, his mouth hardening into a tight white line. She thought he might reach for her, but his arms stayed rigidly fixed at his sides.

"Of course, you could prove I mean nothing to you and find relief another way, but I don't think you'll do that. I think you want me and no other. But go ahead and prove me wrong . . . if you can."

Cate didn't know where she'd found the strength to utter the challenge, but even knowing the risk, she would not take it back. She had too much to lose. Her faith would be rewarded or destroyed *now*—before he married her to another man.

Feeling more battered and bruised than she'd ever been from training, Cate turned on her heel and walked away.

She didn't look back.

Jesus. It was the only coherent thought he could manage, so he repeated it: *Jesus.*

Gregor didn't know how long he'd stood there after she left. She'd done it again: turned him upside-down, inside-out, and all the way around. He felt like he'd been sucked up into a tempest to spin around for a while, before being spit back out onto the ground like a ship scattered on the rocks. A ship that had been sailing along just fine—perfectly fine—until it had run into an unexpected maelstrom.

Cate.

She loves me. After hearing that litany of his character—good and bad—how could he doubt it? It wasn't a girlish *tendre* or an instant infatuation with his face; she really did know him.

Hell, she knew him better than he knew himself. And he didn't know what to think about that except he didn't like it. It confused him. Nay, *she* confused him.

How did she know so much about him, anyway? Undoubtedly his mother had told her some, some she must have figured out from observation, and some was conjecture. *"I think you want me, and no other."* That sure as hell was conjecture . . . wasn't it?

"Prove me wrong . . . if you can." He should. God knew he should. But he wouldn't hurt her like that to prove a point.

He'd hurt her enough with his damned plan. A plan that had seemed perfect before he'd come home but didn't seem so perfect now. He hadn't anticipated wanting her. Hadn't anticipated being unable to keep his damned hands to himself. Hadn't anticipated her response, and sure as hell hadn't anticipated the surge of what could only be called jealousy at the thought of her with another man. *"The next man I am lying under might be my husband."* He swore again.

Nor had he anticipated the guilt he would feel for sending her from her home. For being so eager to be rid of her.

Being rid of her was what he thought he wanted, but when she put it so harshly, damn it, he didn't like how it sounded.

He didn't want to be rid of her. But what other choice did he have? He couldn't marry her.

Or could he? Could he be the man she thought him? The man she deserved?

Ah hell, what was she doing to him? A wife sure as hell wasn't the way to clear his head. Picking up the dagger that was still on the ground and sliding it into his belt, Gregor crossed the practice yard and headed toward the kitchens. A hot bath would clear his head. And if that didn't work, a big draught of ale would make him forget. *"I know you drink more when you are unhappy . . ."* Christ, he had to stop this.

He was walking past the stables when a thin, dark form jumped out to block his path.

Recognizing the miscreant, Gregor's lip curled with distaste. A curl of distaste that was returned in force by the miscreant—along with a menacing glare. "What did you do to her?"

From the way Pip was clenching and re-clenching his small fists, Gregor realized the lad was actually thinking about using them. Another time it might have amused him, but in his present state he was in no mood for the perceived wrongs of a deceitful brat who'd taken advantage of Cate's too-big heart. The lad hadn't been abandoned. According to the information Gregor's seneschal had uncovered, Pip had been sending his mother money—probably since he'd arrived.

"Do to whom?" Gregor said. "Say what you will, Phillip—I'm busy."

Hatred twisted the lad's face into a mask of rage. "What did you do to Cate? Why did you make her cry?"

Ah hell. It felt like someone was pounding a hammer on his chest like it was an anvil. "Cate was crying?"

"If you hurt her, I'll kill you!"

Gregor was taken aback by the venom and intensity of the threat. He did not doubt the boy meant it. "Leave it, Pip. It has nothing to do with you. This is between Cate and me."

"Why are you even here? No one needs you here. I wish you'd just go away and never come back. Everything was fine before you came."

The lad's words packed a surprising punch, perhaps striking closer than he would have liked. Gregor's temper sparked. "Was it fine because there was no one here to question your story? Fine so you could deceive and take advantage of a woman who has been far kinder to you than you deserve? Or fine so that you could continue to send the mother you claim abandoned you coin?"

The boy's face went so white it seemed all the blood had been leeched out of him. "Wait, you don't understand!"

"I'm sure I don't."

Fear had replaced the hatred. In an instant the lad's surly

bravado vanished. It almost looked like fear in his eyes. "Please, you can't send me away!"

Sending him away was exactly what Gregor should do. And he would, but he wasn't as immune to the lad's pleading as he wanted to be. Before he could question him further, however, Gregor had to fend off another attack. This one from a yapping ball of wiry fur that had come tearing out of the barn to attach itself to Gregor's ankle again.

"God's blood!" He reached down to grab the pup by the scruff—mindful of the surprisingly sharp little teeth that snapped at his hand—and held it up to his face. "Quiet."

The sharp command startled the pup, who gave a pathetic little yelp before going silent—*blissfully* silent. It then proceeded to stare at Gregor with what could only be described as a big-eyed puppy-dog look.

Christ, not another foundling on his conscience.

Holding the creature out to Pip, he dropped it into his waiting arms. "Keep the little rat out of my way, Pip, or get rid of it."

"Why am I not surprised that you don't like dogs?"

"I like dogs fine. Find me one—or at least one that doesn't shatter eardrums with its barking or try to sink its teeth into my ankles."

The boy shielded the pup in his arms protectively. If he was trying to make Gregor feel like a bully, he was doing a damned fine job of it.

"Strange how he likes everyone else," Pip said. "But they do say dogs are a good judge of character."

Much as Cate had done shortly before, the boy turned on his heel and left him standing there. And like before, Gregor was left with the distinct feeling that he'd come out on the losing side of the confrontation.

Damn it, he needed to get back to the battlefield. At least there he was good at something. Or used to be good at something. But what if . . .

He refused to contemplate it. There was nothing wrong

with him. He just needed to get back on track. Clear his head.

Hell, maybe he should just marry her so he stopped thinking about her so much.

He shook his head. Christ, he wasn't losing his edge; he was losing his damned mind!

Thirteen

❧

Cate had definitely won all right. Gregor kicked the twisted bed linens off him and jumped out of bed for the fifth or sixth time—he'd stopped counting—to pace around his room like a lion in a cage. The cage of his own mind.

The pacing eased his restlessness, but only temporarily. The moment he climbed back into bed, put his head on the pillow, and closed his eyes, the images would start again. The tormentingly sharp images of Cate in bed with the reeve's son on top of her. Kissing her. Touching her. *Not pulling back.* Slowly lifting the hem of her linen chemise, sliding his hand up her bare thigh . . .

Gregor swore and pounded the side of his fist on the windowsill with enough force to make the glass shake. He bent his head, resting it on the shutter, closing his eyes and willing the maddening images to go away.

Slowly, his pulse returned to normal and the fiery madness cooled, driving the heat from his blood and skin. He lifted his head, took a deep breath, and turned to scan the dark chamber, the soft glow of the peat providing just enough light to see by. His gaze stopped momentarily on the flagon of whisky sitting on his bedside table, as it had done many times tonight.

"I know you drink more when you are unhappy."

He didn't drink too much, damn it. He was always in control, and never drank to the point of drunkenness. But the number of times he'd woken up in the past year with his head feeling as if it were splitting apart told him she wasn't completely wrong.

Christ, now he couldn't even have a drink of whisky before bed without hearing her voice. Actually, it was the drink of whisky he wanted to *not* hear her voice. To blur the haunting images and let him get some rest.

Perhaps he should have gone to the alehouse after all.

Who the hell was he fooling? He didn't want to go to the alehouse and find a lass to take to his bed. *"I think you want me and no other."* She was right, damn her. God knew it probably wouldn't last. He was bound to desire another woman at some point. He had enough of them to choose from; eventually one would catch his eye.

But what if he only ever wanted Cate?

Was that even possible?

All he had to do was think of his married brethren to know that it was. With the exception of MacLean, who'd been estranged from his wife since the start of the war, every one of his fellow Guardsmen was faithful to his wife. Even Raider and Hawk, and they had nearly as many women throwing themselves at them as he did.

Of course, they were "in love" with their wives, which was an emotion Gregor didn't know whether he was even capable of feeling. He'd cared about Isobel—and sure as hell lusted for her—but the kind of flowery romantic love the bards wrote about, or the powerful this-is-the-only-woman-for-me and I'll-do-anything-including-die-for-you emotion his friends had found? He'd never felt that.

You'd die for Cate.

The voice at the back of his mind jarred him. But that was different, wasn't it? She was his responsibility, his family—he was supposed to feel that way.

She was his *family*.

Ah, hell. His heart sank like a stone in his chest. She was his family, and he'd tried to get rid of her with no more thought or care than he would have given to a stray cat—or dog, he thought, recalling his words to Pip earlier. Worse, he suspected he'd unintentionally hit a tender spot with respect to the father who'd abandoned her.

The father he hadn't known about. He'd been surprised—and not a little angry—to learn about her lie, but perhaps he shouldn't have been. He'd always sensed something wrong when Kirkpatrick's name was mentioned. Now he understood why. He didn't like that she'd lied to him, but he supposed he couldn't blame her for trying to erase the "stain" of her birth when given an opportunity. Though he didn't care about such things, she wouldn't have known that at the time.

Actually, he felt more outraged on her behalf. What kind of man could abandon his own child like that? No wonder she hated him. Gregor would kill the bastard himself if he could.

Yet she probably thought he was trying to do the same thing by getting rid of her—walking away from her, just as her bastard of a father had done.

He crossed purposefully to the bed and forced himself to lie down.

Cate wasn't just family, and he knew it. What he felt for her was different. Confusing, frustrating, and maddening perhaps, but different. He didn't know what it meant, but he suspected that if he ever wanted another peaceful night of sleep, he might indeed have to marry her.

For the first time that night, he closed his eyes and the images did not return. He might have been able to sleep if the screams hadn't torn him from his bed.

"Stop!" she tried to shout. "Get off my mother!"

But the soldier kept thrusting, his mail-clad form moving between her mother's legs. He turned, the dark, refined features that should be handsome twisted in an ugly, taunting smile that dared her to try to stop him. She struck him with the hoe over and over, but all it did was make him laugh harder. The maniacal sound rang in her ears, mixing with her mother's screams.

Make it stop! Please, make it stop!

Strong arms grabbed her, and she tried to wrestle free. "No!" she cried. "I have to help her!"

"Cate!" a deep voice penetrated the darkness. She was shaking. Nay, someone was shaking her. "Wake up, sweetheart. You have to wake up. It's just a dream."

She opened her eyes. Gregor's face stared back at her in the shadows. She was sitting up on her bed in his arms. It was he who was holding her, not the soldiers.

She leaned into him, burying herself against his chest, taking refuge in the protective strength of the arms around her, and letting him comfort her. He murmured low, soothing words against her head as he gently rocked her sobs away. Gradually, the breath returned to her lungs and the panicked race of her pulse began to slow.

It was just a horrible dream, a return of one of the nightmares that had haunted her for years after that horrible day. There were different versions, including the one she'd just had where the soldier was raping her mother, and she kept hitting him over and over but he wouldn't die. Another was of Cate in the well, starving and dying of thirst. All the joy and relief she experienced when she heard the rescuers turned to horror when the face that looked down at her wasn't Gregor's, but the soldier's. The worst was the nightmare that actually happened, the replaying in her mind of those hideous seconds of her mother's death, in slow, precise detail.

She thought she'd rid herself of the nightmares for good, but all it took was seeing that man today to bring them back. Deep down, she knew they wouldn't be gone until the soldier paid for what he'd done.

Suddenly, angry at herself for the weakness, she drew back from the wall of Gregor's chest—his *bare* chest, as she was just noticing—dabbing her eyes on the sleeve of her linen chemise. "I'm sorry. I don't know what came over me."

He released her. "You had a nightmare."

His gaze turned to the open doorway. Her embarrassment increased tenfold. It seemed like half the household was standing on the small landing outside her room. In the stream of light coming from the torch mounted outside her chamber she could see the concerned faces of Ete, Lizzie, Pip, and two of Gregor's guardsmen, Bryan and Cormac.

"It's all right," Gregor said. "Return to your rooms. I have her."

I have her. Though she knew it meant nothing, her heart tugged sharply nonetheless.

The light dimmed as the crowd dispersed. Gregor stood to light a candle from the brazier, taking the time to add another block of peat to the fire. Before returning to sit beside her on the bed, he closed the door.

Suddenly self-conscious, she felt her cheeks grow hot under his steady gaze. The temperature in the room seemed to have shot from the dead of winter to the height of summer in a few seconds. She was hot, and she knew it wasn't from the peat; it was from the intimacy of being alone with him in her small bedchamber. Of course, the broad, muscular chest shimmering in the candlelight that seemed to fill every inch of her vision wasn't helping matters.

Good gracious, how did it get so defined like that? There didn't appear to be any spare flesh on the man of which to speak. She could count the lines crossing his stomach, for heaven's sake.

He truly was magnificent.

But he didn't care about her. Reminding herself what had happened earlier—and his plan to be rid of her—she pursed her mouth and forced her eyes from the fever-inducing display of muscle.

"I'm fine," she said briskly. "I'm sorry for waking you. You can go back to bed now."

He took her chin between his thumb and forefinger, lifting her gaze to his. "I'm not going anywhere. You're still shaking." She was, she realized. "Christ, *I'm* still shaking. You scared the hell out of me. You sounded like you were in agony." She had been. The agony of being helpless to do anything as your mother was raped and murdered before your eyes. "The soldier?" he asked.

She nodded.

"Do you want to talk about it?"

She stared into those gorgeous green eyes, felt her heart swell, and then shook her head. The soldier was the last thing she wanted to talk about. Not when Gregor was holding her like this. It might be the last chance she ever had.

The air in the room seemed to change. It grew sharper and filled with a strange buzz. His eyes darkened, and his voice, when it came, deepened. "What do you want, sweetheart? Tell me how I can make it better."

Sweetheart. Her heart thudded. It was the second time he'd called her that. He never used endearments with her— never. Did it mean something? Was the tenderness in his eyes a trick of the candlelight, or could she trust what she was seeing?

There was one way to find out. She told him the truth. "I want you to hold me in your arms and kiss me. I want you to make me forget."

Gregor stilled, cursing himself for a damned fool. What the hell had he expected? He knew better than to ask a question to which he didn't want to hear the answer. But there she was in his arms—practically sitting on his lap— with her big, dark eyes wide and shimmering with tears, her face still pale and stricken by the tortured memories of her nightmare, looking more vulnerable than he'd seen her in a long time, and he'd never felt so bloody helpless in his life. He would have done anything to make it better. *Anything* to wrench those memories from her mind and allow her to forget. So he'd asked his fool question.

God's breath, she had no idea what she was asking of him. *Kiss me. Make me forget.* As if it were that easy, when just looking at her gazing up at him made his pulse race and his blood feel like something churning in a volcano. He wanted to do a hell of a lot more than kiss her. A *whole* hell of a lot more. And he didn't trust himself to touch her. He, the man who never lost control and always knew exactly what he was doing in the bedchamber, realized he was looking at the woman who could break him.

Every instinct in his body was standing on edge shouting *Warning!,* telling him that kissing her in the broad daylight was bad enough; he'd be mad to do so in a darkened chamber, alone, with both of them barely clothed.

But she needed him, damn it. How could he refuse?

Easily. But he didn't want to. God knew, he needed to forget, too. The memory of her scream was too fresh. His blood had run cold. An icy sheen of panic had raced over his skin. He'd thought someone was hurting her, and it had left him weakened, stripped bare, without his usual defenses.

Aye, that was the only explanation for how easily he succumbed to her siren's call. How willingly his lips touched hers, even when he knew how hard it would be to pull away.

He could do this, he told himself. Just a kiss to make her forget . . .

But it was he who forgot every damned thing in his head the moment his mouth touched hers. His senses exploded. All he wanted to do was sink into her and never let go.

How was it possible that anything could feel this good? Her lips were just as sweet and soft as he remembered. So pliant and . . . *open.*

Ah hell, before he could stop himself, his tongue was in her mouth again, and he was giving her those long, deep strokes that made him think of swiving. Lots and lots of swiving. Sweaty-limbs-in-tangled-bedsheets kind of swiving. All he'd have to do was lay her back, untie the braies he'd thrown on, lift her chemise, and he could be inside her. Deep inside her. Plunging in and out in the same frantic rhythm of his tongue. He was hard as a spike just thinking about it.

She was so sweet, so incredibly hot . . .

His arm tightened around her back, drawing her closer. He felt the bead of her nipples against his chest, and just like that, the barely controlled kiss was gone, replaced by the hungry, swirling maelstrom of need that devoured his good intentions and spit them out like the pile of shite that they were.

There was no such thing as "just a kiss" when it came to Cate. He wanted her in a way that he'd never wanted another woman, with an intensity that snapped the steely reins of his control as if they were a few brittle strands of thread. He didn't understand it, didn't really want to examine it—it was just the way it was.

He slid his fingers through her silky hair, cradling the back of her head to plunder her mouth more fully. She responded with a low moan and an insistent press of her chest that went straight to his bollocks and tugged— hard—with a primal urgency that didn't want to listen to reason or honor or any other excuse for not taking this kiss to its natural conclusion.

She wasn't making it easy on him to do the right thing. Cate was kissing him back with every bit of passion that he was feeling, making all those breathy little moans that drove him wild. Her hands weren't helping matters any either. She'd laced them around his neck when he'd first kissed her, but now they'd slid down to his shoulders and were gripping him as if she would never let go, her fingers digging into the muscle with an intensity and fervor that told him exactly how much she liked what he was doing to her. A lot. So much that he knew he could make her shatter with a few strokes.

He groaned, knowing he shouldn't think about that. What he should think about was stopping.

But how the hell was he supposed to resist all this warm, baby-soft skin that smelled like wildflowers, lips that were as soft and sugary as warm honey, and hair—he let it pour over his hands—hair that slid between his fingers like silk?

And then there was that tight little body straining against his chest, the firm mounds of her breasts with the hard pink tips digging into him, that gave him just a teasing hint of what she'd feel like naked against him. But it wasn't enough. He wanted to feel all of her against him. He wanted her under him. On top of him. On her hands and knees in front of him. Any way and every way.

It would be so damned easy to push her back on the bed and give himself all the contact—the naked contact—he craved. Skin to skin. He wanted to see her strong, slender body spread out beneath him like a banquet to feast upon. He wanted to suck the tiny nipples that were raking his chest, lick his way down the slender curve of her belly, and taste the sensitive place between her legs.

God, he *really* wanted to do that. Feel those hard spasms against his mouth . . . taste her pleasure . . .

He groaned deeper into her mouth as the erotic images swirled through him, jerking his cock hard against his stomach.

His body pressed forward, urging her back, as the desire became too much to bear. It felt like a weight pressing him down. *Touch her. Take her. Make her yours.* It hummed through his blood, zipped along every one of his nerve endings, and seemed to have taken command of every bone in his body.

He was breathing hard now, his heart hammering in his chest and ears, his skin hot and too damned tight as need pounded through every muscle and vein in his body. She was practically under him, her body stretched out beneath his. He wanted her so intensely, his body was shaking with it.

Everything about it felt so right. But somewhere in the depths of his lust-crowded brain, he knew it wasn't.

He'd taken precisely one woman's maidenhead in his life and had regretted it ever since. Then, he'd been a seventeen-year-old lust-starved lad whose weak attempt at honor had been rather handily disposed of by a few soft pleas and tender words of love. He was an experienced man now who knew better—and the right order of things. Cate deserved a wedding, a husband, and a marriage bed. Not a frantic, lust-hazed coupling at a vulnerable moment. He was supposed to be comforting her, not seducing her.

With a mumbled oath, he pulled away. "We have to stop."

She blinked up at him, looking half-ravished and eager for the other half—not a good combination for a man fighting for control. "Why?"

"It isn't right. Your maidenhead belongs to your husband."

Christ, he sounded like an old man, or a stern guardian—neither of which sounded right at the moment. And if the crushed look in Cate's eyes was any indication, she'd taken his attempt to do the right thing wrong.

Still, he might have been able to hold to his honorable intentions if she hadn't reached out and pushed him right over the edge.

Fourteen

"Your maidenhead belongs to your husband."

Gregor was the best archer in Scotland; it was no surprise that his arrow struck with cruel precision.

Cate had thought he'd put the ridiculous idea of her betrothal behind him. How could he kiss her like that and still mean to marry her to another man?

He must be the most stubborn, thickheaded man in Christendom! And perhaps blind as well, not to see what was right in front of him. He cared about her—loved her even, though she knew he would run to the nearest battlefield if she told him as much. He showed his feelings in the way he looked at her, in the way he held her, and yes, in the way he kissed her. A man could not kiss a woman with that kind of tenderness and passion and not be at least a little in love with her. She didn't care how good he was at lovemaking, or how many women he'd had in his bed.

Admittedly, she wasn't exactly an expert on the subject, but she'd be willing to stake her life on it—and her virtue as well.

Cate wasn't going to let him pull away. Not this time. She was out of patience. She wouldn't let him marry her off to another man.

Sitting up a little, she reached out and put her palm flat on his chest. Emboldened by the hard slam of his heartbeat that seemed to jump up and meet it, she looked him squarely in the eye. "No."

He appeared too momentarily stunned to reply. Knowing it wouldn't last, she took a deep breath and did the one thing she instinctively knew would put a decisive end to further argument. She let her hand slide down over the warm, hard ridges of stomach muscle to the tie at the waist of his braies.

He sucked in his breath, his eyes dark and predatory, watching her every movement like a hawk daring a mouse to come into his range.

She dared. With a deep breath for courage, she lowered her hand, curving it around the thick column of his manhood.

Oh . . . *my.* She might have gulped, but the swallow stuck in her throat.

Every muscle in his body seemed to tense—an impressive feat for a man who seemed to be built of little else. The low hissing sound that came from between his clenched teeth nearly made her pull away, but she didn't. Instead, she felt a strange flush of what could only be called power—*feminine* power. The feel of him in her hand, so strong and thick, and surprisingly hard, knowing she'd made him that way, gave her courage.

"No," she repeated. "I want you, and I know you want me, too. I don't want you to stop—I want you to finish what you started on the practice yard. I want you to be the one to show me passion. I want you to make love to me." She looked into his eyes, which seemed to be glowing brighter than the fire. "Make love to me, Gregor . . . please."

If someone had asked her for the perfect response to her plea, she would never have thought the sharp curse that came from his mouth would have been it. But somehow the word fit, and not just because it rather crudely summed up what she was asking him to do. Somehow it seemed to encompass the intensity of emotion that he was keeping bottled up and she was forcing free. Somehow it seemed to capture the harshness of his desire, and the base depth of his need for her. And somehow that one wicked word seemed to strip away the last vestiges of pretense and civility, revealing the raw, primitive hunger that he would no longer deny. With that one word, she heard his helplessness, his surrender, and knew that no matter how exceptional a warrior he might be, this was one fight she was going to win.

His mouth was pulled into almost a grimace, the arms holding her had turned as rigid as steel, and every muscle in his body seemed as tight as one of those bowstrings for which he'd become famous. Yet he was so impossibly gorgeous in the candlelight, it make her chest squeeze.

"You don't fight fair, sweetheart. I don't want to hurt you, and I don't know if I can give you what you want." She held her breath when he paused. "But God knows I'm going to try."

Cate sighed with relief. She didn't know what promise he was making, except to know that he'd just made one. He didn't give her time to ask, for no sooner had he finished than his mouth was covering hers in a kiss that left no doubt of his intentions.

He did not intend to woo or entice, he intended to have her, and the knowledge bloomed inside her until warmth and happiness filled every part of her body.

Drawing her hard against him, he claimed her mouth with bold, demanding strokes of his tongue that sent shudders of white-hot need rippling through her body, crashing over her in hard waves. She was drowning in sensation, being dragged under in a riptide of heat and desire. He was kissing her like he could never get enough of her. Kissing her like it meant something. Nay, like it meant *everything*. She returned the kiss with increasing fervency, until it seemed they had dissolved into one another, their mouths, their tongues, their bodies becoming one.

Passion consumed them both—the same as before, yet different. It was just as incredible and just as powerful, but this time there was nothing holding back. It came on her hot and heavy, demanding and unyielding.

It was the same soft mouth, the same spicy taste, the same deft tongue kissing her, but this kiss came with a no-holds-barred intensity that was both utterly dominating and oddly freeing at the same time. He made her feel safe. Protected. *Loved*.

He was on her, in her, surrounding her. His heat enveloped, the granite solidness of his body pressed, his kiss possessed, but never did he take. Rather he gave himself in a way that she suspected he'd never given himself to a woman before. And she took him in with everything she had, opening herself up to him, his kiss, his touch, and the powerful sensations he was stirring inside her.

Instinctively, her fingers curled tighter around his manhood. The husky, deep groan of his pleasure seemed to shudder through her as well. Holding her hand to him with his, he forced her to grip him harder, and then thrust up into the circle of her hand. Once. Twice. The bottom of her stomach seemed to melt between her legs as he thrust again, the raw, ragged sound of his pleasure echoing in her ears.

With a curse that told her he'd had all the pleasure he could stand, he drew her hand away and lowered her back onto the bed.

He came over her, pressing her more deeply into the mattress, his powerful body hard and unyielding on top of her. A warrior's body with the thick, solid muscle that she'd come to crave. Desperately. Frantically. Her hands clutched his shoulders, gripped the rocky muscles of his arms and slid over the hard slabs of muscle at his back forged by years of using a bow, but still it wasn't enough.

She had to be closer, which seemed an impossible quest as their bodies were already fused together.

The same hardness she'd been holding in her hands was between her legs now, and she lifted her hips against him, needing him closer to the part of her that fluttered wildly with need.

The kiss spun out of control, growing hotter ... deeper ... wetter. The determined, demanding strokes becoming less precise and more wild. His hands moved over her body, hot and possessive, claiming her with every touch and caress.

He cupped her breast, rubbing his thumb over the tip until it was taut with need. She wanted to cry out when he broke the kiss—perhaps she even did—but the disappointment lasted only long enough for him to lower his head.

Oh God, his mouth! His hot, wet, wonderful mouth was on her breast. Pleasure shot through her in a bolt of pure molten fire when his lips covered the throbbing nipple. Even through the thin layer of linen of her chemise, the heat and dampness assailed her. Unconsciously, she arched into the gentle pull of his mouth, begging for more, a silent request he was only too eager to answer.

Somehow he'd managed to loosen the ties of her chemise. Barely was she aware of cool air on her fevered skin—her fevered *bare* skin—however, before he took her in his mouth, sucking and circling her with his tongue, until she cried out with pleasure so acute, her body seemed to shake with it.

"God, you are beautiful," he murmured, his warm breath making her damp skin prickle. "So responsive." He flicked her with his tongue, then tugged the turgid flesh gently between his teeth, until she moaned. "Do you like that?"

She might have glared at him, knowing he was teasing her. Of course she liked it. She *loved* it, and didn't want him to stop.

But as their eyes met, she suddenly became aware of her naked flesh between them and flushed. It seemed such a small amount of naked flesh compared to what he was no doubt used to.

She must have given away her thoughts; his face darkened. "You have nothing to be embarrassed about, Cate. You are exquisite." He covered her with his hand, and the look of rapture that came over his face as he groaned gave her no room to doubt him. "Perfect. So round and firm." He squeezed gently. "With just enough to fill my hand. And nipples as rosy red and tight as pearls." He smoothed the hard tip with his thumb. "I could look at you forever."

Forever. Her heart squeezed with longing. It was just a turn of phrase, she told herself, but why when she looked into his eyes did it seem to mean something?

Gregor meant every word. When he looked at her like this—her dark hair spread out on the pillow behind her, her skin flushed, her eyes heavy, her mouth bruised from his kiss, the taut, round curve of creamy flesh bared to his gaze—it wasn't just lust that came over him, although that was undeniably part of it. It was something far bigger and more powerful, a surge of emotion he'd never experienced before. It squeezed his heart, tightened his throat, and filled his chest with a heavy warmth. It was a feeling of utter rightness and happiness, which, given what he was doing, was ironic.

But he wasn't going to think of that. He knew *exactly* what he was doing, and what it meant. He wasn't going to second-guess his decision now. Although admittedly, it hadn't been much of decision. It wasn't the first time a woman had tried to change his mind by putting her hands on him. But it was the first time it had worked.

Christ, when Cate had slid her hand down his bare stomach, coming to rest inches from the throbbing head of his erection, he would have given her anything she wanted to make her go lower. The knowledge that her hand was so close to his cock had made him so hot he thought he was going to explode. He nearly did, when she finally put her hand where he wanted it.

It had been one of the most sensual, erotic moments of his life, and looking into her eyes, so wide, guileless, and full of her unabashed love for him, nothing had ever felt more right.

She belonged to him, and he would have her—whatever the cost, it would be worth it.

Just looking at her was worth it. She was so damned lovely it took his breath away. He wanted to get down on his knees and worship every inch of her—preferably with his mouth and tongue. And he would. Next time. But right now, just the sight of one small breast that fit snugly in the palm of his hand and the turgid pink nipple was too much for him to take.

Where the hell was all that experience he was famous for?

She was a virgin. And not that he didn't appreciate that fact—he did—but making it good for her wasn't going to be easy, especially when just kissing her turned him into some kind of clumsy, ham-fisted squire who had only one thought on his mind.

It was a good thought, though. A *really* good thought. *Slow down, damn it. Pull it together.*

Taking her nipple in his mouth again, he plied it between his teeth, tugging gently, and sucking until she'd forgotten all about modesty and was writhing shamelessly— wantonly, God help him—underneath him. Just the way he liked it. Her body crying out for the pleasure he was about to give her.

She was so primed, so responsive, he knew he could make her shatter just by sucking and teasing her breasts, but he wanted to feel that first shudder of pleasure. He wanted to see her face as she broke apart under him.

Slipping his hand under the edge of her chemise, he slid the back of his finger up her thigh, edging closer to the sweet cleft of her womanhood.

She didn't seem to notice until his hand had slipped between her legs, and then she stiffened for a moment. But only a moment. The second his finger brushed the silken folds, she shuddered and moaned.

Wet. So warm and wet. He gritted his teeth against the violent surge of his own need pressing hard at the base of his spine.

Swearing silently, he knew that whatever control he'd managed to find was quickly slipping away.

He concentrated on her face, watching the shock, and then the pleasure unfurl like a pink rose on her cheeks as he brushed over her. Gently at first, letting her get used to the sensations taking hold of her body.

He gave her breast one last long suck and then released it as his finger slipped inside. Mimicking what he was doing between her legs, he flicked his tongue out over her nipple, circled and stroked. Teasing her with soft breaths of warm air against the damp skin until her back was arching and her hips were lifting in silent plea for release.

She was so damned beautiful, his need for her so intense, he couldn't tease it out any longer. Keeping his eyes on her face, he sucked her breast hard and caressed that sensitive spot with his thumb as he pressed the heel of his hand against her and gave her that friction she needed.

She gasped. Stilled. And broke apart with the sweetest cry he'd ever heard. Her face went soft and dreamy with euphoria as her body shuddered and contracted. He felt the heat, the rush of dampness, and every spasm of the pleasure that claimed her.

It was almost perfect. Next time it would be, because next time he would be inside her. In about two seconds, as that was about as long as he could wait.

*　*　*

Cate felt like she had died and gone to heaven. Surely that was what it must feel like to float among the clouds. Well, perhaps not float. Shoot, soar, and tumble was probably more accurate.

Her body was still tingling when her gaze cleared enough to see him propped over her. His face was strained and tortured in the shadows. She wanted to wrap her arms around him and kiss him, but she didn't have any bones left.

The warmth of his hand left her body as he started to work the ties of his braies.

Curiosity perked her up a little, as she looked down just in time to see him free himself. *Good God!* She flicked her tongue nervously over her lip as she took in the thick column of flesh that seemed even bigger and more powerful than when she'd been holding him. It might have been carved from marble, it was just as shiny, polished, and perfectly formed as the rest of him.

He made a tortured sound low in his throat. "Keep looking at me like that, sweetheart, and this is going to be over before it has started."

She didn't know what he meant, but it sounded like she was doing something right. "Do you like it when I look at you?"

He bit out a laugh, mumbled something like "hell yes," and then looked at her with that bone-melting, knee-weakening smile of his that had probably felled more hearts than she wanted to think about—including her own—and answered simply, "Aye."

A wicked and, she suspected, very cat-like gleam came to her eye. "You liked it when I touched you also, didn't you? Can I do it again?"

He swore, and seemingly incapable of saying anything else, he nodded. She wrapped her hand around him, momentarily shocked by the warmth and velvety softness, which seemed impossible given how hard he was. He was like marble all right, with a thin, velvety layer on top. But hot marble with a life beating underneath.

"Does it hurt?"

"God, no."

The muscles in his stomach and arms holding him over her tensed as she started to explore his length, tentatively at first and then with growing boldness as his increasingly strained growls of pleasure encouraged her. She wanted to grip him, so she did, and the results were rather spectacular. His expression transformed into something so rapturous, she felt like a goddess.

After moving her hand up and down a few times the way he'd shown her how to do before, however, she felt his hand clamp down on hers.

"No more." His jaw was clenched, his gaze was distant yet his eyes were full of concentration, and every muscle of his body seemed drawn up tight like he was fighting some kind of secret battle.

She pulled her hand away. "Did I do something wrong?"

His gaze met hers. "What you are doing is perfect. But I want to make this last, and if you keep doing that, I'm not going to be able to do that."

She didn't know what he meant, but the admission made her heart swell and her body go soft all over. She smiled, reached up, circled her hands around his neck, and dragged his mouth down to hers.

It was as if a dam had burst. All the passion he'd been holding back as he brought her pleasure came rushing out in a torrent of raw need. His body came down hard on top of hers. Instinctively, she wrapped her legs around his as he settled himself between her legs and kissed her.

It seemed the most natural thing to have him on top of her. To have their bodies stretched together, legs twined, chest to chest, hip to hip. To have the thick, solid weight of him wedged between her thighs.

Good lord, he felt good. *Everything* felt good.

The sensations built again. Faster and hotter this time, as she now knew where it was leading. He was kissing her so perfectly, with long, deep strokes of his tongue that beckoned to a primitive place inside her. Her hips started to lift and circle against him. Her body started to tingle. The need for friction and pressure grew at a frenzied pace. She grabbed hold of his shoulders as if he were a rock to anchor her in the storm building around her.

But he pulled her back before she broke apart again. "Not yet. I want to be inside you this time."

Her chemise was twisted around her legs, and it took him a moment to find the edge to lift it.

"This damned thing is in my way." He gave her a boyishly impatient look. "Next time it's coming off."

Despite the blush that rose to her cheeks at the thought of being naked in front of him, she couldn't help but smile. *Next time.*

Positioning himself between her legs, his eyes held hers. She couldn't have spoken if she wanted to. The emotion of the moment had not only swelled her heart, it had also swelled her throat.

She'd dreamed about this for so long, but never had she imagined it would be so perfect.

"It might hurt a little," he warned.

But the warning was lost in the storm of sensation that followed, as the thick head of his manhood started to nudge inside her with a gentle rocking motion of his hips. He moved like a dream. It felt like a dream. The connection was everything she'd imagined and more. She felt possessed. Claimed. Filled. Bound to him in a primitive way that could never be undone.

But it wasn't without some discomfort.

"God, you feel so good," he said tightly, his gaze once again filled with intense concentration. He was being gentle with her—patient—and clearly it wasn't easy for him.

"Good" wasn't the word she would use. He felt . . . big.

As in "perhaps he was the wrong size for her" big. She tensed as her body struggled to take him in.

"Almost there, sweetheart. God, I'm sorry . . ."

She didn't need to ask for what. He held her gaze and gave one last determined push. She gasped, not only at the sensation of him seated fully inside her, but at the sharpness of the pinch.

Hurt a little? Her body screeched at the invasion.

But not for long. He started to kiss her again, murmuring all these sweet things against her mouth and near her ear—which tickled and made her shiver at the same time—about how he was sorry, how it would go away, and how he was going to make her feel good—really good.

He was right.

After a few minutes she forgot about the pain, and no longer felt like a wall that had had its defenses breached with a battering ram. The tension eased with his tender kisses and words, and discomfort was replaced by something else—arousal. A small flutter at first, and then a much larger one as he started to move. Slow and easy in the beginning, getting her used to the motion, and then a little harder and deeper.

He was kissing her still, his body sliding over hers with each stroke. The feel of all that radiating masculine power, all that strength, moving over her—inside her—was incredible. It made her want to move with him.

Which she did. Much, apparently, to his approval. Aye, she could hear the sounds of just how much he liked it with every thrust of his hips, marked by a fierce grunt that sent a wicked shiver of pleasure slithering down her spine.

She'd expected the intimacy and connection—though hadn't realized the intensity—but she'd never realized how *physical* lovemaking would be. Not unlike the training she did in the yard. The more of her body she put into it, the better it felt.

He was working hard, too. His body was warm and

slick with exertion—and getting warmer and slicker by the minute. Surprisingly, she liked it. She liked feeling his muscles bunch under her hands as he thrust into her, she liked bracing herself to absorb the impact, and she liked feeling the fiery heat of his passion under her fingertips.

He even smelled good. Of course he did, she thought with a smile. Even sweat smelled clean on Gregor MacGregor. The heat only seemed to enhance the subtle masculine spice of his skin. It made her want to press her nose against him and inhale, letting the arousing scent pour over her.

He looked so dark and fierce, and so incredibly gorgeous, that when their eyes met—and held—her heart squeezed with so much happiness, the poignancy was so sharp and intense it was almost painful.

He was beautiful, what he was doing to her was beautiful, and she loved him so much it hurt.

He must have recognized the look because his gaze softened.

"Are you all right?"

She smiled. "Better than all right. It feels amazing."

"Just wait," he said with a slow smile. "It's about to get even better."

She knew he was a man she could rely on. He was good to his word.

He slowed his thrusts, moving his hips in a long, circular stroke that started out slow and easy, and then went faster and deeper, making her moan every time their bodies came together and sending a fresh wave of sensation tingling between her legs.

God, he was incredible. His body was like an instrument of pleasure, every move, every stroke, calculated to hit the perfect note.

He knew exactly how to bring her pleasure, and he did—almost more than she could take. She could hear the music building in her ears. The beating of her heart, the quickening of her breath, the echo of their moans as they pounded together toward the final beat. Toward one spectacular crescendo.

"Oh God!" he bit out between gritted teeth.

Their eyes met. She saw the exultation fill his gaze at the same moment the sensation claimed her. Their bodies stiffened together in that one timeless pause before breaking apart in a shattering ray of stars and light. Their cries weaved and tangled together, as a hot rush of pleasure came over them in wave after powerful wave.

When the sensation finally ebbed, it was as if every ounce of energy and emotion had been wrung out of her. Spent and exhausted, Cate curled herself into the warmth of his body and like a well-fed, contented cat, promptly fell asleep.

It took Gregor a moment to realize where he was. The last thing he remembered before closing his eyes was thinking how ironic it was that the first time he actually wouldn't mind hearing how wonderful (explosive, mind-blowing, and earth-shattering also seemed appropriate) their lovemaking had been, the lass snuggled up against him had fallen into the sleep of the dead. When he opened his eyes in the cool, dark chamber, the warm presence at his side was gone.

Where the hell did she go? He looked around in confusion and disbelief, followed quickly by irritation. Bloody hell, didn't she know it was rude to slip out of bed and run away without saying something first? Something like "Thanks for the most incredible night of my life, Gregor," or "You were amazing, Gregor," or "I love you, Gregor." Aye, especially that. He rather thought he would like to hear it again, especially when he was feeling so contented. Nay, not contented, *happy.* Maybe happier than he'd ever been in his life.

Making love to Cate had been every bit as incredible as

he'd thought it would be physically, but it had gone beyond that. *Far* beyond that, taking him to a place he'd never been before. A place where he'd like to be holding her in his arms right now!

Minutes passed—at least twenty of them. Bloody hell, where was she? If anyone should be sneaking away in the darkness, it should be him. This was her room, damn it!

He'd tossed off the bedsheets and was starting to look around the floor for his braies when the door opened. He straightened and turned, seeing the object of his irritation shadowed in the doorway, frozen in her tracks. She seemed surprised, but he wasn't sure whether it was at seeing him awake or the fact that he was standing naked in her room.

He rather suspected it was the latter when after the stunned pause, she made no secret of her interest—her *great* interest—in every facet of his body. Good God, the lass shouldn't look at him like that unless she was prepared to act on all that lust she was casting in his direction. He was liable to forget that he needed to leave, and that she was probably in no condition to be ravished after the ravishing of the night before.

Her face fell as he drew on his braies. "You're leaving? You can't go yet."

The vehemence of her protest took an edge off some of the sting of waking up to find her gone. "It will be morning soon. Where were you?"

She frowned, catching something in his tone. Closing the door behind her, she walked toward him. "I'm sorry if I woke you. I tried to be quiet." She bit her lip, heat rising up her cheeks. "I needed to use the garderobe."

"You were gone a long time."

That probably wasn't the most delicate thing he'd ever said in his life, but damn it, this was a new experience for him, and he was feeling . . .

Uncertain. As if he were sailing in unchartered waters. He'd never been in a situation like this before. A situation where he needed to know that everything was all right. Nay, better than all right. He needed to know that she was all right, that he hadn't hurt her, that it had been just as incredible for her as it had been for him.

The heat in her cheeks deepened. "There was some blood. I used a cloth and the pitcher of water in your room, so as to not disturb you. Did I do something wrong? Are you angry with me about something?" Her mouth trembled as she looked up at him.

"Ah, Christ," he said, drawing her into his arms. The feeling of warmth and contentment that he'd missed upon waking returned instantly. He was acting like a scorned lass. "I'm sorry. Nothing is wrong, and of course I'm not angry with you." He tipped her chin, bringing her luminous eyes to his. "What would I have to be angry with you about?"

She gnawed on that wickedly crimson bottom lip a few more times before responding. "I thought you might be regretting what . . . what we did."

His gaze held hers intently. "I don't regret anything that happened last night." His thumb caressed the part of her lip that had just been bitten. "How could I?"

The smile started out slow, but it didn't take long to light her whole face. The warmth radiated inside him as well.

"I'm glad. It was . . . wonderful," she finished with a sigh. Her grin turned cheeky. "I guess I'd forgotten how cranky you can be in the morning."

He drew back. "Cranky? I'm not cranky."

She arched one delicate, dark brow.

All right, well, maybe he was occasionally—though very rarely—a little out of sorts in the morning. But not today. "I just wasn't expecting to wake up alone."

The second brow shot up to join the other, this time in surprise. "What did you think, that I'd skulked away in shame and left you?"

He frowned—darkly. "Of course not."

"You did!" Amusement danced in her eyes. "You did think that." She put the back of her hand up against her forehead in mock horror. "The most handsome man in Scotland abandoned in bed, what has the world come to?"

His eyes narrowed with warning at her teasing. "Christ, not you, too! I wish I knew who'd come up with that ridiculous moniker, so I could devise some kind of horrible torture to return the favor."

She laughed, lifted up on her toes, and pressed a soft kiss on his mouth. The easy display of affection surprised him. But he suspected he might be able to get used to it.

"Poor Gregor. I'm sure it's been horrible having women falling at your feet all the time."

He grinned wryly. "Aye, well, maybe it wasn't so bad *all* the time, but you haven't met Hawk."

"Who?"

Hell, he'd spoken without thinking. He'd relaxed his guard, he realized. It probably should bother him more than it did, but he trusted her. Cate was entirely without artifice and didn't have a deceitful bone in her body—it was what made her so different, and what drew him to her. She was real. He didn't need to worry about games or ploys or manipulations.

"A friend," he said, waving off the subject.

Instinctively, his hand had slid around her waist when she'd kissed him, but having that warm, taut body pressed against him was beginning to take its toll. He let her go and stepped back. "I should go."

"No, not yet." She had that crushed, disappointed look on her face that hit him squarely between the ribs. "It isn't morning. Can't you stay a little longer?"

Not if he didn't want to make her more sore than she already must be. His gaze flickered to the bed, an unconscious indication of the direction of his thoughts. The smile that crept up her features this time was decidedly more sensual and scheming. Her hands came up slowly over his naked chest to loop around his neck. Her body slid up against him like a wildcat, sleek and dangerous— and every bit as deadly. Especially the pointy nipples stabbing him in the chest. They killed him.

She circled her hips against him. "Please, don't go."

Perhaps she had more artifice than he realized. Who the hell would have guessed she could play the seductive siren? But play it well, she did. He was good and seduced.

She peeked up at him naughtily from under her lashes. "Didn't you say something about my chemise next time?"

He really had to stop swearing around her so much, but the lass really knew how to push him in all the right places.

He could push a few of his own. Pushing her back on the bed, he ripped the offending garment away to reveal a body that had every right to be worshipped.

He'd never seen another woman so perfectly formed. She was all long, lean muscle, slender and strong, with little extra flesh to mar the graceful, feminine lines. For despite the obvious strength in her limbs, she was undeniably feminine with gently curved hips, delicately rounded breasts, and a lush little bottom with an expertly placed dimple or two.

He told her exactly how beautiful she was in words, and then with his mouth and tongue. The feel of her coming apart against his mouth drove him wild. He hadn't intended to take her again, but she had other ideas and didn't seem to mind too much—especially when he was deep inside her, and she was crying his name and begging him to go harder, as he pounded and shuddered inside her.

It would have been perfect if a moment after rolling off her, his brother hadn't come bursting through the door, "Cate, you—"

Seeing them on the bed, John stopped dead in his tracks. Shock was followed by a look of condemnation that made Gregor feel all the guilt that he probably should have felt much earlier.

Fifteen

"You bastard!"

Instinctively Gregor blocked Cate behind him, as if he could somehow shield her from the unpleasantness of the situation.

It would have been bad enough with just John as witness, but his brother hadn't come barging in alone. Ete and Lizzie were standing behind him. Unlike his brother, however, they were considerate enough to back away quickly and not stand there radiating condemnation.

Not that it wasn't deserved, damn it. But Gregor didn't want Cate to accidentally get in the way of anger that should be directed toward him, and him alone.

"I will see you in the solar," Gregor said pointedly.

John ignored him, taking another step into the room, every muscle in his body flaring with outrage. "How could you do this?" He must not have expected Gregor to answer because he immediately added, "You'll damn well marry her. Even if I have to drag you to the church door myself."

Cate made her first sound since her initial gasp on the door opening. "No, John—"

Gregor cut her off with a squeeze of her hand that rested on the bed between them. "Your escort won't be necessary, brother. I have every intention of marrying her."

"You do?" Cate said at the same time as John—with equal surprise.

Gregor ignored his brother and looked at the wide-eyed woman nestled beside him, clutching the bed linens to her neck with her dark hair tumbling wildly around her bare shoulders, looking wonderfully—thoroughly—debauched. Her eyes were pinned on his, searchingly. A wave of tenderness rose inside him.

Tucking a lock of hair that always seemed to be in her face behind her ear, he nodded. "Aye, if my clod of a brother here hadn't interrupted, you would have had a proper proposal." This time John took the hint. But he didn't go without a look that promised this wasn't over. Gregor turned back to Cate when the door had closed behind him. "Surely you could not have thought otherwise?"

His honor demanded it. He'd known that before he'd made love to her and realized what he would have to do.

But he knew it wasn't just honor at stake. He cared about her—more than he'd thought possible. Enough to try to be the kind of man she thought him to be.

She blushed, casting her gaze down in a way that suggested that was exactly what she'd thought. He tilted her chin, forcing her gaze back to his.

"I didn't know what to think," she admitted. "You've made your feelings about marriage quite clear."

A wry smile pulled one corner of his mouth up. "Aye, well, it seems I've been good and trapped this time."

The color drained from her face in a sheet of white. "T-trapped? I didn't mean . . . Oh God, do you think I meant . . . ?"

He grinned. Damn, she was cute. Of course he hadn't thought that. Cate was far too straightforward and honest to do something so underhanded. If he thought she'd had an ulterior motive when she'd touched him last night, he would have walked away. It was ironic that he'd finally found himself in the exact situation he'd always wanted to avoid—being "caught" in bed with an innocent—and he didn't mind at all. The public discovery of what he'd done had only hastened the inevitable.

"You don't need to look so horrified—I was just jesting. Although if I'd known how enjoyable it could be to be trapped into marriage, I might not have resisted for so long."

His levity didn't seem to help. Her smile seemed forced, and her color had turned from pallid white to ill-looking gray.

Suddenly he sobered, realizing why. Christ, he was an unfeeling arse! What had just happened had no doubt been traumatic for her. Of course she wouldn't be ready to jest when his brother had just walked in on them *in flagrante delicto*.

The lass was an innocent maid—or at least had been a few hours ago. She was probably properly mortified. As he should be, and would be, if he weren't so damned *happy*. Aye, he was happy. He hadn't thought she existed, but he'd found a woman who cared about *him,* and not all the superficial shite that other women couldn't seem to look beyond.

He leaned over, cupped the side of her face, and kissed the worry gently from her mouth. By the time he was done, she was lying back on the bed and he was on his side with her tucked against him again—exactly where she belonged.

He lifted his head. Her eyes fluttered open, meeting his.

"You haven't given me your answer," he pointed out. "Although I supposed I never asked you a question. I will get down on my knee, if you like, but it feels a little silly in my current state of dress." And his current state of arousal.

Her cheeks warmed with a soft pink blush, and she consciously or unconsciously—he didn't care which—rubbed against him. "Where you are is just fine."

Where he was was about a hair's breadth from rolling on top of her, spreading her thighs with his, and sinking into her for the third time. That would be a proposal to remember.

His hunger for her hadn't diminished any; if anything, it had only grown more ravenous and insatiable. What had she done to him? Not only had she turned him into a debaucher of virgins, but also a brutish ill-user of one.

His throat was surprisingly tight when he took her chin in his hand and caressed the velvety-soft skin that bore a faint burn from the scratch of his jaw. "Cate, will you do me the honor of being my wife?"

Cate blinked back tears. This couldn't be happening. Gregor MacGregor, the man she'd been in love with for five long years, was leaning over her *in bed,* his tawny hair slumped rakishly across the face that had launched a thousand hearts if not ships, looking at her with a gentleness in his eyes she could never have imagined, and asking her to marry him.

Someone wake me up. For surely, I must be dreaming.

But she wasn't. This was really happening. Everything she'd ever wanted was waiting for her to reach out and take it. To say yes.

But she couldn't—not without being sure of his motivation.

His jest earlier had sent a chill through her veins, reminding her of the conversation she'd had with Seonaid and the thoughtless boast she'd made. She'd been certain that Gregor would marry her because he loved her, not because she'd intended to force him into anything. But she recalled with vivid detail the way she'd boldly—brazenly— touched him. She'd wanted to stop him from leaving, aye, but she hadn't been trying to trap him. Nor could she have known John would come bursting into her room so early like that.

A small furrow of concern gathered between his brows.

"I'd rather hoped my question wouldn't require that much thinking."

She took a deep breath. She had to know. "Why do you wish to marry me, Gregor?"

The furrow deepened. "I would have thought after last night that was obvious."

It wasn't; that was the problem. Was it simply the fact that he'd taken her innocence or was it because he cared about her? The word she most dreaded hearing right now was "honor."

"I'm not a lady, Gregor. You know the manner of my birth. You do not need to marry me if you do not wish to do so." She drew a pained breath through hot lungs. "My father will not come storming your gate with his sword drawn, demanding satisfaction."

His face darkened. "He should. He should be drawn and quartered for leaving you like that. What kind of man—"

"Please, Gregor, I don't want to speak of him—*ever*."

She glanced away, unable to meet his gaze. His outrage on her behalf raised a question she didn't want to ask herself. *It doesn't matter,* she told herself. But what if it did? For the first time, the secret that she was keeping from him felt like a secret and not an irrelevant fact to be pushed under the bed and forgotten like her gown.

He took her chin and forced her gaze back to his. His expression wasn't just dark now, it was also angry. "Do you think the manner of your birth makes any difference to me?"

"Maybe it should. It will to your family. What will your uncle say? No doubt the chief has expectations for you. You have a duty to marry—"

"You know I don't give a shite about any of that. I'll do my duty to my uncle without being bartered to the highest bidder. My position in the king's army will be enough. What's this really about, Cate? I thought you wanted to marry me. I thought you loved me."

"I do . . . I do." That was the problem. "But I don't want you to feel honor-bound or compelled into anything."

"Look at me, sweetheart." She did as he asked. "Hear me well. I knew *exactly* what I was doing last night, and what it meant. I am honor-bound to marry you, aye, but I wanted to marry you before I made love to you."

Her heart seemed to be coming out her throat. "You did?"

"Aye, I care about you, and I'm going to do my damnedest to be the kind of man you deserve." He stroked her chin with his thumb again, then moved it up to play over her lip. "Now will you answer me?"

She smiled, tears of happiness brimming in her eyes. "Yes. Yes, I'll marry you."

His growl of something like "it's about damned time" was lost, as he rolled on top of her and covered her mouth with his.

He spent the next hour telling her without words exactly how much he wanted to marry her. He did protest at a key moment about not wanting to hurt her, but she decided to take matters into her own hands, so to speak. She was becoming quite good with them—if his reaction was anything to go by.

Cate had never been happier in her life. The news of their betrothal was announced at the midday meal and was greeted with a resounding roar of approval. The litany of toasts and cheering that followed turned into a spontaneous celebration with copious amounts of wine, *cuirm*, dancing, and later a few bawdy tunes that made even her ears blush.

Given that it was Christmas Eve tomorrow and they were still in Advent, she was sure the church wouldn't approve of the merrymaking, but Father Roland did appear to be having a good time.

Gregor took all the ribbing and congratulations with a

satisfied, almost smug grin that, when coupled with his unusual attentiveness, put her last doubts to rest. He truly seemed to *want* to marry her. For all intents and purposes he was acting like a man in love, and she couldn't help but wonder whether those feelings that she'd always known were there might finally be ready to reveal themselves.

About the only person who didn't seem happy was Pip. He'd disappeared not long after the announcement, and it wasn't until later that evening that she found him waiting outside the door to her chamber.

"You can't marry him!" he burst out, his dark, overlarge features twisted with a bevy of emotions that ranged from a very manly rage to childish frustration, an accurate reflection of his on-the-cusp-but-not-quite-a-man state.

The swelling in his nose had receded considerably, but there were still black marks under his eyes from the beating he'd suffered at the hands of Dougal MacNab.

A heavy flop of dark hair hung in his eyes. She'd told him after their last practice session to cut it, but it seemed he hadn't gotten around to it yet. He would—when it hampered his vision one too many times.

So far she'd introduced him to sword fighting, archery, and some of the hand-to-hand combat moves she'd learned from John. He hadn't shown great promise in any one discipline, but he was enthusiastic, a quick learner, and a hard worker. All of which spoke well for future accomplishment. He was also stubborn like her, which prevented him from giving up.

Unfortunately, however, that same stubbornness that helped him drag himself out of the mud during practice also made him dig in his heels where Gregor was concerned.

She pressed her lips together in a hard line. Gregor might have made her happier than any woman ought to be, but that didn't mean she didn't wish she could throttle him for a thing or two—Pip being foremost among them. Gregor and Pip had gotten off to a horrible start—in large part due to Gregor's insensitive handling of the boy's situation—but she was determined that would change. They would come to care for one another, even if it killed her.

Ushering Pip inside the chamber, she motioned for him to take a seat on a stool by the brazier. She sat on the bed opposite him and tried to soothe his hurt by calmly responding to his demand. "I know you are not fond of the laird—"

"I hate him!" Pip cut her off virulently. His eyes glinted with proof of his words. "He wasn't supposed to marry you. He was supposed to leave. Men like him always leave."

Cate sensed something important lurking behind his words. She'd assumed that Pip had never known his father—he had professed him to be Gregor, after all—but he spoke as if from experience.

Her heart went out to him. She knew how horrible it was to have one parent abandon you; how much worse it must be to have two. She would know the truth eventually, but she would wait until he trusted her enough to tell it.

"Pip," she said patiently, "you barely know him."

"I know all I need to know," he said with a belligerent thrust of his chin. "I saw the way he was looking at you last night in your chamber when you had a nightmare; I knew what he was going to do. He hurt you!"

Cate was shocked—and embarrassed—by how much the boy had guessed. "He didn't hurt me, Pip," she said quietly.

His mouth drew in a tight line. "I might be a bastard, but I know that what he did was wrong. I know all about him. I know how many women he takes to his bed. Why do you think my mother—"

He stopped, staring at her with wide, horror-struck eyes.

"Why do I think your mother what?" she asked gently.

His face crumpled, and tears he was valiantly trying to hold at bay shone hotly in his eyes. "You're going to hate me, and want to send me away just like him. He knows—or thinks he knows."

"Knows what, Pip?"

The whole sordid tale burst out in a wave of tears and choking apologies. Apparently, his mother, who had been ill-used and then discarded by one of the MacGregor tacksmen a few years after Pip's birth, had seen the money he'd sent to her every month to care for the child end on his death about six months ago. Pip had tried to do odd jobs to make money, but whatever he made was barely enough to pay for his mother's ale, let alone keep them fed and clothed as well.

Turned to bitterness and drink, his mother had begun concocting wild stories about his father, until it seemed even she believed them. Unable to feed them both, she'd forced Pip to go to the man who'd bedded so many women, saying, "Why couldn't he have been your father?" Pip had gone along with it because he'd expected to be turned away at the door. He'd never imagined Cate would take pity on him.

He'd wanted to tell her the truth, but he'd been scared that she would send him away. When his mother found out he'd been taken in—and how well he was being treated— she'd demanded he give her money or she would take him from his new home.

About halfway through the story, Cate had taken him in her arms, holding those scrawny shoulders with all the affection she'd been wanting to show him from the first. She heard what he wasn't saying as well. His mother's abuse had been physical as well.

By the time he was done, they were both shaking: Pip with sobs, and Cate with outrage. She'd known there would be a story, and it would be an ugly one, but what kind of woman could do that to her child? Cate didn't care what she'd been through, or how mired she was in her drunkenness—it was inexcusable. Poor Pip.

"I'm sorry," he choked out. "I'm sorry for lying to you and not telling you the truth. But I knew you'd send me away."

"I have no intention of sending you anywhere, Pip. This is your home."

He pulled back and looked up at her as if she were either deaf or addled. "Didn't you just hear what I said?"

She nodded. "I heard you perfectly."

"But you're marrying *him;* he won't let me stay." He paused, a gleam in his dark eyes. "Maybe you can marry John instead?"

Cate fought a smile, but she returned his earnestness with her own. "But I don't love John; I love Gregor."

His face fell. "You do?"

She nodded.

He didn't hide his distaste. "Does he love you?"

How like a young person to get right to the heart of the matter. She didn't blame him for asking it, when she wondered as much herself. Sometimes it was a little difficult to conceive. "I think so, but I don't think he realizes it yet. Gregor does not form attachments easily."

Pip's eyes narrowed. "Why? What's wrong with him?"

She smiled. "Nothing more than a healthy case of cynicism. He's had so many women offering him their hearts for the wrong reasons, he's become jaded. He does not trust easily," she added. Thinking of Isobel and what happened with his brother, perhaps it was understandable. To say he'd erected defensive walls around himself was putting it mildly.

Pip didn't look convinced.

"Give him a chance, Pip—you'll see. He won't let us down."

Sixteen

❧

It was just before midnight on Christmas Eve when Gregor finally climbed the stairs to his chamber. Between the long masses of the season and his duties as laird, it had been a tiresome day.

He forced his gaze away from the door on the left, but not before noticing the tempting glow of candlelight spilling out from underneath.

She was awake. Knowing that, and how close she was, sure as hell didn't make it easy to do the right thing.

He wasn't a lad in the first throes of passion, damn it— even if she made him feel like one. He could wait until they were married to have her in his bed. God knew, she could probably use the time to recover from the other night.

But he had a feeling it was going to be a very long twelve nights. Assuming he could secure a dispensation with the king's help from Lamberton, the Bishop of St. Andrews, Gregor hoped to marry Cate on January fifth—Twelfth Night—the day marking the end to the winter festival on the eve of the Epiphany.

He could have waited the three weeks for the banns to be read, but with Bruce expected to call him back in early January for the siege on Perth Castle, that would mean delaying their wedding until the next time he could return home.

That he would not countenance. Cate was his, and he wanted it to be true in fact as well as in deed.

He'd never imagined that he would be the one making haste to the altar. But it was as if once the last hurdle in his mind had been cleared, there was nothing stopping him from seeing what he wanted: Cate as his wife, standing beside him in the day and sleeping beside him at night. Although there probably wouldn't be much sleeping for a while.

Just thinking about what he'd like to be doing to her right now was enough to make him hot, hard, and frustrated. It was her fault for being so damned responsive and uninhibited. She made love just like she did everything else: no holds barred, without pretense or artifice and with unbridled passion.

With a little experience . . .

God help him! He didn't even want to think about it. She could bring him to his knees.

Perhaps she already had. What he felt for her was like nothing he'd ever felt for a woman before.

Did he love her? He didn't know if he was capable of that kind of emotion. But her belief in him made him want to be the kind of man who could stay by the hearth, and maybe for now that was enough.

He closed the door, putting temptation firmly behind him. Barely a moment passed, however, before he heard a soft knock. Steeling himself, he opened the door. As he'd expected, Cate stood there in her dressing robe.

"You're up late," she said.

"I could say the same for you."

"I was waiting for you."

His mouth quirked. "So I gathered. But you shouldn't be here."

"I know," she said with a cheeky smile, flouncing in anyway. "But it's been so busy the past couple of days, I haven't had a chance to talk with you alone, and I wanted to give you something."

Suddenly, he noticed the way she was holding her robe

tightly in front of her chest as if she were hiding something. Something like a naked body? His eyes must have flared.

She rolled her eyes, guessing his train of thought, and laughed. "I'm afraid I'm wearing a very thick, very old chemise under here, given what happened to the last one."

He grinned. "I'll buy you a dozen chemises."

She quirked a brow. "The more to rip apart?"

"How did you guess?"

She laughed and opened her gown. "Sorry to disappoint you, but that isn't what I brought you." Taking out the linen bundle that had been tucked in front of her, she handed it to him. "It's this—for Christmas," she explained.

"What is it?"

"Why don't you open it and see?"

After untying the strand of silk ribbon she'd wrapped around the bundle, he carefully unfolded the linen, revealing a linen tunic embroidered with scrollwork in gold and scarlet thread around the neck and—when he held it up—sleeves. Inspecting the embroidery closer, he realized the design wasn't scrolls as he originally thought. "They're arrows," he said, stunned.

She blushed, nodding. "It's to wear under your armor."

It was perfect—he couldn't believe how perfect. He was touched. The stitches were exquisite. He frowned. "You did this?"

His voice must have revealed his surprise.

"I *do* know how to sew."

He lifted a brow. They both knew she found needlework torturous.

"Well, I do." She wrinkled her nose. "Very well, Ete did most of it. But I did come up with the design. And I did this part right here." She pointed to the back of the collar, where the stitches were quite a bit more uneven.

He grinned and pulled her up in his arms. "It's perfect. Thank you."

He kissed her. Softly at first, and then, as always seemed to happen, with far more passion than he'd intended. When he drew back, they were both breathing hard. It took her eyes a moment to focus. His bed loomed too damned close. It would be so easy to push her back . . .

"I have something else for you as well," she said.

"Hiding other treasures under that gown, Caty?"

She laughed. "You never know. But this one is under the bed." When he drew back, she explained. "John helped me carry it up here earlier."

He bent down and dragged out another bundle, this one sturdy, about six feet long, six inches in diameter, and wrapped not in linen, but in hides of leather. "What do you have in here, a caber?"

"Close."

He flipped back the hides and stared in stunned silence at the gift at his feet. He couldn't believe what he was seeing. Bending down, he inspected it closer, paying particular attention to the unblemished grain from end to end. There wasn't a knot or twist in sight.

Unbelievable. Maybe she was the one who should be called a sorcerer. How else could she have procured such a treasure?

She watched him with increasing anxiousness, her hands twisting in her ruby-colored, velvet dressing robe. "It's a stave of yew," she said, obviously worried by his silence.

He knew exactly what it was. It wasn't just a stave of yew; it was a nearly flawless stave of yew. The kind of flawless that was perfect for making a bow and had been nearly impossible to find since the war broke out. With the demand for bows so high, much of the good yew had been felled in both Scotland and England.

His voice was low and full of awe that bordered on reverence. "Where did you get this?"

"From the merchant who brings your wines from Bordeaux."

Gregor frowned. "He told me he couldn't find anything like this."

She grinned. "Well, I encouraged him to look a little harder." Gregor knew better than to ask how. "The opening of the trade routes has helped. It comes from Spain and was cut last winter, so it will only need a bit more seasoning."

He didn't say anything. He was too overwhelmed to do anything other than stare at what had to be the most generous, thoughtful gift he'd ever received.

"Do you like it?"

The uncertainty in her voice knocked him from his stupor. "I love it. I don't know what do say."

She beamed. Lifting on her tiptoes, she slid her arms around his neck. "Perhaps you might think of another way to thank me?"

His arm slid around her waist, as if there was no other place it belonged. "I was trying to be good."

Her dark eyes danced with golden sparks of mischief in the candlelight. "You are good." Her hips rubbed teasingly against his. "Very, *very* good."

"Naughty lass." He gave her bottom a little swat. "What am I going to do with you?"

"I can think of a few things, and I'm sure you could help me think of a few more that I've never tried before."

He groaned, feeling the heat swell in his groin. He sure as hell could. Would he shock her with his requests? Probably, but knowing Cate it would not be for long. He'd been fantasizing about her mouth on him for too long. Just the thought of it was enough to make him hard as a rock.

"You sure know how to shoot my good intentions to hell."

Her eyes lit up excitedly. "I do?"

He nodded and kissed her again. "I used to have a little self-control."

He slid his hands under the shoulders of her robe to slide

it off. She had already started to work the ties of his *cotun* but smiled up at him. "And you don't now?"

"Apparently not where you are concerned."

To prove it, he ripped the chemise she was wearing right off her. It was old, plain, and in his way.

"Gregor!" she screeched, still shy enough to try to cover herself. But the lass had absolutely nothing to hide—nothing. "Not another one," she groaned. "I will have nothing left to wear."

"What a pity. I suppose I will just have to keep you naked in my bed."

He stopped further protests by jerking his tunic over his head, pulling off his boots, and quickly dispensing with his breeches.

She stared at him, taking in every inch of his nakedness. He'd never been self-conscious in his life, but standing there while she studied him came pretty damn close. He wanted her approval. When she eventually looked up at him, it was clear he had it—and more. She was looking at him as if she couldn't wait to devour him. "Tell me what do to. Tell me how to please you."

"You already do."

Just standing there she brought him to his knees. She was adorable—small, compact, and strong, with the sleek grace of a wildcat. Outwardly unimposing but dangerous, with the raw instincts of a fighter. She made every other woman who'd come before her seem flimsy and insubstantial.

She blushed. "I know men prefer more curves, but your mother said I scared them all away on the practice yard, and I was doomed to be as thin as a bowstring."

He chuckled. "Sweetheart, my mother didn't have any idea what men prefer." Her body was toned and sensual, and so damned arousing, he suspected that one day strength and firmness of flesh in women would become prized. "Besides, I have always preferred a bow." He held her gaze. "You are perfect. So perfect that I'm going to have to insist you spend much more time practicing all those hand-to-hand combat moves—although not on the practice yard."

Her brows drew together. "Then wh—?"

She didn't have a chance to finish her question before he catapulted her back on his bed and pinned her with his body.

She gasped with surprise, and then smiled. "There is one problem with your plan."

He lifted a brow challengingly. "What's that?"

"What if I don't want to get up? What if I like it exactly where I am?" She moved her hips so his erection fit snugly between her legs, the fat head nudging temptingly at her entrance. He rocked his hips a little, teasing her until her breath quickened with those throaty little gasps that drove him wild.

"Oh, I think you'll want to get up, Caty." He sunk in just a little, letting her take him in an inch or two before retreating. He felt her shudder with need, and it took every bit of his control not to sink in deep and give it all to her. "Weren't you talking about learning new things? I didn't think you were a quitter."

He'd known she wouldn't be able to resist that taunt. Just as he knew as soon as he gave her an opening he would be on his back.

He was—and more aroused than he could stand. The lass gave new meaning to the word "bedsport." He had a feeling making love with Cate was going to be an entirely different experience—and one that would keep him on his toes for a while.

Maybe forever.

For once he did not push the thought away. He let it sit there, getting used to it.

"Now what?" she asked, looking down at him from her perch lying on top of him. His heartbeat jammed in his chest. Everything seemed to stop. She looked so damned sweet and yet so unconsciously sensual, with her dark eyes fixed on him, her hair tumbling around her shoulders, and her small, pert breasts thrusting proudly in the air. He wanted to hold on to this moment forever.

He drew his hand up to tuck a lock of silky dark hair behind her ear. Cupping her cheek in his hand, he pulled her mouth toward his, kissing her gently, tenderly, with long, slow pulls of his tongue.

But they were both too eager to wait for long.

"Get on your knees and straddle me," he said roughly—huskily.

She looked confused for a minute, but then comprehension dawned. A warm glimmer of understanding spread across her face in a slow smile.

Gregor didn't know whether her quick grasp of the situation should make him curse or drop to his knees in gratitude. How long before she realized who held all the power here?

Not long, if her quick mastery of the position meant anything. She braced her hands on his chest as she moved her hips over him. "Like this?" she said with a slow bob over his erection, which was pounding against his stomach angrily and not in any mood to play games.

Her breasts were too tempting. He had to reach out and cup the firm mounds in his hands, his fingers lightly plying the dark pink tips until they were as hard as two tiny pebbles.

She moaned, arching into his hands, and bobbed over him again, sliding his length between her legs this time, where he could feel the sweet heat and dampness. He made a sound of agonized pleasure and lifted his hips toward the tight, hot glove that he wanted gripping him.

"What do I do?" she asked, her breath uneven.

He could have shown her, but he wanted to let her be in charge and in control of her passion. "Put me inside you."

He groaned when her fingers came around him, and she lifted her hips into position. Every muscle in his body flexed to hold still as she rubbed the heavy head against her slickness, looking for . . .

Oh God, yes. He groaned as she found it and started to lower her body on him, inch by inch. He was slick with sweat and near the end of his rope by the time she was fully impaled.

She drew her hands down the tight bands of his stomach and threw her head back, sinking deeper and savoring the pleasure of their bodies fully joined—connected. "You feel so good," she said. "So big and thick—I love the way you fill me."

He deserved a kingdom at least for not coming right there. The innocently erotic words sent hot bolts of pleasure from the base of his spine to the tip of his cock.

She moved a little and he nearly wept from the effort to stay still. From the effort not to take her hips and slide her up and down on top of him until they were both coming hard.

She was so tight . . .

"Ride me, Cate," he gritted out. It wasn't an order, but more of a plea.

And ride him she did. Slowly and tentatively at first, and then when she found the rhythm, hard and hell-bent for leather.

It felt too good. He could feel the pressure coiling and couldn't take it anymore. He grabbed her hips, digging his fingers into her taut backside, as his body seized. "Oh God, sweetheart, I'm going to—"

She cut him off with her cry, sinking down on him hard. He held her there tight, grounding her against him, letting the hard spasms of her release pull him right over the edge.

He came harder than he'd ever come in his life, shooting his seed deep inside her in a hot rush of blinding pleasure.

When she collapsed on top of him, he had only enough

energy left to roll her to the side and tuck her in against him. He wanted to say something, but all he could think of was a dazed and unimaginative "wow."

She'd brought him to his knees, all right. And it was a damned good place to be.

Cate thought she probably should be embarrassed by her wantonness, but she was too warm and contented—and too wonderfully exhausted—to muster any enthusiasm for the effort. Besides, if she were honest with herself, she wasn't embarrassed at all. She didn't need experience to know that Gregor liked her brazenness and her passion for him.

Ride me. Heat spread over her skin when she thought of how she'd done exactly that. She'd never imagined that kind of freedom—that kind of wildness. It had been incredible. With him inside her, she'd felt powerful enough to storm castles or conquer kingdoms.

She smiled against his chest as her finger absently traced the markings on his arm. It was so different being with him like this. She'd never imagined he could be so lighthearted and playful. He didn't seem remote and untouchable at all, but rather quite wonderfully touchable. She'd never felt closer to anyone in her life.

"What's so amusing?" he asked.

"Nothing," she said, a little embarrassed by how happy she was. "I've never seen a tattoo before. What does it signify? I understand the two crossed arrows behind the shield, but I thought the badge of the MacGregors was a lion's head? The Lion Rampant is the standard of the king." He might have tensed, but she was too busy staring at it. "And what is this design that goes around your arm? It looks like a spiderweb."

He enfolded her hand in his and moved it from his arm to his chest. "So many questions, little one. Aren't you sleepy?"

She propped her chin up on his chest and frowned. "Why do I have the feeling you are trying to avoid my question?"

He held her gaze for a moment in the soft candlelight. He seemed to be debating with himself about something. "You are right; it doesn't have to do with the MacGregors. It's just something I did a while back with some friends of mine."

He tried to dismiss it, but for some reason she sensed it was important to him. "Does it have to do with your role in the king's army?" He looked surprised. "I know you don't like to say anything, but I gather what you do is important."

"I'm a bowman, Cate."

"Aye, but I'd warrant an important one. What exactly *do* you do?"

He paused for so long, she didn't think he was going to answer her. When he spoke, it was carefully. "Sometimes the king needs important targets eliminated. A good marksman can come in handy for that."

She frowned, and then suddenly her eyes widened. "Targets? You mean people?"

He held her gaze, as if steeling himself for her reaction. "Aye. I'm trained to kill, Cate. It's what I do."

He stated it as a fact and without apology, but somehow she knew it wasn't easy for him to admit. "And I'm sure every one of them has been necessary, although I'm sure it doesn't make it any easier."

He looked surprised, as if he'd expected condemnation. He shrugged. "You get used to it."

She suspected he never got used to it at all. But he undoubtedly saw his compassion as a weakness for a warrior, when in fact it only emphasized his humanity. Caring was nothing to be ashamed of.

She'd guessed how much the deaths affected him when she'd realized what the rocks were for. They were his atonement, his acknowledgment of every life that had been taken in the pursuit of Robert the Bruce's ambition.

She thought for a minute. "But what does the tattoo have to do with all of this?"

He sighed and shook his head, smiling. "You are as unrelenting as some warriors I know. I will explain everything to you when we are married."

She liked hearing him say that. "And when will that be?"

"I hope by Twelfth Night. I wrote the king and asked him to help me procure a dispensation." A corner of his mouth lifted. "I wish I could be there to see his reaction. I think Bruce was convinced I'd never find my way willingly to the altar. He'll be disappointed not to be here for the wedding, but I'm sure once Perth is taken he will arrange a great feast at Dunstaffnage."

Cate stiffened. "A *what*?"

He tipped her chin to look at him. "I know you blame the king for what happened, Cate, but that blame is misplaced. He was as devastated by the massacre of your village as he was when news that his wife, daughter, sister, and the Countess of Buchan had been taken reached him. He disappeared into the forest and didn't talk to anyone for days."

Cate refused to allow herself to feel pity for him. She hardened her heart. "Any guilt Robert Bruce felt is deserved. We are all just pawns to a nobleman's ambition. What are the lives of a few villagers in the name of a throne? What is a daughter?" She paused, and quickly added, "Or a wife."

"That isn't Bruce at all, Cate. You don't know him the way I do. He is a great man; there is no one I believe in more. He believed in me when no one else did. When I first came to him, I was young and more braggart and conceited than warrior. But he helped me hone my skills from sport at the Games to the battlefield. He helped make me a warrior."

Cate felt ill. Gregor's admiration for the king went far deeper than she'd realized. God, he almost made him sound like a *father*. And she better than anyone knew the danger in that. She didn't want him to know the same disappointment that she had.

"Scotland needs him. It's staggering to think of what he's already accomplished, and how close we are to victory. Robert the Bruce belongs on the throne, and I will do all in my power to see him there permanently." He took her chin and lifted her face to his. "It's important to me that you give him a fair chance, Cate. Believe me, he never imagined—none of us did—what would happen to your village for helping us."

" 'Us'? You weren't there."

"Two of my closest friends—men I consider brothers— were among the men your village provided shelter to. If you hadn't, they would be dead. They were two of the men who were with me when I found you in the well."

She gazed at him wordlessly. She hadn't realized . . .

"Bruce mourns each loss of life in this war and carries the weight of it with him every day. No one knows more than he does what has been lost in the pursuit of a throne. But it isn't just the three brothers and close friends who he mourns, it's also people like your mother and the other villagers. He was even worried about you, Cate."

Her heart stopped, and then started thudding wildly. Fearing he would notice, she moved off him just enough to break contact. Instantly, she was cold. "Me?"

"Aye, he was very interested in you." Gregor frowned, as if something about the memory bothered him.

"You didn't tell him anything?"

With how anxiously she'd spoken, it was no wonder that he gave her an odd look.

"I told him what I knew at the time: your name and age." He reconsidered. "At least what we thought your age to be, eleven or twelve."

Cate hoped her relief wasn't visible. She'd never expected the king to take a personal interest in her, but it was a good thing that she'd lied about her name—both her names. Bruce wouldn't have known of her mother's second husband. When Bruce left them, her mother had been about to marry her first husband.

Though she wanted to ask more, she feared she'd already said too much. Gregor was too perceptive. She didn't want him to guess that the man he so revered was the same man who'd abandoned her when she was five.

"I was small for my age," she said.

He smiled. "You are still small for your age."

"Big enough to put you on your ar—" She stopped when he gave her a warning glance. "Back," she finished sweetly.

"Aye, well, just don't think the king didn't care. He did. Bruce took the loss of your village very hard. He said it had been some time since he'd visited, but he knew many of the villagers personally." Something seemed to occur to him. "Did you know him, Cate?"

She thought she had. At one time, she'd thought there was no man greater than Robert Bruce, the dashing young Earl of Carrick. But it turned out she hadn't known him at all. The man she'd boasted of as the greatest knight in Christendom had cut her out of his life as thoroughly as if she'd never existed. It wouldn't have been so bad if he hadn't made her love him first. Her heart pinched at the memory of just how much she'd loved the man who'd sired her.

"He came to our village when I was a child," she answered carefully, in what she hoped was a neutral voice.

"And you were not dazzled? I'm surprised. Not many women are immune to the charm of Robert Bruce."

Not many at all. Her mother certainly hadn't been. Cate hadn't been either—at least for a while. And from what she heard, there were at least a few other women with natural children of Bruce who had been quite charmed as well. "Aye, well, maybe it takes a bit more than superficial charms to impress me."

He lifted a brow. "Is that directed at me by any chance?"

She grinned. "Nay, but you might want to keep it in mind. The 'dazzle' of that face is bound to wear off . . . in a dozen years or so."

"Good to know," he said dryly. "And what happens when I need to impress you then?"

She rolled on top of him, savoring the feel of his hard masculine body against hers. "I suspect you will be able to think of a thing or two."

She couldn't believe that husky sound was her voice.

His hand slid down to grip her bottom and fit her snugly against him. Instantly, her body turned hot and liquid. He groaned as he gripped her by the back of her head and kissed her—hard. She reveled in the knowledge that the contact affected him the same way it did her.

She could feel the heat of him growing between her legs, when he suddenly pulled back. "God, you are going to kill me. But you need some sleep. Tomorrow is going to be a long day."

It was Christmas. "You mean today." It had to be well after midnight by now. "Are you sending me back to my room?"

"I'm afraid so, sweeting. I do not want to add to the gossip. In fact, I should probably remove myself to the barracks until we are wed." She must have looked as disappointed as she felt, because he laughed. "It's good to know that I will not be the only one counting the days."

He couldn't have given her a better gift than those off-handed words. "Do you mean it, Gregor? You are looking forward to marrying me?"

His brow furrowed. "I thought we covered this."

"We did. It's just that it's all happened so fast, I feel like

I'm going to wake up and discover you've changed your mind."

He chuckled, brushing the back of his thumb over her bare shoulder. "There is little chance of that. It is you, I hope, who does not come to regret it."

She frowned. "Why would I regret it?"

He paused for a long moment. "I've let a lot of people down in my life, Cate. I don't want to end up doing that to you."

"You won't," she said fiercely. She might not know all the circumstances of his past, but she knew something more important: she knew *him*. Gregor avoided attachment and responsibility away from the battlefield not because he was incapable of it, but because he feared letting people down. But just as the king could count on him, she knew she would count on him, too. He wouldn't let her down.

He laughed and kissed her on the nose. "You remind me of someone when you have that expression on your face. But I can't think of who."

Good thing there wasn't much light in the chamber, because she feared every ounce of color had drained from her face.

Reluctantly, she inched up, clutching the sheeting to her neck, looking for the puddle on the floor that was her robe. "Can you hand me that?"

He sat up, leaned against the wooden panel of the bed, and folded his arms across his chest. She might have noticed the devilish glint in his eyes if she hadn't been so distracted by the bulging muscles of his arms. Good gracious! Her mouth actually seemed to be watering.

"And miss you tumbling out of my bed naked? I don't think so."

She glared at him, ripped the sheet from the bed, and wrapped it around her as she did her best not to "tumble."

He chuckled, obviously amused by her efforts. "Isn't it rather late for modesty? I've seen every inch of you."

She pursed her mouth primly. "Some of us aren't used to walking around stark naked."

He shrugged unrepentantly. "I don't usually get a lot of complaints."

Her eyes narrowed, taking in every inch of a body that could make Adonis weep with envy. *Arrogant rogue.* It was worse because it was warranted. "I bet."

Grabbing the robe from the floor, she purposefully let the sheet drop before securing it in front of her. A quick glance at the thickening column of his manhood made her smile. "Sweet dreams, Gregor."

"Wait." He stood from the bed and thankfully for her peace of mind, drew on his braies. "I have something for you."

She glanced down at his manhood. "I think you already gave it to me."

He grinned appreciatively. "You are turning into quite a wicked lass, Caitrina." She opened her mouth to correct him—*Catherine*—then slammed it shut. She wouldn't disillusion him. He walked to the ambry, opened the door, and retrieved a small wooden box and a leather bag. "I have two gifts for you as well. I was going to give you the first when I came home, but after what happened with Dougal, I wasn't sure whether I should encourage you." He handed her the bag. "Promise me you will not draw this unless you have to."

Knowing he was mostly teasing her, she refrained from arguing about how she "had to" with Dougal. Pulling back the flap of the bag, she retrieved a very thin leather scabbard and what looked to be a small dagger. But it was unlike any dagger she'd ever seen. The blade was about five inches long but it was thin and narrow, coming to a very sharp point. The handle was of horn, and when she put her hand around it, she realized it could have been sized just for her. "I've never seen anything like this," she said.

"A friend of mine made it for me. It's a special kind of dagger." She looked at him questioningly. "It goes through mail," he explained.

Her eyes widened; suddenly the shape of the blade made more sense. It was ingenious. Moving the blade around in her hand, she said, "You had this made for me?"

He nodded. "You can attach it to a leather girdle and wear it at your back or on your side."

Cate was unbelievably touched by his thoughtfulness and by what it revealed. He knew her every bit as well as she knew him. They'd both gotten each other weapons! "It's perfect," she said. "Thank you."

"Aye, well, put it away until I teach you how to use it. You did mention gelding one time."

She laughed and slid it back into the scabbard. "Aye, well, I might have reconsidered. You'll just have to not give me a reason."

The gentle teasing suddenly vanished. His face grew painfully serious. She didn't think there could have been a more awkward silence.

Her heart wrenched. She felt like a fool. He'd never made her any promises. But he wouldn't want to do that . . . would he?

It would break her heart. *Heartbreaker . . .*

That was what he did, wasn't it? *Not to me. This is different.*

"I hope I can do that," he said.

Cate's chest was burning, but she told herself not to overreact. "How long were you with Isobel, Gregor?"

His expression hardened. "What does that have to do with anything?"

"How long?"

"Nearly two years."

"Did you bed other women when you were with her?"

"No." He seemed surprised by the admission.

"That's because when you care about someone you are loyal. And I have every intention of having you care about me very much."

Their eyes held, and something strong and powerful passed between them. Her chest swelled, knowing he already did. It wasn't a promise, but it was the makings of one.

He handed her the box. "This belongs to you now."

"What is it?"

A small smile curved his mouth. He repeated her words back to her, "Why don't you open it and see."

Lifting the top, she drew in her breath. On a bed of velvet was the ring his mother had worn until her death. It was gold, with a large oval crystal in the center and lions' heads engraved on either side. Hand shaking, she took it out from the box.

"It's a charm stone," he said. "There's an engraving on the inside." She held it up to the candle to read it. "'*S Rioghal mo dhream,*'" he said for her.

Royal is my race.

The words taunted her. Stricken, she stared at the ring, not knowing what to do. She couldn't put it on. *Impostor.*

"It's the motto of the MacGregors," he explained.

She blinked at him for a moment in confusion, and then sighed with relief. "Of course it is. I've seen it inscribed on your bow and sword."

The MacGregors claimed descent from Gregor, the son of King Kenneth MacAlpin, the first King of Scots. How could she have forgotten? For a moment, she'd thought it was a cruel jest.

She slipped the ring on, holding her hand up and letting it catch the light. "I shall be honored to wear it."

"My mother would be happy."

Cate's heart tugged at the memory of both women who would have been pleased. She wished they could be here to share this with her—with them. "Aye, she would," Cate agreed.

"Happy Christmas, Cate."

"Happy Christmas, Gregor."

And with one more kiss, he sent her back to her bed— alas, alone.

Seventeen

❧

He grabbed her as she walked by and immediately pulled her into the darkened storeroom. She resisted—as he knew she would—but he was prepared and had her pinned face-forward against the door before she could draw her new dagger.

But her resistance was halfhearted at best. She went lax against him, as he nuzzled her neck just below the ear the way she liked—the way that made her shudder.

"You weren't going to draw the knife on me, where you, Caty? Have you been practicing what I taught you?"

She stretched into him like a cat, letting him feel the pressure of her body in all the right places. Especially her bottom. Aye, that was in exactly the right place. He was hard as a spike, and getting harder by the moment as her tight buttocks nudged him temptingly.

"It would be no more than you deserve, startling me like that. Although I wouldn't have gone for the 'silent kill'— isn't that what you called it? I was thinking something a little more painful."

Gregor couldn't help smiling as his mouth traveled down the side of her neck to the slope of her shoulder. He liked her bloodthirsty. The thought of leaving her alone when he had to return to the battlefield scared the hell out of him, but at least when he left he'd be damned sure she could take care of herself.

"Liar. You weren't startled. You heard me coming and

would have doomed our future progeny with an ill-placed thrust of your knee if I hadn't been ready for you."

She stilled. "Children?" Something in her voice made his chest squeeze. She was trying to sound nonchalant, but he could hear the barely contained yearning. He knew how much a family meant to her. All he had to do was think of the foundlings. Although he had to admit, the fantasy family she'd created wasn't so bad—except for Pip. Something would have to be done about him. But he wasn't looking forward to the argument and tears the subject was sure to provoke.

"That is the usual result of our nighttime activities," he said gently.

"You mean the nighttime activities you put a stop to four nights ago?"

He chuckled, drawing his mouth over the warm, velvety-soft skin of her shoulder, inhaling the faint floral scent that lingered in her hair. "Whinging, Cate? You sound like Ruadh."

"His name is Eddie," she said impatiently. "You can't call him by the color of his hair."

"It's a hell of a lot better than calling him after an English king. Besides, he likes it."

She heaved a weary sigh of resignation, and murmured something about him—and his sex in general—being ridiculous. He could almost imagine her doing the same thing twenty years from now. Bloody hell, they hadn't even reached the altar yet, and they were already acting like an old married couple.

Except for the fact that he had her pinned up against a door in a dark storeroom. Hell, he'd probably be doing that in twenty years, too. The thrill of anticipation running through him didn't seem to show any signs of waning. It just seemed to be getting stronger.

Knowing he could well be taking his life in his own hands, he released one of her wrists and covered her breast instead. Since she didn't try to jab him or reach for her knife, he figured she liked what he was doing to her.

When he was sure she wouldn't try to flip him on his arse, he released her other hand and really went to work, letting his hands roam over every inch of that sweet body, as he kissed and sucked her neck and nape, and rubbed his erection against the bottom pressing against him.

God, he was hot. She was burning him up. It had been too damned long. He should have thought of this earlier.

"It's not nighttime now, sweetheart," he said in a half-groan.

She echoed the sound as he slid his hand from her breast to between her legs.

"I thought you wanted to wait until we were married?"

"Aye, well, it turns out that's too long."

He could almost hear her smiling. "It's eight more days, Gregor."

The requisite dispensation had been procured even faster than he'd anticipated. Gregor had received a missive from the king this morning, informing him that it should arrive a few days in advance of Twelfth Night.

Unfortunately, the king hadn't just been offering his congratulations. He'd had other news to impart as well. News Gregor would rather not think about. He hated keeping secrets from Cate, even if it was for her own good. But it seemed he would finally have his opportunity to give her the justice she deserved. De Bohun was sending men to help with the defense of Perth Castle, under the leadership of his captain, Sir Reginald Fitzwarren.

That wasn't all. The first rumors of Gregor's part in the Highland Guard—or Bruce's Phantoms, as they were known across the countryside—had reached the king's ears. It was only a matter of time before it spread, and the king warned him to be on alert. Gregor had even more of a reason to curse the blown mission at Berwick: Cate. What would this mean for her safety?

But she cleared his troubled mind for him with her next words. "Gregor, can we? Uh . . ." He knew she was blushing, but he was too damned aroused to smile. "Like this?"

Oh God, yes. "Would you like that?" he asked with remarkable calmness, given that he was about ready to explode.

He held her more firmly between her legs. Even through the heavy skirts he knew she was throbbing.

She gasped. "Yes, I think I would."

He tossed up her skirts and untied his breeches faster than he'd ever done before, not wanting to take any chances that she would change her mind.

He made a deep sound of raw pleasure as he slid his cock between her legs and let his length slide back and forth along her dampness.

She was practically panting now, her body shaking with need. "Gregor, I can't wait . . . that feels so good."

Needing to feel how good, he reached around front and dipped his hand between her legs. He slid one finger in, and then another. "You feel so silky soft and wet. I can't wait to be inside you."

She was writhing against him, her whole body begging him. He couldn't wait any longer. He came into her with a hard thrust that jarred her against the door.

She cried out, not in pain but in pleasure. "Yes! Oh please, don't stop."

With every thrust she gave back every bit as fiercely as he did, urging him with the press of her body and her inciting words. *Harder. Make it harder. Faster. You feel so good . . . so big.*

He lost control. He lost where he stopped and she began. He couldn't stop. He drove into her over and over with all the passion and all the unnamed emotion inside him that had been fighting to come out. He held nothing back, and for the first time in his life Gregor felt completely free.

They came together in a conflagration and explosion of

raw energy that rocked and quaked, destroying everything that had come before. There was only the woman coming apart around him. Now and forever.

Two days after the first time Gregor had surprised her in the storeroom, Cate finished the last few adjustments on her clothes and hair. Fortunately, she'd been dressed for practice and the damage he'd done in his eagerness was easily repaired. With the weather clear for the first time in days, she'd been on her way to go for a ride with Pip, when Gregor had caught her in the stairwell and dragged her into the storage room under the stairs that held the casks of wine and ale.

"How do I look?" she asked, letting the end of the plait she'd just finished drop down her back.

He looked her up and down, a distinctly smug expression of masculine satisfaction on his face. "You look like a beautiful, thoroughly ravished young woman who has just come apart three times."

"Gregor!" She blushed hotly. "You shouldn't say such things."

He gave her a wicked smile. "Why not? It's true. That's what I see when I look at you. Other people might just assume you've been sitting next to the fire for a while."

She rolled her eyes. "I doubt it. I don't think we are fooling anyone. Just today Ete asked me if I had counted the bags of grain we had in the storeroom lately. She told me with the feast coming it wouldn't be a bad idea, and I should take as long as I needed—she would watch Maddy later this afternoon."

Gregor grinned broadly. "I always knew I liked that woman."

Cate shook her head. He *was* a rogue. But he was her rogue—or would be soon. "I am glad there are only seven more nights—"

"Six," he corrected. "The seventh night you are mine."

Cate smiled. She'd known that. "You *are* counting."

"Every damned minute," he said, picking up the belt with his sword to fasten it around his waist.

When he finished, he sat on one of the casks to look at her, seemingly reluctant to leave. She knew the feeling. Even though there was something decidedly illicit about what they were doing, it was the only time she had alone with him, and she cherished every moment.

With Hogmanay tomorrow, they'd both been busy with their duties attending to the guests and making sure everything was ready for the big feast. The busyness was to be expected, but that didn't make it any easier. Nor was it any easier to watch the women descend on him like locusts. Or maybe vultures was a better analogy, looking for any scraps left on the carcass of his bachelorhood. Apparently being betrothed wasn't much of a deterrent.

"Where were you off to?" he asked.

"You mean before I was swept off my feet and carried down here by some over-muscled barbarian?"

He grinned unrepentantly. "Aye, before that."

"Pip and I were going to go for a ride, and then practice his archery at some of the butts set up on the moorland on the other side of the village."

He frowned, and she wasn't sure whether it was at the mention of Pip or the mention of her straying so far from the tower house. "How long will you be gone?"

"A few hours. You need not worry—I'm sure your two guardsmen will report back to you as soon as we return."

He didn't bother feigning embarrassment at her discovery. "I'll not apologize for being cautious, Cate. With strange riders about, I thought it prudent to have my men accompany you when you are away from the castle."

"Accompany me? Don't you mean follow me?"

He shrugged as if the difference were immaterial. "It's my job to protect you, Cate."

"I can protect myself."

He didn't argue; he just looked at her with a pleading expression in his eyes. "Let me do this, sweetheart. Just until we are sure the man you saw was nothing."

Did Gregor have reason to suspect the man could be *something*? She held his gaze for a long moment, but he gave nothing away. All she could see was genuine concern.

Good gracious, it was hard to resist him. "If you want to protect me, why don't you come with us?" He seemed about to refuse, when she added, "That is, if you can bear to tear yourself away for a few hours from the bevy of admirers. 'Oh, my laird, I brought you this tart because I know how much you love figs,' " she mimicked, "Or 'Oh, my laird, have you had this cheese from our farm?' " She made a sharp scoffing sound. "Their ploys are so obvious. Does every woman think the way to a man's heart is through his stomach?"

He crossed his arms and grinned at her. "Well, I do like figs and cheese."

"Gregor!" she exclaimed, swatting at him. "That isn't funny."

He grabbed her and hauled her up against his broad chest. Would she ever get used to the feel of his strength? Would the hard shield of muscle ever stop making her skin tingle and her knees weak?

"You have no reason to be jealous, Cate. Those women mean nothing to me; I see through their ploys easily enough. That's why you are so special."

"Because you don't see through my ploys?" she mumbled disgruntledly.

He laughed. "Because you don't have them." He dropped a kiss on her nose. "Now, are you going to smile and be a good hostess to *all* our guests, or am I going to have to bend you forcibly to my will?"

She lifted a brow. "Is that your diabolical plan?"

"Aye, you've found me out. I plan to keep you so well sated, you don't have the energy to argue with me."

She laughed and shook her head. God knew he probably could. Despite the fact that they'd just made love, she could already feel him hardening against her again. "But now I shall be on guard, since you have warned me of your nefarious purpose." She made a face. "Very well, I will smile and be perfectly charming." She demonstrated with a very forced smile. But then her eyes narrowed. "Unless someone does something to annoy me. Tell your admirers to keep their hands to themselves. Especially the willowy blonde—your uncle's henchman's sister, I believe?"

"How about I mention how good you are with a dagger. Do you think that will suffice?"

"It will be a good start. Now, what do you say about coming with us?"

He considered her for a moment. She suspected it was the prospect of spending time with Pip that was holding him back. But that was one of the reasons she wanted him there. She had a plan.

"There are a few things I must attend to, but how about I meet you there in about an hour?"

She beamed. "That will be perfect."

It was working, Cate thought, casting another covert glance at the man leaning against the tree at the edge of the grove, who was doing his best to look uninterested.

But she wasn't fooled. Gregor was going crazy. His hands were practically itching to intervene and put a stop to the travesty taking place before him.

When she helped Pip draw the arrow back about a half-inch below his ear and positioned the lad's elbow down, Gregor reached his breaking point. He came stomping over to where they had set up on the edge of the largest open field in the village.

All around them were the hills and forest, but right in front of them was a fairly wide-open and flat stretch of moorland about three hundred yards in length. As such it served as the place for the annual village archery contest, during the summer fair. Large butts of hay wrapped in hemp were placed at varying distances. Covered in a few inches of snow, they looked like boulders under a blanket of white, but they served their purpose well enough in providing a safe landing place for the arrows.

Coming to a stop next to them, Gregor shot her an irritated glare. "God's blood, Cate. He'll never hit anything if you have him draw like that. Damn it, everything is wrong. Even his stance. His left foot should be pointed more toward the mark." He nudged Pip's toe with his own.

Pip was about to object, but Cate squeezed his arm to stop him. "I have perfect form, Gregor," she insisted. "Ask John. I know exactly what I'm doing."

She did. She was going to force these two to spend time with one another, even if they didn't like it. And what better way than having Gregor teach the lad something he loved?

The famed archer made a harsh scoffing sound low in his throat. "Then why is he putting so much weight on his back foot to start? He should be more balanced when he is first learning. The string should be between these two fingers," he made the adjustment for Pip, "not these two. He's drawing too fast and jerky. His hand should stop at the lower lobe of his ear, his elbow should come out, he should be looking at the mark, not the arrowhead—he's closing one eye, for Christ's sake—and he's holding too long before loosing." He looked furious, as if he'd been personally slighted or she'd just committed some sacrilege. "Bloody hell, at each stage of standing, nocking, drawing, holding, and loosing, he's doing something wrong."

Cate crossed her arms and glared back at him, feigning anger. "I thought I was doing all that. But by all means, if you think you can do a better job, go right ahead."

Gregor's gaze sharpened. Blast it, he was too shrewd. He guessed what she was doing. Perhaps she'd gone a little too

far with all her errors, but she'd wanted to make sure he
noticed.

Conscious of the young boy between them who was
doing his best to look as if it didn't matter to him either
way, Cate held her breath. *Please don't reject him again.*

Gregor held her gaze for a long pause, and then gave her
a sharp nod. It wasn't acquiescence as much as an acknowledgment that she'd won this battle—but he wasn't
conceding the war.

The next hour passed quickly as Gregor instructed Pip
in the proper form and technique of the longbow. It was
obvious Gregor was comfortable in the role of teacher, and
she realized as she watched him that she was probably seeing what it was like when he worked with the men under
his command.

The English had become feared for their bowmen—
especially the Welsh—but the Highlands and forests of
Galloway had also bred bowmen of great repute. When
the time came to face the English, Bruce would not be
without skilled archers. Highly skilled archers, if Gregor
had any influence on their training.

It was clear that not only was he gifted with skill, he was
gifted in the ability to convey that skill to others—the two
didn't always go together. He knew exactly how much information to give, when to make corrections, and when to
give praise.

He demonstrated but did not shoot his own bow, although she was glad to see that he had brought it. When
she mentioned that she hadn't seen him practicing with it
of late and asked him if something was wrong, he brushed
her off by turning the focus to her shooting.

She was surprised when he made a few slight adjustments to her technique that immediately improved her accuracy. Like Pip, she used a smaller, lighter bow made for
her lesser strength. Trying to draw Gregor's bow was like
trying to draw an iron bar. She could barely move it a few

inches. The size of the muscles in his back and arms suddenly took on new meaning and importance. He needed to be that strong to wield the bow.

Pip wasn't the only one disappointed when Gregor put a stop to the practice. "We'd better start back, if we are going to be in time for the midday meal."

With most of the guests already arrived for the feast tomorrow, skipping it was out of the question. She gave a disappointed sigh anyway. "Must we?"

His mouth curved. "Aye, we must." He turned to Pip. "The way to get better is to treat each arrow you shoot at practice the same way you would at battle. This is not a skill that will be bettered by the sheer number of shots. It's making each one count. You need to build up shoulder and back strength—remember it's not in the arm; you are bending into the bow. Shooting when you are tired will do nothing to improve your skill."

The past hour had done what Cate had hoped. Pip was no longer looking at Gregor with veiled animosity and suspicion; he was looking at him like a beaten pup that had just had someone pet him for the first time. He was at once desperate for the kindness, but also leery of accepting it for fear that it wouldn't last.

When Pip nodded, Cate had to look away, fearing one of them would see the tears in her eyes.

It would have been a perfect morning, if it hadn't been marred by what happened on the ride back to Dunlyon.

They were deep in the forest when she sensed a shift in Gregor's watchfulness. As with most warriors, he always demonstrated a high level of alertness and awareness of his surroundings, no matter what the circumstances; but this was different. This was the sharpness and edginess of battle. Everything about him seemed harder.

Pip was riding ahead, and Gregor slightly behind her, when she turned to him and said, "What's wrong?"

His jaw had tensed, and his mouth was drawn in a tight

line. "I'm not sure. I felt something. In the hills to the north." He didn't need to tell her not to look in that direction. "I think someone is watching us."

Her skin prickled, and she instinctively stiffened. Her heart started to pound, climbing quickly toward her throat. "What should we do?"

"When we get to the fork ahead, I want you to ride for the tower house with the lad. I'm going to circle around and see if I can sneak up on our watcher from behind."

"But what if there is more than one?"

For some reason that made him smile. "I will be fine, Cate. You have nothing to worry about." His face grew grave. "But I am trusting you to get Pip back to Dunlyon safely. Tell John what has happened. I will return as quickly as I can. Make some excuse to the guests."

She nodded. Before she had time to argue or panic, he was gone—maybe he'd counted on that.

She did as he'd bid, returning to the castle with Pip and informing John of what had occurred. She did her best to do her duty as the lady of the castle, presiding over the midday meal and seeing that the guests were well attended, but her head—along with her heart—was somewhere else.

She couldn't seem to breathe until Gregor walked through the door of the Hall two hours later, the long meal still going on. He caught her gaze before he was surrounded. Expression grim, he shook his head.

She didn't know whether to be relieved or not. Gregor had not faced danger, but that meant whatever was out there was still there.

Eighteen

✣

Cate's nose was pressed so closely to the wall she was probably getting splinters. He had her hands pinned and was immobilizing the rest of her by crushing her with the weight of his body.

It was hard to breathe. For one moment, she felt a flicker of panic but pushed it back. She tried to move her foot behind his ankle, but he anticipated the move and used his leg and thigh to inhibit her movement.

He pressed her even harder. "That won't work this time, Cate. What else can you do? *Think*."

There was an urgency to Gregor's voice that she didn't understand. But his words only increased her frustration. What could she do? She couldn't do anything, blast it! He was as strong as a bloody ox! She could feel her pulse racing and her blood heating as the sense of helplessness mixed with anger. Every instinct in her body rebelled at this feeling of powerlessness.

But she wasn't powerless. With a sudden clarity of purpose, she stopped struggling. The moment he eased the pressure, she reacted. She bent her knees and slumped just enough to bring her head forward and snap it back hard against his face. Because he was so tall, she connected with his jaw and not his nose, but it was hard enough to make a cracking sound.

He let out a grunt of pain and instinctively bent forward. Taking advantage of the opening, she twisted around, slamming her elbow into his ribs at the same time that her ankle laced around his foot.

He didn't fall to the ground, but the imbalance was enough for her to slip away.

He was rubbing his jaw when she turned back to him. "Are you all right?"

"I'm fine," he said. "That was good instinct. When you're ready we'll try again, but this time we'll practice what to do if someone has you backed against a wall with a knife to your throat."

She nodded, taking in the focused expression on his face. She knew she should be glad that he was taking her training seriously—*very* seriously—but she sensed a larger purpose at work. He was working her much harder than he ever had before. Almost as if he was trying to cram every possible horrible situation she could come up against into a single training session.

Gregor retrieved a skin he'd filled with well water from a pile of weapons he'd brought for practice, drank deeply from it, and then handed it to her. Although it was a cold, overcast day, with an occasional light flurry of snow swirling in the air, her cheeks were flushed and warm from her exertions.

She handed the skin back to him when she was done. "Is something bothering you, Gregor?"

"Nay."

She frowned. "Are you sure? You seem rather *intense* today. I wondered if it might have something to do with earlier? I thought you said you didn't find anyone."

"I didn't. But someone had been there. More than someone—I counted at least five sets of footprints."

"It was probably just travelers passing through."

His mouth fell in a tight line.

"What?" she asked.

His eyes were a very sharp and intense green when they

met hers. "It wasn't anyone passing through. They'd been there for at least a few days."

"How could you tell?"

"What they left behind. They left quickly and didn't have time to cover their rubbish."

She wrinkled her nose at the unpleasant thought. "So even if they were there for a few days, why does it bother you, and what does it have to do with me?"

"It doesn't have anything to do with you," he said. "At least not directly. And it might not be anything. Hell, it probably isn't anything."

He looked so unsettled—so unlike himself—that she reached for him. "What is it, Gregor? What are you not telling me?"

He held her gaze for a long moment. Finally, he sighed and raked his fingers through his hair. "I suppose you have a right to know, and since the secret is already out, I won't be breaking my oath."

"What oath?"

He looked around as if he wanted to make sure no one was close enough to hear. Seeing a few of his clansmen moving around near the barracks, he motioned her a short distance away to the far side of the practice yard near the wooden palisade wall. "I haven't been completely honest with you about my place in the king's army."

Her heart stopped, then started to pound furiously. "You haven't?"

He shook his head. "You were right; there is a little bit more to what I do than serve as a bowman."

She waited for him to continue, feeling mildly vindicated, but far more concerned about what he was going to reveal. The way was acting, so mysterious and secretive, made her wary.

"Have you ever heard of Bruce's Phantoms?"

She smiled. "Of course. Everyone has heard of them, but . . ."

She stopped, her eyes widening and her mouth rounding in surprise. Suddenly, everything fell into place. It was as if her mind clicked, and things that hadn't made sense now were clear. "You are a Phantom?"

His mouth quirked with amusement. "So to speak, although as you can see I am not a ghost. Nor was it our idea to be mistaken as such, but the rumor has proved useful over the years to prevent out enemies from finding us."

" 'Us'? How many of there are you?"

He hesitated. "I do not want to tell you more than you need to know. I would not be telling you any of this, but it seems my place in the Guard has been compromised." He gave her a short explanation of what had happened at Berwick, leaving out the tickets. Hawk was bad enough; he didn't need to hear it from her, too. "We decided to keep our identities secret not only to protect us from our enemies, but also to protect our families. If they could not get to us directly, they might be able to get to us through our loved ones. But this was before most of the men took wives." He smiled. "Let's just say keeping the secret from the wives has worked better in theory than in practice. But we have largely been able to keep our identities from being known by others with a couple of exceptions—and now, it seems, with me."

"So all of this fervor today is because you think I may be in danger?"

He swore. "I probably overreacted, but I don't want to take any chances. If I thought it would have kept you completely safe, I would have sent you off with Farquhar, no matter how badly I wanted you. But wife or 'ward,' it wouldn't have made a difference. You, John, and Padraig are all at risk."

She was still too stunned by what he'd revealed to argue about Farquhar. "Do John and Padraig know?"

He shook his head. "I think John suspects. But they will both have to be told."

Cate just stared at him, as if seeing him for the first time. She'd imagined a lot of things, but not this. "A Phantom? I can't believe it. They say you are supermen who can move through walls and disappear into the mist. They say you can't be killed. That you are all giants and—" She stopped a memory from returning. "The men with you that day when you found me. You were all wearing those ghastly helms and the black *cotuns* and plaids. I thought you were demons at first. They are Phantoms, too, aren't they?"

He nodded grimly. "If I asked you to forget their names, would you?"

"I would try, but I'm afraid I have a very good memory."

He gave her a wry smile. "I figured as much. But I suspect I will not be able to keep the others' identities from you for long."

"I would never betray your friends, Gregor."

"Aye, well, I don't intend for you ever to be in a position to have to do that. What would you think about moving to the Western Isles until the war is over?"

She looked at him incredulously. "You are jesting, aren't you?"

"Partly." He reached out and swept a lock of dark hair from her cheek, tucking it behind an ear. "The thought of leaving you alone when Bruce sends for me makes my stomach turn."

Cate didn't want to think about that either, knowing he would be leaving soon—maybe even days after their wedding. "I won't be alone," she said. "I have John and the other warriors of your *meinie*. I will take care to not wander anywhere on my own. And I might not have the superhuman strength and skill of a Phantom, but I am not unable to defend myself if need be."

He nodded. "I never thought it would be a relief to have a wife who is trained in warfare."

Her mouth quirked. "And I never thought I would marry a ghost."

"Phantom," he corrected dryly. "Well, now you know all my secrets." She paled, but he didn't notice as he leaned over and kissed the top of her head. "Perhaps we can resume your practice with the dagger?"

She nodded, her shock at his news fading with the realization of what it meant. She might know all his secrets, but Gregor didn't know all of hers. And with his place in Bruce's army now revealed—although she still had dozens more questions—it was becoming a foregone conclusion that she was going to have to tell him. She could no longer delude herself that the name of her father wouldn't matter to him. It would. The question—and what she feared— was his reaction when he learned the truth.

Gregor had his arm around her neck from behind, the sharp blade of his dagger pressed to her throat. He'd showed her two ways of escaping. She'd mastered the first, of pulling down on his arm with both hands, as if she were going down to the ground, before driving him back suddenly against a hard surface—in this case, the wall of the barracks—but she was having a more difficult time with the second.

"Tuck your chin to protect your throat," he instructed. "And you still need to pull on my arm to lower the blade so it's more at your shoulder than at your neck. The pivot has to be faster. You can't give me time to react and get the blade back into position."

"I'm trying," she groaned, frustrated. "But I'm having trouble positioning my hands as I turn."

"You're thinking too much. Keep your hands in the same place as you are when pulling down on my arm, and just use your elbow and lean your head into my body as you pivot." She had that fierce, determined, obstinate, pursed-mouth look on her face again that made him want to laugh. God, if she were a man, she could inspire legions with that look. "Ready to try again?"

She nodded.

He'd just gotten the blade into position when he sensed a movement behind him. He turned, but it was too late. His inattention cost him. Cate pulled, pivoted, and twisted the arm holding the blade behind him, forcing him to the ground by pressing against the back of that twisted arm.

He swore. But it wasn't due to the fact that he was eating dirt, her foot was now on his back, and his torquing arm was in pain; it was due to their witnesses. One whose laugh he'd recognize anywhere.

"Watch that face, laddie," MacSorley said, the laughter still heavy in his voice. He'd obviously mistaken Cate for a boy, which wasn't surprising, as Gregor had forced her to wear a mail coif as they practiced with the blade at her throat. "Wouldn't want those ticket holders to be disappointed."

Cate frowned and released him, shooting him a questioning look.

Bloody hell. "I'll explain later," Gregor said, getting to his feet. Despite the fact that he was going to have to tell Cate about the ridiculous tickets, he grinned at the big West Highland chieftain, who looked more like a Norse raider than an elite warrior. It was damned good to see him. "Nothing to worry about, Hawk. If something happens to me, we can always have them come see you and charge two for the price of one."

The two other men with him—Lachlan MacRuairi and Arthur Campbell—snickered. The men had obviously left their horses in the stables and come straight to the practice yard to find him.

"You might have to offer three for one," MacRuairi said dryly. "My cousin has been married for so long, he's out of practice at pleasing lasses."

MacSorley smiled smugly. "There is only one lass I care about pleasing and believe me, cousin, she doesn't have any complaints."

"How is Ellie?" MacGregor asked innocently. "I've been meaning to drop in for a visit next time she visits Campbell's wife at Dunstaffnage."

The taunting grin fell from MacSorley's face. His expression darkened, turning instantly deadly. "You aren't going anywhere near my wife, MacGregor—not unless I'm there with her."

Gregor quirked a brow and smirked. "Worried, Hawk? I thought you hung the moon and stars in your wife's eyes?"

"More like prudent," Campbell interjected dryly. "Even the smartest lass can be a little blinded and act silly around you. Believe me, MacSorley here isn't the only one to be relieved to hear you've finally been snared."

"Aye, so where is the lass who finally got her claws in you, Slick?" MacSorley added. "I'm looking forward to meeting her."

Cate, who'd been standing at his side as he welcomed his brethren, had finally exceeded her patience. She drew off her coif, poked him in the chest with her finger, blew a wisp of hair away from her adorably dirt-smudged face, and glared at him. "Aye, Slick"—she shot a glance to a stunned MacSorley—"a fitting nickname, by the way. Aren't you forgetting someone when you are discussing all these 'lasses'?"

"Bloody hell, MacGregor," MacRuairi said, "it's a lass!"

"A lass pinned you down?" MacSorley said. He looked up as if the gods were smiling on him (which they usually were). "Thank you!"

No doubt the seafarer was thanking them for the future fodder. But Gregor would cure his friend of that belief soon enough, when he let MacSorley be the first one to practice with his soon-to-be bride. The unsuspecting Viking would be on his back in seconds. He couldn't wait.

But introductions had to come first. Once made, not even the normally expressionless MacRuairi could hide his surprise. He could read their minds. This cute, wee lass in a simple tunic, hose, and mail was the woman he'd chosen for his bride? Damned right! He eyed them all challengingly, almost daring one of them to say—or think— anything.

Campbell came forward first and bowed. "It's a pleasure to meet you, my lady. You'll have to excuse our jesting. We meant no offense. It's just that we don't often see MacGregor here bested by anyone, let alone a squire—or a lass," he added with smile.

Cate looked up at his partner warmly. "I am not easily offended, my lord . . . Campbell?" she added, with a confused look to Gregor.

Gregor smiled wryly, guessing the source of that confusion. The Campbells and MacGregors had been locked in a vicious feud before the war broke out, and probably would be again once it was over. Indeed, it was their enmity in the early days of the Highland Guard that had given Tor MacLeod the idea to make him and Campbell partners.

God knew, it wasn't the only unlikely pairing. But it had worked. He and Campbell were like brothers now. Too bad all the pairings could not have worked out so well, he mused, thinking of Seton and Boyd. The Guard was still reeling from the defection of "Sir" Alex Seton. The England-born, Scotland-raised knight had been an ill pairing with the fierce patriot Robbie Boyd from the start. But no one had ever imagined he would betray them.

Turning from this troubling thought, Gregor smiled at Cate. "Aye, you heard that right: Campbell. It turns out this one has a few redeeming qualities. He's a quiet bastard, though, so don't let him surprise you."

Cate looked up at him and said in a low voice, "Are they . . . ?"

He quirked his mouth. He wasn't surprised that she'd guessed.

Giving in to the inevitable, he nodded. He'd known it was going to be impossible to keep the others' identities a secret from her once she knew the truth about him. Although this was certainly faster than he anticipated, as he hadn't known his brethren were coming.

Discovering why they were here, however, would have to wait. Nothing was going to make him miss the opportunity to see MacSorley on his arse.

Hours later, the four men were gathered around the large table in the solar. Gregor sipped his wine, trying not to grin as the seafarer shifted on the wooden bench.

MacSorley's sore backside hadn't been Gregor's only reward. He was also nursing a nice black eye that he'd earned when Cate's elbow jabbed harder than she'd intended. Cate had been horrified, MacSorley had been silenced, and Gregor and the others had laughed until they cried.

"Hell, Arrow," MacSorley said, grabbing a nearby cushion to slide onto the seat. "I can't believe you taught your wee ward all our secrets. I never imagined a lass could learn to fight like that."

"It was John mostly." He grinned. "She's good, isn't she? I wouldn't have believed it unless I'd seen it myself."

"Just don't let my wife see it," MacRuairi said dryly. "I have a hard enough time keeping her away from the battlefield. God knows what she'd do if she got it in her mind that women could fight."

He shuddered reflexively, and Gregor tried not to smile. Talk about unlikely pairings. MacRuairi, the mercenary without loyalties, had wed one of Scotland's fiercest patriots, Bella MacDuff, the former Countess of Buchan.

"Your betrothed is small, but surprisingly quick and agile," Campbell said. "She moves like . . ."

His voice dropped off. They all guessed what he had been about to say, and sobered. *Like Seton.*

"Has there been any word?" Gregor asked quietly.

Campbell shook his head. "So far he's kept his vow."

"Kept *one* vow, you mean," MacRuairi interjected darkly. "He may not have shared our names with the English, but he betrayed us in every other way that matters. 'Sir' Alex had better stay in London and pray he never finds himself face-to-face with one of us on the battlefield. I would enjoy sticking my blade in his back to repay the favor."

No one responded, but MacRuairi was only echoing—albeit in harsher, MacRuairi-like terms—what they'd all thought at one time or another. The man who'd been one of their brethren was now an enemy—and a threat to them all.

Except maybe to Gregor. "Is there any news?" he asked.

"The rumors are spreading," Campbell said. "It's only a matter of time before your name is being bandied about like MacRuairi's and Gordon's. You will need to take precautions." He looked at him. "Has the lass been told?"

Gregor nodded. "Just today, before you arrived." He filled them in on the men who'd been in the forest.

MacSorley nodded. "Maybe Hunter will be able to find something when he arrives."

"I thought he and Striker were in the south with Edward Bruce?"

"They are, but you don't think they'd miss your wedding? Hell, Arrow, there is no man in Scotland any of us are more eager to see wed," MacSorley added with a grin. "They and Raider are bringing your dispensation from the good bishop on their way north." The Bishop of St. Andrews, William Lamberton, was well known to them all. His support had been a huge factor in Bruce's success thus far.

"I'm surprised Raider can tear himself away from the babe."

Boyd's wife—his new *English* wife—had just given birth to their son a couple of months ago.

"He's been in the south with Striker and Hunter, but I suspect he's been making the journey to Kilmarnock often," Campbell said with a wry smile. "Ice and Saint will arrive with Chief in a few days."

"And Angel?" Gregor asked. Helen MacKay née Sutherland—Magnus "Saint" MacKay's wife and Kenneth "Ice" Sutherland's sister—was a gifted healer and had become the personal physician of the Guard. Unconsciously, he fingered the scar at his neck where he'd been shot with an arrow that should have killed him. It *would* have killed him had it not been for Helen. He owed her his life, and it had created a special bond between them—much to her husband's continued annoyance.

Cate would love her. They were actually quite a bit alike. They were both pursuing interests that had been the preserve of men—Cate with her training in warfare, and Helen as a physician.

"Saint left to fetch her as soon as the king received your message. He knew she'd have his bollocks if he let you wed without her being there to see it. The king, Douglas, and Randolph would be here as well, but they are readying the army to Perth to begin the siege."

Gregor nodded. It was what he'd expected. "When?"

"A week," Campbell answered with a sympathetic grimace. "I'm afraid you will only have one night with your bride before we must leave to join him."

Gregor cursed under his breath. He'd hoped to have at least a few days. Cate would be disappointed. Hell, *he* was disappointed.

But at least he'd be ready. It wasn't exactly the way he'd planned to clear his head, but being with Cate had worked. The past week had relaxed him and reinvigorated him for the battle ahead. It wasn't just Bruce now; there was Cate as well. He wanted her to be proud of him—to be the kind of man she could count on—and he wouldn't let either of them down. He hadn't lost his edge. If anything, the time

with Cate had sharpened it. He was eager to pick up his
bow and prove it.

"I don't know," MacRuairi drawled, giving him a long,
knowing look over his tankard of ale. "If the way Arrow
was looking at his wee bride tonight was any indication,
I'd say he's already had quite a few wedding nights."

The black-hearted mercenary who was meaner than a
snake and gave true meaning to his bastardy had obviously
been around his needling cousin for too long. He was beginning to sound like him.

Gregor shot him a warning glare and told him to go do
something that was physically impossible. The bastard
only smiled.

Of course, MacSorley—the needling cousin—couldn't
let the matter rest. "Anticipated the wedding night, did
you? Is that what happened? We wondered how the lass
had gotten those manacles on you so quickly. Although
now that I've met your wee ward, I understand. That
sweet face hides a crafty mind—and I have the bruises to
prove it."

Gregor's eyes narrowed, the muscles at the back of his
shoulders flaring. He leaned forward. "What the hell are
you insinuating, Hawk?"

He wasn't going to let anyone cast any aspersions on
Cate or speculate on his motives for marrying her.

MacSorley held up his hand. "Back down, Arrow. No
reason to get all prickly. I wasn't insinuating anything. I'd
wager you aren't the only one seated at this table who has
been unable to wait for a priest. We all have our breaking
point—I met mine five years ago. We just despaired that
you'd ever meet yours, that's all." He leaned back, crossed
his arms, and grinned. "There's no shame in being trapped
by the right woman. And from what I see, you've been
good and trapped."

Gregor relaxed and eased back in his chair. "Go to hell,
Hawk. It's not like that."

The famed seafarer's grin turned smug. "I'd say it's exactly like that." MacSorley put his hand up to his ear, as if he were listening. "What's that crashing sound I hear? Must be the sound of all those thousands of hearts breaking across the Highlands. The most handsome shark in the sea has been good and hooked."

Gregor shook his head. "Hell, Hawk. I'm saying my vows, not taking them."

MacSorley waved off the protest. "I've experienced the lass's unusual skills firsthand. If I were you, I wouldn't give her a reason to put a knife to my throat—or anywhere else, for that matter."

Gregor's mouth quirked, remembering Cate's words to the same effect.

"He won't," Campbell interjected.

Gregor lifted a brow at the note of confidence in his friend's voice, but he didn't question him. Campbell had an eerie way of seeing things that other people didn't. Maybe that Gregor didn't even see himself.

His partner frowned. "It's funny. She reminds me of someone, but I can't think who."

Gregor felt a cold shiver race down his back. He looked at his friend. "Aye, I've thought the same thing."

They exchanged a glance, and Gregor tried not to be bothered by the troubled look in Campbell's eyes. But it stayed with him. And he would recall it later.

But by then it would be too late.

Nineteen

❧

Cate was pleased when Gregor rode out with the three other Phantoms on the morning of the Hogmanay feast.

She was surprised that they'd managed to keep their identities hidden for this long. All anyone had to do was look for the most terrifying, intimidating, fierce-looking men around, and the search would be over. Had she not been about to marry the most handsome man in Scotland, she also might have noticed that they were all uncommonly attractive. And tall. And muscular. It made sense, given their reputed prowess on the battlefield, but it was rather awe-inspiring all the same seeing them together.

What made Cate happy, however, was not this discovery, but that Gregor had taken his bow with him and intended to use it this time. She'd been more worried by its absence across his back than she'd realized. She couldn't recall a time when Gregor had gone weeks without practicing. But it seemed the unusual break was at an end. Probably because he would be going back to the war soon. Her chest squeezed, recalling what he'd told her last night after the evening meal.

The day after their wedding? It wasn't fair!

Not for the first time, she cursed the man who'd fathered her, albeit this time not for leaving her, but for taking the man she loved away from her.

You have to tell him. She knew she could not keep it from him forever. It might not have made a difference were he just another soldier in the king's army, but he was more than that. Far more.

She would tell him. As soon as she had the opportunity. With all the guests and festivities, it had been difficult—almost impossible—to find time alone. But before Gregor had left, he'd leaned over and whispered "tonight" in her ear. That one word, that one taunting word filled with husky promise, had sent a shiver of anticipation racing through her.

A shiver of anticipation that had tormented her all day. The wretch! Did he know what he did to her? Probably. Definitely.

She found herself flushing at the oddest moments throughout the day. Such as when she was in the kitchens with Ete overseeing the roasting of the pig, and one of the kitchen maids had mentioned how excited she was for tonight. When the girl had asked Cate if she was, too, it wasn't the feast Cate had been thinking about that caused her cheeks to turn red.

Cate's torment had only increased when the long-awaited feast finally began. Though Gregor's hosting duties as laird left little time for conversation between them, she was seated next to him on the dais, and more than once, his hand had "accidentally" brushed hers, his arm had grazed her breast, and his thigh had pressed up against hers, the contact making her jump. His uncle Malcolm, Chief of the MacGregors, who was seated on her other side, had given her more than one odd look and finally asked her if something was wrong. With a chastising look in Gregor's direction, she'd scooted a few inches away from him on the bench.

But putting distance between them didn't help. Every time their eyes met, she'd see that knowing look in his and flush to her roots. She'd lost her train of thought more than once, which left her stumbling embarrassingly through her conversations with the steady stream of people who came forward to offer their congratulations.

The dancing after the meal was even worse. Gregor didn't miss any excuse to touch her. A hand held too long . . . a touch on the waist as he guided her through the steps. By the end of the first reel she was flushed, breathless, and so aroused, she was sure everyone could see how eager she was to strip off that fine dark blue velvet tunic he was wearing and swive the tormenting blighter senseless. The scary-looking pirate Lachlan MacRuairi had caught her eye once and lifted one very dark eyebrow at her with what she swore was almost amusement. She'd been so mortified, she'd wanted to crawl under the table and hide.

Unfortunately, she wasn't the only one looking at her betrothed as if he were a sweet she couldn't wait to gobble up. The usual gaggle of women had dropped around his feet. But Gregor gave her no reason for jealousy. Though he was his usual effortlessly charming self, and polite to all the ladies with whom he danced, the flirtatious glances and touches were reserved for her. Only when she saw him dance with Seonaid did she feel a prickle of something resembling jealousy. Maybe she hadn't forgotten about that kiss as much as she thought she had.

But she quickly realized she had no cause. The shield of untouchability that separated him from the rest of the world had been erected again. It had been gone for so long, she'd almost forgotten what it was like. But he didn't use it with her. She alone had broken through.

By the time the candelabra were lit, she couldn't wait for the feast to be over and the night to begin. She intended to make him pay for his teasing.

But Gregor didn't make her wait. Not long after she'd seen him dancing with Seonaid, he came up behind her when she was talking to John and murmured "wine" in her ear.

She didn't need to ask what he meant. Out of the corner

of her eye, she saw him slip past the partition to the corridor that led to the small room where the wine was stored.

Her pulse raced with anticipation. She could almost smell the pungent, musty smell of the casks now. She could practically feel his lips on her neck, his skin against hers, the heat and hardness of his body . . .

They would have to be quick if they didn't want anyone to miss them. But somehow the hurriedness only heightened the anticipation.

She waited what she hoped was a sufficient amount of time before slipping out after him.

She'd gone only a few feet, however, before she heard someone behind her and turned. She tensed, her body instinctively bracing her for what was sure to be an unpleasant confrontation.

"There you are, Caitrina," Seonaid said innocently, as if the meeting were by chance.

Cate looked behind her, surprised to see that she was without her trusty handmaidens. "Were you looking for me, Seonaid?" She smiled sweetly. "I'm surprised you did not see me. I was seated at the head table next to the laird."

Cate had to admit, seeing the flush of anger on the face of the woman whose jeers and cruel barbs had tormented her over the years gave her a distinct moment of girlish satisfaction. But it was soon replaced by regret. She couldn't let Seonaid get to her like this. Cate wasn't mean-spirited and petty.

At least not usually. But something about the other woman brought out the worst in her. Seonaid's taunts, her verbal jabs, her condescension and disdain, reminded Cate of her childhood and the nameless bastard she'd been—the girl who'd been so desperate to find a place in a world that looked down on her. A place that had been so much worse when the man she'd idolized left her.

Every time Seonaid looked at her, she felt like she was seeing the little no one who desperately wanted to be someone. She felt like the five-year-old who'd donned a pretty dress and believed she could be a princess.

It made her want to lash out. Made her want to gloat and descend to that same unpleasant level that Seonaid trod upon.

But Cate didn't need to gloat. She didn't need to prove herself to anyone. She'd won Gregor because of who she was on the inside. Not because the man who'd sired her was a king—she still couldn't believe the handsome young earl who'd sat on the rush-covered dirt floors of her mother's cottage and played games with her was king!—or because of her beauty, her feminine wiles, or the size of her breasts.

She gritted her teeth. She would be gracious even if it killed her. In a much nicer voice, she added, "Can I help you with something, Seonaid?"

"I underestimated you," the other woman said, her eyes sparking malevolently. She gave Cate a long look, her gaze traveling down her velvet gown—the green one—and up again. "You obviously knew what you were doing when you said you would get him to marry you."

Cate stiffened. "I didn't say that!" *Did I?* She bit her lip. "Well, that's not what I meant."

Seonaid drew back in surprise at her protest. "What else could you mean? Your words were very clear. You said you could get the handsomest man in Scotland to marry you, even if you had to trap him. You sounded very determined and sure of yourself. Weren't your parting words something like, 'If you don't think I can do it, you are wrong'?"

Cate cringed. Dear lord, had she really said that? It sounded so . . . ugly.

Seonaid might not have all her words exactly right— Cate had never spoken of trapping him—but she'd gotten the gist well enough.

"So how did you do it?" Seonaid continued. "Did you strip naked and crawl into his bed so that he was forced to marry you?"

Cate's cheeks flushed hotly—guiltily? It wasn't like that. She'd had a nightmare, and it had just ... happened. *Because you touched him intimately when he tried to leave. You wanted to force his hand. You wanted to seduce him.* But not to trap him, only to prove that he cared about her; she hadn't been thinking of marriage.

But had a part of her known that would be the result?

The blood drained from her face. No! She couldn't let Seonaid do this to her. "Of course not!" she protested. "How dare you insinuate anything so duplicitous! What is between Gregor and me is none of your business!"

But Seonaid latched on to her twinge of guilt like a dog to a meaty bone. "You did! I knew there had to be an explanation. Why else would Gregor MacGregor even look at someone like you?" Her gaze dropped to Cate's chest, and her lip curled. "Unless you have more under there than I thought."

Someone like you . . . The disdain in the other woman's tone made something inside Cate snap. She wouldn't be put on the defensive. Not by someone like Seonaid. "Why someone like me? Maybe because he finds me attractive on the inside as well as the outside. Maybe because I have more to offer than perfectly coiled golden curls and big breasts." Cate returned every bit of her disdain. "You might try not being so *obvious*. That dress leaves very little to the imagination. Some men like a little mystery in what they are getting—especially when there is little else to offer."

Seonaid gasped. Her eyes hardened to ice. "You pretend to be so high and mighty, but you are the one who had to trick a man into marrying you. Had I been willing to sink so low—"

"You would have found yourself alone in bed," Cate snapped. She was so furious, she wasn't even listening to herself. All she could think of was that for the first time, she didn't have to take the other woman's taunts. She didn't have to feel less. "You are deluding yourself if you think differently. You know what your problem is? You're jealous. You can't stand to think that the girl who wasn't good enough to be your friend could have won the man you wanted for yourself." She took a step toward her. "But I did win, Seonaid. He doesn't want you, he wants *me*, and you are just going to have to accept that."

Seonaid's gaze, which had been fixed on her, suddenly shifted to the left, looking past Cate's shoulder and coming to rest on something.

Nay, on *someone*.

The bottom fell out of Cate's stomach. The blood in her veins turned to ice. She didn't need to look behind her to know who it was.

Seonaid smiled. "My laird, I was just congratulating Cate on her coup."

How long had he been standing there? Cate turned and met his eerily cold and blank gaze. It was like looking into a dark cave. There was nothing there but empty blackness.

Long enough.

Every word she'd just said came back to her in one shameful wave of horror. She wished she could cut off her stupid tongue. But it was too late for that. How could she have let Seonaid get to her like that?

Gregor wished he'd stayed in the storage room. But Cate had been taking so long, he wondered if she'd misunderstood his intent. He'd heard the voices as soon as he'd opened the door, recognizing Cate's soft tones and Seonaid's more grating ones.

He'd been standing there the whole time. But both women had been so focused on the hostile game they played between them, they hadn't noticed him.

He wished they had.

"*Get the handsomest man in Scotland to marry you . . . trap him . . . forced to marry you . . .*" He flinched at the words, unable to accept what he was hearing. And Cate's response? Boasts and taunts instead of real denials. Then she served the final coup de grâce, the words that left no doubt of what she thought of him, ". . . *won the man you wanted for yourself.*"

Won. Like he was some damned prize.

He felt his insides twist.

Damn it, not her, too? It couldn't be true. Cate wouldn't do that. She was too honest for such deceit. She wasn't superficial and conniving like Seonaid and her ilk—even if for a moment she sounded like her. He didn't much like this spiteful, boastful side of Cate. Still, he didn't want to believe it.

Don't overreact, he told himself. *Calm down.* This was Cate. His Cate.

But her own words seemed to damn her. Why had she managed only one feeble denial and acceded to everything else Seonaid accused her of? Why was she throwing her "win" back in the other woman's face? And then there was her expression when she turned to him and gave a startled, "Gregor!"

Horror. Guilt. Shame. He saw the mixture of emotions cross her delicate features and felt the doubt inside him begin to harden.

He glanced over to Seonaid, and the satisfied cat-like smile on her face hardened him a little more. He'd be damned if he'd let the she-tiger see how deeply her claws had scratched. "Coup?" he asked lazily.

Seonaid smiled. "Just a figure of speech, my laird. But it is quite an achievement for a girl like Caitrina to secure a proposal from a man of your . . . repute."

Gregor's fists curled in spite of himself. He knew exactly what "repute" she was talking about. "A girl like Caitrina?"

Seonaid flushed, probably realizing how petty she sounded. "I merely referred to her being an orphan, my laird."

He knew exactly what she meant, and it wasn't that.

Cate seemed to have been knocked from her shock. She grabbed his arm, "Gregor, I—"

He cut her off, not wanting to hear her explanation—at least not right now. "I see you let Seonaid in on our wee jest," he said.

Cate looked just as surprised at seeing him smile as she was taken aback by his words. "Jest?"

He turned to Seonaid. "Cate told me all about your conversation. We laughed about the ironic timing of our announcement, but we never thought anyone would actually believe it." He gave her a slow, deadly smile. "Do I look like the type of a man to be trapped by an innocent lass?"

Seonaid flushed hotly, her cheeks turning a bright scarlet red. "Of course not. We were just surprised by the sudden announcement, that's all."

"So you decided to speculate as to the reason?" His gaze hardened. "I hope you have not been spreading lies and rumors about my betrothed, Mistress MacIan."

The lass's eyes widened at the none-to-subtle threat in his voice. "Nay, of course not!"

"Good," Gregor said, not believing her for a moment. "Then I assume I will hear no more of this. And you will correct anyone who repeats such malicious lies?" He leveled a pointed gaze on the venomous blonde, and then turned to Cate, who was looking at him with a relieved expression on her face.

With a frantic nod, Seonaid muttered something unintelligible and excused herself, seemingly unable to escape the corridor fast enough.

"Thank you," Cate said, putting her hand on his arm.

Noticing his stiffening, she looked up at him questioningly. The guileless set of her adorable features seemed to make it worse.

His expression turned to stone. "For what?"

"For defending me. For trusting in me enough to know

that what Seonaid said wasn't true. I didn't intend to trap you, Gregor."

His mouth hardened, the bitterness rising inside him threatening to pour out in hot molten waves. "Didn't you? And yet that's exactly what happened. You seem to have talked about the very thing with your friend—or former friend. She seemed to recall your conversation quite well. I heard a lot of boasting on your side, but not many denials."

He expected a stream of denials, and assurances that it had all been lies. Instead, she flushed guiltily. "If you don't believe me, why did you tell her what you did?" Suddenly the reason came to her. "Oh."

Aye, being duped was bad enough. He wasn't going to confirm it for everyone else to hear. The very idea of him falling prey to that kind of machination—being tricked into marriage and made a prize to be "won"—made his skin crawl. It was what he'd sought to avoid for most of his life.

It was what other women did. Not Cate.

Her hand on his arm tightened. She took a step closer. The warmth of her body and the subtle fragrance of her hair teased his already on-edge senses. He had to steel himself against the desire that even now—when his gut felt like it was being chewed up—raced through him.

"Please, Gregor, listen to me—it's not what you think."

She had no idea how much he wanted to believe her. "Then you did not say that you were going to trap the 'handsomest man in Scotland' into marrying you? Did you not try to best her and 'win' me?"

He could barely even say the words, it sounded so ridiculous. The thought that Cate could have said something so shallow and deceitful made him ill. She wasn't like that. She was different.

So why wasn't she denying it? Why was her face filling

with shame and guilt? Why was she looking at him with panic in her big, dark eyes?

"It wasn't how it sounded. I never said I intended to trap you. That was Seonaid's word, not mine." The sheen of tears in her eyes spoke of her earnestness. "I know I sounded horrible, but you have to understand how it has been with Seonaid and me. She is always finding ways of belittling me and making me feel like I don't belong. I couldn't stand hearing any more about how inferior I am, how I act like a lad, and how impossible it would be for someone like you to fall in love with me.

"So when she cornered me in the churchyard, I'd had enough. It was right after that night in the Hall when you held me, and I realized for the first time that you were attracted to me. I knew we were meant to be together, and that seemed to have confirmed it. So when she taunted me that the only way you would marry me would be for me to trap you, but that I lacked the sufficient enticements to do that, I told her she was wrong. I knew it was petty and silly, but I just couldn't stop myself. Just like what you heard earlier. She brings out the worst in me."

She blinked back the tears and he could see that her hurt was real. "Haven't you ever wanted to throw something back in someone's face who's been cruel to you? I know it's childish, but I'd heard so many of the same things when I was younger that when I had the opportunity, I couldn't resist it."

She'd been teased as a child, he realized, and the injustice of it made *him* want to lash out for her. So aye, maybe he could understand. If it were just the conversation, he might understand. But it was more than that.

He *had* been effectively forced into marrying her when they'd been found together in her bed—a bed he'd tried to leave the night before until she'd touched him so boldly. Touched him in a way that shouldn't have been seducing to a man of his experience, but because it had been Cate, was.

He'd tried to leave again that morning after her strange disappearance and she'd stopped him again. Vehemently. He remembered that now. She'd seemed insistent on him not going. At the time he'd thought she just wasn't ready for the night to end—nor was he—but was there a more nefarious purpose? And he couldn't help but recall her strange reaction to his jest about being "trapped." At the time he'd taken it as innocence, but what if it wasn't? What if it was guilt?

He wanted to believe her, but there were too many questions to ignore. "So the nightmare was just a coincidence? My understanding was that you hadn't had one in a while."

She gazed up at him, the hurt in her eyes making him feel guilty for even asking the question. "I told you why I had the nightmare. It was the man I saw."

"Aye, that's what you said."

She drew back, the first glimmer of anger and outrage appearing in her eyes. "Good God, Gregor! What do you think? That I made him up, lured you to my bed with a nightmare, seduced you, and then arranged for us to be discovered? You give me far more credit than I deserve."

Maybe, maybe not. Though it might sound implausible based on the difference in their ages and level of experience, they both knew that he was far from immune to her and had been fighting a losing battle with his desire, which she'd pushed very close to the edge. "And yet that's exactly what happened."

She held his gaze. "I didn't do what you are accusing me of, Gregor. I didn't plan any of it. What happened just happened. Maybe I wish I hadn't pushed you by touching you—that's why I was embarrassed earlier with Seonaid—but I wasn't trying to trap you into marriage; I wanted you to stop denying how you felt about me. I love you. I would never try to trick or force you into marriage. I would have hoped you would know that without me having to tell you. I'm sorry about the conversation with Seonaid. It was childish and petty, and I never should have spoken of you as if you were a prize to be won. It was unworthy of me, and the love I have for you. But I did not deceive you or dupe you into anything."

She stood there as regally as any queen, waiting for him to say something. When he didn't speak right away, she lowered her gaze, as if he'd disappointed her. "Think about it, Gregor. In your heart you know the truth. I am not Isobel."

No, she wasn't. He watched her walk away, head high and spine straight, wanting to believe her despite everything he'd just heard. She sounded so sincere, and everything he knew about Cate to this point—or thought he knew—told him she was speaking the truth. She loved him; she *understood* him; she wouldn't have done something like this, knowing how much he despised such machinations.

But love didn't preclude betrayal. And it wouldn't mean a damned thing, if he found out she was lying to him.

He took a few moments to let his blood cool and let the sting of the conversation he'd overheard fade. He would give her the benefit of the doubt—for now.

But there were too many things about that night that bothered him. And he wouldn't be able to put his questions to rest before a few of them were answered.

Gregor's questions were answered sooner than he expected. The first person he saw upon reentering the raucous Hall was his brother. In one carelessly spoken sentence, John crushed the last hope that Cate might be telling the truth.

"She sent for me," John said without hesitation when Gregor asked him why he'd appeared in Cate's room that morning. John had been enjoying the free-flowing *cuirm* of the feast and grinned, not realizing the impact his words were having. "Said it was something important."

"And it couldn't wait until morning?"

John shrugged. "I was worried. The boy mentioned something about blood, which is why I woke Ete and Lizzie." He frowned. "I wonder what it was that she wanted?" He smiled lopsidedly. "Ah, well, I guess it worked out all right."

It *had* worked out all right—just as she'd planned. The bitter taste of betrayal filled Gregor's mouth . . . his lungs . . . his chest. It burned like acid in his gut. He called for the whisky to put it out. But the flame only grew hotter.

It wasn't until that moment that he realized how much he'd wanted to believe her. John's confirmation of her perfidy made it all that much worse. Gregor had known something was wrong about that morning. Now he knew why. She must have sent for his brother when she'd left the room for so long. That was why she'd been so anxious for him not to leave when she returned.

What a damned fool! How could he have let himself think even for a minute that she truly cared about him? *Him*. Not his reputation and all the other shite that went along with him.

She was just like Isobel, and he'd been just as blind. Instead of using him to make his brother jealous, Cate had used him as some "coup" to laud over her friends. And she'd done it. Aye, the little "orphan" who'd seemed so genuine and artless had trapped the man who didn't think he could be trapped. She'd turned a jaded, cynical man into a temporary believer.

Gregor would laugh if his chest didn't feel like someone was standing on it. The hurt was what angered him. He didn't want to admit it, but she'd gotten to him. Christ, he'd actually thought he might be falling in love with her.

Isobel had stung his pride, but Cate had done much worse. She'd made him feel. She'd made him want. And if that was what "love" was about, he didn't want anything to do with it. He'd been fine the way he was before, but he'd let himself get caught up in a young girl's game.

No longer. His eyes were open—*wide* open, damn it. And soon enough hers would be as well. She might have forced him into marriage, but she hadn't "won" anything else. She could take him as he was or not at all—he no longer cared.

He drained his cup and poured himself another. It was Hogmanay, damn it. He was getting married in a week. What did he care if the bride had made a bloody fool of him? It was time to celebrate. And he, for one, intended to have a good time.

Cate returned to the Hall and did her best to pretend nothing was wrong. But her smiles were forced, her attention was distracted, and her heart was aching. She felt like someone had just taken a hammer to her happiness and shattered the illusion like glass.

She hadn't realized how fragile the bond she'd formed with Gregor was until Seonaid came along and snapped it with a few carelessly spoken words and half-truths.

Without question, Cate was ashamed of the conversations with Seonaid. She never should have boasted about her relationship with Gregor or spoken about marrying him as if it were a contest and he a prize to be won—especially since she knew how much it bothered him to be thought of in those terms.

In doing so, she'd made herself no better than the countless other women who'd sought him out because he was "the handsomest man in Scotland" or made a game of trying to bring him to heel. But she wasn't like those other women. The ones who tried to seduce him, the ones who wanted to marry him not because they loved him but because of how he looked and his reputation. He had to see the difference—didn't he?

But talking about him like that was wrong, and she deeply regretted it. It wasn't how she thought of him at all, and she hated that he'd overheard a conversation that might have given him a reason to question the sincerity and depth of her feelings.

She wasn't blind. Of course she loved the way he looked. But she saw far beyond that. She saw the man who could have a kingdom but was determined to prove himself on his own merit. She saw the man who no one—not even his own family—had believed in become someone to rely on. She saw a man who'd taken in a traumatized young girl and given her a home, a family, and a way to keep the nightmares at bay by encouraging her to learn a man's skill. She saw the skill that made him one of the best warriors in Scotland, and the depth and compassion for those he killed that made him a great man.

Maybe she deserved his condemnation and anger for her part in the conversation with Seonaid, but a few thoughtlessly spoken words were a long way from the deception and trickery of which he'd accused her. It bothered her how easily he'd been ready to accept her guilt. She would never attempt to trap a man—any man—into marriage. He should know that, no matter how bad her words sounded.

Admittedly, they *had* sounded bad, and given what had happened with John and the others walking in on them, the situation had *looked* bad, too. But it stung that he hadn't trusted her, and the cold, unfeeling look on his face had given her a moment's pause. If he could turn on her so easily, maybe she didn't know him as well as she thought she did?

Heartbreaker. What they said about him came back to her. That wasn't him, she told herself. He did have the capacity to feel. He cared about her—maybe even loved her. When he thought about it, he would realize the truth.

But she was disappointed, hurt, and a little angry—

certainly in no mood for merriment. Still, she forced a
smile to her face as she danced with his uncle, and then
with a steady stream of other guests. *It will be all right,* she
told herself. Gregor would come to his senses. No doubt
he would be ashamed for distrusting her and find a crea-
tive way of making it up to her later.

But as the night drew on, her thoughts of sinful kisses
and passionate apologies became harder and harder to believe. He didn't look like a man who was sorry for anything.

On returning to the Hall, Gregor had gone to the dais,
spoken to John for a few moments, called for the *uisge
beatha,* and proceeded to fill his tankard over and over
with the strong-tasting brew that she'd seen him drink
only rarely—and then in much smaller amounts.

The heavy drinking wasn't the worst of it, though. Those
flirtatious glances and touches that had been reserved for
her were now being distributed freely and indiscriminately.

Gregor hadn't looked at her once since returning to the
Hall. But his friends had. The worried looks cast in her
direction by the other Phantoms and John didn't make it
any easier to bear. When one of the serving maids somehow ended up on Gregor's lap after bending over to refill
his tankard—with her sizable breasts practically right
under his nose—Cate had had enough. She wasn't going to
let him treat her as if she meant nothing to him—no matter what he thought she'd done.

She stormed over to the corner of the Hall before the fire,
where he was holding court like some drunken sultan, and
glared at the two until the giggling servant saw her and had
the good sense to slide off his lap and scamper away.

The crowd of men who had been standing around him—
maybe to protect her from seeing what she had?—slowly
dissipated.

Not wanting to make a scene, she spoke in a low voice

through gritted teeth and a tight smile. "What do you think you are doing?"

"What does it look like?" he replied with a narrowed gaze, and a dangerous glint in his eye that she'd never seen before. "Celebrating the new year."

"It looks like you've done enough celebrating," she said with a pointed glance at his tankard.

His smile was sly and calculating, and it sent a chill racing down her spine. "I haven't even begun. The night is young." He stood with more steadiness than she would have thought him capable after all the whisky, and threw back the rest of the contents in his cup for good measure, before slamming it on the table in front of him. "You aren't my wife yet, Cate. You'd do best to remember that."

She sucked in her breath. Her heart seemed to have stopped beating. Was he saying he no longer wanted to marry her? "What is that supposed to mean?"

He gave her a long look filled with a dark emotion she didn't understand. "It means I know the truth. It means you may have 'won' your little game with your friend, but don't try to get in my way."

There was no mistaking the warning. Clearly, he still didn't believe her. "Gregor, don't be like this. We need to talk."

His gaze hardened to black, unforgiving ice. "Aye, we do, and I shall have plenty to say. But right now is not the time. Do not push me, Cate."

She let him go, watching him walk away with a sense of helplessness. What did he mean, "I know the truth"? If he knew the truth, he wouldn't be acting this way. But it was clear he was in no condition to think rationally. He'd said they would talk. Tomorrow . . . tomorrow things would be much more clear.

Twenty

❧

Tomorrow came and went without anything being re-
solved. The cool light of day, and a whisky-cleared head,
had not imparted to Gregor any sudden epiphanies or rationality about Cate's motives for—or means of—securing
a proposal from him.

Nor did he give her the chance to explain. He skipped
the morning meal and was locked away in his solar with
Aonghus, Bryan, and Cormac—three of his household
men—for most of the morning.

As most of the guests were staying through to the wedding, he could not avoid the midday meal, although she
suspected he would have if he could have found an excuse.
He sat beside her at the high table on the dais, but there
was so much distance between them, he might as well have
been in England. He spoke to her only when necessary,
and then with such blank politeness it cut her to the quick.
The easy rapport and intimacy of the day before had vanished as if it had never existed.

Anger Cate would have known how to fight. But this
seeming acceptance of her guilt and sentencing to a purga-
tory of the unknown—where she couldn't appeal her con-
viction or know her punishment—was far harder to
combat. If she'd thought him untouchable before, it was
nothing to the air of remoteness and indifference that had
gone up like an icy shield around him now.

Still, she tried. She tried throughout the meal to talk to

him, but he either brushed her off or included the people around them in the conversation to forestall the discussion of anything personal. As soon as the meal was concluded, he excused himself and joined the other Phantoms at their table. A few minutes later, they departed. To hunt, she would learn from John later.

She was left to entertain their guests and pretend nothing was wrong. Pretend that she wasn't deeply hurt by his behavior. Pretend that she didn't see the pitying glances sent in her direction.

Pretend that she wasn't worried.

What if he refused to believe her?

By the end of the day, Cate had had enough. She'd hoped that she wouldn't need to defend herself, but she couldn't let it go on like this any longer. If Gregor wouldn't talk to her, then he could very well listen.

After saying good night to the children, she went back down to the second level, but not to her room. Instead, she took up a post at the window in the room where Gregor had slept before he'd removed himself to the barracks. Unlike her room, his overlooked the bailey and gate.

As the chamber was temporarily empty, no one had lit the brazier, and the drafty room was about as cold and desolate as she was feeling. Though far from spacious and modern, the old tower house was a palace compared to the small cottage she'd grown up in, and she loved it. It was comfortable. It was home. Removing the fur-lined coverlet from the bed, she wrapped it around her shoulders, sat on the wooden bench, and waited, watching the gate for any sign of riders.

Surely he would return soon? Though it was only seven or eight o'clock, it had been dark for some time.

But an hour passed, and then another. The number of people moving about the bailey dwindled until only the warriors on the night watch remained.

The castle grew silent. The candle she'd brought with her burned low. Her lids grew heavy.

Reality set in. Gregor wasn't coming back. At least not tonight. Maybe not . . .

She wouldn't let herself finish the thought. With a feeling akin to despair, she curled up on the same bed where they'd made love and tried not to let her mind wander in terrifying directions.

He would come back, and she would talk to him when he did. It had only been a day. Nothing horrible could happen in a day. It would be all right.

But it was a long time before she slept.

Cate startled awake from what felt like a posset-induced slumber. *Jangle. Clop. Clop.* The sounds penetrated her hazy consciousness. She sat up. They were the sounds she'd waited hours to hear the night before . . . horses!

A barrage of yapping followed as she hopped out of bed and raced to the window.

Grasping the wooden frame with white-knuckled fingers, she peered out. Her heart fell with disappointment. It wasn't riders coming in; it was men leaving. She recognized Bryan as he rode through the gate.

Good gracious, what was the matter with Pip's pup? It was tearing back and forth in front of the gate, barking frantically. Finally, one of the men picked him up and started to carry him back toward the stables.

Pip had better keep watch over the poor little mite if he didn't want it to get hurt. The lad was going to have to find a name for it, too. The pup was thriving and well past any danger—assuming it didn't get trampled by horses, that is.

A glance at the sun already high on the horizon told her she had slept late and had better hurry if she didn't want to miss the morning meal.

Maybe Gregor had returned sometime during the night?

If not, she would find John and see if he could tell her anything.

Gregor couldn't just leave. Not with all these guests. Not with their wedding only days away. At least that was what she kept telling herself.

Returning to her own chamber, she quickly washed, tugged a comb through her tangled hair, and changed her gown before racing down the stairs. When she entered the hall, she realized it must be later than she'd thought. The servants were already clearing the trays, and most of the guests and clansmen were gone.

She caught sight of Ete with her head down and darting out the back entrance—probably chasing after Maddy—and would have gone after her if she hadn't seen John talking with Aonghus near the fireplace. Snatching a crust of bread and piece of cheese from one of the trays, Cate managed a few bites while she waited for the men to finish their conversation.

Every now and then she glanced out the window, but the man she was looking for didn't appear. Her gaze kept being drawn back to the two men on the other side of the room. It was clear something was wrong. John looked upset and Aonghus appeared very uncomfortable, as he responded to what appeared to be a barrage of questions from John.

Questions that stopped dramatically the moment John looked up and caught her eye. Something in his expression set the hair at the back of her neck on edge. It was half apologetic and half pitying. He looked like he felt sorry for her, and she wasn't sure she wanted to know why.

God, had he left her?

Her heart thumped in her chest. He said a few more curt words to Aonghus and sent him away.

Cate approached cautiously, having the distinct impression that the conversation had been about her.

John's mouth was tight and his expression strained as

she drew nearer. Finally, she stood before him. Holding her breath, bracing for the worst, she looked up at him. "Is something wrong?"

His mouth drew even harder, whitening his lips and making the muscle in his jaw jump. "My blasted brother will explain. I'll have nothing to do with this."

John was furious. Whatever Gregor had done, clearly John didn't agree with it.

"Gregor has returned?" She hoped she didn't sound as relieved as she sounded.

"Aye. He's a bastard but not a coward," he said grudgingly—very grudgingly.

Cate had no idea what he was talking about, but something was obviously very wrong. Taking a deep breath for strength, she asked the question, "What has he done?"

John swore, dragging his fingers back through his hair the same way Gregor did when he didn't know what to say. "It's my fault. I didn't realize what he was asking. I never would have told him before talking to you, if I'd known."

"Whatever are you talking about, John? Told him what?"

"That you sent for me that morning. I didn't think anything of it until he started acting like an arse that night, and I realized what he thought."

Cate stared at him in confusion. "*I* sent for you?"

"Aye, that morning we walked in on you and Gregor . . . uh, in bed."

Cate was aghast. She stood back, looking at him as if he were deranged. "I did no such thing!"

He frowned. "Pip said you had to tell me something important."

"No." She shook her head. "I didn't send for you. There must be some mistake." Suddenly her eyes widened in horror. She covered her gasp with her hand, realizing what it meant. "And you told Gregor this?"

Dear God, what he must think? What John told him

must have seemed a confirmation of Seonaid's claim that Cate had trapped him into marriage. No wonder he'd been acting so cold.

John nodded. "Aye, he asked me how it was that I came to your room that morning, and I didn't think anything of it. At least not until he started drinking, and . . ."

He left off, clearly not wanting to say what else Gregor had been doing. Flirting—*please let it only be flirting*—with those other women.

"Acting like an arse?" she finished for him.

He nodded. "I'm sorry, Cate."

The way he was looking at her . . .

Her pulse spiked with trepidation. "I didn't send for you, John. I would never try to force him into marrying me. You know that, don't you?"

He hesitated. It was clear that like Gregor, John had thought the worst. But unlike his brother, he had some doubts. "I didn't want to think so. I hoped there was an explanation. I told him so, but he was too angry with me—I told him I wanted to fight with Bruce, not stay here and run his clan for him."

Cate was glad that John had found the courage to tell Gregor how he felt. But how ironic that John gave her the benefit of the doubt her betrothed would not. Yet John had never been manipulated and betrayed by a woman he cared about. John hadn't learned to be guarded and cautious. John didn't fear ulterior motives from every woman he met. And John hadn't heard her in the corridor with Seonaid.

She cringed again. Oh God, how Gregor must hate her! It was a betrayal of the worst kind to him. For all that he pretended that women who set their sights on him instantly upon meeting him or turned him into a notch on the bedpost didn't matter to him, she knew it did.

"There is an explanation," Cate said firmly. "I'll find Pip, and we can clear this all up."

The hard, tight look returned to his face. "I'm afraid it's too late for that."

"What do you mean it's too late—"

She stopped, the reason for John's anger and odd behavior suddenly hitting her full force. She felt like she'd just been crushed under a wall of rocks.

No . . . No! Gregor wouldn't . . .

But he would. The pain cut like a jagged knife, eviscerating her heart from her chest in one cruel slice. He'd warned her they couldn't stay, and she hadn't wanted to believe he could actually send them away. But his anger with her had given him all the excuse he needed. He was making it clear that they wouldn't be a family.

The pup's barking made horrible sense. Pip, Eddie, and baby Maddy . . . they were gone.

Concentrate, damn it. There is nothing wrong with you. Gregor grabbed an arrow from where it was stuck in the ground at his feet, nocked it, drew it back, and let it loose in one smooth motion before picking up the next and the next in rapid succession.

Within seconds, he'd fired off a half-dozen arrows at as many targets that hung from a rope along the wall. All but one of the arrows had hit its mark dead center. The one that missed had done so by less than two inches. Nearly perfect. But for Gregor, two inches was as good as ten feet.

He wasn't the only one who noticed the miss. Although they were trying not to show it, all three of his brethren were looking at him with varying degrees of concern. It had been like this all morning, except that if anything, Gregor's shots were getting worse.

"It was a late night," MacSorley said. "We are all tired. Hell, we probably rode thirty miles last night. Perhaps we should call it a day."

Christ, it was so bad, MacSorley wasn't even trying to jest.

Without a word, Gregor went to the wall to retrieve the arrows from the stuffed bags of linen marked with a black "x."

Gregor *was* tired, and they *had* ridden most of the night—chasing shadows as it turned out, with no sign of the men who'd been in the forest—but they all knew that wasn't why he'd missed a target that a squire would have hit. In fact, it was a training exercise Gregor had devised as a lad and used now to teach young archers.

Two days ago when he'd ridden out with his bow for the first time since returning home, he'd been flawless. Focused. His old self.

But two days ago wasn't today. Two days ago he hadn't known that the marriage he'd actually been looking forward to was a sham. Two days ago he hadn't felt like ripping off someone's head—preferably his own.

God, he couldn't believe what a deluded fool he'd been! He'd actually thought she was different. He'd thought she really loved him, *and* for the right reasons.

But whatever the truth of her feelings, he no longer cared. He didn't need her love, or anyone else's for that matter. He'd had enough games, enough "traps" and boasts, to last a lifetime.

He yanked the errant arrow from the mark disgustedly. He'd missed the target for one reason and one reason only: because he couldn't bloody concentrate. He couldn't get himself to that place he needed to be where nothing else mattered. The narrow zone where there was only his arrow and the target.

He didn't know why he was letting her get to him like this. Why was he still so damned angry? Why couldn't he stop thinking about it? He shouldn't care, damn it. She would be his wife, but that was all. She shouldn't matter to him.

Coming home was supposed to clear his head of distractions, not make them worse. He never should have let himself get involved with her. He should have married her off and been done with it as he'd originally planned. He had a job to do, damn it. The king was counting on him. His friends were counting on him. He sure as hell wasn't going to let them down.

He couldn't afford to lose his edge and let anything interfere. Not when they were so close. Which meant he had to get Cate out of his head for good. He needed to get back to the way he was before he'd been duped.

MacSorley and MacRuairi were already starting back to the barracks when Gregor returned to the line. But Campbell was waiting for him.

The revered scout didn't say anything for a while. He just stared at him with that eerie, penetrating gaze that made you feel as if he were looking right inside you.

Suddenly, Campbell straightened, sensing her arrival moments before Cate walked around the corner. His partner was like that. He could feel things before they happened. It had come in handy more than once.

One glance at her devastated face, and Gregor knew she'd discovered what he'd done. He hardened the fool heart that felt a pang of remorse she didn't deserve and looked back to his partner.

"Whatever is wrong between you and the lass," Campbell said, "fix it. We need you."

Gregor held his friend's gaze for a moment, and then gave a determined nod. He intended to do exactly that.

Twenty-one

Cate barely acknowledged Campbell as she came up to stand before Gregor. Her eyes were only on him. Haunting eyes. Eyes filled with hurt, condemnation, and disbelief. Eyes that begged him to tell her she was wrong about what he'd done.

She was pulled tight as one of his bowstrings, her hands in tiny balls at her sides, her slender figure taut and straining. "Where are they?"

He didn't pretend to misunderstand. "The bairns have been returned to their rightful homes and families."

Her fists squeezed and her lips pursed white. But it was the sheen of tears that made his chest feel too tight and his lungs feel as if they were on fire. She was projecting calm fury, but he could see the hurt and pain and knew just how close she was to losing her composure. *Don't cry, damn it.* If she did, he didn't know what the hell he'd do.

He shouldn't care, damn it. She'd deceived him. Used him. Made him think she loved him for the right reasons. Made him want something he'd never wanted before. And that was something he could not forgive, no matter how remorseful or heartbroken she appeared.

"This is their rightful home. We are their family."

The accusation in her gaze pricked his conscience, letting loose some of the anger whipping around inside him. "Neither is true. It was a fantasy you created that had no place in reality. Those children didn't belong here, they belong with their true family—their real blood relatives."

She drew back, clearly surprised. "What are you talking about? They were abandoned."

"Edward and Mathilda, yes. But both had kin eager to take them in."

He didn't mention the generous yearly allowance he'd offered.

"You found their relatives?" She spoke in a small, soft voice that made her sound about twelve.

"It wasn't difficult. A few enquiries was all it took."

She blinked, staring at him. "And then you got 'rid' of them." Her voice broke, and something inside him twisted—coiled—cutting off his breath. "How could you do that, Gregor? How could you send them away without letting me say goodbye?"

He shuffled a little, unable to completely ignore the discomfort provoked by her question. She might not be able to fault him for what he'd done, but maybe she could for how he'd done it. "I thought it best to prevent a scene. What purpose would it serve to wrench weeping children from your arms? A clean break was easier on everyone."

"Is that what you think? A clean break? At least they would have known I loved them, which was more than I ever knew. My father left without telling me, and let me tell you, there was *nothing* clean about it. What must they think? How could you do that to them? How could you take out your anger at me on them?"

"My decision had nothing to do with you." It had to do with him. He hadn't known whether he could go through with it if he'd had to watch. It was better for everyone this way. Those children didn't belong here, no matter how much she wanted them to. "You knew this would happen at some point. I told you from the start."

Her eyes shimmered with angry tears, but she couldn't

argue with him. "And what of Pip? Was he returned to his kinsmen as well?"

This time he didn't flinch or feel even a twinge of guilt. "There was no need. His mother was close at hand."

She looked aghast. "You sent him back to his mother? How could you do that? God knows what she'll make him do this time."

His eyes narrowed. "So you were aware of the boy's subterfuge?"

"Pip told me everything, but it is you who don't understand. His mother forced him to do what he did, and then threatened to take him away if he didn't give her money."

Whether what she said was true didn't matter. "You had no claim on them, Cate. Any of them. They didn't belong to you."

"I love them. It might mean nothing to you, but it means everything to me."

"Yes, I know exactly how much your love means." He didn't hide his sarcasm. "You might have trapped me into marriage, but I won't take three children from their real families to satisfy some girlish fantasy you have of the perfect family."

He might have slapped her, so jarring was the shock of pain. But she didn't crumple or fall apart. She just stood there staring at him, her silence somehow challenging and condemning at the same time. "I didn't trap you, Gregor. I didn't send for John."

"So my brother is lying?"

She shook her head. "I didn't say that. But I did not send Pip to fetch him. I don't know why he did."

"Convenient that Pip isn't here to explain for us."

Her cheeks flushed angrily. "Whose fault is that?"

They stared at each other in the cold, clear light of day, emotion coiling dangerously between them. And something else. Something else he wanted to deny. The fierce, frenzied attraction that didn't differentiate between love and hate. It flared and crackled between them. Even knowing what he knew, he wanted her still. So intensely that his hands itched to wrap around her arms and haul her against him. To cover her body. To punish her for making him fool enough to care. How could she have done this?

He could almost hate her for it. He straightened. Hardened. "So the fact that I woke and found you gone, and then shortly afterward a crowd appeared in your room, was a coincidence?"

She held his gaze, her eyes unwavering. "Aye."

He didn't say anything but clenched his jaw until his teeth ached.

"I'm asking you to trust me, Gregor. To have a little faith in me. I'm telling you the truth."

He hesitated. For one long heartbeat he actually hesitated. She sounded so sincere. He replayed the conversation in his head, heard her feeble denial mixed with guilt, heard her boasts and damning words, and John's condemning ones.

Looking at her, he could concede that her plea was heartfelt. He didn't even doubt that she loved him. But it wasn't enough. He'd been here too many times before. He had no faith in any of it. "You ask for too much."

He pretended not to see the disappointment brimming in her eyes, but he felt each tear that slid down her cheek like acid in his chest.

"If you loved me, you would know I was telling you the truth."

"Then I would be a fool." He paused meaningfully. "And I am no fool."

She sucked in her breath, taking in his meaning: he didn't love her.

He should be impervious to her hurt. *Should* be. But he wasn't, damn it.

God, he had to get out of here! But he needed to make sure she understood. "You have what you wanted, Caitrina.

You will be my wife. Just leave it at that. Don't expect anything more."

"Like love?"

Especially that. "I will give you my name and in return I will have my freedom."

"What do you mean?"

He held her gaze unflinchingly. "I can only be trapped into marriage once."

She sucked in her breath when his meaning took, looking at him as if he were a stranger. "You do not intend to keep your vows."

It was not a question. He cocked a brow. "Did you think I would? I have a reputation to uphold. But you know that."

Her hurt flared to anger. "So I will be your wife, but you will owe me nothing else, is that it? I will stay here with John, run your castle, and you will return whenever you like? What other duties will I have in this marriage you envision? Am I to share your bed, or will it be too crowded?"

His fury matched hers and he returned her sarcasm with his own. "I will need sons."

"Of course. How could I have forgotten? Those sons that you can have"—she snapped her fingers—"whenever you wish. So you plan to make love to me but not love me, is that it?"

"I told you before: one is not required for the other. Call it whatever the hell you like, but there is very little love involved in shoving you up against a wall and taking you from behind."

He could not have shot an arrow with more deadly accuracy. His words had struck with cruel precision, wounding deeply. He saw it in her eyes and heard it in her gasp of pain.

But Cate was a fighter. She would not go down so easily. She drew herself up and faced him like a warrior on a battleground. "I won't let you do this, Gregor. I won't let you try to convince me that what was between us meant nothing. That it was only lust. Call it what *you* will," she repeated his words back to him, "but even pressed up against a wall you care. I can feel it every time you touch me. Every time you whisper in my ear. Every time you let go inside me, crying my name. *My* name, Gregor, not someone else's. The passion we have is more than lust and you know it. Deny it if you want, but I know the truth. What you feel for me is unlike anything you've felt for another woman. It's special, and you won't convince me otherwise. So if you think you can marry me—*make love* to me—and take other women to your bed, who do you think is the one fooling themselves?"

Gregor fought for control, but his blood pounded in his ears. She was the one who'd betrayed him, and yet she stood there so damned confident, so sure that she had him under her spell. This twenty-year-old girl who'd been a virgin a little over a week ago thought she knew more than he did about passion and lust. Thought she knew what he felt. She was still trying to control him, damn it.

But she didn't know a damned thing, and she'd challenged him one too many times.

She was wrong. And he was going to prove it.

Cate was furious. How dare he try to cheapen what they had by making it sound crude and base!

She knew he was angry and more hurt than he wanted to admit by what he thought she'd done. But he'd gone too far, both in sending the children away without telling her and in turning their future marriage into some kind of meaningless, convenient arrangement. She would never marry him like that—ever. And if she'd really believed he'd meant what he said, she would have told him to go to the devil right there.

But Cate was wagering everything on the fact that she

knew him better than he did himself. That what he was doing was not because he didn't care, but because he did. He was acting like this because she'd hurt him—deeply. Once he realized she was telling the truth, it would be the way that it was before.

She hated that she was being forced to prove her innocence, but she was not ready to give up on him—on them. She had faith enough for them both.

She would make him pay for doubting her, though. Maybe she'd make him write her a love poem or sing her a love song? Or maybe she'd make him take Pip with him as his squire when he left. Aye, that was it. He would personally see to Pip's training.

For she had every intention of getting Pip back—and Maddy and Eddie, too, if she wasn't absolutely convinced the kinsmen Gregor had sent them to wanted them.

She couldn't believe he'd found their families. But maybe she shouldn't be surprised. *You never tried.* Cate felt a stab of guilt, knowing she should have made enquiries herself. But she hadn't wanted to. She'd wanted them for herself.

Yet even if he was right that she had no real claim on them—that it was just "some young girl's fantasy of the perfect family"—the way Gregor had sent them away was wrong. She had to find them to say goodbye. She had to tell them that she loved them and would be here for them if they needed her.

Somehow she made it through the midday meal without her face cracking, her expression like ice as she sat beside Gregor on the dais and pretended everything was all right. She wasn't surprised when he refused to tell her where the children were, insisting that for now they needed time to settle in with their families. Later, he told her—later she could go and visit them.

Cate was too furious to chance arguing with him in public. The meal seemed to go on forever, but the moment it was over, she began making enquiries of her own.

Ete and Lizzie had been just as surprised as she—and were just as upset. They were also in the dark about where the children had been taken. Aonghus, Bryan, and Cormac had woken them at dawn and informed them the children were leaving. They'd been forbidden from waking Cate and letting her know what was happening. They'd made noise above her room, hoping she would hear, but she'd slept in Gregor's room.

Of course, Aonghus, Bryan, and Cormac—as well as John—were nowhere to be found. Most of the men (including Gregor and the other Phantoms) had gone hawking and would not be back before the evening meal.

Suspecting information would not be forthcoming from Gregor's men anyway, Cate took advantage of their absence and decided to see if she could find any clues amongst Gregor's papers.

Slipping into the laird's solar, she lit a few candles (the windowless room was already dark) and began to look through the various chests. She knew that the leather folios holding the household ledgers were in the largest of the chests, so she focused on the others. One contained documents from the time Gregor's father was chief, but the smallest wooden chest, closest to the clerk's table, contained a number of folded missives with their wax seals cracked.

One caught her eye. She sucked in her breath, the burn of pain that seared her chest surprisingly intense even after all these years. She recognized the seal, having seen it many times. The young Earl of Carrick had never been without the ring engraved with the Lion Passant above the St. Andrew's cross. As it wasn't an official document, the king must have used his ring rather than the royal seal.

Learning had not come easily to Cate, but she was grateful that her mother had insisted she be taught how to read and write. Scanning the words, however, she felt her legs turn to jelly. She had to reach for the edge of the table to steady herself, as her stomach and head fought the swirl of dizziness.

No.

Though her skills were rudimentary, they were enough to take in the meaning of the words on the piece of parchment before her. Still, she read it twice to make sure she hadn't misunderstood.

But the truth was there in flourishing strokes of black ink. Her father's missive contained congratulatory remarks about the betrothal, news about the words of Gregor's identity spreading, and new intelligence about the arrival of De Bohun's men to help with the defense of Perth Castle, including the return to Scotland of Sir Reginald Fitzwarren, the captain that Gregor had been enquiring about for years.

For years.

He'd known. All this time, Gregor had known the identity of the man who'd attacked her village—the man who'd killed her mother and the unborn child—and he'd kept it from her. Nay, he hadn't just kept it from her; he'd lied to her, telling her he didn't know. She must have asked him a dozen times over the years. Why . . . why would he do something like that, knowing how desperate she was to know? Knowing how badly she'd needed to put a name to the face of the nightmares that haunted her?

She was so lost in the hurt, she didn't hear the door open behind her.

"What are you doing in here, Cate?"

Still holding the devastating missive in her hand, she turned to face John. "He knew." She held up the letter, her hand shaking. "All this time Gregor has known the identity of the man who attacked our village."

John swore. "You weren't meant to see that."

"Obviously," she sneered. "I guess I don't need to ask if you knew, too. How could you keep this from me, John? How could he? Don't you think I had a right to know?"

John's mouth pursed in a hard line. He took her condemnation without trying to defend himself.

She understood. "He told you not to tell me, didn't he?"

Clearly answering carefully, John tried to explain. "He was trying to protect you."

"Protect me?" she repeated incredulously. "From the truth?"

"Fitzwarren has been in England since the attack—unreachable. But Gregor worried you might try to do something, uh . . . ill-advised."

"You mean foolish. He thought I'd run off and try to kill him myself, that's what you mean?"

"I believe he may have considered the possibility," John said, hedging. "Do you deny it?"

Tears blurred her eyes. It wasn't the lie that hurt as much as it was what it signified. He hadn't trusted—or respected—her enough to think she'd be able to handle the information and make her own decisions. She'd wanted Gregor to think of her as a strong woman—capable of taking care of herself—but he still saw her as the little girl in the well who needed to be protected. Even with their growing closeness the past few weeks he'd kept this from her, *knowing* how important it was to her.

She wished she could be angry, but it was the weight of disappointment crushing down on her that hit her most. "I trusted Gregor when he said he would handle it. I would have listened to his explanations. But he never gave me the opportunity. He has no faith in me at all."

"Talk to him, Cate. He was only trying to protect you. Give him a chance to explain before rushing to judgment. He does have faith in you. It might not seem like it right now, but he does."

John was right. They needed to clear the air between them if this marriage was going to have any chance of working.

She looked at the missive in her hand, the red wax of the

seal catching her eye. It wasn't only the contents of the letter they needed to discuss, but also the identity of the man who'd sent it. Gregor hadn't been the only one to keep a secret.

"Where is he?"

"Washing for the evening meal."

Cate did the same, and then entered the Hall to wait for him. But Gregor didn't appear. None of the Phantoms did.

It didn't take her long to discover they'd gone to the village. But it wasn't until John kept dodging her questions and refused to look her in the eye that Cate guessed why.

Horror descended over her in a smothering mask. Her last conversation with Gregor came back to her. She knew the way he thought. He'd taken her words as a challenge, and he'd gone to the alehouse to prove that what they had wasn't special.

She should have known better than to push him when he was like this. But she'd been so confident—so certain she knew him. So certain he loved her and wouldn't be able to do it.

Her stomach curdled. She wanted to bend over and wrap her arms around her middle, but she hid her pain behind a stony mask of calm as she finished the meal and walked upstairs to change. She would see the truth for herself. Only then would she accept what her heart was already telling her.

"The handsomest man in Scotland *and* one of Bruce's Phantoms? Just wait until I tell my sister."

If there was any doubt whether the news of his place in the guard had spread there wasn't a few minutes after arriving at the ale house. The secret was out.

Gregor's smile hid the flash of irritation caused by the lass's remarks. But rather than nudge her off his lap, he concentrated on the soft bottom rubbing against his cock, the full, heavy breasts brushing the hand that he had wrapped around her waist, and the very talented mouth that he knew from past experience would give plenty of pleasure.

Also from past experience, he knew that she'd shout from the bloody rooftops that she'd had him in her bed. Needless to say, after the first time—no matter how pleasurable—he hadn't gone back.

But what the hell did he care? It was the way it was. Why fight it? She would get something to lord over her sister and the other lasses—war widows, mostly—who took advantage of the rooms above Annie's alehouse for companionship, and he would get a night of mind-blowing, head-clearing lust.

To hell with Cate and what she thought. She didn't know a damned thing. She might have tricked him into marriage, but she sure as hell wasn't going to get anything else from him. He could take whoever he wanted to his bed. Her "special" "only me" shite was exactly that.

Maggie leaned closer. The blast of lavender smote him. Cate used lavender, but on her, the scent was soft and delicate and made him want to inhale and draw it deeper into his lungs. On Maggie, it was cloying and overpowering and made him want to run outside to get a breath of fresh air to clear the stench from his nose.

He swore silently and reached for his tankard. Why the hell was he even thinking about her? Cate was wrong, damn it, *wrong*.

Maggie had leaned in to whisper something to him. "Are they Phantoms, too?" she asked with a tilt of her head.

"They" meaning his three frowning brethren crowded on the benches around the small table with him, who were doing damned fine impressions of Father Roland, the village priest.

Nay, not priests, *monks*. But just because they'd been gelded by their wives and didn't want to have any fun sure as hell didn't mean Gregor couldn't. To hell with them, too. To hell with all of them.

"These three?" He looked over at his disapproving-looking companions. "Do they look like the best warriors in Scotland? They're just West Highland brigands, hoping to make a few coins now that Bruce is poised for victory."

Even MacSorley's eyes narrowed at that. Gregor glared back at him. What did they want, for him to confirm it for her?

Maggie looked unconvinced as she scrutinized the fierce, hulking warriors. "I don't know." She wrinkled her nose. "They certainly look big and scary enough to be Phantoms."

"All muscle," he said. "The Phantoms are clever." *Unlike these three,* he left unsaid. That she seemed to accept. "If I were a Phantom"—the rumors might have reached the village, but Gregor wasn't going to admit anything—"I would hardly be in their company so publicly."

"I guess you're right," she said, snuggling deeper into his lap. When that didn't give her the desired effect, she started to circle her fingers on his stomach and rub her soft, in-danger-of-falling-out-of-her-bodice breasts against his chest.

The lass had fantastic breasts. They were big and lush, and he could remember burying his face in the deep crevice, cupping, squeezing, and then sucking the cherry-red tips until they'd extended a good half-inch and poked against his tongue.

Despite the generous size of her chest, Maggie was slender and dark-haired, the way he liked. She was taller than Cate but her body was too soft, not firm and taut like . . .

He stopped, swore again—this time not so silently—and took another guzzle of his ale. The tankard was discernibly lighter than before. He shot a glare at MacRuairi, who was seated next to him, suspecting that he'd been emptying it when Gregor's back was turned.

Christ almighty! They were treating him like a damned bairn. He didn't need watching over—or saving. He knew exactly what he was doing.

Then why did he feel like he had when he was younger, and he knew he was making a mistake but just couldn't seem to stop himself?

His stomach muscles clenched as Maggie's hand dipped to the waist of his breeches. But it wasn't lust he was fighting.

It felt good, damn it. It *had* to feel good. How could it not? Her hand was only inches from his cock. But his body wasn't responding the way it should to her touch.

Only me . . .

He told that voice to shut the hell up. That wasn't it. He just needed Maggie's hand wrapped around him. Her mouth sucking him. Then he would feel it.

But the anger surging through his veins grew darker and more heated. This was all *her* fault. Cate had done this to him. Messed with his head. Messed with other parts of him as well. But he wasn't going to let her turn him into a damned eunuch.

He wanted other women. Of course he did.

Maggie hadn't lied to him. Maggie hadn't tried to trap him. Maggie hadn't turned him into a blind, besotted fool.

He had nothing to feel guilty about, damn it. Cate had practically thrown a gauntlet down at his feet. Should she be surprised that he'd picked it up?

He drained another tankard of ale before one of his brethren could do it for him.

"I must admit, I'm surprised to see you in here with the wedding and all," Maggie said.

He stiffened, but the lass didn't seem to notice, as she was too busy trying to covertly—or not so covertly—brush her fingertip along the ridge of his cock.

"Some people were surprised when you chose Cate, but I wasn't." She waited for a response from him. Not picking up on his simmering rage, she continued. "She might be a little odd with her sword fighting and all, but she's a real lady. Not judgmental like some of the village women, I'll tell you that." Maggie's mouth pursed with distaste. "Nay, Cate is kindhearted and always has a nice word for me whenever our paths cross."

She frowned, suddenly seeming to realize that what she was doing right now might not be viewed as graciously by Cate.

Gregor's mouth fell in a hard line. He'd had enough. He wasn't going to listen to Cate's finer points from her. He stood suddenly, and barely managed to snag Maggie's wrist to prevent her from falling to the ground. He swayed a little at the sudden movement, his head thick with drink.

But not thick enough. He took a jug from the table and tucked it under his arm. "Come, it's a little too crowded in here. Let's go find someplace a little more private."

Whatever qualms Maggie had vanished. She nodded eagerly and started to drag him away.

But Campbell caught his arm and held him back. "Don't do this, Arrow," he said softly. "I don't know what is going on with you and the lass, but you will regret it."

Campbell didn't know a damned thing. None of them did.

"Go ahead and prove me wrong . . . if you can." That was exactly what he would do, damn it.

"Don't wait for me," Gregor said, ignoring the unsolicited and unwanted advice. "I don't anticipate I'll be making it back to the castle anytime soon."

Determined, Gregor followed Maggie through the crowd to the stairs. He was so focused, he didn't notice the small hooded form sitting quietly in the corner.

Twenty-two

❦

Heartbreaker. Gregor's reputation was well earned. But with all the times she'd heard it, in her arrogant belief that they were meant to be together, not once did Cate think it would be her heart that would be the one broken.

She had been seated at the table for only a few moments before Gregor walked by with Maggie, but it was long enough to see him—*really* see him. The too-handsome heartbreaker in all his roguish glory, drinking, cavorting, and looking every bit like a man without a care in the world.

One tear slid out of the tight tether she had wrapped around her shredded emotions. Furiously, she wiped it away. She couldn't break down yet. She had to do this. She had to finish it so there would never be a doubt. Never again would she be able to delude herself that she meant something to him.

Keeping her head down and doing her best to fade into the background of the crowded, smoke-filled room, Cate wound her way around the perimeter to the door where she'd seen them exit. She was glad she'd taken the time to change her clothing. Dressed in her practice garb, with the hood of her cloak pulled low over her face, no one paid her any mind. She looked like a lad who'd just come in out of the cold.

It *was* cold outside. Bitterly cold. But the chill inside her that had turned her skin and bones to ice had nothing to do with the weather.

She stepped through the doorway and saw the stairs. Her chest twisted. She'd suspected what she would find, but part of her had still held out hope that she was wrong.

Although Cate had never been in this part of the ale-house, she knew what went on here. She knew there were a few solars above where travelers might spend a night, or lonely men might find a companion from one of the women who frequented Annie's.

Normally, Cate did not begrudge women like Maggie who'd lost their husbands to war a way of making a few extra coins. But seeing the lovely black-haired, blue-eyed woman with her generous breasts crushed against Gregor's chest and her hands all over him had changed Cate's mind. She'd felt very grudging indeed and wanted nothing more than to toss the brazen harlot right off his lap.

But she didn't. She'd waited for Gregor to do it. Waited for him to realize that he couldn't do this. That he couldn't make love to another woman because he loved her.

He hadn't, though. Instead, she'd watched in stricken pain as the man she loved—the man she thought she would spend her life with—let another woman put her hands on him.

Now, Cate would see the rest.

Stonily, like a woman condemned to hang climbing the scaffold, she walked up the wooden stairs. Old and rickety, they creaked as she moved, but with all the noise below, she doubted anyone above would notice.

What must have been one large room (albeit a low-ceilinged one) had been partitioned into a few private chambers off a central solar. But with only wooden screens for walls and hangings for doors, there was little privacy. Cate could hear everything. She could hear the couple in the room to her left grunting and groaning in the throes of a very energetic coupling, and she could hear the voices in the room to her right: Maggie's giggling followed by Gregor's deep, rough tones: "I like it just fine."

Like what? Cate wasn't sure she wanted to know. She moved toward the curtain like a ghost. They hadn't bothered to close it completely—why should they, as it hid little of what was going on?—and if Cate stood at the edge, she could see the occupants well enough.

Oh God, no . . .

She drew in her breath as a fresh surge of hurt rolled over her in deep, hot waves. Gregor stood in front of the narrow box bed—the only piece of furniture in the tiny room— facing her. Although there was very little of his face that she could see, as he was locked in a passionate embrace with Maggie. His hand rested at the base of her spine with his fingers spread over the top curve of her buttocks. Maggie's dark hair was loose down her back, the lacing at the back of her kirtle had been undone, and the gown had been tugged down past her shoulders. Her breasts must be bare.

This wasn't like the kiss with Seonaid that she'd witnessed. It was far more carnal. Far more passionate. Far more painful. Far more like the way he kissed her. *Special . . . different.* Her claims seemed to taunt her. She couldn't seem to look away from his hand. Those strong, powerful fingers gripping someone else.

Fortunately, the kiss lasted only a few seconds before Gregor pulled away.

"Is something wrong?" Maggie asked.

Yes. Please say yes.

"No," Gregor said, his voice slurred. He'd obviously been drinking heavily, but that didn't excuse what he was doing; it only added to the unsavoriness.

"Are you sure?" Maggie said, a coy playfulness to her tone. "Maybe it's the drink?"

Her shoulder moved and Cate had to bite her fist to pre-

vent the fresh stab of pain, realizing what she was doing.
Maggie's shoulder had moved because her hand was between his legs. She was stroking him.

Cate's stomach turned in violent revolt.

Maggie giggled. "Let's see if this will help." She dropped
to her knees before him and reached her hands around to
grab him by his backside. "I remember you told me how
good I was with my mouth."

Cate stilled, not understanding. But when Maggie's head
moved forward between his legs, comprehension dawned
in shocked, cruel clarity. She was going to pleasure him
with her mouth.

Push her away. Please push her away.

Instead, Gregor gripped the back of Maggie's head with
his hands, holding her to him. His eyes were closed, his
face a mask of taut lines and intense concentration.

Unable to bear another moment without being ill, Cate
moved away. She'd seen and heard enough. No further
proof was necessary. Gregor had achieved his purpose. She
believed him. God, how she believed him.

What they had together wasn't special. *She* wasn't special. He'd proved it. He didn't care about her—at least not
enough to stop him from seeking out another woman's bed
at the first sign of difficulty between them.

Cate wouldn't marry him, even if he came crawling on
his hands and knees begging for her forgiveness. She didn't
doubt that he would regret it when he learned the truth,
but she didn't care. It was too late. She'd run out of patience, excuses, and faith. Seeing this side of him had shattered every last one of her illusions. She was done making
excuses for him.

She'd wanted to believe that she was the woman for
him, but there was no *one* woman for a man like Gregor
MacGregor. She'd been fooling herself to think he could be
faithful to her—that he could commit. The bond between
them that meant so much to her didn't matter to him. Not

if he could make love to another woman. Maybe he was right. Maybe for him love had nothing to do with the bed-chamber. But for Cate it had had everything to do with it.

Had. But not anymore. Gregor had done what she thought impossible. He'd destroyed her love for him. He'd ripped her heart out of her chest, torn it to shreds, and ground the scraps to dust. There was nothing left. Only the dull, numbing ache of emptiness—as if she were missing a vital piece of herself. The love she'd had for him that had filled her with such joy and hope was gone.

A part of her hated him—but not completely. She also felt sorry for him. Sorry that he was too jaded and cynical, too molded by his past experiences with women, to recognize real love when he had a chance.

It was his loss. Cate would not waste another moment of her life on him.

The man Cate married would believe in her just as much as she believed in him. And it was clear that man would not be Gregor. She did not doubt that he would marry her still. But if he did, he would leave her feeling just as abandoned as her father had. Maybe not physically, but in every other way that mattered.

Gregor wasn't the man she'd thought. She had thought there was more to him than a handsome face. She had thought he was the kind of man she could count on, the kind of man she could trust. But he was no more the noble knight of her fantasies than her father had been. Maybe Gregor was right. Maybe she *had* been trying to create the perfect family to replace the one that she'd lost with him at the center, representing everything she thought a great man should be. She'd wanted him to be something he was not and imagined qualities in him that weren't even there.

She was about to start down the stairs when she heard men below and stopped in her tracks.

"Damn it, someone needs to stop him."

Cate recognized the voice of one of the Phantoms—the big, tall blond one who looked like a Viking, Erik MacSorley. She bit her lip, still embarrassed about the black eye she'd given him.

"We tried, cousin. He didn't seem to be of any mind to listen."

Lachlan MacRuairi, she thought with a shiver, identifying the dark voice and the brigand it belonged to with ease. He sounded as menacing as he looked. Except for the facial hair—they both had unusually shaped, stubbly beards—the two kinsmen looked nothing alike.

"We'll make him listen," MacSorley said. "He doesn't know what the hell he's doing. He loves the lass, and once he realizes it, he'll never forgive himself for doing this."

Cate wanted to tell him he was wrong, but she was more worried about finding a place to hide if they came up the stairs.

"And if making him listen doesn't work?" MacRuairi asked.

"We take him out of there by force," MacSorley said, taking a few steps up the stairs.

Cate was about to dart behind a trunk to hide when another voice intervened in the argument between kinsmen. "Arrow needs to figure this out on his own. If he does love her, he'll realize it. It's not for us to decide."

Arthur Campbell, she realized, the quiet voice of reason. He was right, too. Unfortunately, Gregor had proved that he didn't love her.

After a few more moments the men moved away from the stairs. Cate debated following them—it was dark, and she'd imagined more than one shadow in the woods on the way here—but not wanting to risk discovery, she exited the building and slid into the stables to wait.

When it started to snow a short while later, however, she decided she'd waited long enough. It didn't take her long to reach the edge of the village. She hesitated; the darkness of the forest ahead proved vaguely unsettling. Though she was tempted to borrow a torch from one of the village cottages, she didn't want to draw attention to herself.

It was a decision she would regret a short while later, when the darkness of the forest seemed to swallow her up like a snowy dragon.

She looked over her shoulder more than once, swearing she heard something. A snapped twig. A rustled branch. Then she decided she was only imagining the sounds, her fear causing her mind to play tricks. But once she was deep in the forest, Cate realized it wasn't her imagination. At first she thought she was being tracked by a pack of wolves. But the beasts that surrounded her were horrifyingly human.

Cate fought with everything she had. But in the end, against five soldiers, it wasn't enough. Forced to the ground with a knife to her throat and voices swearing to kill her if she didn't stop struggling, she surrendered.

Two men hauled her off the ground—none too gently— pinning her arms behind her back to face the others. They'd taken her sword, but she still had the dagger Gregor had given her in a scabbard at her waist. If she could just reach it . . .

Her fingers extended toward the hilt. Feeling her movement, one of the men tugged one of her arms harder, making her groan in pain, but also aiding her cause by bringing her hand an inch closer to the hilt. She could just about reach it.

A torch was brought forward and held to her face by a third man. She sucked in her breath, recognizing him: the man on horseback in the woods. The man who looked just like the soldier who'd killed her mother.

"I told you it was her," the man said. "She might dress and fight like a man, but it's MacGregor's bride."

"You were right, Fitzwarren."

Cate froze at the mention of his name. It couldn't be—he was too young.

Nay, it wasn't the captain, she realized, but it could well be his son.

"What do you want with me?" she asked.

"Nothing," Fitzwarren said slyly, his eyes dropping to her out-thrust breasts with a cold, lecherous look that told her he might be like his father in more ways than just appearance. "It's what you are going to do for us. You are going to give us one of Bruce's Phantoms."

Cate froze, but she quickly tried to cover her reaction. "You don't think that rumor is true, do you?"

She cried out as Fitzwarren grabbed a thick tress of hair that had come loose in the struggle and twisted it hard against her scalp. "Don't bother denying it, gel. We know it's true. He's been under suspicion for some time, but has proved elusive. But thanks to you, we won't need to try to capture Gregor MacGregor; he'll walk right through the gates of Perth Castle all on his own to secure his beloved bride's freedom."

Cate was about to argue with his premise—she wasn't his beloved or his bride for much longer—but she clamped her mouth shut. If these men thought she wasn't worth anything to them, they would kill her. And the way young Fitzwarren was eyeing her, she would be lucky if they just killed her and didn't rape her first.

She shuddered with revulsion. But not with fear. Gregor had given her that at least. She wouldn't go down without a fight. She bit back a smile of satisfaction as her fingers closed around the hilt of the dagger. The moment they released their hold, she would be ready.

Suddenly, the other part of what he'd said hit her: *Perth Castle*. The same place the missive from her father had said the captain was heading. The captain who'd escaped punishment for too long.

Gregor had said he would handle it—and maybe he

would if given a chance, even with all that had happened. But Cate didn't want him to. It wasn't his responsibility; it was hers. She wanted to do it herself, maybe even needed to do it herself. Right now it was the only thing that mattered, and the only thing she wanted to think about. For so long, her entire world had revolved around Gregor and the perfect life they would have together that she'd lost sight of anything else. How could she have forgotten the duty she had to her mother and the other villagers? The price of living was to see justice done. Cate might never have another chance to get so close to the man responsible for their deaths, and she would not waste it.

All the hurt, all the hatred, all the heartbreak, she turned to vengeance. Nay, embraced it. It gave her a purpose.

Loosening her grip around the hilt of the dagger, she let it go. For now.

Gregor woke to the sound of snoring and the stale stench of whisky-laden vomit. His stomach rolled at the smell and bile shot up the back of his throat, threatening reemergence.

The vomit was his, he realized, the unpleasantness of the night coming back to him in surprising clarity given the amount he'd imbibed and the current throbbing state of his head.

He felt like hell—which was probably no more than he deserved. He blinked up at the ceiling first, and then at the face of the woman on the pillow beside him.

He winced. God, he needed to get out of here. But as the slightest movement caused extreme pain and threatened what little control he had over his stomach, he unfurled himself from the lass's vice-like grip with painstaking care.

It wasn't Maggie snoring, he realized, but the man in the room beside this one.

Christ, what the hell was he doing? Looking around, he felt a blast of self-loathing and repugnance. Was this what he wanted? Drunken, meaningless liaisons in an alehouse where he woke up to the sounds of another drunkard's snores?

He was a fool. Last night had served no purpose. He'd failed. Miserably. Even with Maggie's mouth around him, he'd seen Cate's face in his head, heard her voice, and knew he couldn't go through with it. Didn't want to go through with it—even if Maggie had been able to get a rise out of him.

He'd blame the whisky, but he knew that wasn't all of it. The moment her mouth had come around him, he'd wanted to push her off. He'd tried to concentrate, tried to think about what she was doing, tried to force back the revulsion, but it hadn't worked. After a few seconds he lost the battle, barely making it to the chamber pot in time.

He'd lost the contents of his stomach from a woman trying to pleasure him with her mouth—that had to be a first.

Maggie had been surprisingly understanding, telling him to lie down and that they would try again when the whisky wore off.

Gregor had passed out knowing it was never going to happen. Not sober, not drunk, not ever.

Cate was right. He loved her. Even knowing what she'd done, he loved her. He loved her resilience, her fight, her determination. He loved her strength and independence. He loved how she made her own way and didn't rely on what was given to her like most noblewomen he knew. He loved kissing her, he loved holding her in his arms, and he loved making love to her.

And just touching another woman—or letting another woman touch him—was enough of a betrayal to make him physically ill.

He'd done nothing wrong, he told himself. Cate was the one who'd betrayed him.

Then why did he feel like emptying his gut all over again?

With a grim look at the woman sleeping in the bed, he fished a few coins from his sporran and left them on the bed. He would apologize later, but he needed to get away from here or he was going to embarrass himself again.

He hurried out of the alehouse, fortunately not running into anyone. It was barely dawn, and most of the occupants were probably still sleeping off last night's festivities.

Gregor needed to wash them off. Taking a slight detour on his way back to the tower house, he stopped at the river to swim. That there was snow on the banks and the river was a few degrees from frozen seemed somehow fitting. But not even the icy dunking could wash away the stain of guilt that clung to him. No matter how many times he told himself that he'd done nothing wrong, that he owed her nothing, he couldn't convince himself that it was true.

He might not have gone through with it, but he'd done enough.

The only way he was going to feel clean was to tell Cate what he'd done—or tried to do. Would she understand? Things were so buggered up between them, he didn't know, but he would tell her the truth and apologize. No matter how bad things were, he shouldn't have done—or attempted to do—what he did.

She'd hit a tender spot, and he'd reacted badly. But he loved her. He was going to have to try to trust her. If she said she hadn't tricked him into marriage, he was going to do his damnedest to believe her.

With grim resolve, he pulled himself out the river and quickly—very quickly—donned his shirt, hose, and braies. He was reaching for his *cotun* when he heard a noise behind him.

His head still foggy from the aftereffects of drink, and his movements slow from the cold, he barely deflected the knife aimed for the lower right side of his back. A stab that given the location could have killed him in a minute or two.

He could feel the edge of the blade brush past his side as

he twisted, slammed his hand against his attacker's wrist, and swung his leg around to knock him off his feet. A move that was easy given the size of his attacker.

Pip! The boy reached for the knife, but Gregor stepped on his wrist before he could get it. Leaning down, he dragged the lad up by the collar. "What in Hades do you think you are doing? You could have killed me."

Pip's face was an angry contortion of frustrated rage. "I wanted to kill you! I wish you were dead."

"Well, I'm sorry to disappoint you, but you'll have to get in line. Most of the English army is in front of you. I know why they want to kill me, but what have I done to deserve a knife in the back from you?"

"You weren't supposed to marry her. You were supposed to leave. I just wanted you to go, so you wouldn't send me away. But you sent all of us away, and you hurt Cate. I never meant for her to get hurt."

Gregor released the boy and took a step back. The heat in his blood from the attack chilled. A shiver of premonition trickled down his spine. The boy's words didn't make any sense, but somehow he knew what had happened. "It was you. Cate never sent for John. You did."

Pip nodded, tears streaming down his cheeks. "I saw her come out of your room that morning and saw the blood on the cloths that she tried to hide. I wanted John to marry her, not you. I thought you would leave. You were supposed to leave. John is honorable, not you."

As the full ramifications of what the boy was saying hit him, Gregor had to sit down. He found a rock and stared wordlessly at Pip, feeling like he'd just taken a knife in the gut.

She hadn't set a trap for him; the boy had. She'd been innocent of any true wrongdoing, and he'd called her a liar. He'd nearly . . . *ah hell*, he almost got sick again, knowing how close he'd come to doing something he would have no right to ask her to forgive. "Do you have any idea of what you've done? What I've done?"

Pip looked at him uncertainly, his reaction obviously not what he'd expected. "What?"

"I love her, and I might have destroyed whatever chance at happiness that we had."

Pip stared at him as if he were a stranger. "You love her?"

Gregor didn't answer him. His mind was on one thing. He donned the rest of his clothes quickly and strapped on his weapons. Noticing the blade on the ground, he picked it up and handed it back to the boy. "You might have need of this yet. If Cate won't forgive me, I'll let you plunge the damn thing into my heart."

Pip's eyes widened, but he remained silent on the short walk back to the tower house.

Gregor hadn't taken a step into the hall when his brother blocked his path. "Where have you been? Or do I want to know?"

Gregor gritted his teeth, ignoring the unwanted questions. "Where's Cate?"

"I was hoping you would know. When Ete went to her room this morning, she wasn't there and her bed hadn't been slept in. No one has seen her since last night."

"What do you mean, no one has seen her since last night? Where the hell could she be?"

His brethren must have heard the commotion and left their meal to come over to help. "What is it?" Campbell asked.

"Cate is missing," Gregor answered.

"Where would she go?" MacSorley asked.

MacRuairi asked the one question all of them were thinking. "Did she know where you were?"

Gregor looked to John. His brother nodded. "But that isn't all. She saw the note."

"What note?"

"The missive in your solar about Fitzwarren."

Gregor swore. The panic running through his blood turned to a full gallop. He quickly explained about the letter to the others.

"Would she go after him on her own?" Campbell asked.

"I don't know, but I think we have to assume yes."

Wasting no time, Gregor quickly organized a few parties of riders to go after her. John and Campbell would lead one, MacSorley and MacRuairi another, and he a third. But before they left the Hall, one his men found him and handed him a crumpled piece of parchment.

"What's this?" he asked.

"One of the village lads brought it this morning. He said a man had given it to him last night but told him not to bring it until morning."

There was something inside. Unwrapping it carefully, Gregor's heart stopped beating when he realized what it was. The familiar ring stared back up at him. The betrothal ring he'd given Cate. The words on the parchment swam in front of his eyes. He handed it to John to read, but he knew what it said. "We have something that belongs to you. If you want her back alive, come to Perth Castle."

The blood drained from his body. For the first time in his life, he felt like he might faint. They had her. The English had Cate. It was just as the Guard had feared if their identities were ever revealed. They would use her to get to him.

If anything happened to her . . .

He couldn't let that happen. He *wouldn't* let that happen. Cate was the most important thing in the world to him. He would give his life to save hers a thousand times over. And it looked like he was going to have to do exactly that.

Twenty-three

❧

Cate was ready to collapse by the time they reached the outskirts of the royal burgh of Perth, one of the most important and wealthiest burghs in all of Scotland. Located on the River Tay—making it an important city for trade—and close to Scone Abbey, Perth was considered the capital of Scotland by ancient Scottish kings.

The castle had been partially destroyed by floods about a hundred years ago but rebuilt by King William the Lion. Less than ten years ago, the city had been fortified with stone walls, towers, and gates by Edward of England after he'd taken the city during Wallace's rebellions.

The wall was how she'd guessed that they'd reached their destination, as the party of riders drew up on the crest of the last hill. She'd never seen anything like it. The massive stone fortification that surrounded the city shimmered like golden alabaster in the dawn's first light. Surrounded on three sides by a *lade*—the wet ditch was the town's only previous defense—the east side butted up against the natural defense of the Tay. Seeing those daunting walls—and knowing that she would soon be imprisoned behind them—gave her a moment's pause.

Cate looked at the men who were sitting on their horses discussing something among themselves, paying her little mind, and glanced over her shoulder at the wide expanse of forest just beyond the next hill. If she were going to try to escape, this would be her last chance. But she couldn't. Not with the opportunity for vengeance so close at hand.

The weapon hidden under her cloak at her side bolstered her courage. The soldiers hadn't searched her—probably figuring one weapon was unusual enough on a woman. She had to hope they didn't conduct a more thorough search when they arrived. She did not deceive herself. Her chances at success or escape were not good, but they were even less without the element of surprise the dagger would give her.

She knew she had to act quickly. No matter what he'd done, Cate would not allow Gregor to give himself up for her. Not if she could help it. She was counting on her father to force caution upon him. Even though Gregor thought she'd betrayed him, she did not doubt he would come charging through those gates as soon as he was able. As her "guardian," he would feel responsible for her. But Robert the Bruce wouldn't allow one of his most important warriors to give himself up to the English for a woman. Bruce might have let her down as a father, but she could not deny that some of those same qualities made him a good king. Ruthless decisions—not emotional ones—were what had placed the crown upon his head, and thus far had kept it there.

Unless she was mistaken about the identity of the army of men taking position on the far side of the river, Gregor wouldn't be able to avoid him. From the looks of it—and what seemed to be concerning the soldiers who'd taken her—Robert the Bruce had arrived at Perth to begin his siege. Along with Berwick, Roxburgh, Edinburgh, and Stirling, Perth—or St. John's town, as it was also known— was one of the key castles left for Bruce to take back from the English. What must be especially galling to Bruce was that Perth Castle—like Stirling Castle—was being held by a Scotsman, Sir William Oliphant, and defended by a garrison comprised of mostly Scots.

The knowledge that her father was so close brought an unexpected pang to her chest. Even after all these years, she wanted to know one thing: why. Why had he left her like that? Was it because of his new bride? He'd married his first wife, Isabel of Mar, shortly after he'd left. Had she demanded he stop seeing the woman who'd fathered one of his "bastards," or had he merely tired of his Cate and her mother?

She turned away from the army of men beyond the gates. She would never know; as she wasn't marrying Gregor, she no longer had to face the prospect of seeing her father again. It had been so long, he probably wouldn't even have recognized her. She wondered if she would have recognized him. The handsome young earl was now a man of nearly two score and a king. Yet somehow she knew she would know him. He'd loomed so large in her past. But that was where he belonged: in her past. Along with Gregor. Her mouth tightened with residual anger and bitterness that not even her exhaustion could erase.

One of the men, a young soldier by the name of Gibbon, who had taken pity on her over the last day and a half of their journey, handed her a skin of water. Cate was a competent rider, but to prevent Gregor from catching up to them they had ridden over forty miles with only brief stops along the way. She could barely sit on her horse, she was so tired.

"How will we get in?" she asked, noting the closed gates. "I assume those are the king's men on the other side of river opposite the drawbridge?"

"Aye, King Hood has begun his siege earlier than we expected. We won't be able to use the red gate near the bridge or we'll run the risk of encountering some of his men. But he hasn't had a chance to position his men around the city yet, so we can use one of the other gates. They'll admit us when they see the banner."

The men rode under De Bohun's arms. She guessed they

were not knights but ordinary men-at-arms, although from what she'd caught of their conversation, it was obvious that young Fitzwarren hoped to be made a knight as reward for capturing one of Bruce's Phantoms.

"We are fortunate that we arrived when we did," Gibbon said with a kind smile. "Or we might have had a more difficult time making it back inside."

"I would think inside would be the last place you should want to go with a siege about to start."

He laughed. "Normally you would be right. But this won't last long. Look at that wall. King Hood doesn't have the siege engines to bring it down, and we are ready for his trickery. The city has fresh water and stores enough for six months. But it won't take nearly that long. Mark my words, King Hood will pack his carts and slink back into his foxhole soon enough."

Cate couldn't have realized how prophetic his words would prove to be.

Two weeks after riding into camp, Gregor stood before the King of Scotland looking very unlike one of the most elite warriors in Scotland—and even less like the most handsome. He'd slept little in the days since Cate had been taken, and every moment that he was awake he was tormented by thoughts of what was happening to her. He looked as horrible and on edge as he felt.

He was done being patient—no matter who was asking it of him. "I can't wait any longer."

The king eyed him from behind the long table that had been set up in his pavilion. The tent was sparsely decorated for a royal lodging—even a temporary one—but Bruce was more warrior than king. It was one of the things Gregor and his fellow Guardsmen most admired about him. The tent itself was a colorful scarlet and gold, reflecting the royal arms, but inside they stood on rushes, not expensive carpets from the East, and in addition to the table there was only a chair, a bench, a bed, and a painted wooden screen for privacy where the king might wash and change. After living on the run for so many years, the king had learned to travel light, unlike his English counterparts, who seemed to campaign with endless carts carrying furnishings and the royal plate.

"I understand what you are going through better than anyone, Arrow. Do you not think I would like to ride into England and free my wife and daughter if I could? But I will not let you go like a lamb to the slaughter. I need you too much. Nor will I risk the others."

Gregor tried to bite back his frustration, but the king's refusal to let him attempt a rescue—or exchange himself for Cate—was driving him past the edge of reason. He'd never felt sorry for MacRuairi before, but the past week had given him an inkling of what the famed mercenary pirate–turned–loyal Guardsman must have gone through for two years. God forbid Cate was being kept in a cage like MacRuairi's now wife had been for part of her imprisonment. Isabella MacDuff was free (as was the king's young sister Mary), but Bruce's queen and heir were still being held in English convents. Gregor also understood the king's fear of Gregor breaking under English torture, but Angel—Helen MacKay—could give him something to ensure that didn't happen. Monkshood or another poisonous plant would ensure the safety of the others, if it came to that.

Gregor turned back to the king and tried to use what rationality he had left to argue his point. "But Cate isn't in England—she's here in Scotland, in one of our castles. And they weren't threatening to kill your wife and daughter." His voice broke, and he looked at the king with hot, dry eyes behind a face that had to be as haggard-looking as he felt. "They said they would kill her by the end of the week if I don't surrender. I won't let that happen."

Over the past two weeks, Gregor had exchanged a series

of missives with Sir William Oliphant, the former Scot hero who was now keeper of the castle for the English and governor of Perth. But after Cate had been brought out on the battlements yesterday to prove that she was alive and in good health, Gregor had nothing more with which to delay. The sight of her—even from a distance—had nearly brought him to his knees with relief, but it had also instilled a new urgency in him.

"I won't ask you to. I'm only asking that you be patient for a few more days. That is all we will need to be inside the castle, if my plan goes as I hope. Nor do I believe Oliphant will sanction the killing of a lass—no matter what the English would like."

Given how unsuccessful their limited siege weaponry had been so far against the city walls, Gregor thought the king optimistic about their chances—to say the least. But they'd succeeded against far worse odds too many times for him to completely dismiss the king's words. Nor would he wager Cate's life on Sir William's honor as a knight. "How do you intend to do that?"

Perhaps sensing Gregor's doubt, the king leaned back in his chair and crossed his arms smugly. "By retreating."

Cate could hear the cheering of the soldiers the moment she exited the tower.

Sir William Oliphant, the former Scottish commander who'd fought alongside Wallace, and the man now tasked with holding the city of Perth for the English king, walked beside her on the parapet. When he reached the place where he'd brought her the day before—to prove her good health to Gregor—he stopped and let her see for herself why the men were celebrating.

She was no less stunned than when he'd come to her tower room a few moments ago and told her that Bruce and his army were on the move. "They are giving up?"

Sir William nodded. "It appears so. We will follow them,

of course, to make sure this is not another of Bruce's tricks. But with what little progress Bruce has made since he and his army arrived, I'm not surprised. He'll not want to waste the time and provisions it will take to starve us out. He'll find an easier target—though not one that is as important."

In the two weeks of her captivity, Cate had grown to admire the gruff old warrior—as well as feel sorry for him. He was a former Scottish patriot who now found himself through circumstance, family allegiances, and vows of fealty in the unfortunate position of fighting against his countrymen.

Like many early patriots, Sir William Oliphant had been taken prisoner by the English after the disastrous battle of Dunbar and eventually released. Also like many of his fellow patriots, he'd broken his promise to Edward of England and "rebelled" again to join Wallace in his uprisings.

Sir William had earned hero status among the Scots when he'd held Stirling Castle with only a few dozen men against Edward of England and the might of his infamous siege engines—War Wolf, the Ram, and the Vicar—for over three months. Ironically, as the old warrior had pointed out to her, it was Bruce who'd been fighting alongside the English at that time.

King Edward repaid Sir William's broken promise with one of his own, when Sir William surrendered Stirling under favorable terms only to see himself stripped naked, paraded around with his men for the amusement of the English, and then imprisoned in the Tower of London for four years. Released under *mainprise* with the promise to fight for the new King Edward II, he'd been given command of Perth earlier this year, after the king's favorite, Piers Gaveston, the Earl of Cornwall, had returned to England only to be executed shortly thereafter.

With no love of Bruce, who Sir William viewed at times

with grudging admiration for what he'd achieved and at others as little better than a usurping murderer (first for taking the crown from the ineffectual but anointed King John of Scotland, and then for killing the king's kinsman— and probable heir to the crown—John "The Red" Comyn before the high altar of Greyfriars), Sir William found himself fighting alongside his former English enemies.

But it was clear the old warrior—probably ten years her father's senior—resented the English "nursemaids," as he called them, from De Bohun, who'd been sent to watch over him and ensure he was not tempted to switch sides. The Fitzwarrens—father and son—in particular, he could not abide.

In that they were of one mind. Cate had barely been able to hide her hatred of the man who'd raped and killed her mother the one time she'd been brought before him, shortly after arriving at the castle. Had "Sir" Reginald Fitzwarren not been armored and surrounded by a half-dozen men-at-arms, she might have been tempted to draw her dagger. She was tempted—more tempted than she should have been, given the circumstances—but she wasn't going to prove Gregor right by doing something foolish. She would bide her time and wait for a better opportunity.

But one had yet to arise, and she knew she was running out of time. The negotiations for her release had already dragged on longer than she'd anticipated.

For that she had Sir William to thank. He, and not the Fitzwarrens—much to their fury—had taken charge of her imprisonment and the negotiations for her release. He'd also seen that she was given a small, sparsely furnished, but relatively comfortable chamber in the tower, and taken charge of her "interrogation." A fact that she'd been glad of when she stumbled through an explanation of how she'd come to live with the MacGregors of Roro. Realizing she could hardly mention her connection to Lochmaben for fear Fitzwarren might recognize her—she already thought he'd looked at her too long that first meeting—she'd claimed to be the orphaned daughter of one of Gregor's father's guardsmen.

On learning that she hadn't left Roro since she'd arrived, and that Gregor rarely returned home—and when he did, it was alone—Sir William dismissed her as a possible source for any useful information about the Phantoms. Despite his kindness to her, the old warrior, like the majority of his sex, thought women of little importance and hardly likely to be confided in about something so important.

Fitzwarren had been furious and mentioned the skills she'd demonstrated on being captured, arguing that she must have been trained by the Phantoms. Cate had vigorously denied it, truthfully claiming that John had been responsible for teaching her how to defend herself against cowardly Englishmen who thought raping women made them men.

She'd held the captain's eye a little too long, her words a bit too pointed, and Fitzwarren's gaze had narrowed.

Sir William had been amused both by her show of spirit toward the English captain and by the idea of a lass learning warfare. He made the young Fitzwarren seem foolish and incompetent when he tried to explain how he and his men had had a difficult time capturing her, and how "a wee lassie" had clobbered one of the men on the head with the hilt of her sword and nearly taken off the leg of another.

Though Sir William was obviously busy with the defense of the city, he seemed to have taken a liking to her and ensured that she was fed, given suitable clothing (a gown), and allowed out once a day to walk with a guard around the yard. It was far more freedom than she would have been given if the Fitzwarrens had been charged with her keep, and it bothered her that she would eventually be forced to take advantage of it.

Mistaking the source of her distress, Sir William took her hand in his big paws—he reminded her of a bear with his hefty frame and graying whiskers. "You have nothing to fear, lass. Your betrothed has not deserted you. Bruce might be in retreat, but MacGregor has promised to surrender himself on Saturday at dusk."

"Saturday?" she echoed. That was only three days away!

He nodded. "I believe he has returned for a few days to Roro to put his estate in order."

Cate paled. "Do you mean to kill him then?"

The old warrior's expression hardened with distaste. Cate knew that he did not approve of using a woman to force a surrender—no matter how important the prisoner. "Not me, but I will not lie to you, lass. King Edward has been chomping at the bit to get hold of one of Bruce's Phantoms, but once MacGregor gives him what he wants, Edward will not have a reason to keep him around— indeed, he'll have many reasons not to."

Cate chilled, telling herself it would not come to that. But she knew she could not wait much longer. She must act before Saturday.

Yet as she stood beside Sir William on the battlements and watched her father's men prepare to leave, she also knew that something did not feel right. Robert the Bruce would not give up so easily. She would need to be ready for anything.

Sir William was obviously pondering the same thing. "As glad as I am to see him go, I have the feeling this is not the last we will be seeing of Robert Bruce."

Twenty-four

❦

The wait was agonizing. Finally, two nights after they'd "given up" the siege and marched away from Perth, Gregor, most of the rest of the Highland Guard, Douglas and a handful of his men, and the king himself were on their way back to Perth.

It was Bruce's stubborn insistence on joining them—rather than wait nearby with a larger force for when they opened the gates—that had nearly caused them to abandon the plan altogether. Gregor thought Chief was going to burst a blood vessel in his temple, he'd been so furious. But the king would not be dissuaded, even by the fearsome Island chief. It was his plan, and he was going, Bruce had insisted. This was how legends were made, he'd added, ignoring Chief's rejoinder that it was also how fools were killed and thrones lost.

Not many men could get away with calling the King of Scotland a fool, but Tor MacLeod, the Chief of the Highland Guard, was one of them. Bruce had just laughed and told Chief that was why he was going along—to ensure that he wasn't.

Gregor took his turn along with the others in trying to talk sense into the king, but he would not be dissuaded. If they wanted a king who would be content to wait someplace where he could be "protected" while they fought for his crown for him, they could have Edward II. Bruce was a warrior, and he would lead his men into battle, even if it meant his cause died with him. God would protect him—and if not, the Highland Guard would. It was hard to argue with that logic, even if it was blasphemous.

Leaving about a hundred men in the forest nearby—the bulk of the army had remained at Dundee Castle, which was taken by Bruce the previous winter, to maintain the illusion of a retreat and not alert the English spies—the small party of warriors approached the north end of the city where the castle was located. There were several gates into the city, including the Red Brig Port, Turret Brig Port, Southgate Port, and Spey Port, but their plan was to cross the *lade* near the castle, scale the wall, and open the small gate at Curfew Row to admit the rest of the army and take the garrison by surprise. Once the castle fell, the city would be theirs.

It was well after midnight when the score of warriors approached the icy black waters of the *lade,* carrying only the rope ladders fashioned by Douglas that they'd used for the first time at Berwick and very light weaponry. Not coincidentally, it was a moonless night and the skies were dark as pitch. With the soot and seal grease blackening their faces, the men were hard-pressed to recognize the man standing next to them. For the soldiers standing watch on the rampart they would be nearly impossible to see. Hearing them was unlikely, as even from outside the wall the sounds of revelry were unmistakable. Apparently, the garrison and townsfolk were celebrating their victory. A bit prematurely—not that Gregor was going to complain, particularly if it meant the soldiers were not keeping good watch.

Bruce was the first man in the water, much to the shock of a French knight who'd recently joined Douglas's retinue and was unused to seeing a king lead his men from the front. Chief followed closely, with Gregor immediately behind him.

Murky, and cold enough to freeze your bollocks off, the

lade was about twenty yards of oozy, smelly, slimy hell. At times the water was high enough to nearly reach their mouths, and, given the pungent scents coming from it, Gregor was glad it didn't.

When they finally reached the far side of the *lade,* they had to crawl on their bellies up a bank of mud and rock at the foot of the wall. Once the others had made it across, the two Island chieftain cousins, MacSorley and MacRuairi, began tossing the grappling hooks of the rope ladders.

No one spoke. They didn't need to. They all knew their roles. Any necessary communication was done by hand signals.

Chief had won one small victory before they'd left. Bruce would *not* be the first man up the ladder; MacRuairi would go ahead of him. Gregor would be the first man up the second ladder to take his position along the wall.

Slowly—silently—no more than two men on the ladder at one time, they started to climb. MacRuairi was about five feet from the top, with the king a few steps behind him, when disaster struck. The rope on one side of their ladder snapped near the top. Both men barely managed to grab hold of the remaining side of rope as the boards under their feet dropped sideways, and they went careening into the wall—which was a hell of a lot better than landing on the rocky bank about twenty feet below.

The clatter of wood and metal against stone was enough to attract the attention of even the most lax of guards. From below, Chief whispered, "Arrow, on your right."

Over halfway up the second ladder, Gregor didn't have time to think. A soldier on one of the turrets had stopped to investigate. He was about twenty yards away, looking in their direction—a faint blur of a target in the darkness. Wedged against the wall with only his feet for balance, Gregor let go his grip on the ladder, notched an arrow, and sent it careening into the darkness in seconds. The shot was more prayerful than realistic, and given that one wrong move would have him careening backward off the ladder, one of the most difficult he'd ever attempted. But there was no way in hell he was going to let this attack fail. Before the soldier could shout out a warning to the rest of the watch, he fell harmlessly to the ground.

MacRuairi had managed to pull himself to the top. The king was still hanging from the broken ladder with the men in position below to catch him if necessary. But Bruce didn't fall. Like MacRuairi, he climbed the broken ladder up and over the wall. Thanks to Gregor, disaster had been averted.

With Chief cursing the whole time, in the kind of valiant act that earned Bruce the heart of the people and the admiration of his men, the king led the small party of warriors in a surprise attack. Though Gregor wanted nothing more than to go in search of Cate, he held his position at the wall overlooking the bailey to ensure that no one was able to alert the rest of the garrison before the castle could be taken and the gate opened.

Gregor didn't have to notch another arrow. The garrison was woefully unprepared, and Bruce's men met little resistance. Within the space of a half-hour the castle and city were theirs, and Robert the Bruce had added one more improbable feat in an improbable reign that was quickly becoming legend.

But Gregor wasn't ready to celebrate yet. Unable to wait a moment longer, he turned to Campbell. "I'm going to find Cate."

"I'll go with you."

He nodded. "We'll check the guard towers first."

They had just started down the stairs of the rampart when Gregor heard a shout. Recognizing the voice as Bruce's, he turned to the bailey below. In one glance, Gregor took in the situation and cursed. Bloody hell, one of the English soldiers was using a woman as a shield, and

Bruce—who never could forget his knightly roots—was going to go to her damned rescue and get himself killed!

Not hesitating, Gregor notched his arrow, raised his bow into position, and drew back his hand. It wasn't a difficult shot. The bailey was lit with torches and the soldier was only about twenty yards away. As soon as the woman got out of the way . . .

His gaze flickered back to the woman, and his stomach dropped. *Bloody hell.* It wasn't just any woman; it was Cate.

Cate recognized the man coming toward them an instant before Fitzwarren did. Most of his face was hidden behind a helm, and his skin seemed to have been darkened with something, but the arrogant swagger and aura of confidence and authority were the same as they'd been the last time she'd seen the handsome young Earl of Carrick ambling away from their small cottage fifteen years ago.

For fifteen years she thought she'd hated him. But all it took was one look—one moment when their eyes met—for her to realize that no matter what her father had done, she would not be the instrument used to destroy him. Instinctively she knew that was exactly what Fitzwarren would try to do.

Frustration and rage tangled inside her. By all that was holy, it never should have come to this. She'd been ready. All day she'd been waiting in her chamber for someone to come so she could put her plan into motion. She would have had plenty of time to find Fitzwarren and exact her vengeance before attempting to escape the city.

She'd even had a backup plan. If escape proved impossible, she'd intended to take sanctuary in a church. Sir William's honor as a knight would not let him violate it—as the Earl of Ross had done when taking Bruce's queen, sister, daughter, and the Countess of Buchan—or trick Gregor into surrendering without having her as leverage.

But her anxious pacing all day had been for naught. For the first time since her imprisonment, no one had come to take her on her walk or even to bring her food. From the sounds of revelry outside, they were too busy celebrating.

Of all the days to be forgotten! She'd banged her fists on the door, cried out, and pleaded for someone to come for her until her voice was hoarse. She'd almost given up hope when the door had finally opened—well after midnight— and the very man she'd hoped to find came bursting in.

Shocked to see the elder Fitzwarren standing there, it took her a moment to react.

"You didn't think I would forget you, did you?" He laughed cruelly. "It took me a while to remember Bruce's whore and her mongrel." Frozen with shock that he knew who she was, Cate gasped as he stepped toward her. For a moment she was the young girl in the cottage again, seeing her mother raped and then murdered by this evil man. "Did you climb out of your tomb? I should have let them fill it with water as they wanted. But I thought it would be more fun for you to starve." He shrugged indifferently. "I knew there was something about you that was familiar, but it wasn't until one of the serving maids proved a little resistant tonight that it came back to me. I never forget a screaming woman I've fucked, especially one as pretty as your mother. You look like her. Who the hell would have guessed the scrawny whelp would grow so fair? Bruce had good taste in whores, I'll give him that."

Cate cried out like a wounded animal. "She wasn't a whore, you murdering bastard!" Hatred for the man who'd killed her mother and thought to taunt her with the memory of it consumed her. The shock of his recognition—and the realization that he knew who she was—fell away, and her only thought was to kill. She forgot her training and let emotion lead.

But in a horrifying repeat of the past, her effort with the knife proved just as unsuccessful as it had with the hoe.

Fitzwarren saw the knife a fraction of a second too early. Before she could sink it through the mail into his gut, he slapped her hand away. The tip of the knife caught on a bit of mail before falling harmlessly to the ground.

She hadn't killed him, but she'd pricked him—surprised him—and given herself that second she needed to get away. Yet she couldn't just let him go. He had to pay. He had to. She couldn't have come this close only to fail.

She reached for the knife on the ground. It was a mistake—a huge one. Fitzwarren kicked the dagger away and brought his knee up hard against her chin, momentarily stunning her. Her head swam as the ground swayed under her feet. She recovered, but not fast enough.

"You stupid bitch!" He hauled her up against him, wrapping one arm around her neck, cutting off her breath before she had a chance to tuck her chin. "If I didn't need you, you'd be dead for that. But my men and I are getting out of here."

He dragged her outside, still squeezing her neck with enough force to cut off her breath. She grabbed his arm and pulled, fighting for air, but his steel-clad arm was unrelenting. The last thing she remembered was thinking that the chain mail digging into her throat hurt.

When she came to, they were in the courtyard. Fitzwarren was dragging her in front of him like a shield with one arm around her, pinning her arms to her sides, and the other digging the sharp tip of a dagger into her back. Men were moving all around them. She recognized the younger Fitzwarren and some of the other English soldiers gathered in one corner.

It took her a moment to realize that the castle was being attacked and that the English and Sir William's men were surrendering.

That was when she recognized the man striding toward them as her father.

"Let the woman go." The deep voice penetrated the depths of her memory.

"Not so fast," Fitzwarren said. "Where is your leader?" Suddenly, he stiffened with recognition. An evil chuckle rumbled out of his chest. "Well, how do you like that. Today must be my lucky day. Well met, *Sir* Robert—it's been a long time, but I seem to have found something of yours."

Fitzwarren jerked her toward the torchlight, causing the knife to dig into her back. She cried out in pain as the blade penetrated her flesh. Blood oozed down her back.

Her eyes met her father's, and she could see the realization dawn. "Caty Cat?" He sounded as stunned as he looked. His face seemed to have drained of all color behind the black smudges. Oblivious to the danger, he took a step toward her, his eyes never leaving her face. "My God, Catherine, is that you?"

He reached for her.

Oh God, no! Cate felt the dagger leave her back and sensed what was about to happen. Fitzwarren was going to plunge the blade into her father's chest, which he'd left open and vulnerable by reaching for her.

Every protective instinct in her body flared. This was all her fault. She should have escaped when she had the chance, and now her father . . .

Stop him. I have to stop him.

The moment Fitzwarren released his hold, she reacted. This time, she remembered her training. Just as she'd done with Gregor on the practice yard, she bent forward a little bit and threw her head back into Fitzwarren's jaw with all her strength. The mail of his coif blunted the blow, but it gave her an opening long enough to twist out of his hold.

He grunted in pain and swore, but let her go. His attention was still focused on her father, who had just moved within arm's length.

Cate caught the glimmer of the silvery blade in the torchlight as Fitzwarren swung the dagger around toward the king. *Her* dagger. The one that penetrated mail.

He was bringing it forward, intending to thrust it deep into the king's gut, when she screamed, "No!"

She knew what to do. Gregor had taught her well. He'd pounded it into her that one day on the practice yard until the movements had become almost second nature. With both hands she grabbed the wrist holding the knife, twisted Fitzwarren's hand back, and plunged the dagger into his own chest.

She saw the surprise in his eyes for only a second before her body jerked forward with a loud, sickly thump. Pain caused her to stiffen with as much shock as Fitzwarren, as they both collapsed to the ground.

Get away. That was what he'd taught her. That was what he expected her to do. As soon as Cate was free, she was supposed to run away.

The moment Cate slammed her head back, extracting herself from the soldier's hold, Gregor was ready. He saw the knife coming toward the king and reacted, letting loose the arrow that would save the king's life. But as his fingers released—too late to call it back—he was distracted by a movement.

By Cate.

Gregor cried out in tortured horror as Cate lurched forward into the path of his arrow.

Too late he anticipated what she was about to do. It was what he would have done. She had the instinct of a fighter, and he'd taught her too well.

He wanted to shout for her to get out of the way, but it was too late. It felt like his heart was being ripped out of his chest and burned before his eyes as he waited for the inevitable.

Miss. God, please miss.

But his prayer was only partially answered. The arrow

meant for the soldier—the one that should have struck him right between the eyes—found Cate's back as she leapt forward to wrest the knife from the soldier's hand.

He was already racing toward them when he heard the sickening thud, her pained gasp, and then the king's cry. An instant later Cate crumpled to the ground, and he wanted to die.

Any pride he might have felt that the soldier she'd struck—and from the looks of it, killed—had followed a similar path was lost in the fear that had turned his blood to ice.

He pushed people out of the way mindlessly as he raced toward her. *Let her be all right. Please, let her be all right. I couldn't have . . .*

Refusing to think the words, Gregor stumbled forward through the crowd that had gathered around the king, who inexplicably had fallen to his knees and was holding Cate draped across his lap.

Her head was back, her face bloodless, her eyes closed; she looked . . .

Gregor made a harsh choking sound, "Cate!"

He would have reached for her, but Bruce stopped him. "Cate?" The king's eyes flared with a kind of rage Gregor had never seen before as he looked at him. "By the rood, stay away from her!"

Gregor stared at him in shock, not understanding. "But that's my—"

"Do you know what you've done?" The king cut him off. "You've shot my daughter!"

It took a few minutes for the words to resonate. When they did, Gregor staggered back as if struck by a powerful blow.

Daughter? It couldn't be.

He must have spoken his thoughts aloud. Bruce pinned him with another deadly gaze. "Do you not think I know my own child? You told me she was dead. All this time, I thought my sweet little Catherine was dead." Bruce held her to him, stroking her dark hair. *Cate's* dark hair.

Gregor's eyes flickered back and forth between the pair, his stomach twisting as he saw the similarities that had only teased the edges of his consciousness before. The same dark eyes and hair, the same mulish pursed mouth and determined jaw.

He heard Campbell mutter a curse beside him. "Damn it, I knew there was something familiar about her."

Suddenly, Gregor realized what that meant. He seethed with anger against the man he'd always admired. "You bastard, you left her. How could you do that to her?"

Robert the Bruce shot him a glare of warning, reminding him with that one look that he addressed a king. "Not willingly, but I do not owe the man who told me she was dead an explanation."

Gregor didn't have the opportunity to respond. The king was finished with him. Bruce lifted Cate's limp body and started shouting orders to find him a bed in the castle and the best physician in the city.

Feeling as if his heart was being wrenched out of his body, Gregor watched helplessly as the man he'd thought like a father to him carried away the woman he loved and might have killed.

Nay, not helpless. There was something he could do. Gregor looked around for MacKay, finding the big Highlander in the bailey with the other members of the Highland Guard. He could tell by their concerned expressions that they'd heard at least some of the exchange with the king. But he didn't care. Not right now. There was only one thing that mattered now. "Where's Angel?" he asked. "I need her."

If anyone could save Cate it was Helen MacKay. She'd given Gregor his life back once, and now he would ask her for something far more important: to give him back Cate's.

Twenty-five

✣

Gregor's arrow hadn't killed her, but the fever nearly had. Were it not for the pretty redheaded healer who'd arrived a few days after Cate was shot, she might never have woken from the delirium to which she'd succumbed.

She might never have known the truth. Aye, Cate had much for which to thank Helen MacKay. She'd given her her life *and* her father. The king had been at her side when she woke initially after being shot—before the fever had taken hold—and had told her everything.

She still couldn't believe it. He hadn't abandoned them. It had been at her mother's insistence that he stayed away. She wanted to give her marriage a chance, and her betrothed—the man that would become Cate's first stepfather—had been deeply jealous of the king. Her mother had thought her former lover's absence would give them the best chance for a happy future.

She was supposed to tell Cate the truth when she was old enough to understand, but for some reason never had. Maybe she'd thought Cate had forgotten him? Maybe she'd thought it best not to open old wounds? Maybe it had been too hard for her to have Bruce around, she'd loved him so much? Cate would never know.

Her father had never intended to stay away forever, but the war had come and he'd been fighting—and fleeing— for his life. By the time he'd returned to Scotland to reclaim his throne, her village had been attacked, and it had been too late.

At least he thought it had been too late. Despite her insistence that she'd lied to Gregor, her father put the entire blame for their long separation squarely on his archer's shoulders, and nothing she said would change his mind. Bruce was just as intractable as her mother had accused her of being. Cate, of course, didn't see the similarities. *She* was reasonable.

The maidservant had just finished tying the ribbon that bound the bottom of her plait, when her pixieish doctor entered the chamber.

Used to the other woman's intense scrutiny, Cate gave Helen time to study her from head to the toes that were peeking out from beneath the edge of the fine linen night rail and velvet robe her father had given her.

When she'd finally satisfied herself, Helen's gaze returned to hers. "You look much improved. The bath was not overtaxing?"

Cate shook her head and smiled. "On the contrary, I feel like a new woman. I can barely feel the soreness in my shoulder."

Helen's eyes narrowed, as if she knew she lied. "You are not leaving this room for a few more days—soreness or not. It's only been a week. You need more time to gain back your strength. You bullied me into letting you take a bath, but that's as far as I will go." She sighed, as if she was much put upon. "You are much like your father, you know. He was a horrible patient, too."

Cate's mouth quirked in an effort not to smile. The comparison—even an unflattering one—pleased her.

She was surprised that anyone could bully Helen MacKay. Despite her fey appearance, the skilled healer seemed to have a will of steel, and from what Cate had seen, she ordered the king about as if he were a recalcitrant squire.

"I hope I will not need to force-feed you vegetables?" Helen asked dryly.

Cate shook her head, recalling her father's distaste for almost anything that grew on a tree or out of the ground. "I like vegetables—except for beets." She wrinkled her nose.

Helen harrumphed. "Let me guess, they taste like dirt? I've heard that before. Just last night I caught the king trying to pass the carrots I had made specially for him off to the hounds. To the hounds, if you can believe it!" Shaking her head again, she moved closer to where Cate sat on the edge of a trunk to address Lisbet. "You were careful?"

The maidservant nodded nervously and Cate interjected, "Lisbet was very careful not to let the bandages get wet and followed all of your instructions."

Helen nodded. "Good. Then let's see you back into bed. There is someone who wishes to see you."

Cate stiffened.

As she was holding her by the arm, Helen sensed her reaction. "I refer to your father."

The tension immediately dissipated. Cate could see the other woman's unspoken plea but would not heed it. Helen didn't understand her refusal to see Gregor, and Cate was too proud to enlighten her, but Helen respected her wishes, and that was all that mattered.

Cate knew Helen was married to Magnus MacKay—one of the Phantoms, she suspected, from the glimpse she'd had of him when he'd come to fetch Helen for something—but it was Gregor who'd brought her here. Helen never said anything, but Cate sensed there was something between them. She could see it in the other woman's eyes every time Cate refused to see him. Helen cared about him.

Knowing Gregor, Cate could guess what had been between them. The prickle of jealousy only reminded her of what she'd seen and the lifetime of jealousy she would have faced had she married him. Still, she was grateful to Helen. Whatever the circumstances, she owed her her life.

Cate allowed the two women to help her back into bed and tried not to wince as they propped the pillows up behind her tender back.

The arrow had struck the bone of her left shoulder blade. As any movement of her arm caused extreme pain, Helen had suggested she use a sling. It helped immeasurably, but the jostling of getting comfortable reminded her that no matter how anxious she was to leave the sickroom, it would be some time before the wound was fully healed.

She'd been lucky she wasn't taller, Helen had told her. A few inches lower and the arrow would have found her lung or heart.

Cate refrained from correcting her. Gregor's arrow *had* found her heart, albeit a couple of weeks before the second had struck. The first had been far more painful.

As it was, Helen assured her that she would be good as new in a few weeks—if she didn't overtire herself and allow the fever to return.

"Shall I send him in?" Helen asked. "He was pacing rather impatiently in the antechamber when I came in."

Cate laughed. "Aye, it's probably best not to keep a king waiting."

While Helen went to fetch him, Cate arranged the heavy fur bed-covering around her. Though there was a fire in the brazier, the stone walls were lined with fine tapestries, and glazed glass filled the two windows, it was January in the Highlands and the tower chamber in the castle was drafty.

A moment later, the door burst open and the King of Scotland strode through. His gaze scrutinized her almost as intensely as Helen's before the smile reached his eyes. She thought there might have even been a sheen of dampness when he looked at her. "Ah, Caty, you look so like your mother it brings back so many memories. What a beauty you've become."

Cate blushed. Though she knew he exaggerated, she could not help but be flattered by the comparison. Her mother had been beautiful, and even the slightest resemblance to her was enough.

He sat on the edge of the bed beside her. Fifteen years of warfare had aged Robert Bruce. There were lines around his face and a hardness to his visage that hadn't been there before. The loss of three brothers, countless friends, and the imprisonment of his wife, sister, and daughter no doubt explained much of it. But when he smiled and his eyes twinkled, he didn't look all that different from the handsome young knight who'd filled their small cottage with such light and laughter. She'd been right about him after all.

"You are feeling better." He tipped her chin, turning her face to the light streaming through the window. "I think I see some color in your cheeks."

"I feel vastly better after the bath. As soon as I'm permitted to walk outside, there will be much more color in my cheeks."

Her father smiled but held up his hand, fending off her not-so-hidden plea. "Don't look at me. That's between you and Helen. She's mad enough at me as it is. Apparently, you became too distressed the last time we spoke."

Cate's heart stopped. "Sir William is well?"

His mouth pursed with distaste. "Aye, thanks to you. Without your intervention, the traitor would have been put to the gibbet. Instead, he will be sent to the Isles so I won't find myself facing him over another castle wall. Consider it repayment for saving my life."

Relieved to hear that the old knight's life had been spared, Cate eased back on the pillows. She didn't ask about the others. She already knew what had happened to them. The English had been released and sent back to

England. Except for the Fitzwarrens. The son had been slain during the short battle, and the father had been killed by her hand. Cate would not regret it, but neither did she feel the satisfaction she'd thought she would. Gregor's words of warning had come back to her. She'd killed someone, and though it had needed to be done, she knew that doing so had somehow left a mark.

Her father shook his head. "Who would have thought a wee thing like you could learn to move like that." He grinned. "You always were more like me than your mother." His expression turned chastising. "Not that I'm not appreciative, but you shouldn't have done what you did. You could have been killed."

As this was something they weren't likely to ever agree upon, Cate switched the subject. They spoke of far more inconsequential matters for a few more minutes, before he finally came to the reason for his visit.

From the way his mouth pulled into an angry frown, she could guess the subject.

"Have you reconsidered your decision?"

As Cate held his gaze, the chill that was centered in her heart permeated through her bones. "No—nor will I. Gregor MacGregor is the last man I wish to marry."

"But you were betrothed. He said you loved him."

She turned away; despite her vows to not shed another tear for the scoundrel, she felt the prickle of heat in her eyes. "Please, do not ask me to talk about it. Suffice it to say the betrothal is over. If I ever loved him, I do not any longer."

Whatever else Cate might have said was cut off as the door burst open and the last man she wanted to see strode into the room. "What the hell do you mean, 'if' you ever loved me?"

Cate startled, her eyes widening. Not from the shock of seeing him—she knew she would not be able to put off this conversation forever—but from how he looked. Unkempt was putting it nicely. His eyes were bloodshot, his hair rumpled, his jaw unshaven and dark with the shadow of a week's stubble, and there were deep lines gouged in his not-so-stunningly-handsome face. The most gorgeous man in Scotland looked like hell. More specifically, like a man who was one step away from entering it.

The king jumped to his feet and turned on him angrily. "I told you to wait outside."

But Gregor was looking at her. Their eyes locked for an instant. She could see the almost visceral relief, the longing that seemed to pour out of him as he gorged on every facet of her face and figure. But when she turned harshly away, she felt the heat of his frustration and ire.

"I'm done waiting. She's refused to see me for days. Cate—*Catherine*," she heard the sarcasm, "and I need to talk."

Her father's fury matched Gregor's. "You will talk when and *if* she wants and not before. Need I remind you that you are only here by Helen's request, and if I had my choice you'd be in the south with the others."

Gregor's mouth clamped until his lips were white.

She looked back and forth between the two men, seeing the tension between them where before there must have been mutual respect and admiration.

No matter how strongly she wanted to send Gregor from the room and tell him to go to the devil, she would not. There might be nothing to salvage between them, but she would do what she could to mend the break between the king and his once favored Guardsman. She knew how much her father's approval meant to Gregor, and no matter what he'd done to her, she would not take that from him. Her father would never hear from her how Gregor had betrayed her. Gregor might not be the kind of man a king might wish his daughter to wed, but he needed him in his army.

She put her hand on her father's arm. "It's all right. I will speak to him."

Her father looked back and forth between them, a hard expression on his face. How much he knew about what had happened between them, she didn't know. But from that look, she gathered that he suspected most of it.

His gaze met hers with concern. "You don't have to do this now if you are not up to it. I will not see you over-tired." The last he directed to Gregor.

"I will be fine," she assured him. Then, turning stonily to the man who'd broken her heart, she added, "This will not take long."

Gregor felt like he was holding on by a thread. Since the moment that arrow had left his bow, he'd experienced every kind of unimaginable torture. My God, he'd almost killed her! Just knowing how close he'd come to killing the woman he loved was enough to send him into a fit of frantic desperation and panic.

He'd been so despondent, so close to losing his mind to grief in those dark hours of her fever, that Helen had drugged him to force him to sleep. Drugged him, damn it. With her husband's help.

He'd spent days in the chapel praying, and his prayers had been answered when Helen found him and told him the fever had broken. He'd waited for Cate to ask for him and had been stunned—and then angered—when told that she refused to see him.

How could she refuse to see him when she'd lied to him about her identity? He still couldn't believe his wee "ward" was Bruce's natural daughter. The king was furious with him, blaming Gregor for the years he thought her dead, even though they both knew it wasn't Gregor's fault. But Gregor was guilty of something. He'd taken the king's daughter's innocence, and he wasn't looking forward to confirming what Bruce no doubt already suspected.

Damn it, why hadn't she told him? Cate had a lot of explaining to do. But if there was one thing of which he was damned certain, it was that they were going to be married.

He kept a tight rein on the emotions whipping around inside him as the king took his sweet time in exiting the chamber—and not before sending a glare of warning in Gregor's direction. A glare that Gregor was too damned furious to heed.

Helen had taken pity on him and allowed him a few glimpses of Cate when the king wasn't looking, but this was the first time they'd been in a room together alone for weeks. She looked so lovely—and so wonderfully alive—that for a moment he didn't know whether to fall on his knees in gratitude or take her in his arms and shake her until she swore to never scare him like that again.

He'd been terrified that he would lose her. Hell, he was still terrified. That was part of what made him so angry. She seemed to have no sense of the torment going on inside him. She looked almost bored. *Bored,* when he was hanging by his last damned thread.

Her eyes when they looked up at him were perfectly blank. "Is there something you wished to say?"

Her very nonchalance pushed him over the edge. He stormed over to the bed, looking down on her. He wanted to pull her into his arms, but conscious of her injury, he kept his hands at his sides. "Damn right I have something to say. I think there are a few things we need to clear up, *Catherine.*"

She flushed, apparently not completely unashamed of her lie. "Such as?"

He leaned down so their eyes were level. The scent of lavender that filled his nose was so heart-stoppingly familiar, he almost lost the battle not to take her into his arms. But the cold indifference of her gaze stopped him. "Such as what name you want on the marriage contract. Because despite what you have just told your father, we will be married, whether you like it or not." He dragged his gaze down her body. "Need I remind you why."

He sounded like an arse, and he knew it. But she was provoking him by *not* provoking him. By sitting there as if she didn't care. As if she didn't want to be in his arms as badly as he wanted her there.

All she did was quirk a brow. Quirk . . . a . . . damned . . . brow!

"As you of all people should know, that is not necessarily a precursor to marriage."

God's blood, the woman knew how to infuriate him. "Damn it, Cate, will you not even apologize for not telling me the truth about your father?"

"Do you mean like you not telling me the name of the man who killed my mother and tried to kill me?"

He winced. Fair enough. They'd both kept secrets. "I was trying to protect you."

"You didn't trust me," she said calmly—too calmly. "Believe me, I understand. You proved that quite effectively."

He knew what she meant, and also realized why she was so angry. Hell, he supposed it was deserved. "I'm sorry for not believing you about what happened that morning with John." He explained how Pip had confessed everything—leaving out how how he'd tried to kill him. "I should have trusted you. I should have known you wouldn't try to trick me. I did know it, but I was just too proud to listen."

He paused, waiting for some kind of response. He'd just apologized; shouldn't she say something? Shouldn't she be glad that he knew she was innocent of any subterfuge?

Through the confusion of emotions swirling around inside him, he felt a prickle of unease. Somewhat nervously, he continued. "This thing with Bruce is awkward. I wish you'd told me, although I suppose I can understand why you didn't—given what you thought about why he'd left. I'd like to think it would have made a difference had I known, but it probably wouldn't have. God knows, I wanted you too badly. I still want you so badly. Once he gets over his initial anger, I do not think he will object. There is no reason we cannot be wed as soon as a priest can be found. Helen said you were not with child, but—"

"How dare you!" He flinched back a little from the venom she shot toward him. "Whether I am with child is none of your business. Nor did you have a right to discuss it with your former . . ."

Her mouth tightened, not saying the word. But he knew what she was thinking. He stiffened. "Helen is my friend, nothing more. She saved my life a few years back. She is with child, and it made me fear that you might be as well. Do not be upset with her. I was . . . not in a good state."

She held his gaze as if trying to decide whether to believe him. "It makes no difference. It would not induce me to marry you. *Nothing* could induce me to marry you. I would rather my child be called a bastard than have you for a father."

Gregor drew back. He'd expected anger from her about what had happened. He'd behaved ignobly and should have trusted her. But this level of animosity was completely unexpected.

Was she in more pain from the wound than he realized? His anger fled. He sat on the foot of the bed and tried to take her hand. "God, I'm sorry, Cate. You have to know I didn't mean to shoot you. You were supposed to move away, damn it. I never meant to cause you pain."

She laughed. He had no idea what could have provoked the seemingly illogical reaction until she spoke. "Didn't you? The arrow in my back might not have been intentional, but why did you go to the alehouse if you did not wish to hurt me? Did you not think proving to me how little you cared for me would cause me pain? I loved you, Gregor, *loved* you with all my heart. Worse, I believed in you. And how did you reward that belief? You took the first woman who you could find to your bed."

"I didn't take any woman to my bed."

"Don't!" she said. "Don't lie to me. I *saw* you."

"How could you have seen me when it didn't happen?"

"I followed you to the alehouse. I saw you take Maggie upstairs. I saw you in the room together."

Gregor felt all the blood in his body drain to the floor, landing with a hard thud. Horror, shame, and panic descended on him in a maddening rush. Christ, what had she seen? Too much, if the look on her face was any indication.

He'd planned on telling her what happened, but he never dreamed she could have seen it. How was he going to make her understand? "Nothing happened, Cate. I swear to you. I didn't take her to my bed."

"No, what you were doing didn't seem to require a bed." The words seemed to break her. The next came out in a sob. "I saw her take you in her mouth, Gregor. I saw everything."

Shite. Gregor felt ill just thinking about what that must have been like for her. What must she think? What he'd done was inexcusable.

He knew just how badly he'd erred, and he fought with everything he had to hold on to her. To not let her slip away. But he felt like he was trying to grasp a cloud that was floating away from him.

"I tried to do it, Cate, but I couldn't. It was wrong—God, I know it was wrong, but I swear to you it only lasted a few moments before I pushed her away. I became ill, and passed out. When I woke up, I realized what a horrible mistake I'd made and planned to tell you everything. I knew then that I loved you and didn't want any other woman but you. You were right, sweetheart."

She wiped the tears away from her eyes angrily. "And when did you have this great epiphany? Before or after you let her get on her knees before you? Am I to be relieved

that you stopped? Should I give you a reward for not finishing what you started? Is it any less of a betrayal for not
reaching completion? What if you'd found me in another
man's arms? What if he kissed me and touched me intimately? Would it matter to you that I did not find pleasure?"

His eyes flared. "I'd kill any man for touching you."

"Even if I wanted him to?" she taunted. "Even if I needed
to prove my feelings for you?"

"That's ridiculous. You love me, that isn't how—"

He stopped.

"Exactly," she said softly. "That isn't how you prove
anything, most of all love." She held his gaze. "I'm done
fighting for something that isn't there. Maybe your father
was right. Maybe there *is* nothing more than a pretty facade. You've spent all this time becoming an amazing warrior, building muscle until you look like a rock, but inside,
where it counts, you are weak."

He flinched, the words hitting hard, striking old scars
that hadn't healed as much as he'd thought. *Weak.* He felt
like a midge crushed under her heel. Small and utterly destroyed. Worse, he had only himself to blame. Of all the
mistakes he'd made when he was younger—and he'd made
a hell of a lot of them—he'd never done something so de-
structive. He'd never held something precious in his grasp
and then tossed it away.

God, what had he done? He'd reverted to a man he didn't
want to be. She'd believed in him and he'd let her down.
He'd let himself down.

He had no right, but he asked anyway. "Forgive me,
Cate. What I did was wrong. I will spend the rest of our
lives proving to you how wrong and how much I love you,
if you will let me."

She held his gaze. For one long heartbeat, he thought she
might give him another chance.

But he'd hurt her too much. She looked away, silence her only response.

Refusing to accept the truth that was staring at him, Gregor tried the only thing he could think to do. But when he put his lips on hers, hoping to reawaken their love—to prove that what they had couldn't be denied—all he felt was the poignant ache of loss.

As his lips touched hers, he felt the warmth, tasted the familiar sweetness and hint of mint, but the most important thing was missing: her response. She didn't want to kiss him. She didn't want him at all.

This wasn't a faerie tale. A kiss didn't heal wounds or make everything all right.

He feared nothing he could do would ever make it right. But damn it, he was going to try.

Twenty-six

❧

As soon as Helen declared Cate well enough to travel, the two women and a small retinue of her father's men removed to Dunstaffnage Castle in Lorn on the west coast of Scotland. A good portion of the king's army—including her father himself—had gone south to Galloway to join in the battle against the MacDowells. What remained of the king's men had been left behind in Perth to help in the slighting of the castle, continuing with the king's policy of destroying Scotland's fortresses so they could not be used against him.

In addition to Cate and Helen, there were about forty men on the *birlinn* that sailed from the River Tay to the Firth of Tay, out to the North Sea and around the northern coast of Sutherland, and into the Atlantic. The captain was none other than Erik MacSorley (whose war name of Hawk became clear when she saw his ship), who along with his terrifying kinsman Lachlan MacRuairi, the fierce warrior Tor MacLeod (whom she remembered from her rescue), Arthur Campbell, and—much to her constant irritation—Gregor, comprised the Phantom portion of her escort.

The royal castle of Dunstaffnage was kept by Arthur Campbell and his wife, Anna, but with most of Scotland's major strongholds still in the possession of the English—including the castles of Edinburgh, Stirling, Berwick, and Roxburgh—it served as the temporary seat of the king's court. As such, it was a beehive of constant activity, buzzing with courtiers and other important nobles.

For the first time in her life, Cate found herself feted, and openly acknowledged as the king's daughter. Along with the endless parade of nobles through the gates, there were feasts, fine gowns "fit for a princess," and even a jeweled circlet for her twenty-first saint's day.

It was as if her father was trying to make up for the fifteen years they'd lost together in a few weeks. She suspected she was also serving as a substitute for the family that was still being held in captivity. She wasn't the king's only natural child, however, and she was looking forward to meeting a couple of her five half-siblings in the ensuing weeks.

She did have a family, as it turned out, although her heart still pinched at the thought of those whom she'd lost. She had not forgotten her vow to ensure that the children were well cared for. It was the only thing she'd asked of her father, and he'd promised to look into it. As soon as it could be arranged, she would be reunited with Pip, Eddie, and Maddy.

Although Cate enjoyed all the attention, it was a bit overwhelming and at times even a little intimidating. She was worried about doing or saying the wrong thing. Despite her recent foray into "acting like a lady" to attract Gregor, Cate wasn't used to all the rules, expectations, and accoutrements of the nobility. For that, Lady Anna had been an enormous help.

Still, three weeks after arriving at Dunstaffnage, Cate found herself missing the freedom of her life at Roro and chafing at the bit to resume her training. Her back was still a little sore when she lifted her arm, but she feared that if she sat around pretending to sew for any longer, her fighting skills were going to be completely atrophied. But despite her father's obvious pride in what she'd done to save his life, she wasn't sure how the king would react to his daughter taking to the practice yard. Moreover, she suspected who would insist on overseeing.

Gregor had not tried to approach her or speak with her privately since that day in her chamber at Perth, but he was an ever-present source of watchfulness hovering around her like an unwelcome, forbidding dark cloud. The other Phantoms traveled with her father to Galloway, but Gregor hadn't gone with them. What she didn't know was whether it was his choice or her father's.

Either way, she didn't like it. When she found herself enjoying the company of a dinner companion, one of the dozens of young knights and lords of the royal castle—she suspected her father's involvement in this—a servant would appear or the music would stop unexpectedly, and she would catch him glowering at her with one of those dark, dangerous stares he was getting so good at.

She had to admit that maybe once or twice (or maybe more than once or twice), she'd egged him on a little with her flirting. Thinking of all the times she'd been forced to watch him do the same, it was rather fun to be on the other side.

For a while. But as it was clear from the number of times she'd told him to leave her alone that he wasn't going to listen, she did the only thing she could do and ignored him.

It wasn't working very well. Despite the firm resolve in her head, she was too blasted aware of him everywhere else. If he would just leave her alone, she could get on with her life. Forget about him and move on.

He'd broken her heart, hadn't he?

But she couldn't help noticing that the charming rogue wasn't so charming anymore. She hadn't seen him talk to any woman except Helen or Lady Anna since they'd arrived. He didn't have time. He was too busy staring at her and trying to intimidate anyone who came near her.

Day after day, he was there. Her own personal sentinel.

Dark, forbidding, and maybe a little rough around the edges with the unkempt brigand look he seemed to have adopted, but still undeniably the most handsome man she'd ever seen.

And sometimes at night (very well, *many* times at night), she would think of everything else. How it had felt to be in his arms. The way her heart had jumped when he surged inside her. The warmth and possessiveness of his hands covering her body. How much she'd liked to touch him, to feel the granite-hard muscles of his chest and arms under her fingertips. She remembered the heat of his mouth, the lash of his tongue, the heady taste of mint. She remembered how the bottom had fallen out of her stomach every time he'd kissed her.

She still felt ill when she thought of what she'd seen at the alehouse, but she'd been more relieved by what he'd told her than she wanted to admit. He *had* stopped. Maybe not soon enough, but he hadn't been able to go through with it. Did it mean something?

Good God, just listen to her! She was a fool. She couldn't soften. He didn't deserve her forgiveness.

Why couldn't he just leave her alone?

She redoubled her efforts to forget about him. A distraction was what she needed. Surely she could find one in the bevy of young knights and lords her father brought before her?

That night she danced with every unattached young man she could find and whittled it down to a few possibilities. But inexplicably the next day, at what was to be her belated saint's day celebration, two of the men were nowhere to be found, and the third—one of her father's most vaunted knights, Sir David Lindsay—appeared to be nursing a very ugly-looking black eye, among other cuts and bruises.

Suspecting who was responsible, Cate's gaze slid to the dark corner where her sentinel stood watch. He wasn't alone but talking to her father, who'd just returned from Galloway. Although "talking" was putting it nicely. From the look on her father's face, Gregor was getting an earful.

It wasn't hard to guess why. Her eyes narrowed, even from across the room she could see that Gregor's nose was about twice the size of normal and had a new crook at the bridge.

She might have been amused at the irony of his sabotaging her flirtations as she had done to him previously, if she weren't so angry and exhausted from the effort to ignore him. This had gone on long enough. She and her surly, overbearing sentinel were going to have a little talk.

Squaring her shoulders, Cate marched across the room ready to do battle.

There was a reason they called it penance. It wasn't supposed to be easy; it was supposed to hurt. And God's blood, it did.

For Gregor, standing to the side while Cate blossomed like a rose in the sun, watching her shine and captivate everyone around her—not just because she was the king's daughter, or because she was about the most adorable thing he'd ever seen all dressed up like a princess, but by the sheer force of her personality—was self-flagellation, a hair shirt, and whatever else monks used to torture themselves all rolled into one.

For God's sake, did she have to smile so much? She was too damned pretty when she smiled.

Not interfering, not putting his fist through the teeth of every one of the men who'd vied for her attention or dared—*dared*—to even think about touching her was the hardest thing Gregor had ever done.

But she deserved the attention, and by God, if he had to chain himself in a room to see that she got it, he would.

Apparently Bruce had reached a similar conclusion.

"You are fortunate I do not toss you in a pit prison for attacking Lindsay like that."

Gregor clamped his jaw down tight. "The bastard deserved it."

"The 'bastard' is one of my best knights and did nothing more than dance with her."

Gregor gritted his teeth. Lindsay had done far more than dance—the young knight had let his gaze drop down to her chest and lingered for a full three seconds. *Three!* Gregor had counted every blasted one of them.

He wouldn't apologize. Hell, no. Lindsay was lucky Gregor hadn't blackened both his eyes and had left him with a few unbroken ribs.

Bruce studied him. "At least he seems to have given as much as he got. You aren't looking so pretty. How are you planning to win my daughter looking like that?"

Gregor turned from his view of Cate across the room to shoot him a glare. "Cate doesn't care about things like that."

She loved him for who she thought him to be. He just had to prove to her that he was that man.

"You'd better hope so. Do it again and I'll banish you to the Isles. You can be the most handsome man on the Isle of St. Kilda." The king laughed at his own jest, but then took a look at his broken nose and grimaced. "I knew this was a bad idea. I never should have agreed to let you stay here. You were needed with us in the south."

Gregor felt a twinge of guilt but pushed it aside. He was the only member of the Guard who hadn't been in Galloway to watch the MacDowells fall. "I needed to be here." With Cate.

"Your brother is skilled," the king said in a more even voice. "But he is not you."

Gregor wasn't sure *he* was himself anymore. He hadn't picked up a bow since the day he'd shot Cate, and he didn't know if he would ever want to again. He wasn't sure he had the stomach for it anymore. Any of it.

"John will improve," he said. His brother deserved a chance to fight. For too long he'd been doing Gregor's duty for him. Gregor was laird, and it was time he started acting like it.

The king gave him a long look. "I hope you know what you are doing. I'm not convinced she'll have you back—or that you deserve to be forgiven after what you told me." Gregor clamped his mouth closed. To get the king to agree, he'd been forced to confess the basics of what had happened. It had been a risk, but he'd escaped with his body parts intact—all of them. Bruce might not have been faithful to the women in his life himself, but he wouldn't tolerate anything else for his daughter. Illogical or not, for Gregor it wasn't an issue. Cate had his loyalty and fidelity for life, if she wanted it. "Be assured that if you hurt her again, I'll run you through myself."

Catching a glance of the expression on the face of the woman who'd just started toward them, Gregor said wryly, "You won't need to."

It seemed the princess was finally deigning to speak to him.

A slow smile turned the king's mouth as he saw his daughter. There was undeniable pride in his face when he spoke. "If she weren't so cute as she is, I would almost wish she'd been born a lad. I'd have made her one of the best knights in Christendom."

Gregor didn't doubt it. But he was rather glad she was a lass. *His* lass. For if it was the last thing he did, he would win her heart back.

He could see the outrage on her face as she stopped before them, sent an angry glare in his direction, and turned to lift on her tiptoes to give her father a kiss on the cheek.

"Are you having fun, Caty?" Bruce asked. "I wasn't here

to celebrate your actual saint's day with you, but I hope today will make up for it."

"It's perfect, Father, thank you." She glared at Gregor again for good measure. Putting a hand on her head, she said, "And thank you for the circlet as well—it is beautiful."

Gregor shot a warning glance to the king not to say anything.

Surprisingly, he heeded it. "I instructed the piper to play nothing but reels tonight after the feast." With a sly look to Gregor, he added, "I have a special guest who just arrived and has requested to sit next to you for the meal. I don't believe you've ever met my half-sister Isabel's son, Sir Thomas Randolph?"

Gregor had to bite back a curse, but Bruce must have seen his balled fists—the sadistic bastard grinned. He was making Gregor pay, all right.

Cate shook her head. "I've heard of him, of course."

"Aye, I'm not surprised," Bruce added. "He's become quite renowned for his prowess on the battlefield. And off as well—he's a great favorite among the ladies of court, isn't that so, MacGregor?"

Gregor smiled through teeth that were grinding together. "I believe I've heard something to that effect."

Bloody hell, Randolph? He was a bigger rogue than Gregor had ever been. Gregor didn't understand the fascination with the pompous bastard, whose knightly armor was so shiny you could clean your damned teeth in the reflection, but who could account for taste? The fact that Cate was a cousin of sorts wouldn't stop the young knight from flirting outrageously—and driving Gregor half-crazed in the process.

It was going to be a long night.

"If you don't mind, Father, there is something I would like to discuss with my *old* guardian."

Gregor didn't miss the jab at his age. His mouth tightened. Christ, he was one and thirty, not one and eighty. He'd be more than happy to prove just how spry he was, if she would let him.

The king's smile suggested he was taking far too much pleasure in this, blast him. "Aye, but don't take too long. There's Randolph now. Wouldn't want to keep him waiting."

The sweet smile she gave her father turned frosty when it fell on him. "Don't worry, I only need a few minutes."

As soon as Bruce walked away, she wasted no time. "I won't have any more of this, Gregor. It has to stop. All those menacing looks were bad enough, but how dare you strike Sir David for dancing with me!"

His mouth fell in a hard line. "It wasn't for dancing."

She put her hands on her hips, waiting.

He shrugged. "I didn't like where he was looking at you."

She made a sound of outrage and looked very much like she wanted to poke him in the chest. If there weren't people milling around, he suspected she'd be doing just that.

"Are you crazed?" she seethed in a low voice. Aye, he was. But she was obviously not expecting an answer. "You have no right," she continued, eyes blazing. "*I* will be the one to object if I don't like the way a man is looking at me, not you. I don't need a protector, a guardian, or a bad-tempered, sotted, unkempt, grizzled ruffian with a broken nose who is acting like a spoiled child who didn't get what he wanted. What do you expect me to do, throw myself at you in gratitude for saying you love me?"

Maybe not gratitude, but acknowledgment would have been nice. He'd never uttered those words to anyone, and having them ignored had stung. Realizing she might not appreciate that honest of an answer, however, he said, "Maybe not, but you don't need to take so much pleasure in torturing me."

The flush that rose to her cheeks suggested she wasn't

unaware of how much her flirting bothered him. But she lifted her chin and looked regally down her nose at him. Christ, she was a natural. It must be in the blood.

"What makes you think what I do has anything to do with you at all?"

"Because you love me," he said simply.

Cate was loyal and steadfast and true. When she gave her heart to someone it would be forever. He'd hurt her deeply—unconscionably—but not irreparably. She was a fighter. He was counting on it. He had faith in them, even if she no longer did.

She opened her mouth to protest, but he cut her off. What he wanted to do was push her into the laird's solar behind her and kiss her, but she had a few more days. "One month, sweetheart. That's all I can take. Enjoy what you have left."

She blinked in confusion as he started to walk away.

After a few steps, he turned back. "You might be right about everything else, but I'm not sotted. I haven't had more than a glass of wine or watered-down ale to drink in weeks."

The arrogant beast! How dare he walk away and leave her standing there after saying something so outrageous! Cate was tempted to drag him back and tell him every reason she most certainly did *not* love him. He'd broken her heart, and even if it admittedly didn't feel quite as broken right now, she wasn't going to let him hurt her again.

How could she trust him? Just because he said he loved her and was doing his best impersonation of a stalwart, only-have-eyes-for-you swain, how could she be sure it would last? One month wasn't a lifetime.

But it is a start.

Telling the little voice in the back of her head to be quiet, Cate concentrated on all the things she didn't like about him. The crooked nose, to start. God knows, it would

probably only make the blighter more handsome—as if
that were what he needed!

She stormed over to the dais to join her father and Sir
Thomas. But her mind was still on the conversation with
Gregor. What did he mean by one month, anyway? It was
just like him to be purposefully vague in order to make her
curious. Which she was, blast him.

She did, however, manage to have a thoroughly delight-
ful time with her "cousin." Sir Thomas truly was an outrageous flirt, and undeniably handsome with his refined
features, dark hair, and blue eyes. Had she not vowed to
not think about the man who'd resumed his post as her
forbidding watchdog, she might have speculated that this
was probably how Gregor had been when he was younger.

When she caught Sir Thomas's gaze dropping down to her
bosom during one of the reels (the tight bodice did rather
demand attention), she let it linger a full ten seconds before
drawing his gaze back up to hers with a question. The white-
ness around Gregor's mouth when she cast a surreptitious
glance in his direction proved surprisingly satisfying given
his curious "one month" comment.

She was smiling when her gaze met her partner's again.

"Are you enjoying yourself?" Sir Thomas asked, a mis-
chievous sparkle in his deep blue eyes.

"Immensely," she said with ill-concealed relish.

He laughed. "I don't think your former guardian is having much fun. Why do I have the feeling I should watch my
back as I leave here later? Let me guess—you danced with
Lindsay last night?"

Cate instantly sobered. She bit her lip, looking up at him
worriedly. "I'm sorry . . . I wasn't thinking. I'm afraid you
are probably right."

"I was only jesting. If MacGregor wants a fight he will
have one. Besides, I owe him. He and his friends put me
through hell when I rejoined my uncle a few years back."

The gleam in his eye turned decidedly wicked. "What's say we make him suffer?"

Cate thought a minute—well, more like two seconds, really—and grinned back at him. "You don't mind?"

"Dear cousin, it will be my pleasure. Watching that one squirm with jealousy is worth *two* black eyes."

Fortunately, it didn't come to that. Whatever her father had said to Gregor earlier seemed to have worked. And she did have her month—whatever that meant.

Having her suspicions, the next day she hunted down her father in the laird's solar to find out. He dismissed the hulking Island chief who never seemed to leave his side, Tor MacLeod, and the handful of other men with whom he'd just finished meeting. She'd heard her father refer to him as Chief a number of times, leading her to suspect that he was the leader of the Phantoms. He was certainly big and intimidating enough. Fierce-looking was putting it mildly.

Leaning back in his chair behind the table, her father watched her pace back and forth a few times, waiting for her to begin.

She stopped and turned to face him. "You were furious with Gregor after I was shot. To what did he agree to make you forgive him?"

He quirked a brow in a way that was vaguely familiar. "What makes you think I've forgiven him?"

She bit her lip. "Haven't you?"

"It depends." His expression softened. "Have you?"

Cate pursed her mouth. "Of course not—why should I?" Realizing her father didn't know the details and not wanting to go into them, she added, "Did you force him to agree to stay away from me for a month?"

His mouth quirked mischievously. "Not exactly."

Her eyes narrowed. "What do you mean, 'not exactly'?"

"I did not force him to do anything; it was his idea."

Her brows drew together. "His idea?"

"Aye, he thought you deserved to have some time as my daughter." His voice softened. "He wanted you to feel special. To have all of those things that would have been your due had we not been separated."

Cate's eyes widened. Of all the things she'd expected him to say, it wasn't that. Rocked, she swayed on suddenly unsteady legs. Locating a bench behind her, she sat. "He did? Then all this . . . ?"

"Was his idea. I'm ashamed to say that I didn't think of it. He was right, Caty—you deserved to be treated like a princess."

They both knew a natural daughter wasn't a princess, but she understood what he meant. What she couldn't believe was that Gregor had done something so sweet . . . so thoughtful . . . so *caring*.

"The circlet?"

"He had it designed specially for you in Oban."

Cate didn't know what to say.

"He cares about you, Caty."

She could not argue. But was it enough? Could she forgive him?

"What happens after a month?"

"I gave him permission to court you—that is all. And only if you agree."

Cate felt her chest tighten as the ice around her heart began to crack, and a glimmer of the love she'd once held for Gregor crept back in. "When is the month over?"

"Wednesday."

Two days. She looked up at her father with despair. "What do I do?"

His eyes were gentle. "What do you want to do?"

Trust him. She didn't speak the words aloud, but her father must have seen the thought in her face.

"I think you already know what you want to do. I can't

say I'm not pleased. I hope this means I will get my archer back."

She frowned. "What do you mean?"

Annoyance crossed his noble features. "My best bowman claims he doesn't want to fight anymore."

Twenty-seven

❧

After being pushed to the very edge of his restraint the night before, it wasn't surprising that Gregor found himself at the practice yard early the next morning. He felt like killing someone and needed an outlet. Nay, not just someone—the smug bastard who'd had his eyes and hands all over Cate last night. Just the memory of the way Randolph's palm had rested on the small of her back and then slid down one very inappropriate inch made every muscle in Gregor's body flare.

Gritting his teeth, he swung his sword and let it come down with all the frustration and anger teeming inside him.

He was fortunate his sparring partner was the best swordsman in Scotland and didn't know the meaning of the word "practice." With MacLeod it was always full-out, no-holds-barred combat.

MacLeod blocked the blow, albeit with some effort. The Chief of the Highland Guard drew back to take a break, breathing heavily. "Christ, Arrow, keep swinging a sword like this and we might find a new place for you with or without your bow." He gave him a long look. "I guess I don't need to ask what has gotten into you? I saw Randolph with your lass last night."

Suddenly, MacLeod's gaze shifted past him. Gregor turned just as Cate stomped up beside him.

"I'm not his lass," she said to MacLeod with gritted

teeth. Gregor was so glad to see her, so busy drinking in every sweet inch of her, that he didn't even mind when she scowled at him. "Why aren't you practicing with your bow? And what is this my father says about you not rejoining the, uh . . ." She looked about uncertainly at the men gathered around. ". . . army?"

Unfortunately, his place in the "army" wasn't exactly a secret anymore. Gregor sighed, pulled off his helm, and dragged his fingers through his sweat-drenched hair. Damn Bruce for bringing her into this! "Can we talk about this later, Cate?"

"I don't know, Slick," MacSorley piped in from his position leaning against the wall of the armory, where he'd been watching the sword practice. "I'm rather interested in what you have to say on the subject as well." He looked around at the other members of the Guard gathered there: Sutherland, MacKay, MacRuairi, and Campbell. "We all are."

Feeling more than a little cornered, Gregor might have snapped back angrily, but Cate unexpectedly came to his rescue. She turned to MacSorley. "You know, I think you are going to have to come up with a new name for him. He doesn't look very slick right now. He looks rather a mess."

Some rescue. Gregor repressed a groan.

MacSorley grinned. "Ah, you might be right about that, lass. I'll have to think of something. But don't worry about that pretty face of his—it will heal up just fine. Did he ever tell you how he was dipped in the River Styx as a child?"

Gregor muttered a not very low "go to hell" under his breath, while Cate laughed.

"Like Achilles with the arrow? How appropriate! Did his mother hold him by the heel as well?"

It was MacRuairi who answered, shaking his head. "We didn't think he was vulnerable anywhere. But turns out he is."

Cate searched the faces of the men around them, waiting for an explanation.

Finally, Gregor let out an exasperated sigh. "You, Cate. He means you."

Their eyes met and for the first time in a long time, she was not looking at him with hatred and anger. She blinked widely. "Oh."

"Aye, 'oh,'" he repeated. Conscious of too many eyes upon them, he drew her away. "Come, we can talk inside the armory—where we won't have any interruptions."

"Ah, hell, I was hoping for a rematch," MacSorley said. "I'll be ready next time, lass. Although you might not want to wear such a pretty gown. This time I won't be the only one to get dirty."

Cate was laughing as he dragged her away. "He's amusing," she said. "I can see why you like him so much."

"Hawk's a pain in the arse," he grumbled. "Wait until he comes up with a nickname for *you*."

The smile that lit her face stabbed him with a longing so intense it stole his breath. How could he have been such an idiot? How could he have thrown away the most important thing that had ever happened to him? She meant everything to him. He should have trusted his feelings. Committed himself to her, heart and soul.

"Do you think he will?" She couldn't hide her excitement. "What do you think he will call me?"

"I don't even want to guess. But you can be assured it will be hilarious to everyone but you or, more likely, me."

Before they went into the armory, he washed some of the grime off his face and hands with a bucket of fresh water from the well.

Entering the armory, he could see that there was enough light coming through the wood slats, so he closed the door behind them. Clearing off a wooden crate that was used to reach the weapons stored higher on the walls, he motioned for her to sit, but she shook her head. "I'd prefer to stand."

He'd prefer she do her standing a few feet away from him because in the enclosed space, with only a few feet between them, he was finding it very hard to keep his hands at his sides. It had been so long since he'd touched her—really touched her—that he ached with the need to feel her soft skin under his fingertips again. And as if the thought of that wasn't enough to test the limits of his control, a moment later the subtle scent of flowers teased his senses. She'd used lavender in the water to wash her hair, and all he could think about was unbinding the two coils secured under her veil and burying his nose in the silky softness.

But he'd lost that privilege. He'd have to earn it back—if she let him.

Taking a step back, he cleared his throat. "What did you want, Cate?"

Unaware of the fragile command he had on his control, she stepped toward him until she stood only inches away. Christ, all he had to do was bend his head and her lips would be under his. His muscles tensed. A rush of heat pounded through his veins, but he kept his arms pinned to his sides and tried not to think about how badly he wanted to kiss her.

Maybe she was more aware of what she was doing to him than he realized. Her voice was slightly husky. "What's wrong, Gregor? Why have you not been using your bow? Why are you contemplating quitting?"

His jaw hardened. It wasn't quitting; it was merely that what he wanted had shifted. He no longer felt the need to prove himself. He no longer had the drive to be the best and nothing else. He no longer wanted to avoid his other duties.

"This isn't because of me, is it?" she asked. "I know you didn't mean to shoot me. It was an accident."

He gritted his teeth against the tight swell of emotion in his throat. When he'd let loose that arrow, for the first time the full import of what he did hit him. "I could have killed you."

"But you didn't. And even if you had, it wouldn't have been your fault. You couldn't have anticipated what I was going to do. In fact, I think you'd instructed me many times *not* to do what I did."

The sympathy in her eyes undid him. He had to tell her the truth—no matter how shameful. "You don't understand. If you hadn't done what you did, the king might be dead." His mouth hardened. "I missed, Cate. The arrow I shot was too low. It wouldn't have killed Fitzwarren."

The surprised doubt on her face only made it worse. "You can't know that. And even even if it's true, I imagine you were unusually distracted."

He clenched his jaw in silence. She was right. He had been distracted—by her—but that was no excuse. "It wasn't the first time. It's one of the reasons I was sent home." He described the hesitation at Berwick and the small mistakes he'd made leading up to it. He gave voice to his fear for the first time. "My skills are slipping."

"Your skills are exceptional. But you are not perfect. So what? You are the only one who expects you to be, and you don't need to be. Even with a few not-perfect shots, you are still the best archer in the Highlands. What about the shot you made from the ladder? From what my father said, it saved the attack from discovery."

"I was lucky."

She looked at him as if she knew better. "Luck or not, no one else could have made that shot, Gregor. No one. Think about that."

His jaw hardened. Whether she was right really didn't matter. "You don't understand. I'm . . ." He just said it: "Christ, I'm losing my edge. I don't feel the same intensity."

She gave him a long look, considering his words but seeing far beyond them. "How could you? You must be mentally exhausted. You've been fighting for my father for . . . ?"

"Over seven years," he filled in.

"So seven years of functioning at the highest levels, under the most extreme of conditions, with constant pressure? That would be difficult for any archer, let alone with the type of precision required for a marksman. I'm not surprised it has begun to wear on you; actually, I'm surprised you lasted this long." She paused, cocking her head to study him. "Do you still believe in my father?"

"There is no one I believe in more. He is a great man—and a great king."

She looked up at him with far more understanding and compassion than he deserved. But it was what she did next that nearly brought him to his knees. Slowly, she reached up and cupped his jaw in her hand. He regretted the roughness of the stubble scratching her soft skin, but she seemed not to mind as she rubbed his chin against her palm.

"You won't let him down, Gregor. Even if you never hit another mark again, you have proved yourself many times over." She made a face. "You don't know how many stories of your escapades I've been forced to endure the past few weeks."

She'd shocked him. "He's been furious with me."

"Aye, so maybe that should tell you something. His faith in you is as unwavering as yours is in him." She smiled. "Even after shooting his daughter."

Was the fear of losing Bruce's faith in him what was holding him back? He suspected it might be part of it. For so long his focus on being the best—proving himself by his skill—had been all that mattered. But what happened when it was gone? Maybe he was fighting too hard against finding out.

That was Cate. Cutting through the chaff to get to the wheat. She seemed to take the jumble of confusing emotions inside him and make them clear.

She wasn't done. "I suspect this might have as much to do with Father Roland's offertory basket and the stones on your father's grave as it does about your skills. Taking a life—any life—is not easy, even when it is deserved. You were right in that." He wished he could have spared her that knowledge. "Not being eager to take a life is nothing to be ashamed of; it just ensures that when you do, it is necessary. And what you do is necessary—I know you know that. You just need to remind yourself. My father needs you, Gregor."

He took her hand and brought her dainty fingers to his mouth. Some of the tightness squeezing in his chest relaxed when she didn't pull it away, but allowed him to press his lips on her fingers. "But I need *you*. None of it means anything without you. For so long, I've been fighting against someone else's image of who I am that I lost sight of the man I wanted to be. You reminded me of who that is. I want you to be able to count on me, Cate. I want my clan to count on me. And I want our children to count on me. Give me your trust, Cate, and I swear I will die before I ever break it again."

He could see the indecision in her eyes, the vacillating between longing and fear. She wanted to trust him, but she was scared. He couldn't blame her. His chest tightened—burned—knowing just how much he'd hurt her.

But it was the longing that snapped the last tethers of his restraint. He couldn't see that fragile plea of hope and love in her eyes—that tenderness that he'd feared would never reappear—and not respond.

He kissed her. It was a kiss unlike any he'd ever given a woman before. It was a kiss to destroy all indecision and all fear. It was a kiss to woo, a kiss to persuade, and a kiss to convince.

It was a kiss that didn't allow any room for protest or argument. With every gentle caress of his mouth, with every long stroke of his tongue, with every groan and sweep of his thumb on her cheek, he told her how much he loved her and how much she meant to him.

She had to believe it.

Cate's knees went weak when he kissed her. Everything else went weak as well with the tender onslaught of his mouth and tongue. Her resistance melted under the warmth of his love.

He did love her. It wasn't just words or a kiss that convinced her. It was in everything he did. It was in the way he looked at her when she first walked into a room; it was in the way he'd forced himself to stand aside for a month while she enjoyed some of the benefits that might have been hers by birth had tragedy not intervened; it was in his haggard appearance and in that ridiculous broken nose.

Suddenly, recalling what else he'd said, she pulled back. "What do you mean you want your clan to count on you?"

"I might not have been born to be the laird, but I am, and it's time I started acting like it. I had John fill in for me in Galloway. There is no reason he cannot do so again."

Cate was glad for John, knowing how eager he'd been to return to battle. "But not all of the time, Gregor. They need you."

He didn't say anything.

"Don't you want to be a Phantom anymore?" she asked.

"Of course, but I have a responsibility."

She knew that was only part of what was weighing on him. She had not yet fully convinced him that there was nothing wrong with him that rest and the realization that he did not need to be perfect would not cure, but she would. He had plenty of faults, and she'd be happy to remind him of them whenever he needed her to. "Aye, but don't you think there is a way to do both? Perhaps we might come up with a compromise?"

His eyes held hers. "'We'?" He stroked her cheek with

the back of his finger. "Does that mean you will give me another chance?"

She lifted a brow. "I believe I still have two more days in my promised month. I'd hate to lose them when Sir Thomas has asked—"

She didn't get to finish. He cut her off with a very unflattering curse about her cousin and hauled her up against him. The feel of her body pressed against his was at once familiar and new, and as always, it made her gasp with shock.

This time when he kissed her, he kissed her hard. Possessively. And very, very thoroughly. He left her no doubt of exactly what he wanted to do to her and all the pleasures that awaited her in their marriage bed.

When he pulled away a long time later, they both were breathing hard and about one minute away from experiencing those pleasures up against a wall in the armory.

"Did I say a month?" he said huskily. "I meant twenty-nine days. One more night like last night, and I'll be calling St. Kilda home."

Cate laughed. "Is that what my father threatened you with? I wondered." Her expression turned serious. "But thank you, Gregor. Twenty-nine days or a month, what you did . . ." She looked up at him. "You don't know how much it means to me."

He swept a lock of hair that had tangled in her lashes from their kiss behind her ear. "I think I do. You are special Cate, and you deserved far more than a month. I wish I could give you everything you missed."

"I think you've made a fine start."

He grew troubled for a moment. "Are you sure, Cate? God knows it's selfish of me to ask you to give me another chance after what you've been through. I nearly lost my mind when I discovered you'd been taken. They could try it again—using you to get to me and the others. I swear I will do everything I can to protect you, but being with me is not without risk."

"I'm Robert the Bruce's daughter, Gregor. I'm going to be at risk with or without you, and I like my odds better with." She smiled. "When I cannot defend myself, there is no one I would count on more."

She could see that her words meant something to him.

"You proved that well enough with what you did to save the king. I'm proud of you, Cate."

She beamed, smiling broadly. His praise meant more to her than he could know. "I'm proud of myself, too. I guess all that dirt you made me eat that day was worth it."

He laughed, and then gave her a cryptic smile. "I told you I wanted our children to count on me. Aren't you curious to know what I meant?"

She rolled her eyes. "I assumed you were anticipating all those sons again."

He grinned back at her. "Not exactly. I'm afraid I was referring to something a little more immediate than that."

It took her a moment to realize what he meant. The blood drained from her face. She gazed at him wordlessly, not wanting to say the words that might crush her hope.

"They are waiting for you—for us—at Roro, my love."

He'd brought the children back. "But how? What about their relations?"

"They will be a part of their lives if they want to be, but I convinced them that they belong with us. You gave them a home, Cate."

She couldn't believe it. Eddie ... Maddy ... "All of them? Even Pip?"

He nodded. "I think with my nose we even look like father and son now. What do you think?"

She gave a half-cry and sob and launched herself into his arms again, just letting him hold her. The feeling of those strong arms around her was like nothing else. She didn't realize she was crying until she looked up, and he wiped the tears from her eyes.

"What's wrong?" he asked.

She shook her head. "Nothing. I'm just so happy, I don't know what to say."

"Say you'll marry me. Say you'll be my wife. Say you'll be the mother of my children—even ones I didn't know I had right away. Say you'll stand by my side during the day, and sleep by my side at night. Say you'll grow old with me. Say you love me as much as I love you."

"I do love you. And yes, yes, I will marry you." She paused, tugging her bottom lip between her teeth. "Although I was looking forward to a month or two of courting."

When he smiled that long, slow smile that curved his sensual mouth and set every drop of green in his eyes sparkling, the most handsome man in Scotland had never looked so dazzling. But it was that other glint in his eye—the one that promised another kind of dazzling—that made her shiver with anticipation. "That depends on the kind of courting you have in mind."

She pulled back. "A very proper one, of course, under my father's watchful gaze."

He groaned. "Christ, that's what I was afraid of."

She quirked a brow. "Do I take it you are not enjoying celibacy?"

"Not when I am near you. Right now, I'm not enjoying it at all. After a month—or two—of this, it's not going to be pretty."

She patted him on the cheek. "Poor, Gregor. I think you'll live."

He captured her hand in his much bigger one and brought it to his mouth, pressing a warm kiss upon her fingers. "I will, but it won't be easy."

He looked as bent out of shape as his nose. She slid her arms around his neck and lifted on her toes to press a kiss on his disgruntled mouth. "Don't worry; I think we might find a few storerooms in Dunstaffnage."

A shadow crossed his face. "I haven't apologized for what I said, Cate. I never should have said that about taking you against a wall. I didn't mean it—"

She stopped him with a press of her fingers to his mouth. "I know. And I will let you apologize to your heart's content later, but right now you'd better hurry if you don't want someone to come in here and discover us."

His eyes lit up like green flames as soon as he took in her meaning. It was clear from how quickly he started removing her clothing that he wasn't going to wait for her to change her mind.

When they were both undressed, he slide his gaze down her appreciatively and let out a low whistle. "Hell, sweetheart, if it means I could trap you into marrying me faster, I don't care who walks in. Maybe you should call John?"

For that, she slipped her ankle behind his and pushed him to the ground. But when she fell down on top of him, he didn't seem to mind so much.

He was a rogue. But he was her rogue. And when he made love to her that day and for every day afterward, he never let her forget it.

Epilogue

❧

"Yap, yap, yap, yap . . . *yap*!"

The frantic barking at her heels made Cate start to giggle—in spite of her current position with her back up against the door and her legs wrapped around her husband's waist.

Gregor put his forehead to hers exhaustedly and swore. "Damned dog. Add better latches to the list of things to do in the new tower."

They'd started the stone castle a few years after Gregor had returned to Roro permanently at the end of the war—or mostly permanently, as her father still used his "Phantoms" for "delicate" situations—and it would be completed soon. Cate had convinced Gregor to pick up his bow again and continue the fight for her father's crown, albeit for fewer missions. He spent much of his time at Roro with her, but whenever the king needed him, he was ready.

Hands still cupping her bottom, he gradually eased her down. Cate needed a moment to find her feet, her limbs weak from the force of her release. Even after nearly twelve years of marriage and the birth of five sons—blast him!—to add to the five "foundlings" they'd added to their large brood, Gregor never seemed to tire of surprising her in storerooms.

Not that she was complaining. At three and forty, he took her breath away even more than he had at one and thirty. She'd been right. The crook in his nose only added to his appeal—as did the craggy lines of time and battle-fields. There might be other claimants to the title, including some close to home, but to her he would always be the most handsome man in Scotland.

She shook her head, readjusting her gown and hair, which had barely been disturbed. Twelve years of practice—not to mention a few innocent questions by children about why mummy's cheeks were flushed and hair mussed every time she went to the storerooms—had taught them something.

She shook her head. "I think you are going to have a hard enough time explaining all those extra storerooms as it is." She laughed. "Besides, at least Berry waited for you to finish this time. The poor thing is just jealous. He doesn't like it when you don't pay attention to him."

Gregor shot the dog a glare. "He's a nuisance, that's what he is."

Cate bent down and scratched the little terrier's head. "Don't listen to him, Berry—he loves you."

Berry was the name Pip had given the tiny pup all those years ago, when he heard about the botched attack at Berwick Castle from Hawk. Not surprisingly, as they shared the same sense of humor, Pip and the seafarer had become fast friends. Much to Gregor's annoyance over the years. Indeed it was Pip who'd come up with her name—Crush—for what she'd done to women's hearts and men's pride (namely Hawk's, after he landed on his backside again on their rematch).

Gregor grinned wickedly. "It's a good thing the blasted beast did wait. I need another son."

Cate wasn't so out of practice that she couldn't flip him on his backside when she needed to, so he wisely moved out of her reach. She didn't spend as much time on the practice field these days, but when the girls needed her she would be there. Even at four and ten, Maddy could defend herself if necessary. The pretty young girl might look like a porcelain poppet on the outside, but she was tough. She had to be with all these *men* about.

"Don't you even jest about it—I just finished weaning your last son. I swear, Gregor, if you don't give me a daughter, I'm going to put a lock on our door! Maddy and I would have had to move out long ago without Beth and Jeannie." The two little girls—sisters—had come to live with them two years ago after the death of both their parents from a fever. "Living with all these lads is like living with a bunch of noisy pigs. How is it that every one of them has been born with the inability to pick up clothes off the floor?"

He shrugged, not bothering to hide his amusement. "Life is a never-ending mystery."

"Never-ending mystery my—" She stopped before the word fell from her lips. "If I'm sick the entire way to Scone it will be your fault!"

He sobered. "Ah hell, Cate. I didn't think about that. I wish you didn't suffer so every time."

She hadn't meant to upset him. "I was jesting. It's not so bad. It only lasts a few months. Besides, in the end it is worth it." Her eyes filled with tears as the memory of her mother swept over her. It didn't seem fair that her mother had struggled for so long to have another child, yet all Gregor had to do was look at her and Cate found herself with her head in a basin. But she knew how happy her mother would have been for her to be surrounded by so much love.

She had more family than she'd ever dreamed of, including a new, much anticipated half-brother who was the reason for their journey. After ten years as the undisputed

King of Scotland and the release of his queen from captivity, Robert Bruce finally had his legitimate son. David had arrived in March, and the king and queen were planning a celebration unlike any that had taken place in Scotland for years. The country—and the throne, with the birth of David—was stronger than it had been since the death of King Alexander III.

They were taking the entire family, even baby John. For the first time in years, they would all be together. As had Pip before him, Ruadh (she'd given up that Eddie battle years ago) was being fostered with Arthur Campbell, and Pip had been a knight in her father's army for almost five years now. Who would have believed that the skinny, funny-looking urchin could have grown up to rival his father in good looks? A foot of height, a few stone of muscle, and a face that grew into the nose had made Pip a heartbreaker. It didn't hurt that he was one of the best horsemen in Scotland and highly skilled with a throwing spear, thanks to his foster father.

He also had a wicked sense of humor—for which Gregor blamed Hawk. One of his favorite things was to introduce his mother to the young women who couldn't seem to leave him alone. Cate had to admit it was fun to watch their faces as they looked back and forth between them, trying not to show their shock. As Pip grew older, they looked even less than their six years apart.

Gregor must have known what she was thinking. He gazed at her tenderly, brushing a lock of hair from her forehead. "I'm sure they are as anxious to see you as you are to see them."

"I can't wait. It will be good to see all the Phantoms again, and their families. I think Arthur and Anna's eldest daughter has her eyes on Pip. Not that he seems to notice."

Gregor frowned. "The lass is only . . ."

"Fifteen, and he's seven and twenty." She lifted her brow, daring him to say anything. "Sound familiar?"

He laughed, shook he head, and pulled her into his arms. "He won't go down easy."

"They never do."

But when they did, they fell forever. Cate ought to know.

AUTHOR'S NOTE

The character of Gregor MacGregor is fictional. I wanted to base him on a real person, but I was ultimately defeated by the lack of primary source material, and the inconsistencies and gaps in the genealogical charts and clan histories of the time.

The first accepted Chief of Clan Gregor is "Gregor of the Golden Bridles," who appears on the scene sometime in the mid-fourteenth century. However, there do appear to be "MacGregors" (possibly referred to as MacAlpin at that time) in the traditional three "MacGregor Glens" of Gelnstrae, Glenorchy, and Glenlochy in the thirteenth century, and there is a reference to a John of Glenurchy (Glenorchy), who fought on the patriot side with Wallace and the Lord of Lorn at Dunbar in 1296. John of Glenurchy was taken prisoner after the disastrous Scot defeat, ordered to fight for King Edward in France, and died there, leaving only a young heiress, Margaret (Mariota).

This is where the record becomes very confusing. Margaret, who would have had to be born before 1296/7, was supposedly given in wardship to Neil Campbell (one of Bruce's staunchest supporters and the brother of Arthur "The Ranger") and was eventually (again supposedly) married to Neil's son with Mary Bruce (the king's sister), Iain/John Campbell, who gained with the marriage the lands of Glenorchy and possibly the barony of Loch Awe—in other words, the MacGregor lands. (Other sources suggest that the barony was given to Sir Neil and then passed to his first son [by a Crawford wife], Sir Colin.) This will be the first claim by the Campbells to MacGregor lands, which in later centuries will spawn a vicious feud and serve as the subject of my Campbell Trilogy.

Neil Campbell and Mary Bruce weren't married until after her release from imprisonment (she was one of the women hung in the cages by King Edward), which means John couldn't have been born until c. 1314. This John Campbell was named the Earl of Atholl by the king after the defection of David Strathbogie (Mary's son in *The Recruit*), and most records have him married to Joan Menteith (with no reference to Margaret). If John was married to Margaret before Joan when he was very young, she must have died before he married Joan. John Campbell died at the Battle of Halidon in 1333, without issue from either wife, and it seems at this point the lands returned to the MacGregors. In 1390, another John MacGregor of Glenorchy was back on record as the owner of the property at his death.

So what were the MacGregors doing between the death of John of Glenurchy c. 1297 and the appearance of Gregor of the Golden Bridles in the mid-fourteenth century?

The short answer is that it's hard to say. Clan histories, historical sources, and genealogical sources are all over the place.

A couple of the sources suggest that the MacGregors were not happy about the Campbell claim to their lands through the heiress Margaret and elected a nephew of John of Glenurchy's named Gregor as chief. At this point, the MacGregors held the glens by "right of sword," but they were eventually pushed off their land until they were mostly limited to the area of Glenstrae.

Still other sources, including the great historical fiction novelist Nigel Tranter, assert that there was a chief named Malcolm at the time of Bruce who came to the king's rescue on his white steed when fleeing the kingdom in 1306, fought at Bannockburn carrying the relics of St. Fillan, and was gravely injured in 1318 at the battle in Ireland when Edward Bruce died. He was possibly the father of Gregor of the Golden Bridles. This Malcolm "the lame lord" is said to have died at an advanced age in 1364.

There are a couple of big problems with this. Aside from clan histories, the evidence of these MacGregors is a mention of Malcolm and Patrick of Glendochart in Ragman Rolls of 1296 ("Malcolum de Glendeghrad" is how the name actually appears). An early nineteenth-century Scottish historian, Donald Gregory, believed they were MacGregors—and apparently many later historians jumped on this—but my go-to historian for the period, Barrows, suggests they were MacNabs.

There are two questions I can't answer. Even assuming that this hero Malcolm was a MacGregor, how was he related to John of Glenurchy (the chief who was taken prisoner at Dunbar and later died in France)? Was the Glendochart family a different branch, or was Malcolm the son or brother of John of Glenurchy, as some suggest? A son seems very unlikely, given Margaret as the heiress, so a brother makes more sense.

The more difficult question, and why it doesn't make sense to me that "Malcolm MacGregor" could have been tied so closely to Bruce, is that if he had been, why weren't the MacGregors rewarded for his support and loyalty like everyone else? It's clear that the MacGregors (like the Lords of Lorn and MacNabs, with whom they were associated) lost their lands and standing after the Wars of Independence, with Glenorchy going to to the Campbells, at least for a while, and Glendochart going to the Menzies. The really frustrating thing is that many historians write about Malcolm MacGregor as a loyal Bruce adherent, and then in practically the same sentence talk about how the clan's fortunes changed after Bannockburn without explanation.

Ultimately, I decided to steer clear of the whole thing by making my Gregor the chieftain of a cadet branch of the family—Malcolm's nephew—and leaving out references to Chief Malcolm's alleged heroics. I did, however, get a little inspiration from a possible grandson of Gregor of the Golden Bridles named (surprise!) Gregor—his sobriquet was Gregor Aulin, meaning "perfectly handsome." How about that! Gregor Aulin was the progenitor of the MacGregors of Roro ("Ruath Shruth," meaning red stream) in Glenlyon, so that's where I put my Gregor.

The Dunlyon tower house in the story is fictional, as I couldn't find any references to early MacGregor strongholds in the area.

The character of Cate is loosely based on Christian of Carrick, one of Robert the Bruce's six (at least) natural children by various mistresses. Little other than her name is known—making her perfect for my purposes—except that she was receiving a pension in 1329.

I'm often asked why I haven't written about Bruce himself, and the existence of Christian and her siblings is the reason. To my mind, Bruce is a great hero and would make a wonderfully complex historical *fiction* subject, but the presence of the natural children (some conceived when married to Elizabeth de Burgh) made it hard for me to envision him as a historical *romance* hero.

My descriptions of the attempted taking of Berwick Castle on the night of December 6, 1312, and the taking of Perth Castle the following month in January 1313, borrow heavily from the historical accounts, including the supposed first use of the inventive ladders and the barking dog at Berwick, and the broken ladder and the French knight who was in shock to see Bruce take the lead at Perth.

Ronald McNair Scott, in his book *Robert the Bruce* (Barnes & Noble, 1982, p. 134), quotes the French knight as saying, "What shall we say of our nobles in France who think only to stuff their bellies when so renowned a knight will risk his life for a miserable hamlet?"

I pushed back the siege of Perth by a week or two, to give Gregor and Cate a Christmas together. The siege of Perth was said to have lasted several weeks (one source said as long as six), before Bruce broke camp and appears to have retreated, returning on the night of January 8 to take the town.

As is probably obvious from the story, I have a great deal of sympathy for men like Sir William Oliphant. By all accounts, honorable Scots found themselves through various understandable reasons on the side opposite Bruce. If you've read *The Recruit*, Sir Adam Gordon is a similar figure. These are men who were on the "right" side early in the war, fighting along Wallace for the patriot cause, but then for reasons of family alliances, honor, or circumstance found themselves on the "wrong" side against Bruce.

If Sir William was a little gun-shy to switch sides, I can understand why. Imprisoned in England for a year after Dunbar, he was released, rebelled again, heroically held Stirling Castle with a very small force against Edward I (and Robert the Bruce), and then, when he surrendered under what he thought were favorable terms, he was publicly humiliated before being tossed in the Tower of London for four years. When he was finally released under *mainprise* (kind of a medieval bail), it was with the promise that he would fight for Edward II against Bruce.

Although the tide had definitely changed for Bruce at this point, his ultimate victory was by no means assured. Bruce's successes against the English in the period from 1306 to 1313 were mostly in minor skirmishes and through trickery. He had yet to test his army against the English in the pitched battle that would put a decisive end to the question. Were I Sir William, I think I'd be cautious about jumping ship, too.

There is some confusion about what happened to Sir William after the fall of Perth. Some sources say he was banished to the Isles, where he eventually died, and others have him as the William Oliphant who was given a barony by Bruce, signed his name to the declaration of Arbroath, and had a son (Walter) who would marry Bruce's daughter Princess Elizabeth.

ClanOliphant.com had a good explanation, suggesting that there were actually two Sir William Oliphants at the time, who were cousins and both fought at Stirling. The "gallant knight" Sir William who was in command and later held Perth was sent to the Isles, where he died, and it was the cousin who went on to lead the clan at Bannockburn, and later be warmly taken into the Bruce fold.

As I mentioned in the story, a high percentage of the garrison at Perth were Scots. What happened to those Scots after the surrender to Bruce is uncertain. Some sources say they were put to the sword while the English were allowed to go free, in a rare instance of Bruce executing those who stood against him. Others suggest that only a few of the leaders were killed.

When thinking of a fitting inscription for Gregor's sword, I couldn't resist the clan motto *S Rioghal mo dhream*—Royal is my race—given the identity of my heroine. One of the traditional origins of Clan MacGregor is that they were descended from Gregor, who was a son of Alpin and brother to King Kenneth MacAlpin (King of the Picts and first King of Scots). Another royal origin claim is that the clan descends from the kings of Alba. DNA data is supposedly consistent with the first Alpinian contention rather than the second.

Medieval sermons could apparently get quite graphic in order to frighten the listeners into compliance. The nun who gouges her eyes out and sends them to King Richard when he is lusting after her, which I refer to in chapter six, is one of them.

And finally, the term Hogmanay to describe the Scottish New Year's celebration was first recorded in the sixteenth century, but as one of the speculated origins is Norse, it conceivably could have been used much earlier.

Romance ___ 129 / 727

McCarty